Misappropriate

A Death Dwellers MC Novel

Book Two

By

Kathryn C. Kelly

Misappropriate by Kathryn C. Kelly

Published by Makin Groceries Media
24200 SW Freeway, Suite 402, #353
Rosenberg, TX 77471
www.katkelwriter.com
www.deathdwellersmc.com

ISBN: 979-8-88630-001-7 (ebook)
ISBN: 979-8-88630-000-0 (paperback)

Misappropriate
Blurb

Meggie. The beauty who tamed the biker.
She believes her future is bright. Her baby boy. the love of her man and the affection of the Death Dweller brothers fill her with contentment. Now, the only thing she wants is to have her marriage blessed in a church ceremony.

Outlaw. The bad boy who fell for the beauty.
When a new threat rides into town and puts a target on his woman's back, Christopher "Outlaw" Caldwell is forced to confront a past that has him questioning if Megan belongs with him or not. Standing in a sanctuary reciting sacred vows suddenly seems a useless exercise. He wants vengeance and blood. Love and romance have no place in a world of violence and vengeance. The more he pushes her away, the more Megan lures him in. She sees him as Christopher, but Outlaw is in his blood. Just as he always feared, the man she believes him to be and the one he is collide, risking the most important thing of all: Megan's life.

Dedication

To my Facebook fans for your love and support.
To Outlaw's ladies—this one's for you.

Chapter 1

Meggie

"I DON'T THINK THIS IS A GOOD IDEA," MEGAN CALDWELL said. She glared at the three men surrounding her after listening to their suggestion that she go away so her husband, Christopher "Outlaw" Caldwell, could enjoy the bachelor party they'd planned for him. They'd waylaid her on her way from meeting with the lady she'd hired to help her decorate her and Christopher's house. Meggie only had time to open the door to the room she shared with Christopher at the MC, thank her mother for babysitting, and watch Dinah scoot through the wall of men Meggie now faced. "CJ and I will stay in the room and—"

Mortician, Enforcer of the club and the man with a variety of handy skills, folded his arms, muscles rippled on his brown skin, while the skull ring he never seemed to remove leered from his middle finger. Though cold outside, he wore short sleeves under his cut. "C'mon, Meggie," he persisted. "You think Prez'll enjoy himself knowing you and his kid right down the hall?"

She glanced back at her sleeping son. Judging from her achy breasts, his feeding time was approaching. Only seven months old, he was the size of a baby twelve or thirteen months and already a smaller version of Christopher with the blueness of his eyes changing to a deeper shade of green with each passing day. Her hair might've been golden, but her son's was just as black as his daddy's. A daddy who didn't let him very far out of his sight. Besides, she didn't have time to just leave with the near completion of their house and their church wedding ceremony coming up soon, scheduled to happen in a month. In the beginning, the service was to have taken place on Valentine's Day. *Now,* February 14th was two days away. The wedding had been pushed back to March 14th; Christopher's bachelor party hadn't been. As much as she loved Valentine's Day and would've enjoyed having her church ceremony coincide, their new wedding date would be even more special. CJ would turn eight months the same day.

"Christopher isn't going to like this. He won't want us—"

"Is it him or you, girl?" Digger, Mortician's real brother, asked, cocking his head to the side.

All right so maybe it was her a little as well. But they wanted to throw her husband a bachelor party, complete with the Bobs— those women paraded out for special occasions and their exceptional oral skills.

"We're already married," she pointed out, jabbing Digger in the chest. He was taller than his older brother, a little less broad in the shoulders, arms, and chest. Mortician was ripped. Digger was muscled but…she frowned. Was she actually sizing up her husband's officers?

"Why does he need a bachelor party?"

"Right, Meggie," Val, the bald RC, grunted. His mouth kicked up in a smile, revealing the sexy dimple that made him irresistible to so many girls.

Umkay. Yes. Yes, she was sizing these men up. Men she'd known for over a year and thought of as friends and older brothers.

"Why you need some big fucking church wedding?" Val went on in the steely voice he adopted for intimidation. "You already married, huh?"

She'd walked right into that one. She stepped farther into the hallway, so their voices wouldn't prematurely awaken her son. She'd be so glad when their house was finished because she was sick to death of living day-in and day-out at the MC. "Where am I supposed to go all of a sudden?"

"I'm with Megs," a voice to the right of her said. Johnnie, Christopher's cousin, and the club VP, leaned against the wall next to her.

Meggie looked at the ankle boots she wore, not wanting to stare at Johnnie. The one glimpse she had seen of his chiseled face, when she'd glanced between the space created by Mortician's head and the wall, proved enough for her.

"Christopher will have your balls if he knows you're pressuring his wife to leave," he continued.

Johnnie's blond hair, longer on top than on the sides, made his silver-gray eyes stand out. The heat of his gaze lasered her profile and she shifted her weight beneath his scrutiny. She didn't have to look at him to know he studied her. He always did. And not in a brotherly way.

"I'm suggesting you asswipes back off," he said lazily.

Meggie rocked back on her heels, satisfied at his defense. "He's known about this bachelor party all along. He's never once said he didn't want me there. Or, at least, on the premises."

"Prez wouldn't want to upset you," Mortician went on. His dreads had grown even longer in the months since she'd met him. Today, they were queued, and his strong neck flexed with his movements. "But we gonna have associates, hangers-on, and brothers from our support clubs as well as dudes from our out of town chapters. You know if you're here Prez's either gonna want you out there with him or he's gonna be in here with you. How's that gonna make him look to the other brothers?"

"Like he loves and respects his wife," she snapped.

"Who the fuck are you?" Johnnie snarled, drawing everyone's attention to a man who'd just walked out of the main room and into the hallway where only members and their guests were allowed.

Sardonic green eyes studied them, and Meggie frowned when she caught a brief glimpse of him as Mortician shifted and turned to the side. A blue bandanna covered the man's head and a leather jacket that might very well conceal a weapon.

He raised his hands. "Sorry, brother. Looking for the shitter."

The men now hid her, their backs to her in a semi-circle of towering, muscled protection. Behind them, she stood on her tiptoes to get another look at the interloper, placing her hands on Digger's shoulders to balance herself.

"This ain't the fucking way," Digger growled.

"Yeah, fuckhead. Public shitters in the other direction," Val added, raising an arm.

Meggie guessed it was to point toward the public shitters. They were on the other side of the main room, in the area of the pool tables and dartboards.

"Sorry," the man said again, though something about his mocking tone told Meggie he wasn't sorry at all.

"You forgiven this fucking time," Mortician called. "Make a mistake like this again and we not responsible for where the fuck parts of you end up."

Meggie poked Mortician in the back at the threat, though she knew the score. She sighed and thought of Christopher's bachelor party. Men like the stranger would overrun the place and Christopher's well-earned reputation as a badass meant everything to him. At the thought, her defenses crumbled. Mortician was right. To her, Christopher was everything she could ever want—a wonderful father and a very dedicated husband. To everyone else…he was both feared and respected because of the way he carried himself and the way he handled things. She wouldn't want him to lose face because she couldn't allow him to enjoy his bachelor party without her around.

They turned back to her, and she knew the man was gone. She heard the first stirrings of her son. On cue, her breasts opened like a faucet. "Fine," she said before they started in on her again. "I'll call Farrah and Lacey and go to Seattle."

"Seattle?" they chorused, glancing between one another with consternation. She hadn't seen her friends since forever, so, maybe, this would be a good time to visit. At least, they'd serve as a distraction about her husband's bachelor party.

Digger recovered first. "Meggie girl, well, I guess that'll be cool. We know you won't change your mind and decide to come back during the party with you being so far away."

"Seattle, huh, babe?" Val rubbed his jaw, his mouth downturned. "Just don't call Prez every ten minutes, telling him you miss him. That'll be just as bad as you being here."

Meggie shook her head. "I won't call him every ten minutes, but I will call him—"

"No, girl," Mortician insisted. "No calls at all 'til the next day. If he hears your voice, he won't have fun."

"What planet have you three been living on?" Meggie bit out, tapping her foot in agitation. "I won't like not being able to talk to Christopher at all after just deciding to fly out of town, but he really won't like not hearing from me."

Johnnie cleared his throat and pushed off the wall. He reached in his cut for a cigarette, his gaze falling on her swollen breasts. Meggie lowered her lashes and gritted her teeth, flushing to her toes at the lust in Johnnie's eyes. He didn't light his cigarette, just held it between his fingers and used it to emphasize his words.

"The woman sleeps next to him every night. She knows him better than we do. I say you three idiots listen to her."

"You've known him all your life, John Boy," Val said in defense of his argument.

"My point exactly," Johnnie said. He pointed between the three of them. "And you fucks have known him ten, fifteen years."

Meggie backed out of the doorway and a little farther into the room. "One call to let him know we've gotten there safely."

"Meggie, c'mon," Digger said with frustration, "that won't fly. He's not going to die without hearing from you for one day. And neither will you."

She had no time for this. CJ was making his little baby babbles. "Fine."

Not wanting to hear anymore, she turned, finished talking, needing to get to CJ so she could nurse him. Right before she closed the door, she heard Johnnie mutter, "Don't say I didn't warn you bozos."

Chapter 2

Christopher

CHRISTOPHER "OUTLAW" CALDWELL REARED BACK IN HIS CHAIR in the office of his MC, checking the clock for the millionth time and wondering where the fuck Megan was. Swiveling the chair sideways, he sidled a glance out the big window. The last rays of the sun slipped through the canopy of trees, creating shadows and giving him a sense of the time, even if the fucking clock hadn't been around.

It was time for her to feed his son and she usually came and sat with him in the office during at least one of CJ's feedings. Today, she'd been busy with shit to do with their house, so he kinda understood why she hadn't come in earlier and shared a private lunch with him. Kinda. Now? Some-fucking-thing brewed.

Christopher shifted in his seat, his cock hardening as he fantasized about the milk beading on the tips of Megan's red nipples. Fuck him, but CJ's lease on Megan's tits was set to expire soon. On the other hand, Christopher liked suckling her tits himself and, if he revoked his son's privileges, Megan's milk would dry up. He rolled his shoulders, glanced at the clock, glimpsed the baby thing Megan laid CJ in once he fell asleep, his gaze lingering on the old, brown leather couch where he fucked her once she saw to their son.

She'd been quiet and distant during lunch and just pushed around her food during dinner. Now, this. A no-show. He would've thought she'd be excited as a motherfucker to get her big ass church wedding she'd some-fucking-how talked him into. Yeah, he knew he'd have to do more than the City Hall shit, but she was making him and his boys wear fucking monkey suits and all. The very least she could do was keep him calm with her tits and pussy.

Grabbing his bottle of tequila, he rose to his feet, and stomped out of the office. The moment he opened the door, the noise hit him full force. A lot of motherfuckers were on premises for the bachelor party his boys were giving him the next night. Motherfuckers he hadn't seen in months—and Megan never met—was here.

Christopher swigged his drink and scowled as he drew closer to the opening of the main room. Noise already pounded in the place, the bright lights glinting off the huge mural of the Grim Reaper slapping motherfuckers in the face the moment they stepped inside and looked right.

Cigarette smoke clouded the air, the scent of alcohol, sex, sweat, perfume, cologne—just a fucked up brew of smells— swirled in Christopher's head. He thrust his hands through his hair, frustrated like a motherfucker. He knew Megan was tired of living here, even though this place meant a lot to him. At one time, it had been everything. Not now.

Another swig and a pulsing need for a smoke. Megan had taken center stage in his heart, became the air he needed to breathe and…Fuck him. Fuck. Fuck. Fuck.

And pussy-whipped the fuck out of him. End of fucking story.

Christopher really couldn't figure out what the fuck had crawled up her ass and why she'd been so distant with him for hours now. Had she gotten tired of his lifestyle and decided to leave? He was building a big ass house for her when he was quite content to live right the fuck where he was. He'd agreed to a big ass wedding when he was content as a motherfucker with their civil ceremony.

Valentine's Day was two days away and she'd planned some big ass dinner in their almost-fucking-finished house. A motherfucker that should've been finished fucking months ago.

Laughter drew him and he stepped closer to the entryway. He was always up for a good time—as long as Megan was with him. Call him an obsessed motherfucker, he didn't give a good fuck. Where Megan was, was where he wanted to be. And he knew if he passed the main room on the way to his bedroom, some eagle-eyed motherfucker was going to spot him and then he'd have to socialize.

Another tequila taste and a few more curses fell from his mouth. Just as he was about to move, he saw Megan walking down the hall, his mini-me in her arms, his boy's chubby little hands fisting Megan's golden hair. Every time, Christopher saw his son, Christopher Joseph Foy Caldwell, aka CJ to him and Megan but Little Man to the boys, his heart did a strange little flip.

What Megan held in her arms was the fucking best of him and he thanked the fuck out of his lucky stars every-fucking-day for her.

The moment she stepped in front of the mural, greetings rained her way. Christopher bit back a satisfied smile at the genuine affection for her that he detected from those who knew her.

"That's Megan. Outlaw's old lady," Derby called. He was the president of the Burning Hounds, one of the Dwellers' local support clubs. Derby had visited with his old lady—and without.

Christopher grimaced and brushed the 'without' part aside. Usually, when Derby went without his old lady, he went with Club Ass. Something Megan hated.

"I ain't responsible for where a motherfucker puttin' his fuckin' dick, Megan," he'd snapped the first time she'd seen Derby go off to fuck a girl who wasn't Gypsy, his old lady.

"I know Gypsy. How can I look at this woman and socialize with her, knowing her husband's a pig?"

"Motherfucker ain't her 'husband'," he'd snarled, "so he can stick his cock in whatever cunt he wanna."

Megan had punched his jaw. Actually. Fucking. Punched. His. Motherfucking. Jaw. He'd been madder than a motherfucker and stormed out. They'd just started fucking again after she'd healed from giving birth to his boy. And the reckless little bitch had shut him out of her pussy for two fucking days. She'd won that fucking argument hands down and Christopher had felt like cutting Derby's dick off himself.

Now, when Derby visited, Christopher tried his fucking best to get Megan the fuck to their room before the man fucked over Gypsy.

"Megan, babe!" another male voice yelled, snapping Christopher back to reality, just as she floated toward him again. Instead of ratcheting back up after Derby's and Megan's brief exchange, the noise screeched to a halt. "Come keep us some company. You gonna be off the market soon, so take advantage of it now and have a little fun with me."

Motherfuck him, was some fuckhead hitting on his wife?

"No, thank you," she called back, glancing in Christopher's direction. "I'm already off the market." She started forward again.

And, fuck, if that motherfucker didn't start in on her again. "Just one little kiss."

Who the fuck was that anyfuckingway? Not a motherfucker whose voice Christopher recognized.

"All right, get the fuck out of here," Johnnie snarled. "Fucking with Outlaw's old lady is the quickest way to get yourself dead."

Christopher crooked his finger in Megan's direction and, this time, she reached him. She beamed a smile at him and stood on her tiptoes to kiss his lips. "Hey, you," she said.

"Hey me?" He narrowed his eyes at her. "Where the fuck you been? And who the fuck that fuckhead harrassin' you?"

She shrugged. "I don't know. Then, again, there are a lot of guys here I've never met."

No fucking shit, genius. He scowled at her. "Wait in the office for me, baby." He shoved his bottle of tequila into her hand. "Be right back."

"Christopher!"

Ignoring her call, he went into the main room he'd wanted to avoid. He caught the attention of Bowlie, who was on monitor duty, and the man thrust his chin toward the door. No motherfucker needed to be asked who he was looking for, it seemed, because everyone was suddenly very interested in his movements and not too interested in talking to him.

Before Christopher reached the door, Johnnie appeared, massaging his knuckles.

Disappointment rose in Christopher. "Who the fuck was he?" he asked, cracking his own knuckles and flexing his fingers. His brain understood he wouldn't get the chance to pummel the motherfucker. The rest of him hadn't gotten the message yet.

"No clue," Johnnie answered. "Said he's from the East Coast. Never seen him in my life before earlier today."

"Name?"

"Cee Cee."

Christopher frowned. "What the fuck kinda name that is?"

"Fuck if I know. But the boys won't let him back through the gates. Don't worry."

"Wait a fuckin' minute. Some assfuck walk the fuck in here. Know my girl's name. Proposition her and all he gettin' is a punch and a 'he-ain't-welcome-through-the-gates' no-fuckin-more?" he barked. Megan's strange behavior already had him on edge. Now, this bullshit sent his temper skyrocketing. "What kinda shit is that?"

Digger stepped between him and Johnnie and patted his shoulder. "Yo, Prez, you figured out if Meggie driving herself to the airport or if you driving her there?"

Christopher paused and turned his gaze to Digger. "What the fuck you say?"

"Oh, um." He glanced at Johnnie, then backed up. "My bad."

This day was going from bad to fucking worse. He yanked Digger to him, using his shirt and cut rather than his throat like he really wanted to. "What the fuck you talkin' 'bout?"

Not surprising, Mortician came up to them. Christopher knew Mortician didn't want to see his younger brother snapped in half, a distinct possibility if the motherfucker didn't clarify his words.

"Outlaw," Mortician began in calm tones. "Wassup?"

"This motherfucker askin' me some shit 'bout Megan goin' to the fuckin' airport."

Amusement danced in his cousin's silver eyes and he scratched the five o'clock shadow on his jaw. "I guess Megs didn't tell you, yet, then?"

He shoved aside the apprehension prickling his skin. "What the fuck she gotta tell me?" he asked. Though he spoke to Johnnie, he glared at Digger. He was the motherfucker who'd brought this shit up in the first fucking place.

"That she leaving so you can enjoy your bachelor party," Digger explained. He spoke low and slow, choosing his words with care.

As well he fucking should. "No fuckin' way," Christopher snarled. He looked at the three of them. He might not have understood every-fucking-thing they were thinking, but one thing he did read was the truth in Digger's words. He shoved the man away, knocking him into a table overflowing with glasses and surrounded by bikers with women in their laps. Not that he gave a fuck.

When he reached his office, Megan sat on the floor and already had CJ in the baby thing, rocking him back and forth and cooing to him. CJ was wide awake and playing with some little noisy cloth motherfuckers that amused the shit out of his boy.

Some of Christopher's anger and bad mood evaporated at seeing the two of them. The tightness in his chest eased up and he closed the door behind him. She looked up, her gaze roaming from his head to his boots. He supposed she was checking for signs that he'd kicked the shit out of the fucker who'd been calling out to her.

"Everything okay?" she asked.

"You tell me. Everyfuckinthing okay, Megan?"

"Of course. We'll be married in church in a month. As far as I'm concerned, everything is great."

He glowered at her, the lamplight gleaming off her diamond and sapphire wedding set depending on which way she moved her slim hand. "So why the fuck Digger talkin' 'bout you goin' to some fuckin' airport?"

"Moron," she mumbled around a groan. Unfastening CJ, she scooped him up and hopped to her bare feet. The tips of her hair skimmed her waist, and her tits twitched the ears of some ugly fucking dog on her T-shirt with each breath she took. "Me and the baby are going to Seattle tomorrow, Christopher."

Instead of commenting, he made his way to his seat and dropped into it, glad she'd put his tequila bottle close. He didn't want to jump to conclusions, nor did he want to get into a screaming match with her. She was the only one who always found a way to win against him all the fucking time, he thought sourly.

"What the fuck you gotta do in fuckin' Seattle on this short fuckin' notice?"

"Nothing much," she admitted. "I'm going to visit Lacey and Farrah. Momma's coming with me, too." She shifted her weight and lowered her lashes. "I-I just want to be out of your way, so you can enjoy your bachelor party."

"What the fuck make you think I'ma enjoy that shit with your lil' ass three hundred fuckin' miles away?"

"The time apart will do us good. You don't let me or the baby very far out of your sight and—"

"And fuckin' what? I ain't realize you wantin' away from me for a long time? The last time I left you alone, you was fuckin' pissed and your feelins was fuckin' hurt. Next time you was alone, you got a fuckin' knife plunged in your chest. I thought I was fuckin' doin' what the fuck you want keepin' you fuckin' close."

Having her near all the time was certainly what he wanted. That she felt different shocked the shit out of him.

"You left me for three weeks. Remember?" she huffed.

That was old news. Her sudden decision to leave now had nothing to do with his decision to leave her then.

She bounced CJ on her hip in agitation. "This is just two days and I'm doing it for you."

Something wasn't fucking right. He wasn't sure what. But this fucking idea came out of no-fucking-where when Megan had had every-fucking-thing planned right down to the little pillow things the little kids would carry. Now, she was suddenly flying to Seattle to see two bitches who was supposed to be flying to Hortensia in two weeks for a final fitting?

He smelled a big fucking rat that stank to high fucking heaven.

But from the set of her jaw and the determination in her eyes, he knew he wouldn't get her to budge on her decision. He nodded. "Okay, baby. If that's what you want. You have reservations already?"

"Um, yes." She swallowed, a hint of uncertainty flashing in her eyes.

He had to remind himself she'd only turned nineteen several months ago. He'd already made her a mother and a wife, but that didn't mean she still didn't have some growing up to do herself.

Besides, the words bachelor party put fear in the hearts of many women when it had to do with their man. He could only imagine how Megan was feeling given his history.

He winced. "What time your plane leavin'?"

"Nine tomorrow morning."

"And you comin' back the next day?"

"I couldn't get a reservation then." She sighed. "I have an early morning flight for the day after."

"On fuckin' Valentine's Day?" he asked for clarification. She'd been killing herself to have the kitchen, dining room, and bedroom ready for the dinner she'd planned and…what the fuck was going on?

"I did the best I could," she gritted, raising her chin. She'd gone from bouncing his son to alternating between kissing the top of his head and patting his back.

Muttering a curse, he got to his feet and took his son into his arms. CJ blinked, surprised at the sudden change in terrain, going from resting against Megan's petite softness to being surrounded by Christopher's muscles. The baby looked at Christopher's shoulder and whined.

"I feel you, boy," he said gruffly, kissing the tip of his nose. "You want your gorgeous ma not your big, ugly old man. But you ain't gonna sleep no time soon and Daddy 'bout to burst outta his fuckin' pants—"

"Christopher!" Megan screeched behind him.

Ignoring her, he pulled open the door and carried his boy to the main room. Tonight, the Bobs were out. These were new chicks, not the ones who'd been sent to him for the final fucking interview a couple years ago. He'd fucking considered Megan when he'd passed the other bitches off to some other clubs and he didn't need a degree in psychiatry to know seeing those bitches around all the time had fucked with Megan's head.

He nodded here and there, clapped Derby on the back, and reached his destination. It was Johnnie's turn to watch over CJ, so Christopher headed for his cousin when he spotted him near the pool tables talking to May and Gurly, two girls who had elevated from infrequent visitors to regulars…aka…Club Ass.

May was the color of caramel with skin that looked edible. She had blonde-streaked dark hair styled into little braids, while Gurly was older, about forty-five. If she was younger than that, then her life had been one rough motherfucker judging by the lines on her face and the bags under her eyes. She'd probably been pretty at one time, but life had chewed her the fuck up and left…her.

Both May and Gurly smiled at him when he got to them. He nodded, then turned his attention to Johnnie.

"Get the fuck to your fuckin' room 'til me and Megan come get the lil' motherfucker."

Johnnie finished his beer and wiped the froth from his lips, before whispering something to May and patting Gurly's ass. He didn't seem to mind that he'd have to leave behind some sure pussy. None of the guys did. They doted on his boy because they doted on his ma. Besides, as long as she was happy, Christopher was happy.

With the baby's sitter seen to, he got back to his office—and found it empty. Was he ever getting Megan's fucking pussy tonight? He thrust a frustrated hand through his hair and turned on his heel. A few moments later, he opened his door and walked inside the bedroom, hearing a hard guitar riff resounding from his CD player.

Megan rose to her knees in the middle of their bed, wearing nothing but a hot pink thong. She met his gaze, her blue eyes captivating him. Raising her hand to her breast, she squeezed, for his pleasure because she disliked the sensation of the milk sliding down her champagne-colored skin. Thin lines on her belly, thighs, arms, and legs, reminded him of the cuts she'd given herself to cope with all the bullshit that had been going on in her life at one time. She had the slightest little belly pooch left over from her pregnancy that Christopher only noticed because she pointed it out. Where pussy was concerned, size, age, or race had never mattered to him. Add in how much he loved Megan, she could've turned into the female version of the Incredible Hulk, and he still would've wanted to be with her. Seeing her now, in nothing but her thong, made his dick turn to stone. She was teasing him with her body, taunting him with the vibrating lead guitar, and increasing his suspicions that some bullshit was going on.

He wouldn't bring the shit up now. He wanted to fuck her too bad.

Only about fifteen footsteps separated him from her but, by the time he sat on the edge of the bed, his shirt, cut, and belt was already off and his pants were unzipped. He didn't waste time getting everything else off, her hands roaming his body and the kisses she planted along the way ratcheting up his need for her to animalistic. With a hard pull, he ripped off her thong.

He turned and guided her back onto the pillows, climbing over her and pressing his cock stand against her belly. He took her mouth in a hard kiss, spreading his fingers through her pussy curls and tasting her tongue with his, wanting to devour her. Still kissing her, he opened her pussy lips and thumbed her clit, slipping one finger into her. She was slick and hot, ready for him.

He added another finger and she groaned against his mouth, lifted her hips, searching for her orgasm.

For some reason, he was fucking pissed with her. No, not some fucking reason. One fucking reason. She'd decided to go to Seattle without even asking him if he wanted her away for his bachelor party. She fucking knew him. If he didn't fucking want her there, he would've told her to get the fuck away while his party was going on. Even more fucked up was, if he had told her he wanted her gone, she would've turned into a jealous little bitch and would've been madder than a motherfucker.

He brought her to the brink of coming before pulling his hand away. Her dazed eyes and swollen mouth made him grit his teeth against plunging into her and letting her come all over his dick.

"Christopher," she whispered. "Don't stop. I want you inside me."

He kissed the tender skin behind her ear and slid his tongue across her throat. "You like my dick, dontcha, Megan?"

"Yes."

Oh, yeah, infuckingdeed, she did. She twisted and pushed her pussy against his thigh, grinding against him.

"That ain't my dick, Megan," he pointed out, unable to hold back his laughter. He grabbed her hips and stilled them. His cock throbbed. Demanding he shove this bullshit aside until after he got inside Megan.

She growled in frustration, her hazy passion deserting her when she lifted her head and glanced at him, her hair pooling onto the pillow, her body already flushed from arousal. "You're angry."

"No fuckin' shit, genius." He glared at her, refusing to allow her big, blue eyes to suck him in. "If I woulda told your fuckin' ass to leave, you woulda turned into some psycho bitch. Yet, you make that fuckin' decision and I'm supposed to be fuckin' happy about it."

"You're so frustrating," she complained, flopping her head down. "If I would've stayed here for your bachelor party, everyone would've accused me of being clingy and not wanting you to have fun. Not trusting you."

"Fuck everyone," he yelled, his eyes drawn to her opened thighs and her glistening pussy, begging to be licked. "I've made up my fuckin' mind and you ain't fuckin' leavin'. Case fuckin' closed."

She blinked and narrowed her eyes, her entire body stiffening. Fuck him. He knew the belligerence dropping into her features. His nostrils flared, her anger overwhelming him with the need to possess her.

"What did you just say, jerk?"

He threw her a dirty look, fisting his hands so he wouldn't pin her arms above her head and fuck her senseless. "As if you didn't fuckin' hear me."

She scrambled up, her breasts heavy with milk, her nipples swollen. The sight of her golden pussy hair, wetness glistening off the curls closest to her cunt lips and her thighs, made his mouth water.

"You don't own me, Christopher. I'm your wife, not your child. I love you as a grown woman, not a little girl."

He scowled. "I know what the fuck you is, Megan."

She raised her chin and folded her arms, lifting her succulent tits. "You can't stop me from going wherever I want to go."

He glowered at the ceiling, unsure why he was acting like such a controlling motherfucker with her. Well…Okay, so, maybe, he was slightly controlling where Megan was concerned, but fuck him, he didn't want anything to happen to her. She crossed over him, her intent to get out of the bed quite clear.

Nope, wouldn't fucking happen.

Before her feet hit the floor, he grabbed her around the waist and pulled her back against him. She tried to squirm away, but he pinned her arms above her head, flattening his other hand against her belly to hold her in place. Nothing worked until he bent his head and suckled one of her nipples. Hard.

She groaned and arched her back. Her milk was sweet and watery and the way her body provided for their son fascinated the fuck out of him. Assured of her compliance, he released her arms, still latched onto her nipple, and spread her legs.

His kissed his way down her belly, grasping some of her pussy hair between his teeth and tugging.

"Christopher."

He ran his nose along her seam, smelling her essence. "Ain't nothin' I love more than eatin' this pussy, Megan." He ran his tongue along the same path his nose had taken, and she shivered against him. Opening her lips, he licked her tender pink flesh, swirling his tongue around her clit, inserting it into her pussy and lapping her inner folds. "I could worship at the feast of Megan's pussy for hours." He wrapped his lips around her little clit and sucked, careful not to bite too hard, but still applying pressure. She trembled against him, and he worked his mouth, tongue, and teeth faster until her pussy juice dripped down his chin and her breath were nothing but short, little pants and cries.

Fuck, his balls were so full, the moment he buried himself in Megan, he would fill her up with his cum. But, fuck, if it wasn't worth it, to have her body flushed and limp beneath him, sweetly open to take every inch of him inside her. He inched back up her body, kissing every patch of skin he met, until his body covered hers. Bracing on one arm, his other hand met hers at his dick and they guided him to her entrance. He thrust into her and grunted at her wet heat. She dug her nails into his biceps and canted her hips.

"Fuck, Megan. Fuck. Fuck. Fuck."

"Come in me," she whispered, her intense regard holding him captive.

He slammed into her, his body shaking when his cum began to pour from him. He squeezed his eyes shut, trying to focus, but his head was filled with the scent and taste of his wife. The more he thought of her, the more he shook. The more he shook, the more he felt little droplets of cum seep from him and into her. She licked the sweat from his shoulder, and he wanted to fuck her again. Instead, he opened his eyes and found her staring at him.

"I love you," she murmured.

"I love you, too, Megan," he said hoarsely, brushing strands of her damp hair behind her ear and rubbing his nose against hers.

She licked his nipple. "My turn, Christopher."

She pushed at his shoulder, his cue to lie on his back. Clutching her ass, he reversed their positions. Disappointment surged through him when she lifted herself off his dick and fell to his side, then raised herself up on an elbow. He supposed she wanted to talk.

"Did the priest really say we can play the Wedding March?" She laid between his legs and kissed around his navel, wrapping her hand around his cock and funneling him in her hand.

How the fuck did she expect him to concentrate with his dick in her hand and her mouth so close to it?

"Christopher?" Her hand slid up and down his dick again, still slick with her pussy juice. "The Wedding March?" Another tug and pull. A pass of her thumb over his cock head. "The priest flat out refused me to allow a secular song in the church."

God. Fuck. Jesus. He couldn't even think of fucking words to explain why the fuck that fat motherfucker gave in. Even if he'd been inclined to, which he fucking wasn't. He didn't need Megan pointing out how threatening to gut a Man of God was probably a sin. She still didn't get that he'd lost his soul ages a-fucking-go because she saw past all the bullshit and found his heart. Fuck, yeah, he had a heart for her and their baby. Any other motherfucker? All bets were off. Well, except for Johnnie, Val, Mortician, and Digger.

She squeezed his dick and he groaned, clutching the sheets to keep from yanking her by the hair and shoving his dick down her throat.

"I can have the Wedding March?"

Each diocese had different rules and this one didn't vary much from others in that the Wedding March was considered secular music and wasn't usually played within the confines of the sanctuary. But Megan wanted it, so Megan got it. No one had to know of the threats and dire warnings, especially her. That wasn't important. Only the end result was.

He choked. "Yes."

"Thank you." Her breath fanned his skin and goose bumps ran along his body. "I love being your wife. I just want our marriage blessed. And, now, I'm going to have a perfect wedding. All because of you."

"Anything for—"

The word 'you' flew right the fuck out of his brain when Megan dropped her saliva onto his dick and slurped him into her mouth. His eyes crossed at her hard sucks. She cupped his balls, and he gripped her hair hard enough to fucking scalp her. Jerking his dick up and down, Christopher realized he'd corrupted the fuck out of her and turned her from an innocent virgin into a little firecracker in bed. Not that he'd change that, but still…

His dick went back into the haven of her mouth, her head bobbing up and down, her face flushed. Her hand wrapped around his cock base and, as her head went up, so did her hand, giving him a blowjob and a hand job at one time.

"Megan, baby," he moaned, near the edge, hoping like a motherfucker he didn't blow the back of her head off when he shot his load. Fuck! He pulled out of her mouth, grabbed her, and flipped her over. He buried himself so deep inside of her, he was probably touching her tonsils. He growled and pounded her like a fucking animal until his seed exploded inside of her and he saw fucking stars.

Chapter 3

Meggie

"**W**HERE ARE YOU GOING, MOMMA?" MEGGIE CALLED AS Dinah squeezed past her in the cramped airplane cabin.

Her mother paused and glanced back, discomfort in her features. She pursed her mouth. "I'm switching seats, Meggie."

Meggie shifted CJ in her lap, looking at his little sleeping face. She was already suspicious that her mother had given her son something to make him sleep so soundly. Dinah had taken him to the bathroom while they waited to board and, by the time the twenty minutes had passed, her son was asleep. Now, they had barely pushed back, and her mother was switching seats with someone else?

"No," Meggie ordered. "I could've taken the window seat, but I gave it to you because I know you'd prefer that. I want you next to me." She wanted to find out what Dinah had given her baby. It was one thing to totally leave her to hang dry as she had after she'd married that monster. It was quite another thing to do it to her son.

"Sorry, Meggie," Dinah said quietly.

"Ma'am, excuse me. You need to take your seat," the stewardess said in a stern but kind voice. She had a casual look with a Polo shirt banded at the collar and sleeves in blue and a pencil skirt.

It was the type of outfit Dinah would've once worn and looked great in as an assistant high school principal. Meggie suspected with a little maintenance to her hair and care to her face, her mother would still look fabulous. Maybe, she'd buy a few outfits for Dinah while they were on vacation and use the excuse of splurging during their girls' trip.

"Ma'am?" the stewardess prompted when Dinah stood, unmoving, a doe caught in the headlights with nowhere to run.

"Sorry, we got it mixed up," a man said. His voice was familiar but before Meggie could look at him, he slipped past her and sat in her mother's vacated seat.

"No, wait!" Meggie called. But the stewardess was already leading Dinah away.

"Nice boy," the man next to her said.

She glowered at him, startled to see a cut peeking out from his leather jacket. His face was weather-beaten, his head covered with a blue bandanna. But he sounded familiar and something about him looked familiar. She didn't know what and felt like pitching her shoe at her mother's head for leaving her in a lurch with this man.

He gave her chills with the way his green eyes studied her and stared at CJ. Thank God, the flight wouldn't last long. Still, it was going to be an uncomfortable seventy-five minutes. CJ's little mouth moved, and she smiled at him, her heart just not big enough to hold all the love she felt for her son. Or her son's father.

She was already sorry she'd agreed to what the guys asked her, but she also knew it wasn't normal the way she and Christopher were attached to one another. Still, it was going to be difficult until she saw him again. She hadn't slept anywhere but next to him for over a year.

"I'm Cee Cee, by the way."

She cleared her throat. "Nice to meet you." Not. She wished he'd shut up if he couldn't go away.

"You from around these parts?"

Meggie's nerves were frayed. Between already missing Christopher, being upset with how easily Dinah had given her seat to a stranger, and Meggie's suspicion that Dinah had drugged her son, she didn't feel very mannerly. "Cee Cee? That's your name, right?" She didn't give him a chance to answer. "I'm not in the mood to talk, so if you have to sit next to me, please don't talk to me."

Soft laughter rumbled from him, and he shifted in the narrow space, his leg touching hers, his arm brushing her breast. She stiffened and remembered Thomas, her stepfather. Christopher had taken care of him, but Meggie still carried the memories. And her husband wasn't there now to protect her while she had a son to protect and a mother who hadn't healed—might never heal—

from the abuse she'd suffered at Thomas's hands. In this, she had to take care of herself and her son.

He flexed his fists, and she noticed the tattoos on his fingers. He had big hands, and, from his demeanor, Meggie suspected he'd used those hands in violence. He was tall and broad with a weathered face, sharp features, and an earring in his left ear. She realized he also had a black eye and a lip scabbed over.

"You Outlaw's old lady, aren't you?"

"And?" she asked with as much venom as possible.

"Meggie, right?"

The moment he said her name, she remembered where she'd heard his voice. He'd been the one calling out to her last night.

"I'm not from around here, Meggie," he continued. "Not anymore."

No use in beating around the bush. "What do you want, Cee Cee? Tell me and I'll relay the message to my husband."

He smiled at her. A mean, nasty smile that Meggie didn't like at all. Yet, the curve of his mouth lured her. It was so eerily familiar, almost a mirror of Christopher's.

He shrugged. "He doesn't really know me. Heard his mother got popped."

Meggie gasped. Speaking of Patricia's death so casually told her he didn't care one way or the other about the poor woman's death. And thinking of Patricia made her think of Ellen and Kiera, two women who had been shot point-blank by Meggie's lunatic brother. She shook a little, hating to think of that day. So many times, she'd wondered if she'd done something different could she have saved them. Either of them. All of them.

Christopher always said 'no'. Nothing could be done.

She squirmed in her seat. The man smelled fresh and clean with the scent of leather and alcohol clinging to him. She glanced across the aisle to her mother. Dinah was two rows back on the opposite side in an aisle seat. She looked unhappy and tired. Then, again, when had her mother been happy? Not any time in Meggie's recent memory.

"You're not too talkative, are you?"

Not when I'm dealing with morons. No.

Instead of blurting that, she held her tongue, pretending to ignore him under the guise of shifting the baby. She watched the rise and fall of his little chest and slanted another evil glance to her mother.

"You need me to hold your boy?" Cee Cee asked, already reaching for CJ.

Meggie didn't think. She just reacted and swatted his hand away. "Don't touch my baby," she snarled. He paused and lifted a black brow, but she wouldn't back down. Not where her child was concerned.

After another sweeping glance at her, he nodded and dropped his hands to his lap, balling them into fists. "I didn't know you two was already hitched."

Somehow, she'd missed the entire safety procedures the stewardess's had gone over. Because it was such a short flight, there would be no food service. Not that Meggie cared. Food was the last thing on her mind, right now.

"I don't bite."

Meggie jumped to her feet and stomped to her mother. "Go to that seat and sit next to that pervert yourself," she hissed.

"Meggie, please," Dinah whispered. "You're going to draw attention to us. I-I don't want any trouble, so just go back to your seat. We're not going to be on the flight much longer."

"I'm going to tell the stewardess. I want police waiting for him at the gate. I don't like him. He gives me the creeps."

"No, don't, baby. You're just paranoid. He might be overly friendly, but he means no harm. Please," she whined. "Don't cause a scene."

She gritted her teeth, not sure why she listened to a woman who had zero protective instincts in her. Her guard up, she returned to her seat, wanting to smack the man's ridicule off his face. Time for a different approach.

Two minutes passed before he spoke again. "How long you been Mrs. Christopher Caldwell."

The way he said her name raised the hairs on Meggie's nape. "How did you get all this information?"

Whenever he smiled, his thin lips took on a cruel twist. Like now. "Word travels through the clubs about your rivals, your allies. Everyone. We have to keep tabs on folk, don't we? Can't be too careful."

"No, you can't," she said with meaning.

He barked a laughed. "Quite right, Meggie. Quite right. Let me give you an example of how word travels: I know you're Big Joe's girl."

She frowned and swallowed. Another sore spot with her, simply because of Christopher's involvement in her daddy's demise.

"You're no fun," Cee Cee complained, getting to his feet. "I'm gonna send your mama back to you."

He slid past her. Within a moment, her mother was scuttling past her and dropping in the seat next to Meggie.

"Meggie—"

"What did you give my baby?"

Dinah swallowed. "A little Tylenol and a little Benadryl."

Meggie's heart nearly stopped, and her gaze dropped to her son. He was still breathing at a steady rate, his little mouth still moving like he was nursing. He had that baby scent that she adored. But her mother had drugged her son. She stood to go to the stewardess to ask if he needed first aid. She'd never given him medicine in his short life, and anything could happen to him.

Her mother grabbed her arm and Meggie jerked away, cradling CJ in her arms. "Don't. Touch. Me."

Dinah released Meggie's arm, her eyes filling with desperation. "Please. He's going to be fine. It was just a quarter dropper of Benadryl and a quarter dropper of Tylenol. Sit back down. Please."

Cee Cee smirked at her from his seat and Meggie slid next to her mother. "I should report you," she hissed.

"It wasn't a lot," Dinah said defensively, and bit down on her lip. "I did it for him. He would've been screaming from the pressure in his little ears. Disturbing everyone. Getting men angry."

"Don't talk to me," Meggie spat, angry. She shouldn't have said anything else until she calmed down. But Dinah's refusal to get in touch with reality continued to amaze her. Why? She didn't know. "I should never have brought you with me. What have you ever done for me but made my life miserable?"

Tears rushed to Dinah's eyes and added to everything else, guilt surged through Meggie, and she groaned.

What a great frigging start to her trip.

CJ STIRRED JUST A LITTLE WHILE MEGGIE WAITED AT SEA-TAC for Farrah's arrival. She'd already collected her overnight bag, filled mostly with baby things. It sat next to her while she contemplated how to maneuver her son and her phone, so she could search the Internet for the effects of the medicine her mother had administered.

"Need help?"

"NO!" Meggie screeched to Cee Cee. "I need you to leave me alone." She glanced over her shoulder at her mother. Dinah stood a few feet away, staring straight ahead, dejection and defeat screaming from her. Her blonde hair was in a messy bun. She'd stopped bothering with makeup years ago. Black sweats made her look old and sallow. Meggie could readily forgive her mother anything. Except putting her son in danger. "You need someone to talk to, keep my mother company."

He rocked back on his steel-toed boots, and she glanced up at his taunting green eyes and thin mouth. He laughed and started off. "See you round, Meggie girl," he called over his shoulder, his chuckles trailing behind him.

A slamming car door drew Meggie's attention away from Cee Cee's retreating back.

"Meggie!" A voice screamed.

Farrah barreled into her in a blur of motion and grabbed Meggie in a tight hug, her blonde-streaked chestnut hair ruffling around her.

CJ gurgled, and Meggie almost fell to the ground in relief. His eyes opened for a moment, his mouth made the rooting movement, before he went right back to sleep.

"Oops, sorry," Farrah chirped. She removed CJ from her arms without permission. "Omigod, he's gorgeous!"

"Is he okay? My mom gave him Benadryl and Tylenol," she said in a rush. "Should we take him to the emergency room?"

Farrah wrinkled her nose, her whiskey-colored eyes filled with disgust. "He'll be fine, Megster. My mother did it to my little sisters all the time."

Meggie picked up her overnight bag, sincerely wishing she had it in her to leave her mother right there. It didn't matter if Farrah's mother doped up her little sisters. They were her children, and she made the choice to abuse them. CJ was Meggie's son and Dinah didn't have any right to make such decisions.

Farrah opened the cargo bay of her Range Rover and Meggie dropped her bag in, then glared at her mother so Dinah could do the same. Once the car was loaded, Meggie glanced at the back row and smiled.

"Thanks," she called to Farrah when she saw the car seat. "Tell me how much I owe you, so I can reimburse you."

"Are you kidding me?" Farrah handed Meggie the baby so she could secure him in the car seat. "Repay your son's aunt?"

Meggie giggled. If only she and Farrah were related.

"All set," she called and started to climb in.

"You sit in the front, Meggie," Dinah suggested. "You girls can catch up. I'll sit in the back with CJ."

In response, Meggie gave her mother the evil eye and slammed the door shut.

"It's fine, Dinah," Farrah assured her, opening the front door for her. Her mother obediently got in.

They rode in silence, giving Meggie a chance to look up the effects of the medicine. CJ met the weight requirements for the Benadryl but not the age requirements for the dosages her mother had given him. She kept a close watch on him and saw that he showed no signs of distress.

Glancing out the window, it surprised Meggie how far removed she felt from the life she'd led here before she'd become a wife and a mother, when she was still a frightened little girl who hadn't known what to do to save herself or her mother. She'd grown up since she'd run away and couldn't wait to get to her hotel to unwind and curl in bed with CJ to catch up on Farrah's life. Lacey was going to meet them later and they'd spend the next two days exploring Pike Place Market, which held so many happy memories for Meggie. Visits there with her mother had been before Dinah became this shell of a woman.

"Uh, Farrah?" Meggie called, frowning when she realized they were on I-405, not I-5. "You're going the wrong way."

Farrah waved a careless hand. "Not! We're going shopping then we'll get to the hotel."

Meggie blew out an irritated breath and settled back in her seat. No use in wasting her breath to dissuade Farrah. The girl's middle name should be Shopping.

She glanced at the phone, wanting to text Christopher but remembering her stupid promise. Since he hadn't called her, yet, maybe, the guys were right. Maybe, he was happy for this time apart. She wasn't. Call her obsessed but she loved staring into Christopher's green eyes and slipping her fingers through his black hair. Her man was big and strapping with corded muscles in his arms, ripped abs, and hard thighs.

She squeezed her legs together, her clit swelling, her core hot and wet. Shameless.

While fantasies of her husband enthralled Meggie, Farrah found a parking spot. Meggie took CJ into her arms since she hadn't brought his stroller, or the baby carrier Christopher liked to use. Chuckling at the thought of CJ strapped to Christopher's chest, she followed Farrah and her mother to Neiman Marcus.

"May I use your phone?" Dinah asked and held her hand out.

Without answering, Meggie handed her mother the cellphone and then continued behind Farrah, who was model-thin and had grown up in wealth. It showed in her every move, by the flick of her wrist, as if she expected the world to bow down to her. Still, she was Meggie's friend and had never been anything but kind to her.

"I have to buy my nephew some rags," she announced, stopping here and there to look at a purse or test perfume.

Meggie liked to wear heels and looked halfway stylish in her winter white heeled booties with pants and a form-fitting top the same color. Her subconscious knew Farrah and had prompted

Meggie to dress accordingly. If CJ had been awake, chances were high he would've slobbered all over her.

"He doesn't need new clothes, you know, Auntie Farrah?" Meggie called in amusement once they reached the children's department.

Farrah ignored her and continued to hold up outfit after outfit.

Meggie cradled CJ in her arms, rocked him back and forth and kissed his head. "If you don't stop, I'm going to have to buy another suitcase."

"I'll just shove his clothes in my bag and bring them when I come in for the rehearsal dinner."

Once Farrah satisfied herself with the number of baby things, she decided CJ needed, they headed for the dresses. Her mother rejoined them as a tuxedo dress with a leather hem caught Meggie's attention. By now, CJ's deadweight resembled two tons, no matter how many times she shifted him from arm to arm.

"Cute!" Farrah called. "That'll be great for tonight."

Dinah strolled to the dress and grabbed the tag, then gasped. "Did you see the price of this?"

One thing at a time, Meggie thought, a very intense headache setting in. "What's going on tonight?"

Farrah lifted a brow and shook a piece of hair out of her eye. "The strip club, of course."

The what? "I'm not going to watch men take off their clothes. Especially tonight. I'm tired and, in case you've forgotten, I have a baby to look after."

Farrah rolled her eyes. "Dinah can watch him."

Meggie gave her a-bitch-are-you-stupid look and turned to her mother when Dinah tugged on her shirt.

"This dress is almost a thousand dollars, Megan. There's no reason for any woman to own something so expensive."

"Meggie, you're going to that frigging club." Farrah slapped her hands on her hips and glared at her. "We haven't hung out together in months. No, years."

"You don't have the money to buy this dress." Dinah pocketed Meggie's cell phone and sniffed. "You'll only embarrass yourself at the register."

Meggie blinked at the barrage of words, hitting her from both sides and aggravating two different nerves. The one reserved for annoying mothers and the other reserved for cheeky friends. "Momma, stop talking out of my wallet."

"You don't have a job," Dinah pointed out through tight lips.

So, maybe, her next move was juvenile, but Farrah and Dinah shoved her to her wit's end. Glaring at her mother, she found the dress in her size, grabbed it from the rack, and stomped to the cash register. Once she completed her purchase, she bit out, "Take me to the hotel. Now!"

She'd channeled the way her husband barked out his words very well, satisfied when Farrah scurried to do her bidding.

Chapter 4

Christopher

CHRISTOPHER REARED BACK IN HIS CHAIR, GLANCING AT the naked girls fanning out in all directions of the main room at the clubhouse. Extra women had been brought in for tonight's festivities because the two dozen Bobs hadn't been enough to handle all the men on hand. This bullshit was the reason Megan had left with her whiny ass Ma early this morning. It amazed the fuck out of Christopher how he appreciated the beauty of other girls, but only wanted to fuck one in particular. He couldn't even imagine laying a hand on no other bitch now that he had Megan. She'd turned his life upside down from the day they met. Not only did she stand up to him, she stood up for him. Saw him as a man worthy of love.

His cousin's laughter rang out and Christopher saw Johnnie leaning on the bar, chatting up two tall, black-haired chicks. Megan had turned his cousin's life upside down, too, the big fucking elephant in the room, always hovering between them. Christopher gave a mental shrug. Tough shit. She was Christopher's. Case fucking closed. Not to say he didn't wish Johnnie shitloads of fucking happiness—he did. Just as long as he stayed the fuck away from his wife with his refined fucking shit, preppy fucking look and smooth fucking words.

He hated the resentment stewing inside him. After all, he'd been the stupid assfuck that left his girl with John Boy. Yet…fucking *yet*…somewhere inside of him, he'd expected the same respect he'd given Johnnie. Not once had Christopher ever tried to make a play for Iona. When they fucking argued, Christopher listened to her. If she needed a ride and Johnnie couldn't make it, Christopher was there. The times Johnnie went out of town for the medical lab, Christopher made sure Iona didn't need anything. Because of her, he'd gone Nomad. Supposedly. In truth, Christopher knew Johnnie's decision had to do with Boss.

At times, that motherfucker threw Christopher and Iona together as a fucking test. He'd never been fucking sure if Johnnie was testing his ass or his bitch. None of it fucking matter anyfuckinway cuz she was *Johnnie's*.

He'd always been everybody's Golden Child, especially Logan Donovan's, their grandfather. And Christopher had been so fucking proud of his cousin. He'd admired and respected him and wanted nothing but the best for him. It had never occurred to Christopher that, before Megan, the motherfucker had never gotten rejected. This was fucking why rejection did a motherfucker good. A rebuff here, a spurn there…when that shit happened efuckinnuff it became just a fucking thing.

Christopher tasted his beer, wishing like a motherfucker he'd convinced Megan to stay and wondering why the fuck she hadn't fucking called him, yet. She'd been gone ten fucking hours, twenty-eight minutes and—he glanced at his watch—seven seconds.

He pulled at his hair. Maybe, she had a fucking point. If she'd stayed, everybody would've noted his pussified behavior over her. Just because she had him pussy-whipped like a motherfucker—paranoid, and, yeah, fucking insecure—didn't mean he wouldn't hesitate to do his job to keep motherfuckers in line.

Take now, for instance. His boys had overlooked Christopher's faithfulness and dedication to Megan. Maybe, some of the others didn't know how much of a weakness Megan was for him—but his fucking brothers in his club knew. So why did strange bitches keep coming up to him offering a dick suck or a quick fuck?

He was getting more pissed by the second, his mood worsened because he hadn't heard from Megan at all today. He was still a fucking killer. Still rude and crude as a motherfucker. He was still him. Had she gotten tired of it and took this opportunity to leave him?

You fuckin' losin' it, fuckhead.

Was he?

She was stronger now. She'd gotten her GED and even talked about college. Some of the brothers saw how happy he was and already had old ladies themselves and kids on the way. Megan had made friends with a lot of the new chicks. She stayed out of Official Club Business, but she'd managed to glue a frayed club back together. They celebrated things, even his birthday. Did more than throw pussy, herbs, and assignments at newly patched-in members. They were a family again, brothers in every sense of the word. Because of her. Because he sure as fuck didn't have a clue what the fuck a family did. His maternal grandparents had despised him and his sisters loathed and shunned him. All Christopher knew about families were that they blamed you for shit that couldn't be controlled—by them or him—and they didn't stick around in times of need.

Somehow, the former president, Megan's father, knew what it took. Christopher thought he'd learned it, too, but, with the man's death, he hadn't been able to pull his shit together.

"Yo, Outlaw, what the fuck you sitting in this big ass leather chair for looking like you lost your best fucking friend?" Digger pulled up a chair, commandeered from a nearby table. He'd cut his dreads and now they just touched his shoulders. It seemed as if the dude was stepping out of his brother's shadow and, little by little, changing his hair. Couldn't do fuck all with his face, though. He shared a striking resemblance to Mortician, just a little leaner and taller. "At least, you can fucking smile, Prez."

He glowered at Digger. "Ain't got to do shit if I don't fuckin' feel like it."

Mortician sauntered up to him and patted Digger's cheek. Digger knocked his brother's hand away.

"I don't want your dick fingers on my pretty face, fool."

Mortician laughed, wearing his trademark skull ring and diamond ear studs. "Just touched the base, bro. Had to guide it to that Bob's mouth."

Christopher rubbed his eyes and emptied his beer. "Still got dick fingers, Mort."

Mortician shrugged. "Mixed with pussy." He signaled a chick over. Her face was as round as her body and Mortician checked her out from head to toe. "Umm, you one fine motherfucker, girl."

She giggled and Christopher rolled his eyes. Give him fucking strength.

After Mortician gave the girl his order, he went behind Christopher and leaned his arms on the top of the office chair. Apparently, this was some fucking signal because Val and Johnnie joined the group. He supposed if K-P and Stretch hadn't been somewhere getting fucked, they would've joined him, too, and then he'd have all his officers at his side. As if he needed baby-fucking-sitting.

"What's up, Prez?" Val asked. He thrust his chin out to one of the brothers, ordering the man, without words, to give up his seat. Once he sat, he drew out a bud, lit it, took a couple puffs, then began passing it around. "You not enjoying your party?"

"No. I ain't enjoyin' my fuckin' party," he snapped.

Mortician took his drags, then poured himself a glass of tequila, after passing the herb to Johnnie. "That's what the fuck I'm talking about. Young pussy. I'm gonna stay far away from that shit. A man get too addicted to showing a young bitch how to fuck. She gets his nose wide open and the next thing you know, a man hooked on one pussy."

"Fuck off," Christopher growled. Yeah, he'd taught Megan all about fucking and shit with her—how fucking sensitive to his touch her body was—continued to amaze him. But Mortician sounded too fucking amused. "Ima bet you a fuckin' G, you gonna end up with some young pussy yourfuckinself." After he puffed on the roll, he kept it, needing another hit before he passed it to Digger. "When your ass do, my ass gonna laugh in your fuckin' face, motherfucker."

Mortician shifted behind Christopher. "Not happening, Outlaw. Not in a million fucking years."

Johnnie flicked a lighter to light the cigarette hanging from his mouth. Once he did, he blew out smoke and grinned. "You're fucking sure about that, Mort?"

"I'm so sure I'm willing to up the ante to five Gs."

Digger finally got his turn with Aunt Mary. "What the fuck the bet?" he asked once he'd released the smoke.

"That assfuck here fall in love with a young bitch like Meggie," Val answered.

"I'm in," Digger announced, grabbing the tequila from Mortician and drinking straight from the bottle. "You talk too fucking much, Mortician. That shit got to come back and bite you in the ass. Straight up."

Mortician cursed as Val and Johnnie cast their bets on Christopher and Digger's side.

"I'm not losing," Mortician grouched. "I'm not handing out twenty large over no woman."

"Why not go all in?" Johnnie challenged. "Make it twenty-five apiece."

Digger squinted. "What the fuck you mean, John Boy? If that mother—" he pointed to Mort— "got to give us twenty-five Gs, we got to ante up, too."

"Only if we fuckin' lose, Digger," Christopher said. He smirked at Mort. "We ain't."

"Yeah, Prez, you will," Mort countered, scowling before remembering expressions like that might get him fucked up. "I'm never falling in love again. I could meet a woman ten years older than me or ten fucking years younger. It won't make a fucking difference."

"No motherfucker here talking about a broad older than you," Val said. "The bet state a young bitch going to bring you to your fucking knees."

"Fuck, you want to up the fucking bet to twenty-five?" Mort snarled, glaring at Johnnie. "Bring it, motherfucker."

Johnnie grinned. "It's brought." He looked at Christopher. "You in."

"Fuck yeah," Christopher said.

"Count me the fuck in too," Val chortled.

Mortician lifted a brow at Digger. "What about you, fool?"

"Bet, Mort," Digger said. "Murphy's Law, bruh. Law of averages. Whatever you want to call your being so smug and certain. That's just when the fuck shit go fucking sideways when you think everything right side up."

Christopher agreed wholeheartedly.

"If Meggie was here, you'd be partying like fuck," Digger pointed out, changing the topic and getting back to his girl.

Yeah, he would. If she'd just *called,* he'd be partying like a motherfucker. But she hadn't and she wasn't answering his calls. Too much fucking worry consumed him for him to think about fucking partying.

"Megan left for nothing if you just sitting around, looking like something from *Paranormal Activity.*"

Christopher opened his mouth to say something when he noticed a tall redhead bitch heading for him. At least six feet, the beauty had endless legs, heavy breasts, a slender waist, round hips, and a shaved pussy, while her red hair flirted with her ribcage and curled at the ends.

The surety of her movements and the heat in her big, brown eyes made Christopher's head pound. This bitch better have been sent by motherfuckers who didn't know Megan. Or the fact that she trusted him enough to leave town with her mother and Christopher's son, so he could enjoy this shit the boys had planned for him.

The redhead sat on Christopher's lap and grinded against his crotch. The fact that his dick jumped pissed him the fuck off even more. But he was a man with a well-functioning cock. Having pussy grinded on him would get a response from almost any motherfucker.

He surged up…and shoved her back so hard she landed not only on her ass but flat on her back, staring up at the ceiling. He shot to his feet and pulled out his nine, fed fucking up. Everything screeched to a motherfucking halt. Just like the fuck it should.

"I told all you fuckheads don't send no bitches to me. Bring me the motherfucker who want to smile in my wife's face then send me a whore to fuck while she away?"

"Outlaw, calm down," Johnnie said. He kept a smile on his face, so the words sounded like they came from some talking fucking puppet or some shit, then glanced at the gun. Christopher knew his cousin was debating on whether to touch him and try to force his hand down.

He kept fucking still, which, in Christopher's opinion was a wise fucking choice.

"You know the boys didn't mean any harm," he continued, closer to Christopher so he could speak in low tones, instead of through his teeth. "Don't ruin your own fucking bachelor party by shooting some dumb fuck."

Christopher narrowed his eyes, but Johnnie didn't waver, holding his ground—out of stupidity or sheer determination.

"Yeah, Outlaw, let it go," Digger said. "We didn't tell the stupid bitch to go to you. She done that on her own."

The girl was sitting up now, still looking at Christopher with come-fuck-me eyes. Johnnie scowled at her, walked over and yanked her to her feet. She looked too refined to be a whore, but, what the fuck did Christopher know about bitches? Enough money bought off years of wrinkles and hard living with plastic surgery and all that other bullshit.

Val's tear-drop tat on his left cheek crinkled when he frowned. "We have a bunch of bitches here, Prez. The Bobs and our Club Ass know not to fuck with you, but the outside girls wouldn't."

Christopher thought about what Megan would say if she found out he'd put a hole in some stupid motherfucker for disrespecting her by sending a whore to him while she was gone. Fuck. She wouldn't like it. His piece disappeared inside his cut and he nodded. "Then clue them the fuck in because not a motherfucker alive disrespectin' my girl like this." He glared at the room in general. "You hear me, fuckheads? You wanna continue to be welcome on premises, not get a bullet in your ass, you fuckin' keep it straight with my wife. Fuck as many bitches as you want. Fuck 'em 'til your dick drop the fuck off. Ain't no other bitch gettin' me except Megan. Now, I ain't gonna fuckin' repeat myself. Get the word out. Take out a ad in the newspaper: *Outlaw Caldwell only fucks Megan Caldwell.* I don't give a rat's fuck. Just don't let there ever, *ever* be a repeat of this shit afuckingain."

"Not like we'll ever get the chance, Outlaw," Mortician reminded him. "In the months since you and Meggie girl been married, this the first time you two been apart for more than half a day."

"And she fuckin' lucky she got to go this time," Christopher snarled. "Took CJ with her, too."

"Give Megs a break," Johnnie protested. Not loud, though. He valued his fucking teeth. "On a good day, you're a fucking Neanderthal with Megan."

Then, again, maybe, he didn't value the motherfuckers.

"Outlaw, we promise we gonna do better about getting the word out, brother," the barrel-chested president of their bigger support club called. He raised a shot glass. "Now, I propose a toast to you and the missus."

Hollering and congratulations competed with the sound of glasses, bottles, and cans clanking together. The toast appeased him, but he was fucking through. He couldn't take one more minute of this bullshit.

"John Boy," Christopher called, baring his teeth in dislike at the girl he'd all but forgotten about until she peeped from behind Johnnie. "It's gonna be a long fuckin' two days. I'm goin' to my fuckin' room."

Johnnie smiled at the girl. "Turn the corner, go left and head to the last room on the left hand side of the hallway. Wait for me there, gorgeous."

She nodded and scampered away. Christopher realized she hadn't spoken one word. Of course, whores weren't there to talk. They were there to fuck. But, hell, the way a bitch sounded could make or break the deal, too.

"Let's go have another smoke," he ordered and turned, coming face-to-face with the gigantic mural of the Grim Reaper holding a bloody scythe while his eye sockets burned like hellfire. A smaller version was on his left forearm. Covering the scar on his shoulder left by his most recent bullet wound was an intricate tattoo with a dove, a heart, roses, and Celtic knots with the name *Patricia*, in memory of his ma. He'd already had a tattoo on his right forearm to honor her.

At his door, Christopher rifled through his keys until he found the proper one. Once all five of them were in the room, he locked it again.

A huge, framed photo of a pregnant Megan greeted Christopher. She stood sideways, her gorgeous face looking into the camera, her hands covering her breasts. In the photo, he stood behind her, leaning into her, his hand resting on her bulging belly. In size, coloring, and age, he was a stark contrast to her and he figured that's what drew him the most to her—their differences. Her innocence and youth dug into his darkness and lit him up, dredging up emotions women older than her couldn't reach because Christopher figured they knew the score. And, even if they hadn't, so fucking what? Experienced bitches came a dime a dozen and saw in him what he saw in them—a body to fuck.

Looking at the painting now, hearing Johnnie's sharp breath as he paused next to Christopher made Christopher wish he'd waited until their house was completed before he hung it. As usual, though, Megan had prevailed and gotten her way.

"Why the fuck ain't you called, baby?" he asked, like the photo had fucking answers. He ran his knuckles along his jaw, his wedding band speeding up his heart. "You decided you couldn't take this shit no fuckin' more and skipped out on me?"

"Stop being dumb," Digger snapped. "She didn't leave you, Prez."

"If she hasn't left you yet, why would she now?" Johnnie asked. He walked to the entertainment center and pulled out a bottle of whisky, along with five glasses. "She loves you."

Christopher accepted a filled glass then sat on the side of the bed. "God know fuckin' why."

"We got yet to figure the shit out either," Digger said with a shrug, "but the bitch do and that's what should be important."

"Maybe, I keep her a lil' too fuckin' close," Christopher reasoned after downing the whisky. "She been gone eleven fuckin' hours, twenty-two minutes, and—" He raised his wrist up and looked at his watch— "fifteen point seven seconds and I ain't had one fuckin' call from her. She ain't fuckin' answered my fuckin' calls neither."

"Let me just start off by saying I don't mean no disrespect in what I'm about to say," Val began, backing closer to the door. Perspiration appeared on his bald head and upper lip. "But your behavior with her a little possessive. I-I mean like a stalker or something."

"You forfuckingot what the fuck happen to her, assfuck?" Christopher snarled. If they had, he sure the fuck hadn't. "My girl got stabbed in the fuckin' chest. I coulda lost her."

"Yeah, but you didn't." Mortician paused to allow the statement to sink in. He gave Christopher an under-eyed look, then chose another fact to bitch slap him with. "And, since then, you've gone on short runs on club business where you couldn't call her."

"She ain't on fuckin' club business. She left with my son cuz of this weddin' shit. A weddin' we ain't fuckin' needin' since we already fuckin' married. It was her idea to leave. I ain't fuckin' ask her to do it."

While he raged through all the possible scenarios, the other three assfucks glanced at Johnnie, who shrugged. Christopher didn't like that fucking shrug. It meant something was going the fuck on and he wasn't yet in on it.

He rubbed his eyes. Did these motherfuckers *like* to have his ass fuck them up?

"What the fuck goin' on with you motherfuckers? Why you assfucks fuckin' lookin' green?"

Before anyone answered, *Love in an Elevator* by Aerosmith blared through the room and relief swept Christopher's entire body at hearing Megan's ringtone. About. Fucking. Time.

"Megan," he growled by way of answering, "where the fuck you at, baby? Why the fuck you ain't call me all day?"

"Christopher, I'm sorry to disturb you," she responded, sounding as down as he felt. "I know I promised the guys I wouldn't disturb you, but I-I miss you."

"What the fuck you talkin' 'bout, baby? What the fuck you promisin' these motherfuckers?" And why the fuck was she just telling him now?

Unless…Christopher narrowed his eyes at his boys.

Val choked, and Mortician's dark brown skin turned ashen.

"They…I…we wanted you to enjoy yourself without—"

"Been through this shit. Ain't fuckin' needin' you to go through it afuckingain. That ain't got fuck all to do with some fuckin' promise."

She went silent and Christopher waited, knowing only moments stood between him and the fucking reason she'd jetted on the spur of the moment. She sighed. "The boys asked me to leave, and I promised them I would and not disturb you today but—"

"Come fuckin' again?"

Judging by Johnnie's disgust, Christopher guessed he hadn't encouraged Megan to leave. The other fucks, though? *Those* fuckheads shifted and looked between one another.

"Them fucks told you to do what?"

"I think I left some bitch behind—" Digger began, creeping away.

Rocketing from his seat on the edge of the bed, Christopher grabbed Digger by the scruff of his collar and halted him, but his heart and his head was settling now that he was talking to his wife. He guided the man to the chair near the bed and shoved him down.

"I miss you so much. I shouldn't have listened to them. I knew it was a mistake from the moment the flight took off. There was…Momma…"

He'd hear about whiny Dinah in a fucking minute. At the moment, he wanted the fucks to hear his girl's voice, so when he fucked them up, they'd be fucking clear about why. "Wait, wait, baby. I gotta put you on fuckin' speakerphone. I need a fuckin' drink." Truth. He also needed his fucking fists free. "Repeat what the fuck you said. I wanna make fuckin' sure I heard you right." Setting his phone down and tightening his hold on Digger, he glowered at Val and Mortician, daring them to move. "Now, spill. Tell me afuckingain why you fuckin' left."

"Christopher!"

Unable to stop himself, he smiled at the exasperation in Megan's sweet voice.

"I'm trying to tell you what Momma—"

"Ain't givin' a good fuck 'bout that right now. I wanna hear—"

"Fine," she said with a sniff. "Val, Digger, and Mortician didn't think you'd enjoy your bachelor party as much if you had to worry about me and CJ. I know I promised them I wouldn't disturb you until tomorrow, but I really missed you." She paused and the sounds of his mini-me reached him. She was cooing to his boy, fussing over the baby just like she fussed over him. He could see her now. Opening her bra and pulling her delicious tit out, guiding his son's little mouth to her nipple. His dick swelled just as she spoke again. Hearing her voice beaded his cock with pre-cum and he gritted his teeth. "CJ has been really fussy," she went on. "I think he misses you just as much as I do."

Christopher gave Val, Mortician, and Digger the evil eye before his gaze landed on Johnnie. "What 'bout John Boy? He ain't had fuck all to do with this?"

Johnnie stiffened and annoyance spread across his features.

"Of course not," she said easily. "Why would he?" Before he could answer, she sighed and asked in a small voice, "Are...are there a lot of girls at the party?"

Fuck him. He thought about that red-haired bitch. Just like they had strange fucking women here tonight, new bitches could show up at any time. They might know about that dick-grinding whore and tell Megan. "Look, baby, befuckinfore you hear 'bout this bullshit from some fuckin' bitch, this cunt grinded all over my dick. I ain't like that shit, so I shoved her flat the fuck on her fuckin' ass. Ida fuckin' capped the motherfucker responsible for sendin' that whore to me. Nofuckinbody fessed up, though."

Silence. "Megan?" he asked when a few more seconds went on and she still said fuck all. "You hung up on me?" Nothing. "Megan?" In agitation, he swigged from the whisky and grabbed Digger by the throat. Shit. Maybe, the Herb and Al had loosened the fuck out of his tongue. Because if he wanted to be honest with her, he could've done it in person, not when she was hundreds of miles away from him in Seattle.

"I, um, I have to go, Christopher," she said finally, a little tremble in her voice. "Go enjoy the rest of the party and I-I'll see you Saturday."

"Aww, fuck, Megan," Christopher called, squeezing Digger's neck at the sound of her uncertainty, "stop fuckin' bein' like that, baby. I miss the fuck outta you. If Ida been clued in 'bout these three fucks tellin' you to go, I swear I wouldna letchaleave. I ain't wantin' no other bitch but you. And I ain't at the party. I fuckin' left after that bitch dry fuckin'. My ass in the room, missin' the fuck outta you."

Megan pulled in a breath. "Okay. And d-don't be mad at the three of them. They just wanted to make you happy—"

Nice try, Megan. They were still in for ass whippings.

"You make me fuckin' happy, Megan. You." With each word, he shook Digger. "Motherfuckers 'round here know that shit, so I ain't listenin' to you tellin' me I ain't needin' to be fuckin' mad at them assfucks cuz you there thinkin' I'm fuckin' some bitch—"

"Only because you told me what happened while I'm here," she snapped. "You could've waited until we were face-to-face."

If he tightened his hold on Digger once more, he was going to strangle the man. He shoved him away and Digger grabbed his neck, doubling over.

"I ain't thinkin' straight," Christopher muttered. "I'm so fuckin' pissed with these motherfuckers. It's cuz of them, you ain't fuckin' here."

"Christopher," she drawled softly, after a moment, "please be nice to them. They didn't mean any harm. I know I can't be around you all the time, but it just shocked me a little to hear the first time I'm not there at a function, you have women grinding on you. I-I mean…" Her voice trailed off.

Her pain and insecurity were like fingers, reaching out and touching him, choking him with a painful grip.

"What, Megan? Talk." Christopher yanked Digger back to a sitting position.

"How'd she get in your lap in the first place? You c-could've stopped her before she got that far."

Yeah, no doubt about it. Herb and Al had made his fucking mouth run like a fucking motor. He had to make this shit right. "No, I couldna. That fuckin' bitch had to get up close and fuckin' personal so I could shove her the fuck away and make my fuckin' message loud and fuckin' clear."

She sniffled, and Digger hung his head. The other two had the fucking decency to look ashamed.

"Megan, please, baby, stop cryin'. You askin' me to be nice to motherfuckers, then you tryna get them laid up in fuckin' traction for months cuz I'm hearin' your tears. Where's Farrah and Lacey and your whiny fuckin' ma?"

"They're out."

"Lemme call you back in 'bout half an hour. I gotta take care of somethin'."

"Don't, Christopher," Megan said. "I know what you have to take care of and I'm asking you to let them be. I'm just tired. Momma drugged CJ with Benadryl and Tylenol and I haven't spoken to her since."

That fucking bitch did fucking… *"What?"*

"And there was this man. She changed her seat with him. And he gave me the creeps. He was the same man who was at the club the other night. He said his name was—"

"Cee Cee," he snarled.

"You know him?"

No, but he fucking would and shortly. "He bad news, baby. Stay the fuck outta his way. Hear me?"

"It wasn't as if I had a choice. Momma gave him her seat. I told her I was going to tell the stewardess to have police waiting for him."

Police, huh? And he was going to have a long fucking talk with that bitch, Dinah. She had abso-fucking-lutely no motherly instincts. Drugging his son? And, just as bad or worse, letting some fuckhead sit next to his wife where shit got so out-of-hand Megan wanted to call the police?

"Yeah?" he asked casually. "You was gonna call the badges? For fuckin' what?"

"I've handled it, Christopher. Don't worry. I don't need you to fight all my battles." She sighed. "Hold on."

"Uh, hey, Prez, can we leave now?" Val asked, hooking his thumbs in his pockets, and rocking on his heels.

Christopher glowered him into silence. He'd get Megan off the phone, fuck these motherfuckers up so they never talked his wife into doing some shit like this again, and then call her and talk to her for the rest of the night.

"I'm back," Megan said. "I had to lay CJ down. Anyway, once we landed, we decided to go shopping and Momma complained about the price of a dress I wanted. Farrah got mad at me because I refused to go to a strip club. But I made the choice to leave you, so it isn't anyone's fault the trip is going so bad."

Uh, if Megan was trying to plead these motherfuckers' cases, she was just digging their fucking graves. Christopher leaned down and punched Digger. Flesh connected with flesh and Digger slid to the floor.

"What was that?"

Christopher kicked Digger. "Nothin', baby," he called.

Silence again. "So you're alone?" she asked after a moment.

He kicked Digger once more and the man groaned. "Ain't I said I was?"

Christopher guessed she didn't believe him because she wasn't saying anything. She was probably listening for sounds.

"Gimme fifteen minutes, Megan." Five minutes to fuck each of them up. He already had a head-start on Digger. "And answer the fuckin' phone when I call you the fuck back." Not waiting for her response, he disconnected the call.

Mortician held up his hands. "Prez, we can explain—"

"Exfuckinplain?" he yelled. "Exfuckinplain why you motherfuckers told Megan to fuckin' leave? Stickin' your fuckin' nose in my business?"

"Outlaw," Val started, "we just wanted—"

"Christopher—" Johnnie began.

He jerked Digger to his feet and shoved him toward Val and Mortician. "All you shut the fuck up. You motherfuckers payin' for this shit. For fuckin' now, your ass whippins goin' on the back fuckin' burner. We findin' that motherfucker name Cee Cee."

Grabbing his smokes and his nine, he glanced at his phone. He'd call Megan back in a bit. First, he needed to socialize and discover what he could about Cee Cee Whoever-The-Fuck.

Chapter 5

Johnnie

WONDERING WHO THE HELL CEE CEE WAS AND what he wanted, Johnnie walked into the room he used at the clubhouse whenever he slept on the premises. While the others spoke to some of the other brothers, he'd intended to make some calls and try to get a bead on the asshole who'd shaken Megs up enough that she wanted to call the police. Instead, he had company. The whore who'd sent Christopher over the edge. He'd expected the whore to have found another brother to fuck. Instead, he found her, knees drawn up, and fast asleep.

He withdrew a cigarette from his cut and lit it, his gaze never leaving the nude woman on the bed. Releasing the smoke, he thought about leaving her alone. He didn't want her. First, he and Megan had shared a heated kiss, then he'd finger-fucked her while she jerked him off. In between those two encounters, he'd spent enough time with her to discover the person she really was. And he wanted every inch of her. But she didn't want him, not that way at least.

So be it.

After finishing his cigarette, he walked to his stereo system and slipped in an old Creed CD. The whore stirred and sat up. Hard nipples tipped peach-colored, quarter-sized aureoles and she stretched, thrusting her breasts out further. She blinked when she saw him standing in the room. Her shock and panic didn't escape him. Who the fuck was she? She'd been ready to seduce Christopher, but now, looked like a deer in the crosshairs of a hunter's gun.

"H-hi."

A husky voice to go with a lush body. The prospect of fucking her grew more appealing by the second.

"Hello."

She combed her fingers through her hair, arranged the entire length over one shoulder, covering a breast.

He folded his arms and crossed one ankle over the other, leaning against the desk holding the stereo system. He didn't have much in the room because he rarely spent nights there. A bed. A chest of drawers. A desk. That was about it.

As she continued to stare at him, Johnnie walked around, checking beneath the lamp on the desk for a hidden microphone or camera. He pulled out the drawers in the chest, eyed the inside, before rubbing his fingertips against every inch of the wood. He repeated the process at his desk and the headboard of his bed.

She studied him, confusion drawing her copper-colored brows together. She chewed on her full, bottom lip.

With Arms Wide Open began to play and Johnnie stilled, listening to the passionate words about the desire to show his son everything. Christopher had played this song for Megs at the wedding celebration they'd had after their civil service, even though he hadn't known she was having a boy. The thought was still the same had she had a little girl. His nostrils flared.

"Are you alright?"

Johnnie narrowed his eyes at her. "Who the fuck sent you?"

Her brown eyes widened. "Whoever sent the other girls," she answered without hesitation. "I'm not sure. Just say I'm a freelancer and one of the other girls couldn't make it, so my friend called me. Asked me if I wanted to take the chick's place. And here I am."

Useless to ask for names, since they weren't regulars and, instead hired whores.

"No one hired you to fuck Outlaw?"

She frowned. "Why would someone hire me to do that?"

"To fuck with his relationship with his wife."

"Seems silly. She's not here, is she? How would that interfere with their marriage?"

Either she was a damn good actress, or she really didn't know that all someone had to do was tell Megs Christopher had fucked another woman and their marriage would be interfered with.

"Besides," the whore continued, "she's a biker's wife. I'm sure she understands infidelity and betrayal." She spat the last word. "I was on his lap. I felt his erection. He wanted to fuck me and would have if there hadn't been all these people here."

"If you think that, then you're a goddamn fool. He couldn't help but get a dickstand with the way you were grinding your pussy against him. But, if he wanted you, he would've fucked you and not cared who was here."

She lowered her lashes and laid back on the bed, opening her legs. Her bare pussy lips and glistening clit winked at him. He could lose himself in this woman, forget the torment of Megs for as long as it took him to fuck. No names would be exchanged. No more talk. Nothing, but the sound of the music filling the room and the memories of Megs's cries in his head.

Undressing in silence, he watched as she rubbed her pussy. He took a condom out of his desk drawer and gloved his cock in it before climbing on top of her and settling between her legs.

Surprise entered her eyes. "We aren't going to kiss?"

No. He hadn't kissed one woman since he'd tasted Megs's mouth. Instead of answering the beauty beneath him, he thumbed her clit and she groaned. He bent his head and licked her nipple, rewarded when her pussy heated a little more. He inserted two fingers inside her juiciness, and he sucked in a breath. She arched against him and moaned, rocking against his hand. He bit her nipple, increased the pressure of his thumb on her clit, the in and out speed of his fingers. A keening wail began to escape her, but she bit down on her lip, catching the sound in her throat that his kiss could've captured.

Holding her hips in place, he sank into her, and she expanded around him, her velvety softness just the haven he needed. Her lips brushed against his chest and a shiver went through him. She wrapped her long legs around his waist, clutching him tighter to her body, and lifting her hips to take him deeper.

"Just one kiss," she whispered. "Please."

Her voice sent him over the edge, and he shuddered and groaned, filling the condom and going still. He was breathing hard and heavy, but it surprised him at how sated he felt. More sated than he'd felt in months.

He rolled off her and stared at the ceiling, at a loss for words. He covered his eyes with his forearm, hoping she got the message and leave him now that they'd fucked. But, no, of course things wouldn't be so simple. He felt the condom being pulled off his cock a moment before she wrapped her mouth around his dick, allowing the head to hit the back of her throat. She relaxed her throat, took him deeper, and Johnnie grunted, lifting on his elbows to see her lips stretched around half his dick, her cheeks hollowed as she sucked him hard. He fisted her hair and wrapped it around his hand, pulling on her head, hoping the slight pain he caused encouraged her to suck him harder and faster. He pumped his hips to her deep slurps and his head lulled back.

"Ah! Fuck!" He tightened his grip on her hair and held her head in place, thrusting into her wet mouth as cum jetted from him. He kept his dick in her mouth, her head in place, until his breathing slowed. Only then did he pull away and release her hair.

"Now will you kiss me?"

Hands behind his head, he popped an eye open. "You want a kiss, baby?"

She nodded.

"Come here."

She crawled next to him, her heavy breasts hanging, hovering near Johnnie's mouth. He sat further up and sucked a tight nipple into his mouth while guiding her onto her back. She moaned and he raised his head.

"If you want a kiss, gorgeous, I'll give you a kiss you won't forget."

Her breath caught. He knew she expected him to roam up instead of heading south. There were kisses and there were kisses. Some were the sweet, romantic kind with romance in the air and oh-so-gentle seduction involving two mouths, two sets of lips, two tongues. Others were hot, wicked kisses containing one set of lips attached to one mouth, one tongue, and a pair of slick pussy lips.

He ran his tongue along the creamy seam of her folds, pushing her legs wide open. He circled her bare outer lips before opening them and licking his way around the inner folds, circling her clit but never quite touching it. He speared his tongue into her pussy, and she screamed.

"My God," she groaned. "Who taught you to eat pussy like this?"

He didn't answer her, instead enjoying his cunt feast. Removing his tongue from her hot body, he pushed the hood of her clit back, exposing the most sensitive part of her and gave her what she asked for, a kiss. He pressed kiss after kiss against her before lapping. She thrashed against him, tugging at his hair, her legs trembling through her orgasm.

Oh, he wasn't halfway finished eating her pussy. She wanted a kiss, then a kiss she'd get. Her juices clung to his lips, his chin, his nose. She'd come all over the place. Showing her just a slight bit of mercy, he blew on her clit, lubricating his fingers with her wetness and spreading her ass cheeks. He inserted a finger in each part of her and began swiping his tongue over her clit, massaging the thin membrane separating her pussy and ass, keeping her in place by pressing his other hand against her belly.

Her screams and sobs gratified him and when she came again, he removed his finger but not his mouth, sucking her pussy until she begged him to stop and he pulled away. He sat up to get another condom. He took her fast and hard, her feet resting on his shoulders, the sound of his movements in her soaked pussy spurring him to harder drives into her. Burying his head against her shoulder, he closed his eyes and breathed in her scent, flowers and sex and sweat. He bit her ear, fingered her clit until she reached her orgasm, then emptied into the condom.

He remained inside of her for a few minutes, before withdrawing and getting to his feet to discard the condom in the bathroom. When he returned, she had sat up and looked so sad. He got his cigarettes and offered her one but she declined with a shake of her head.

"I-I need to leave."

Johnnie nodded.

"I…my clothes are in my car and my jacket is somewhere out in the main room."

He sucked on his cigarette, thinking about what would happen to her if she went back out there with no clothes on, looking as thoroughly used as she had been. He doubted Christopher remained in the main room. He'd only wanted to gather some information and then get back to Megs and he didn't have any idea what Val, Mortician, and Digger might be up to by now.

Silent, Johnnie grabbed his jeans and slipped them on. He yanked open a desk drawer and stopped short as a photo of Megs greeted him. Swallowing, he snatched his gun and slammed the drawer shut. He turned, the.38 still gripped in his hand. The woman let out a frightened cry. With a sigh, Johnnie shoved the weapon into the waistband of his pants.

"I don't kill or hurt women. Who the hell knows what's going on out there by now? I might have to pistol-whip some asshole or shoot the shit out of them as I escort you to your car."

After finding her a shirt and a pair of his shorts, he led her out of the room. Just as he suspected, the festivities had elevated to an orgy with brothers fucking the hired whores wherever and however while the Bobs sucked dick. Walking through the crowd, two naked girls approached him, ignoring the prostitute he was leading away.

"Not tonight," he said with a wink, pausing when one of the brothers approached the woman he'd just fucked. "She's with me, Bowlie."

"Th-thank you," she said when they left the noise of the clubhouse behind and reached the outdoors. Worry for her safety made him frown. It was cold and foggy. Though he'd probably never see her again, he'd just spent hours having sex with her. For now, in this freezing night, he felt a sense of responsibility for her.

He followed her to her car, impressed by her late model Mazda Miata MX-5. "Are you sure you're going to be all right to drive?" he asked. Whatever other part of his soul he'd lost, he still protected women, thought they were the most amazing creatures on the face of the earth. "We can go back to my room. Spend the night together." He shrugged. "Talking. Drinking. Having sex. Your choice." Especially because he wasn't sure what he wanted or needed right then.

She stared up at him, the spotlights glaring around them burning through the low fog and outlining her perfect features. "Kissing?"

He scowled, then sighed, wondering why it was so important to her that they kissed. The wind howled and she hugged her arms about herself. "No. I'll kiss your pussy. The lovely globes of your ass cheeks. I'll lick you from your toes all the way up to your thighs. But kiss you? No. That I won't do."

Her lips parted and the cold air chafed her skin red. Still, he knew his words had affected her.

"Not even to keep me out of this weather? Keep me here and safe?"

Johnnie lifted a brow, amusement dancing through him. "It's your life, gorgeous. If you want to gamble with it by trying to manipulate me into giving you your way, that's your business."

She lifted her chin, her lips thinning.

"I want you safe," he reiterated.

Vulnerability and genuine shock shone in her brown eyes as if the idea of anyone concerning themselves with her safety was shocking. And, maybe, it was. For all her refined beauty, she was a whore. High-classed, but a whore all the same. Yet, he'd never hold her past against her—or any woman. Not when he had so many sins of his own staining his soul.

On impulse, Johnnie pulled her into his arms and hugged her, kissing her temple. "Thank you, gorgeous," he whispered, caressing her cheek. She was making her choice and he'd abide by it. "I had a wonderful time with you."

She nodded. "Same here."

Once she used her keyless entry, he opened the door and held it until she got in. She smiled at him, and he gave her a two-fingered salute before she started the car and drove away.

Chapter 6

Meggie

THE COVERS TANGLED ABOUT HER, MEGGIE TOSSED AND glanced at the clock. 3:00 AM. CJ had awakened at midnight, falling back to sleep about thirty minutes ago. She was happy that the effects of Dinah's actions had worn off long enough for him to remain awake more than fifteen or twenty minutes. But, as he was awakening, she was controlling her disappointment that Christopher hadn't called her back. Farrah and Lacey had gone to the strip club, then called and said they'd picked up a couple guys and were going home with them. Instead of sharing the king-sized bed with her girlfriends, she had the bed all to herself while Dinah was on the sofa in the living area. After a hellish day, she needed a moment to unwind.

Turning toward the closed draperies of the hotel window, she debated whether to get up and glance outside. Maybe search for the moon and glimpse the shadow of the Olympic Mountains rising in the distance since the darkness would swallow the beauty of Puget Sound.

She twisted again, the core of her feeling empty and unfulfilled. Neglected. She groaned, flushing with desire and embarrassment. Lovemaking had become a daily part of her life and she enjoyed it as much as Christopher did. There wasn't one part of her body he'd left untouched. The only times he hadn't made love to her was the six weeks she'd needed to heal after giving birth to CJ and the two days he'd pissed her off over Derby's blatant cheating. They even made love during *that time of the month*.

She pushed her heels into the mattress, her legs falling open, bare beneath her short nightie. She pressed her palm against her sex and bit her lip to keep from moaning, her nipples hard.

Opening herself, she fingered her clit and shivered. She caressed the swollen nub, applying pressure, closing her eyes and imagining Christopher's touch and rough words.

"Your pussy feel so fuckin' good, Megan."

She whimpered and arched her back, licking her lips.

"Fuck! Suck every drop of cum, baby."

"All of it," she breathed, as if he were there to hear her, her juices slipping onto her fingers, her orgasm closing in on her and tightening her belly. Pleasure washed over her in waves, and she groaned Christopher's name, rocking her hips to the rhythm of her fingers.

Before she had a chance to spiral down, the sound of her cellphone pealed through the quiet and she jumped. Not wanting CJ to wake up, she answered the phone, her voice still breathy from her orgasm.

Instead of a response, silence met her. "Christopher?" She knew it was him because he had a special ringtone—*One and Only* by Adele.

"What the fuck you doin'?" he asked.

"Trying to sleep," she responded and frowned at the annoyance in his voice.

"Why you sound like you just got fucked, Megan?"

She sighed. "Because I just got through touching myself." Why bother with trying to hide it from him? He'd get the truth from her eventually.

Silence, then a hoarse, "Fuck me. You playin' with your pussy, baby?"

"Yes," she whispered, her clit swelling in need all over again. "I want you."

"Yeah? Whatcha want from me?"

She loved the deep rumble of his voice. When they were intimate, the timbre pitched lower and drove her crazy. She liked his dirty talk and learned to do it herself. But she was usually in his arms, staring into the intensity of his green eyes.

"I want your cock deep inside me, Christopher," she responded. Her nipples had swelled and overflowed with milk. The material of her nightie clung to her, the throbbing deep in her core pulsing through her entire body.

"Put your fingers in your pussy, Megan," he ordered, and she nearly came just from the roughness in his voice.

She opened her legs, slid her hand across the satin of her outfit, the lace edging, the soft curls covering her sex and found her slippery heat. She inserted her fingers and released a little cry.

"Fuck, Megan. My dick hard as stone, thinkin' 'bout your delicious pussy all hot and swollen. I want inside you, baby."

"I want you inside me, too. You make me crazy, Christopher. I love the way you taste." She thrust her fingers deeper and expanded them, opening her tender walls. "The way you smell." She whimpered and arched her back. "The way you feel."

"Lick your pussy juice from your fingers and lemme hear you suckin' them. Like you slurp my dick."

"You make me—" lick, slurp— "feel so—" slurp, lick— "nasty."

He chuckled. "Come for me, Megan," he demanded.

She bit down on her lip to keep from crying out too loud.

"Your pussy drippin' for me, ain't it?"

God, instead of helping her through it, he was making it worse.

"I could just slide my dick in you you so wet, yeah?"

Her body jerked and her chest heaved, the hand holding the phone shaking. Somehow, she managed to gasp out, "Yes. You make me so wet."

"Ima fuckin' pound your pussy all night, Megan. Hear me?"

Her brain told her to shut up, but her body didn't allow it and she let out a wail, her eyes rolling back in her head, her breathing harsh and heavy.

CJ started to whine just as the door swung open. "Megan, what's going on in here?" Dinah asked.

Megan squeaked in surprise. Her mother's voice and her son's cry dousing her haze of pleasure. "Oh my God! Momma, get out," she almost snarled, pulling the covers over the lower half of her body.

"What the fuck that bitch doin' in your room, Megan?" Christopher growled.

"Can I call you back?" Megan whispered, mortified.

"No!" he barked. "But you can come open the fuckin' door."

Christopher

I**T TOOK FIVE MINUTES BEFORE MEGAN OPENED THE** fucking door, during which time Christopher grew more and more pissed. He'd gone back to the main room at the club to check with some of the other brothers about what they knew about a Cee Cee motherfucker. As it turned the fuck out, none of them knew a motherfucking thing.

Restless, Christopher decided to hit the road, after ordering Johnnie to meet them here tomorrow evening, so they could ride back in his Navigator while his cousin drove Christopher's Harley. Christopher had been unable to get any information on Cee Cee. All he knew was the motherfucker showed up at his club, and then somehow ended the fuck up on the same fucking flight as Megan. Shit wasn't fucking flying.

He wanted Cee Cee and he wanted the motherfucker who'd brought him to the club in the first goddamn place.

He'd called Megan to tell her to open the door, then she'd answered the phone in her I've-just-fucked voice, and he hadn't been able to stop himself from bringing the freak out in her. One thing for fucking sure was his girl was a freaky little nymphomaniac, and he loved—fucking loved—it, especially since he was responsible for it.

She stood there, in a pink floor-length silk robe, cradling his boy in her arms. CJ seemed wide awake. Christopher stepped inside, pausing to slant his mouth over Megan's and drink in her sweet taste. She smelled like sex and the cherry blossom scented shampoo she favored.

A voice cleared in the background, pulling him away from Megan's lips. He lifted his head, grabbed his son, and sauntered past his wife. He narrowed his eyes at Dinah, and she swallowed, stepping back toward the fancy chocolate-covered sofa with an abandoned pillow and blanket. Megan was very protective of the woman and didn't like Christopher to frighten her. Too fucking bad.

"Listen up, Dinah," he began, smiling at CJ when he saw his wide baby grin. "You ever let a strange motherfucker sit next to Megan again, I'm barrin' your fuckin' ass from bein' 'round her."

She bit on her lip and gazed passed him to where Megan stood, her eyes pleading for rescue. "You wouldn't allow that, would you, Meggie?"

Probably not, which irritated the fuck out of Christopher, but it was what it was.

"Not because of you exchanging your seat with that awful man, no," Megan said, confirming what he already knew. "But for what you did to my son, I'm tempted to bar you myself."

Dinah's blue eyes widened, and Christopher snorted. He needed to sit the fuck down in that wingback chair and enjoy the fucking show of Megan blasting Dinah.

"Meggie—"

"Don't Meggie me, Momma. You sold your house to be near me and I was glad. I thought it was a chance for us to start over. But you're not the same mother I remember and I'm not the same girl I was. The time for following my every move was when your husband was climbing in my bed and feeling me up. Or, maybe, standing by me when I called the police to help you and you denied he'd hit you then stood by while he beat the crap out of me, then knocked you senseless."

Megan swiped away her tears, the sight snatching away the fury rising in Christopher at the reminder of her step fuckhead. The memories of what Megan had gone through would stay with her for the rest of her life. He'd always believed she'd never confront her mother because Dinah seemed so broken, so it was hard for him to believe she'd ever been the strong woman Megan claimed.

Megan shuddered. "I'm giving you one, last chance, Momma. Your mothering gene might've been beaten out of you, but you better find your grandmothering one. If you ever do anything to CJ like you did earlier, I'm never talking to you again."

Without another word, Megan stomped to the bedroom and slammed the door shut, leaving her whiny ass Ma staring at him with huge, teary eyes.

"I didn't mean any harm," she said on a sob.

Christopher snorted. "We ain't givin' our boy no drugs, Dinah."

"I just wanted—"

"Ain't much givin' a fuck what you wanted. CJ mine and Megan's son."

"Megan's the last person I have. If she stops loving me, I'll have no one."

Motherfuck him, if her pathetic statement didn't touch Christopher's heart. He sighed. "Megan ran away to find Big Joe to help you. She love you. She just sick of your fuckin' ass. You the adult and for too many fuckin' years, you made her take care of you. I might've made her grow up by takin' her to my bed and givin' her my kid, but it ain't no one sided shit. I have her back and she got mine. Does she act like a spoiled little bitch sometimes? Yeah. Throw tantrums like a little girl? Fuck yeah. The way I fuckin' see it, she deserve it cuz when she shoulda been able to do that shit with you, you was lettin' that fuckhead take away every-fuckin-thin' you meant to yourself. Everything Megan remembers 'bout you. And, most of all, you was failin' your baby girl." Yeah, he felt sorry for her, but, fuck, the bitch needed to be told how much she'd fucked up. Only by holding onto the words of her father—and harming herself with knives—did Megan get through the abuse.

Christopher didn't think he'd ever respect Dinah for leaving Megan so unprotected.

He started past her, and her shoulders slumped. Fuck, fuck, fuck. He thought about his own mother and how he missed the fuck out of her. Patricia had had her faults as well, but he'd never wanted to see her cry. She'd been his mother and he'd loved her. Just like he knew Megan loved her mother. Megan didn't have hate in her. A bad fucking temper? Yeah. Hate and grudge-holding? No.

He slanted a sour glance at Dinah, thought about Big Joe. Boss hadn't known how to handle how he felt about this woman, but it had broken his heart when she'd stopped him from coming around. Christopher really believed he'd been as hurt that he couldn't see Dinah as he'd been about not having easy access to their daughter. Despite that, Megan knew Big Joe would've dropped everything to rescue Dinah.

He scowled and reached out to grab her in an awkward hug. She sniffled and he prayed she wouldn't leave snot on his cut.

"You gotta get past this bullshit, Dinah," he said gruffly. He pulled back from her and patted her shoulder. "Megan ain't gonna let nobody hurt you. Just don't fuck with our boy." He hoped he'd said that enough that it got through Dinah's thick fucking skull. Since Megan had covered just about everything he would've thought to say and more, he didn't feel like he needed to add nothing else. He'd intended to fuck Megan into oblivion, but he should've just let her finish coming without adding shit, since he hadn't been there to swallow her screams.

Fuck him, but he couldn't wait 'til their honeymoon when he had her all to himself.

"Get some sleep," he told his mother-in-law and started toward Megan's bedroom.

"You're not saying anything about what I did?"

Her question made Christopher want to scream so much shit at her that her eardrums popped. And, he could, too. Megan was pissed with her, so she wouldn't give a shit what the fuck he told Dinah. This was his chance.

He lifted a brow. "Nope. My wife covered all the shit I coulda thought about without threatenin' to bury your fuckin' ass."

Not waiting for her to respond, he walked the fuck away and left her standing in the middle of the suite.

Chapter 7

Meggie

"WHAT DO YOU THINK?" MEGGIE ASKED AROUND A yawn, holding up two negligees for Lacey's and Farrah's approval.

Farrah sat with her legs crossed, her sunglasses covering her bloodshot eyes. Lacey's shades were pushed back in her purple hair, her leg thrown over one of the chairs she sat in. A saleswoman hovered in the background, ready to jump to Meggie's bidding because Meggie had already chosen a few bras and panty sets and other sexy nightclothes now piled behind the register up front and guarded by the other saleslady.

"Have you gotten everything else for the wedding taken care of?" Lacey asked, the question prompting Meggie to drop her arms.

"Yes," Meggie confirmed with a wide smile. Because the ceremony was originally set to happen in two days, she'd paid for almost everything, even her wedding gown. She just had to go in for her final fitting. The personalized items with the date of her marriage had to be reordered. Changing the date also gave her extra time to think of things she'd previously forgotten. "I've even chosen our China pattern."

Farrah laid her head back. "Christopher didn't help you?"

"Of course not. He's happy to let me handle all the details." Although he had suggested the colors for the wedding—peach, blueberry, and cream—and helped with the guest list.

Lacey flicked her nails together, then wrinkled her nose. "You don't feel funny he's so much older than you?"

Meggie rearranged the two negligees and straightened them on her lap. "Not at all. Do you?"

"Kind of," Lacey confessed with a shrug. "I mean—" She blew out a breath. "Sensible girls just don't get married so young and get saddled with a kid. That's plain stupid."

"What I do with my life is my choice," Megan said evenly, the underlying concern in Lacey's tone keeping Megan's temper in check. "I'm happier now than I've ever been, and I don't regret one minute of my life with Christopher."

She fanned herself, a small pain in her belly a reminder of how well—and how hard, at times—Christopher had pleasured her.

"If you say so."

"I do say so, Lacey. From now on, unless I ask for your opinion about my husband, keep them to yourself."

Farrah yawned. "Calm down, Megster. Ignore Lacey and let's talk about your honeymoon. Have you planned that yet?"

A distant chime sounded in the air, the signal another customer had arrived, but Meggie and her little group sat in a partitioned area, way in the back where plush seats were grouped near the dressing rooms.

"Christopher's handling the honeymoon. We're going to London," she announced with excitement. She'd never been out of the country and had never traveled no further than Disney Land in Anaheim. She'd only been ten and it had been a real family trip, one of the few with both her mother and father.

Lacey shifted in her seat and tucked one of her legs beneath her. "Er, London? Like, um, London, Minnesota or something?"

"Piss off," Meggie snapped. "London, England. Great Britain. The UK. Excuse me, I mean the United Kingdom. I forgot people with narrow, little minds like yours wouldn't understand the abbreviation."

Lacey's eyes widened, her mouth covered in black lipstick forming an 'o'. "Scary, wrong-side-of-the-law, biker dude is taking you to Europe?"

"Let's see the negligees again," Farrah rushed out when Meggie growled.

"Let me get something straight," she snarled. "Don't talk about my man and don't talk about my son and I won't bitch slap either of you. I might be an old married lady, but I'm still me."

Lacey sighed. "I know what that means. You're about to turn into a raving bitch" She made the motion of zipping her lips. "So zip and onto the next subject."

"I don't remember you caring about my ravings when I was defending you," Meggie bit out.

Lacey looked away.

"Dinah asked us to assist with the guest list," Farrah said, lowering her lashes and pulling bobbling from her Cashmere sweater. She rolled the fuzzy little ball between her fingers, not meeting Meggie's gaze. "I hope you don't mind."

"Why would I?" Meggie asked with suspicion. "Momma and I have known you both since I was in eighth grade, so you'd know who to invite as much as her."

"That's why she asked, Meggie," Lacey said with a short, nervous laugh.

"She wants to wear black to my wedding," Meggie revealed, watching her friends' reactions. "I'm begging her to reconsider. I found three gorgeous gowns for her to choose from. One's peach, the other's cream, and the third one is blue. I'd prefer if she pick either the peach or the cream, but anything is better than black."

"Dinah's against your marriage too," Lacey stated. "She's only nine or ten years older than he is, so that makes sense."

"No," Meggie snapped. "That isn't her reason. Momma would be against any man I chose. She wants me all to herself."

"Well, you are her only child," Lacey pointed out. "She wants the best for you, just like Farrah and me. Don't you think she's been through enough? Thomas left her. You ran away for reasons I've never figured out. Your mother gave your everything, loved, *loves* you to pieces. Thomas accepted you as if you were his biological child."

Meggie had never told her best friends the hell she lived in at home. Before she'd run in search of her father, she'd been afraid of revealing too much. In part because she followed her momma's lead, but it was also due to her own fear of being taken away from Dinah. Her feelings and behavior had always been so erratic toward Thomas's abuse. She hadn't wanted to leave Dinah in the clutches of that madman, yet she'd wanted to escape him with everything in her.

Eventually, she had. Thomas hadn't let her go as easily, following her to Hortensia and almost taking her life. Christopher had sent for Dinah and made Thomas disappear. Meggie knew what that meant. She tried not to think about it. From time to time, Dinah bombarded her with questions about her missing husband. Meggie had become adept at evading direct answers, though she sometimes resented her mother's concern about a man she should've been happy no longer posed a threat.

Officially, it was said Thomas walked away from Dinah.

"Is everything still good?" the saleswoman asked, smiling.

Meggie handed the saleswoman the two negligees in her lap before asking her to show her the last two she'd chosen for a closer inspection while she decided if she'd purchase the sexy nightclothes.

"I think I'm ready to eat," Farrah groaned, once the sales lady handed Meggie the negligees. Her head lulled back again. "I feel like I'm going to puke at any moment, and I think food will soak up some of the alcohol."

"Or make you puke faster," Meggie added. "Drink a lot of water. That'll help."

"As if you've ever been drunk," Lacey chirped, folding her arms. "You have to get sloshed once in your life. It's like a rite of passage. But you're too busy dropping babies and planning weddings to live like a normal college-age girl."

"Lacey, I'm like two point five seconds from knocking you on your ass," Meggie warned, jumping to her feet.

"Ooooo, please, the arguing is hurting my head worse," Farrah moaned.

"You're such a lightweight." Lacey rolled her eyes while Meggie reseated herself. "I'm sorry and ignore, slut puppy, Megster. She didn't sleep at all last night."

"I didn't either since Christopher surprised me and kept me awake," Meggie announced, heat flushing her skin. Maybe, the argument, sleep deprivation and too many orgasms had taken away her brain-to-mouth filter.

Lacey squealed in approval. "Shut. Up. You mean you're our new slut puppy?"

Meggie knew her friend would warm up at the news. In school, Meggie had been the odd girl out when Lacey and Farrah discussed their sexcapades.

If they knew all the things she and Christopher did in bed—or wherever—they'd definitely crown her with the Slut Puppy of the Year Award. She held the negligees higher, covering the extra heat creeping into her face.

"I say take both," a voice announced.

Meggie's arms went slack, and her gaze met Cee Cee's green one. The light bounced off his tattooed head and he gripped the bag indicating he'd made a purchase from this store.

"Who the fuck are you?" Lacey asked, narrowing her hazel eyes.

"Someone who wants to go to jail," Meggie snapped. "You're following me."

He shrugged. "Maybe. Maybe not."

She turned toward the saleswoman who'd stepped up with a disapproving frown. "Is there a problem?"

"What the fuck you gonna do if there is?" he asked, folding his arms. "Free country. I'm not harming anybody."

Her heart was pounding, and she was glad Dinah was at Lacey's mother's house with CJ. If Lacey's mom wasn't with them, Meggie doubted she would've left CJ, leaving her at a bigger disadvantage facing this man if she had to worry about her son's well-being.

"Am I right, Meggie?" he continued.

"Stalking is a crime," Meggie gritted. "So is harassing."

He hooted with laughter. "We just happen to be showing up in the same places."

"Sir, please, if you've completed your purchase—"

He stared at Meggie for long moment, a range of emotions rushing over his features. If she studied him too long, she pictured Christopher resembling him as he grew old—

The thought crashed to a halt, and she gasped.

He sniffed and a half-smile twisted his mouth. "Always heard you were a smart little thing." He winked at her. "I can see you already got the connection."

She reached out blindly and grabbed someone's hand—Lacey's, Farrah's, the saleswoman's. She didn't know and she didn't care.

Dizzy, she watched as Cee Cee pulled everything she'd chosen, tainted all her pretty panties and bras with his touch. He threw them at her. "Welcome to the family, baby. Tell my son it isn't nice not to share his good fortune with his old man and the new president of one of his local support clubs."

He glared at her a moment longer before he turned and sauntered away.

SOMEHOW, CHRISTOPHER DIDN'T GET ARRESTED. HE merely got them banned from ever setting foot in the hotel again after incurring so much damage Meggie cringed every time she thought about it.

Her shopping had been ruined by everything Cee Cee, from his appearance to his putting his dirty hands on the things she'd chosen. To her dawning realization and his sneering announcement. While Farrah went and got the car, Lacey decided to purchase the last two negligees for Meggie.

"Once this is passed, you'll regret not purchasing them."

Doubtful. Every time she looked at them, she'd forever remember Cee Cee. The man who'd raped Patricia Donovan and gotten her pregnant with Christopher from that violence.

Once Meggie had gotten in the car, she'd called Christopher. By the time she'd arrived back at the hotel with CJ and her mom, she'd found their suite destroyed and Johnnie doing everything but tying Christopher to what was left of the chair.

Between Meggie, Val and Johnnie, they'd talked hotel management into not calling the police, but it had been a close call. Now, they were three hours into their six-hour drive with Johnnie at the wheel of his Navigator, Christopher in the front passenger seat and her, CJ, and her mom in the back. Val's arrival had been unexpected, but she discovered he hopped in Johnnie's ride just to get away. Which worked out because it gave Christopher the chance to calm down without having to concentrate on driving. Instead, Val hit the road on Christopher's Harley and Johnnie chauffeured them back to Hortensia in his Navigator.

Meggie sighed. She had several weeks before her church wedding. She'd wanted her union with Christopher blessed. Now, she said a quick prayer that they would all stay safe. A chill went through her, and she knew her prayer would go unheard.

Cee Cee had begun a cat-and-mouse game that Christopher was determined to finish.

Chapter 8

Dinah

DINAH NICHOLLS SHRANK BACK WHEN THE BIKER WITH the bald head, silver beard, and eye patch swung the car door open and held out his hand to help her out of Johnnie's Navigator.

"Babe, I don't have time for this shit," he snapped. "Give me your fucking hand so we can get you the fuck inside."

She thought his name was K-P, but she wasn't sure. He was one of the more mature bikers, a little older than her forty-three. For some reason, he felt familiar to her, as if she'd met him before.

Johnnie gazed at her from the other side of the door, keys hanging from his fingers, his silver-gray eyes narrowing. "I'm tired, Dinah. We need you to get your ass out the fucking car and go see to your daughter and grandson."

She saw Christopher clutching Meggie's hand and cradling CJ in his other arm, hustling her toward the club. For once, Meggie didn't pause and think about her, Dinah noted, a pang of fear and remorse going through her. Meggie's words had hurt, more so because she really hadn't meant any harm. Men were so violent, though. A crying baby might have—

K-P grabbed her hand and yanked her out. Dinah let out a frightened cry and raised her hand to shield her face. The man froze.

"I got this, John Boy."

"Better you than me," Johnnie grumbled and stalked away.

Dinah's heart banged against her ribcage. She was alone with the barrel-chested biker, and he might choose to hit her now. That's what Thomas always did. She licked her lips and lowered her eyes, unable to hide how frightened she was. Her legs actually shook.

A gentle finger lifted her chin, but tears slipped down Dinah's cheeks. Her heart hurt. Her head hurt. The memories of the humiliation and pain she'd suffered wouldn't leave her no matter what she did. She felt like a failure. She felt stupid. Unloved. Unworthy. Everything Thomas had ever said about her.

Sometimes, she wondered at his whereabouts, though she had her suspicions. She was familiar with club justice. Once, she'd been Big Joe's old lady.

"Look at me, babe."

Her trembles fanned out to her entire body.

K-P caught her arms. "Steady, Dinah," he rasped. "Take a deep breath."

She blinked, so startled he knew her name her gaze flew to his.

A half-smile lifted one corner of his mouth. "Yeah. I know your fucking name, even before John Boy said it a minute ago." Heat crept into her cheeks at his wry tone. "We all do. You're Meggie's momma and Outlaw would have our balls if we didn't keep watch over you since you so important to his girl."

She swallowed. "Not anymore," she admitted. "I've finally made her stop loving me."

"No. Meggie will never stop loving you."

"I—" Her throat worked.

If she told him the truth, he might punish her. Their priority was Meggie. Not her. The very thought of the pain she'd endured during her marriage made her trembles return. Nausea churned in her belly. God, the painful sex and the awful punches and cruel words. And she didn't even want to begin to think about all that Meggie endured. Dinah hadn't known how to save herself. She'd thought not running was the best protection she could give Meggie. Every time she'd tried to escape Thomas and get her baby girl to safety, Thomas found them. Calling the police had always been a mistake, too, so Dinah had decided to accept her fate. Her Meggie had been her protector, her warrior princess. Now, she'd left her to the wolves, not caring how the bikers felt about Dinah.

"None of you like me," she blurted, cringing at how pathetic she sounded. She wanted Thomas to be wrong. She wanted someone to think she was worthy to be liked and loved.

He rubbed his bald head and glanced away. "We don't bullshit around here, babe. We don't really know you to feel one way or the other about you. We don't like the way you left Meggie to fend for herself." He rocked back on his heels. "I suppose we don't respect you too much for that."

She bowed her head, her shoulders shaking with the force of her sobs.

"And babe? You do that shit a lot."

"What?" she whispered.

"Fucking *cry*. That's nerve-racking shit, babe. Grates on everybody's asses."

She sniffled. "I don't know what to do."

He gazed up at the cloudy sky and hooked his thumbs in his jeans. "What do you like to do?"

What did she like to do, anymore? She had no clue. At one time, she liked cooking. And kissing. The thought sank her spirits further. She wiped her hands across her lips, still feeling the sting of bites and the cruel laughter when Thomas had bit her and drew blood.

"There has to be something you enjoy?"

"C-cooking."

"Any specialties?"

"Mac and cheese. Chocolate Chip cookies. Two of Meggie's favorites."

"When was the last time you cooked for her?"

Years. Thomas didn't like her cooking anything special for Meggie.

K-P grabbed her hand, his grip gentle. "Let's get inside, babe. If you feel up to it, maybe, you can help me out in the kitchen this evening. Surprise your daughter with your mac and cheese."

He winked at her, and Dinah nodded slowly. He gave her hand a squeeze and she felt…protected. What an odd concept.

Meggie

"**H**APPY VALENTINE'S DAY, MOMMA," MEGGIE GREETED, the next morning, carrying CJ in her arms. With her sudden departure to Seattle and all the following chaos, she hadn't purchased any candy for Dinah to give her as a present, one of the things she intended to remedy during her errands. She started forward. "I'll see you later."

"Aren't you leaving him with me?"

Meggie frowned. "Uh, no."

"I promise I won't do anything to him." Dinah bit her lip and looked down at her toes. She reminded Meggie of an errant child, instead of a mother and a grandmother. "Give me a chance, Meggie."

"Momma, you'll get your chance when Christopher and I go on our honeymoon." Even though the thought sent chills down her spine. She was considering the possibility of taking her son with her rather than leave him with Dinah so her mom could drug him to keep him from disturbing anyone. As far as she knew, the airplane incident had been the one and only time. But who knew when it would happen again? "I have errands to run, and he can come. And, tonight, at the Valentine's dinner, he'll be no trouble."

Although Christopher would. She knew he wanted the alone time with her in their new house where CJ wouldn't pull her away from or distract her attention toward him.

"Meggie, babe, I'm gonna hang out here tonight," K-P called, appearing at her mother's side. "I can help Dinah with Little Man."

Meggie cocked a brow and narrowed her eyes at the blush creeping up Dinah's cheeks. "That's not—"

"Babe, I got a daughter myself and she's grown. Me and her mama did a pretty good job looking after her."

"You have a daughter?" Meggie asked in surprise. The man continued to amaze her. She'd met him when he'd been cooking for a club event, chopping onions like he'd been born to do the job. Who would've thought the man who resembled a cross between a big biker and a bad pirate had cooking and parenting skills?

He nodded. "Her name's Bailey."

Meggie plastered a smile on her face, not because she didn't like K-P, but, because she didn't want to throw her mother to the wolves. Dinah wouldn't take too well to having K-P so close without other people around.

"Thanks, K-P, I really appreciate it. I'll just keep him with me."

"Can I hold Little Man, Meggie?" Val's voice rose from behind her.

She turned and saw the man already had his arms out. Not that she'd turn him down. She smiled. "Sure, Val." Carefully, she placed CJ in his arms, admiring the skull tattoo on one arm and the cross tattoo on the other. It always amazed her how the gentleness surfaced in these tough bikers whenever they dealt with her son.

Val and CJ stared at one another, and a wistful regret washed over the man's features. He had a son, too, almost seven months old now, whose mother happened to be Christopher's sister.

Someone tugged her sleeve and she glanced over her shoulder. "Momma?"

"I-I…if you're thinking about me when you turned him down—" She pointed in K-P's direction— "I'll be fine. He…he seems really nice."

Meggie gazed passed her mother and noticed K-P's heartening smile. A plea mixed with his encouragement. She gazed between her mother and K-P. Dinah still wore the same haggard, frightened expression, her blonde hair more than a little gray, the wrinkles in her face making her appear older than she really was. Dinah's gaze skittered between the floor and K-P in a curious way.

Meggie cleared her throat and rocked back on her heels. Umkay… "Okay. But no drugs, Momma. No Tylenol. No Benadryl. Nothing."

K-P folded his arms. "What the fuck does that mean, babe?"

Dinah flinched at K-P's growl, although Meggie suspected the tone was for her and not her mother. However, he dropped his hands and scowled when he noticed how Dinah shrank back.

"It means just what I said, K-P," Meggie returned. "If CJ gets too fussy or whatever, make sure you call me and not ply him with whatever to make him sleep."

"Babe? Hey, babe?" K-P frowned at her mom. "You did that to Little Man?"

Her color leeching from her skin, Dinah swallowed and stepped back. Meggie's heart sank to her toes because she knew her mom expected retaliation from K-P. Drawing in a calming breath, Meggie inserted herself between them. She grabbed Dinah's shoulders and hugged her. "No one here is going to hurt you, Momma. They'd have me to deal with. K-P wasn't asking you that to chastise you like you're a child—like Thomas would—" *More like beat her to a pulp.*

"Aww, Dinah, babe, you can't think I would hit—"

Meggie glanced with meaning at K-P, cutting him off. "It's okay, Momma. I promise. You're among friends and family."

Laughter rumbled from Val. Meggie stepped away from Dinah and saw Val enraptured with CJ while her son laughed at the faces the man made. An idea formed in her head. Maybe…well, she had to run out for some last-minute grocery items for the dinner she needed to start cooking in a kitchen she'd never seen. She couldn't believe the master bedroom, kitchen and dining room were finally finished and they'd soon move into their new house.

Meggie kissed Dinah's cheek, unable to ignore the anticipation of both Val and K-P. "I have to get going, so I can start cooking."

"You're allowing him to stay with me?" Dinah asked, hope flaring in her eyes.

She nodded, actually leaving CJ with the boys, but Dinah didn't need to know that.

Soon, Meggie was on the road in her Beetle. Christopher had surprised her with the car for Christmas and she adored it. It gave her mobility and proved just the right size for her, since whenever they traveled together, they took a bigger vehicle if CJ accompanied them or went on the Harley if he didn't.

Twenty minutes later, Meggie pulled up in front of the neat, little white house with red shutters. Shrubbery grew on each side of the five concrete steps that led to a railed porch with a red entry door. She didn't have Zoann's cell phone number because her sister-in-law owed Christopher all types of apologies. Meggie would prefer to never have anything to do with the mean, spiteful witch. However, Zoann wasn't only Christopher's sister, but she was CJ's aunt and her son CJ's cousin. Children shouldn't have to suffer because of idiotic adults.

Walking up to the door, Meggie rang the bell, wondering if Zoann was on duty at the hospital. A moment later, the woman swung open the door, answering the question. Her eyes widened in surprise when she saw Meggie while Meggie stared back, halfway expecting Zoann to slam the door in her face.

Instead, her lips thinned. "Megan."

Meggie sniffed. "Zoann."

"What do you need?"

Not to stand on the porch freezing half to death. Judging by the satisfaction in the other woman's whiskey-colored eyes, she knew it, too. Meggie clenched her jaw and mumbled bitch under her breath.

"Obviously, I need to talk to you," she snapped.

Zoann glowered at her, the stubborn set of her jaw reminding Meggie of Christopher, even though brother and sister looked nothing alike. While Christopher had black hair and green eyes, his sister had a wealth of chestnut hair and whiskey-colored eyes.

"Do you want to come inside?" she asked sourly, stepping aside a fraction, the small space she cleared cuing Meggie in on the other woman's preference.

Not answering, Meggie scooted past her and closed her eyes in bliss at the warmth of the house. Baby things were scattered here and there, a play yard in one corner. A blue diaper sat on the patterned sofa. A huge photo of Patricia, Zoann, and the four other girls stood front and center on the wall above the sofa, irking Meggie to no end because another face belonged with them.

"Aren't you missing someone?" She folded her arms and thrust her chin toward the picture.

Zoann shut the door with a definitive thud and leaned against it. She lifted a brow. "Am I?"

Enough was enough. "I'm sorry about Patricia, Zoann. I didn't know her very long, but I've grieved for her, too. She never met my son—"

"Or mine," Zoann spat, rocketing forward, and stopping inches away from Meggie.

Perfect distance for Meggie to slap some sense into her head. She narrowed her eyes. "Or yours. But the way you treated Christopher is unforgivable. You owe him an apology. All of you do." All five of his sisters had been complete bitches to him at their mother's funeral. "At this point, I don't think groveling at his feet and begging his forgiveness would be too much to ask."

"If this is what you came to talk about, *leave*. Christopher is responsible—"

"Oh my God," Meggie shrieked, jabbing Zoann's shoulder. "You're such a bitch. Christopher isn't responsible for anything. And if you ever say something like that to him again, I'll make you sorry." Forgetting her purpose for visiting her sister-in-law, Meggie stormed to the door. A baby's cry halted her, and she yanked the door open. "I came here on behalf of Val, *not* Christopher. Whatever's going on between you and Val, get over it. He has every right to see his son just as if you were together."

Zoann turned on her heel and stomped toward the other room with a "hold on a moment" tossed over her shoulder.

As good as her word, she returned holding a little boy who had a mop of brown hair but eyes the color of Val's, his mother's full mouth and the impression his nose would take of the shape of his father. Plopping down in the rocking chair near the window, Zoann led her son to her nipple, then glared at Meggie.

"You're sticking your nose where it doesn't belong—"

"I beg to differ. My nose is exactly where it belongs. Those guys are my family, and I won't stand for anyone treating them less than they deserve. *Especially Christopher,*" she bit out.

"How do you know I haven't given Val permission to visit—"

Meggie snorted.

"I resent the insinuation of that snort."

"As if it matters to me what you resent," she retorted.

"If he wanted to see his son so bad, he could've tried to reach me again himself instead of sending you."

"He didn't send me," Meggie said on a whisper-yell, aware of the little boy laying with such contentment in his mother's arms. Her own breasts tingled. "I came on my own when I saw him with CJ."

Zoann blinked and turned her head. "CJ? Your son?"

"Yes. Christopher Joseph Foy Caldwell."

When Zoann fell into silence, Meggie turned to leave. There would be no happy ending here and time was fast slipping by. This had been a wasted trip, but she'd given it a shot. Over the months, she'd caught snippets of conversations between Val, Christopher, and the others about Val's son, so she'd already guessed he'd been after Zoann to visit the baby and she'd turned him down again. And again. And again.

"Christopher married you."

The dull statement once again halted Meggie. "At City Hall. We're having a church wedding in a month."

Tears returned to Zoann's eyes, and she blinked them away—again. "He loves you."

"And I love him."

Her jaw tautened and bitterness turned down her mouth. "He's a lying, murdering, cheating, stinking biker," she spat. "Just like Val."

"I'm here to appeal to you to allow Val to see his son," Meggie began, just as tight and fierce as Zoann. "I'm not here to listen to you disparage my husband. Your brother."

She glared at Meggie and eased the baby's mouth away from her nipple. "Here, then. Take a photo of him and then, please get out."

Yanking her cell phone from her jacket pocket, Meggie found the switch to the overhead light, pushed the button for the camera, and then leaned in to take shots. "Unless you're trying to give Val a thrill, cover your nipple."

Zoann shot her a nasty look, then fastened her nursing bra and shoved her shirt down.

"He's beautiful," Meggie said in an off-handed manner, snapping shots of the little boy from different angles.

"He was born a few weeks earlier than he should've been, but he…he's thriving now."

"I'm so happy to hear that," Meggie responded, wondering just what Zoann had gone through to reveal such stark pain in her tone and expression.

"He looks like his daddy," Zoann whispered and bent down to kiss his forehead.

Kinda. But if that's what Zoann saw, then Meggie wouldn't argue.

"His name is Ryan," she went on quietly. "Ryan Matthew Taylor."

"So Val's last name is Taylor?" Wow! It dawned on Meggie that she hadn't known Val's real name until then. Satisfied with the number of photos she'd taken, she pocketed her cell phone again. "Valentine Taylor. That's an interesting name."

Zoann glanced away. "His road name is Valentine. His name is Matthew. Matthew Ryan Taylor."

Typical Zoann. She'd denied Val the pleasure of allowing his son to have his first name.

"I'll see you around," Meggie said with a sigh. She wished Zoann didn't have such a chip on her shoulder. Obviously, something had happened with the MC—besides the issues with Christopher—for Zoann to carry such enmity.

"D-does V-val have an old lady?"

So it did matter to her. Of course, it did. She wouldn't be so bitter and angry if it didn't. "Not that I know. He's too busy being a murdering, whoring, stinking biker," she added dryly.

The doorbell sounded again and, since Meggie stood right in front of the door, she pulled it open, surprised when she found Ophelia on the other side. Ophelia was Christopher's youngest sister, twenty-three, the closest in age to Meggie. Like CJ and Johnnie, Ophelia had also been born in July.

Her eyes, a darker brown than Zoann's, widened. When Meggie had spent time with everyone two Christmases ago, she and Ophelia had really taken to one another. All that vanished with the death of Patricia and their treatment of Christopher and Meggie hadn't seen the woman since Patricia's funeral.

"Meggie?" Ophelia greeted with a tentative note. She'd allowed her hair to grow from the two-inch spikes it had been when Meggie met her. A headband pushed her hair back, accentuating her heart-shaped face.

"Ophelia."

Ophelia pursed her mouth at Meggie's chilly greeting. "H-how's Chris?"

"Perfect."

"Would you tell him—" She licked her lips and glanced nervously in Zoann's direction.

"Go ahead, Fee," Zoann said glumly. "It doesn't matter."

"Tell him…tell him 'Hi' for me?"

Meggie shook her head. "Not unless an apology is included in that 'hi'."

"I miss him, Meggie."

And she was sure Christopher missed his sisters, which she had no problem telling them.

"Really?" Zoann called. "We hadn't seen him in a year before my mother was killed and—"

"And that ship sailed and is never returning to port," Meggie called. "So get over it. He had his reasons for not visiting. You had no excuse for your attitude—"

"We did," Ophelia put in. "We were grieving."

"So was he. He needed you and you all let him down."

"Would you tell him I'm—"

Meggie cut Ophelia off. Maybe, she was opening old wounds and maybe she was creating a bridge for the future, but these women were part of her family, and someone had to extend the olive branch. Might as well be her since they shared some of Christopher's DNA, especially the stubborn strand. "Some of the ladies are giving me a wedding shower at the club. I want you to come and you can apologize to him yourself."

"Really?"

She nodded. After giving Ophelia all the information and discovering she was Zoann's babysitter when Zoann went to work, Meggie got in her car and sped to the grocery store. While all the problems hadn't been solved with this visit, it was a start.

Chapter 9

Christopher

CHRISTOPHER GLARED AT MORTICIAN AND VAL, who, along with a bunch of the other brothers, sat among some bitches. He flipped Mortician off when the man rolled his eyes and pointed to the big bouquet of red roses Christopher held.

He didn't know all Megan's plans, but he did know she was excited about this Valentine's dinner she was planning for him. He couldn't act like a dick and go to her without some of the bullshit girls liked to receive on Valentine's Day.

When he stepped outside, he felt for the little jewelry box he'd hidden in his cut, the cold air blasting him. He paused to pull out a cigarette, then his lighter. Doing this shit one-handed irritated the fuck out of him. But he would've had to stomp one of those motherfuckers for some smart-ass comment if he'd stayed in the clubhouse to do this shit, though it would've been easier because he could've set the roses down for a minute.

Bin waved at him from where he lounged against a bike, talking to a new girl. Christopher nodded to the brother, released the smoke through his nose, wondering what the fuck about Bin pissed him the fuck off. Brought in by Traveler, Bin had patched in a few months ago, and he seemed reliable. He did what the fuck was asked of him, never complaining about assignments. And, yet the motherfucker just rubbed Christopher the wrong fucking way.

Much like Cee Cee. Fuck. That motherfucker did more than rub him the wrong fucking way. Christopher imagined strapping fuckhead down and borrowing his extremities to send to their rivals as a little 'if-you-fuck-with-the-Dwellers-motherfuckers-this-could-be-your-fucking-arm' message.

Or leg. Foot. Hand. Finger…

What the fuck ever.

Pushing Bin, Cee Cee, and all other fuckheads to the back of his mind, Christopher turned toward the thick stand of trees. The house he'd built for Megan rose up along the pathway. Their bedroom was on the third floor because Megan liked floor-to-ceiling windows and balconies, and Christopher wanted to keep her safe. CJ's room was on that floor, too, but without all the glass and missing the balcony.

Fuck. This dinner meant a lot to her, so he couldn't bring workplace bullshit to the table. He'd outline his plans for parts of Cee Cee later. Right now, he'd focus on his gorgeous, little wife.

The light gleamed from their bedroom, brighter amidst the canopy of trees. The cold air bit into his nose and cheeks, and he sniffled, shifting the flowers and flexing his fingers to bring warmth back to his arms and hands. Another light shone from the first floor, the kitchen where the back door was located. He suspected he'd find Megan there.

Enjoying his cigarette, he looked at the bare grounds. His girl had big plans for that, too. Once the house was built and the construction crew gone, he'd gotten the fuck out the way. He didn't want to interfere with how Megan's whole face lit up whenever she talked about how she'd decorate a certain room or what appliance she'd place in the kitchen. So he'd stayed the fuck out of it and, tonight, would be the first fucking time he'd set foot inside in weeks.

Taking one, last drag on his cigarette, he found his key and unlocked the gate. Once they moved in, he was going to choose some of his most reliable brothers to serve as security here. K-P had already volunteered to help with the guard dogs and, so far, the man was doing A-o-fucking-kay.

Climbing up the wraparound porch, Christopher headed for the back door, trying the knob, and cursing when he found it unlocked.

"Megan!" he called, some delicious fucking smells invading his nose. His stomach growled as he propelled through the mudroom and into the spacious kitchen. The black refrigerator door stood open, and he saw Megan's hand holding onto the handle. "Why the fuckin' door unlocked?"

She slammed the door shut and Christopher's mouth fell open, his hold on the bouquet slackening. He just managed not to drop the motherfuckers. She wore…nothing. Absofuckinglutely nothing.

Her eyes lit up at the sight of the flowers. "Those are for me?"

No, she wore something. Red heels, he realized, hearing the motherfuckers clicking on the tiled floor. He hadn't paid attention to her feet, too fixated on her beautiful tits and her delicious pussy. She tugged the flowers out of his hand, then pulled his head down to plant her mouth over his for a quick kiss.

"Ain't we eatin', Megan?"

She laid the flowers on the counter and turned to him with a saucy wink. "You're telling me you're not going to eat?"

Wicked little bitch. He laughed, all the other bullshit from the past two days floating the fuck away. "Oh, yeah, baby. Im a fuckin' feast."

He wedged her against the marble and wood island in the center of the kitchen, snaking an arm around her waist while tweaking one of her nipples and slanting his lips over hers. She opened to him so sweetly and he slipped his tongue into her mouth, his breath catching in his lungs and expelling in a big burst of air, her taste and scent leaving him lightheaded as a motherfucker. He lifted her off her feet. She wrapped her arms around his neck, and groaned into his mouth, grinding against him. Their tongues met and twirled out all kinds of words in each other's mouths: *More. Fuck me. Now. Pussy. Met. Dick.*

For some reason, the stupid fucking idea cracked him the fuck up and he barked a laugh against her mouth.

Megan nipped his lip. "What's funny?" she asked, her fingers roaming along his jaw and down to his neck.

He laid his forehead against hers and told her about the words he imagined their tongues spelling out. She giggled and nuzzled his throat.

"Can you guess this one?" Her tongue swept against his with little brushes and pokes.

"Fuck. Baby. Tell me."

"I spelled eat me."

"Megan, baby," he breathed, bending his head and taking a nipple into her mouth, sucking hard.

She whimpered, her fingers sliding through his hair. "Christopher."

Her milk filled his mouth and Christopher let the sweetness slide down his throat, holding her in place when she began to squirm. Focusing on the other tit, he widened her legs and slipped a finger inside her pussy, wiggling it inside of her.

She cried out and Christopher lifted his head, her flushed features and darkened eyes hitting him right in the balls. Cum threatened to detonate them with the force of dynamite. He gave her a heavy-lidded look.

He lifted her onto the counter and nipped her neck, licking at the tender skin near her ear, tracing the shell of her lobe. "What the fuck you want from me, baby?"

She kicked her heels off. "Your tongue between my legs."

"You want me to lick your pussy?" he growled, feathering her mouth and hairline with kisses. She threw her head back, her hair raining around her like golden silk.

"Yeah." She leaned back on her elbows, using one hand to open her pussy lips. "Lick my clit."

Hooking his arms around her thighs, he bent and lifted her pussy to his mouth. "Roll your cunt on my tongue for me, baby." As if he had to tell her, but his words made her hot as fuck. He sucked her clit between his teeth, then soothed it with the tip of his tongue. She gasped and gripped his hair, wriggling against his lips and the flat of his tongue.

She jerked against him and cried out his name, bathing his lips, tongue and chin in her pussy juice. He kissed the inside of her thigh, resisting the urge to sniff her pussy—for now—and straightening to his full height. She spread her legs and fingered herself.

"I want you inside of me, Christopher. Now."

He began freeing himself and stepped between her legs.

"Want my dick in your sweet pussy?"

Her fingers worked her clit and her head lolled to the side. "Yeah. Put your…your…dick inside of me."

He'd take those words. Bracing one arm on the side of her, he slid his dick tip over her swollen clit. "Put my cock in you, baby."

Groaning, she widened her legs and guided him to her hot entrance, lifting her hips to draw his wide crown inside.

Christopher grunted. "Fuck, Megan." He thrust into her, buried in her pussy right to his balls, and stuck his tongue out. She lifted herself up, raising her hips to meet his hard thrusts, and meeting his tongue with hers, their wet, sloppy kiss expanding Christopher's dick. Gripping her hips, he pulled her closer and swiveled against her to brush her clit. "I ain't gonna last, baby. I'm about to come all in your pussy."

"God!"

He bit her neck and she shivered. "You want that, Megan? You want my cum in your pussy? I'm gonna give you every last drop, baby. I ain't gonna stop comin' in your pussy 'til my balls empty."

She dug her nails into his back and screamed out her release. Her quivering body drawing his cum out of his balls and pulsing into her belly.

Meggie

NERVOUS, MEGGIE CLASPED HER ARMS AROUND CHRISTOPHER'S neck as he carried her down the hallway toward the center of the first floor. She'd wanted only two floors—and she definitely didn't need such a huge house—but her husband had insisted on both the square footage and the third floor for the family bedrooms. They hadn't even eaten yet, but she'd been wanting Christopher all day and knew the best way to get his attention. Instead of dressing after she'd soaked in her bath, in her lovely cream-colored tub big enough for two, she'd decided to forget about putting on the dress she'd purchased a couple days ago.

"Okay, stop," she ordered, reaching the door where her surprise lay on the other side. Her heart beat very hard when her brain raced through all the various scenarios of Christopher's reactions. She squirmed out of his arms and faced him, very conscious of her nudity with her body so sated. Besides, he still wore a long-sleeved crew shirt beneath his cut, every ripped inch of his shoulders and torso defined through the fitted material. He rarely wore his leather pants, but, tonight, black leather clung to his thighs and legs, gathering his penis into a very delectable package. Heat rushed through her at the fire in his eyes, the intensity of their mutual awareness scorching through her. She licked her lips. "Close your eyes."

Impatience tightened his hot study of her. She knew Christopher didn't believe in mushiness, but he'd consented to a romantic evening. Though she hadn't expected the flowers, it reaffirmed her belief of her importance to him. She'd met him in the nude because of her own lusty need to feel his big body moving inside of her. Now, the gesture seemed right and a very satisfying compromise.

"Instead of closin' my eyes, I'd prefer to flip you over and bury my face in your pussy, Megan." He grabbed her by the neck and pulled her closer, kissing her with enough desire and passion to make her spontaneously combust. "While I'm lickin' your pussy, you can suck my dick, yeah?"

"Yeah." She sucked on his tongue before pulling away from him and shifting from foot to foot, staring at him through the sweep of her lashes. "I wanna show you my gift first. Please?"

"Fuck." He squeezed his lids shut and balled his fists at his side.

Heaving a deep breath, Meggie swung open the door and guided Christopher inside the room, flipping on the light, finding everything in place. "Now, open them."

Christopher's eyes flew open, gazed around, and blinked. "Fuck me."

He zeroed in on the bar, shaped and fashioned after the one at the clubhouse, all the same alcohol stocked in the recessed mirrored space behind it. Instead of a panel of monitors, a huge flat-screen television hung on the wall above the liquor. Replicas of the bar stools and tables stood around the room. Megan had only one pool table, not three, cordoned off with wooden railings—just like at the club—and one dartboard. Her addition was a sofa and a card table, along with cards and a set of dominoes. Around the corner of the railing were two bathrooms, one for women and one for men, the signs of *Chicks* and *Dicks*, another clubhouse carbon copy. Not that she expected many women to be allowed in this room. If Christopher liked it, he'd probably bar her from coming in here, too. The final touch was the Grim Reaper mural dominating one wall of the room.

"You recreated the bar at the club."

His tone and inscrutable expression gave her no sign of his feelings. Did he like it or loathe it?

"Yes," she mumbled.

"I can't believe you did this shit." He three-sixtied again, turning in slow degrees. His gaze burned into hers. "Why, baby?"

She *really* should've greeted him with clothes on. She'd feel so much more confident if she wasn't bare-assed naked and would handle his rejection of her gift better. Instead of showing her insecurity, she shrugged. "Because you've made a lot of changes for me, Christopher. I know how much you love the club and, sometimes, it gets so noisy there." She wrung her hands. "Which, thinking about it, you probably love, too. But, sometimes, if you and your officers wanted privacy or—"

He wrapped his arms around her, his shoulders shaking with laughter. "Megan, shut the fuck up, baby, cuz you ain't even knowin' what the fuck you sayin'." He touched his forehead to hers. "Know why the fuck you doin' this shit?" he asked gruffly.

"Because—"

He placed a finger on her lip. "Cuz my ass a lucky motherfucker with a girl that want him so fuckin' happy, she takin' space in her fuckin' house to give him a fuckin' room she know he gonna fuckin' love. You did this shit cuz you love my ass."

She nodded, glad he'd gotten the meaning behind the gesture.

He pulled away from her and his laughter deepened. "You also did it cuz you a jealous lil' bitch and you figure if you got a room in *this* motherfucker lookin' like my bar in *that* motherfucker—" he nodded his head in the direction of the clubhouse— "you control the bitches 'round my fuckin' ass."

She opened her mouth to deny it, but he sounded so amused, she couldn't help but laugh herself. "Caught," she admitted.

"Fuck, Megan. I ain't got nothin' near like this shit for you. I mean, fuck, you greetin' me with your pussy made my ass fuckin' delirious with happiness. Then, you gotta add a whole fuckin' room after giftin' me with the golden Promised Land."

"I wish you'd stop referring to my vagina as the Promised Land."

He glared at her. "Stop ruinin' my Valentine's present callin' your pussy a vagina. We been through this shit befuckinfore. Vaginas for lil' ninety-year-old ladies and fuckin' the last thing on their mind. *Any* pussy still gettin" fucked *ain't* a vagina, Megan. Pussy. Cunt. Hole. Twat. Slit. Snatch—"

"All right!" she yelled, holding up her hand. "I get the frigging point. Will lady bits or vajayjay suffice?"

He folded his arms. "Vag."

"Vag?" She frowned. "That sounds worse than vajayjay. Vag?"

He nodded.

She sighed. "All right. I can live with vag."

The moment she capitulated, he was upon her, snatching any more conversation from her head with his gaze refocused on her. Meggie kissed his chest, still covered with his long-sleeved T-shirt and his leather cut. The ridges of his six pack bumped her fingertips as she slid her hands lower and dropped to her knees, helping him to bare himself to her.

He fisted his rigid flesh. "Whatcha 'bout to do to me, Megan?"

She slid closer to him and licked one of his testicles, his hand bumping her nose.

"What, Megan?"

"I'm about to suck you." She wrapped her lips around his other testicle and suckled. "Make you come in my mouth."

"Play with your pussy while you suckin' my dick," he demanded, guiding his manhood to her mouth, which she greedily accepted.

She slurped him into her mouth, closing her eyes in bliss at the scent of him, the smell and taste of her own body clinging to him. Gripping his base with one hand, she slid two of her fingers inside herself, pressing her thumb on her clit, caressing it to the rhythm of her sucks. Christopher's grip on her hair and deep grunts ignited her blood and pooled in her core. The tips of her breasts tingled, and she tongued the dark, mushroom-shaped crown, the fluid already bubbling from him sticky in her mouth. The nub between her legs tightened against her fingers, the pressure building low in her belly. Her womb clenched and she quaked against the movement of her hand, the taste of Christopher driving her wild.

Bright light exploded behind the lids of her eyes, and she released his hardness from her mouth, crying out in pleasure, the touch of Christopher's fingers massaging her scalp combined with the sensations rocketing through her.

He lifted her to her feet and dragged her toward the barstool. "Bend over," he rasped.

The red vinyl of the seat cooled her flushed skin and the grooved chrome surrounding it pressed against her belly. Christopher laid one hand on her back, spreading her legs with the other one. He circled her clit, dug into her entrance, and spread her juices, stroking up, opening her butt cheeks and aligning his erection to her.

He stroked her back, crooning to her, preparing her for the invasion she still found foreign. He eased the head into her, and she tensed.

"Relax, baby," he whispered. "Remember, what I told you? It hurts worse if you stiffen up."

She nodded, felt him push a little more of himself into her and she drew in a deep breath, the sound of his voice grabbing her out of the depths of her fear and loosening her muscles.

"Good girl." He pushed further into her, found her clit again and she groaned, pain and pleasure slicing through her. "You feel so fuckin' good, Megan."

Inch by inch, he eased into her until he'd embedded himself deep within her. He bent over her and began moving in and out of her cautiously, taking more care with his thrusts while he was inside her this way.

He licked her ear, then bit her neck and her shoulder, fisting her hair into his hands. "I love you, Megan. So fuckin' much. You for me, baby. Every part of your beautiful fuckin' body mine. *You* given me that fuckin' gift."

She twisted against him, and he sucked in a breath.

"Every fuckin' part of me belong to you, too, 'specially my fuckin' heart and dick."

His body covered hers, her back pressed against his wide chest and hard stomach, his heat and power surrounding her, owning her. She gasped and sobbed his name, his continued stimulation between her legs and his thrusts into her merging the pain and the pleasure into something powerful and explosive, her body a slave to his.

"Yeah, baby," he growled, easing into her again, his testicles slapping against her clit and making her tremble. "I'm fuckin' comin', Megan." He yelled her name and shuddered against her, his manhood jerking inside of her. He went limp against her, breathing heavy.

She squirmed under him, and he raised up, pulling out of her. She groaned and came to her feet, wincing at her wobbliness. He steadied her and they stared at each other, the awe in his eyes sending heat rushing to her face.

He bent and kissed her lips. "Thank you."

"I**F YOU TELL THEM MOTHERFUCKERS THE SHIT WE doin',** they ain't ever lookin' at me the same again."

Meggie giggled, her third glass of rosé champagne tingling through her veins and combining with Christopher's lovemaking. She felt boneless and giddy and stuffed from the crab cakes and French fries she'd cooked. They'd enjoyed their first glass of champagne while they chomped on fresh Rainier cherries, and then went upstairs to their bedroom and indulged in a bath, where they washed and massaged one another with a bath oil she chose for its spicy scent. Christopher would never have agreed to smelling like any type of flower.

Now, they sat at the round table in their bedroom. *Bedroom* was a little understated because of its size, sitting room, walk-in closets, and huge bathroom.

"The fuckin' shit you get me to do."

"You shouldn't have told me you played Monopoly, Christopher," she said calmly. "And it isn't like this is the first time we've played the game since you let slip you remembered playing the game with Johnnie years ago."

"Seein' as how this Valentine's Day, we gotta play strip Monopoly. Every fuckin' time one of us land in jail, we take a piece of clothin' the fuck off."

She narrowed her eyes and frowned. "Aren't we already naked?" She couldn't be that drunk that she'd imagined neither of them bothering to dress after they'd finished with the bath.

Christopher leaned back in his chair and grabbed the second bottle of champagne, chilling in the silver bucket next to him. He popped the cork and Meggie squealed, clapping her hands. Cork popping always made her think of happiness and celebrations and she'd had so little of that until she'd met the beautiful man across from her.

"I'm callin' a fuckin' rain check 'til we play Monopoly my fuckin' way." He swigged from the newly opened bottle.

Meggie drained her glass and held it out for Christopher to pour her more champagne.

"Watch it, lil' girl," he teased, licking his fingers when the bubbly fizzled over. "A fuckin' dirty old motherfucker tryna get you drunk and fuck your brains out."

"I better not tell my husband then. I don't think he'll like that too much."

His gaze on her breasts, he drank more champagne, then sat it aside and folded his arms. "I gotta talk to you, Megan."

The seriousness of his tone straightened her spine and she swallowed. What caused the sudden change in his mood? She knew he still had the incident with Cee Cee lurking in his mind, but they'd been having such a wonderful time, she didn't believe he'd bring it up tonight. "Okay. What's up?"

While he studied her, Meggie focused on Christopher's face so she wouldn't salivate over his chest. His hair had the *I've-been-fucked* style guys got after women pulled and caressed their strands during sex. If she got up and slipped her hands through the dark mass, she'd—

"You willin' to learn how to shoot guns?"

His topic relieved her because he'd sounded so harsh. "No."

"What the fuck you mean? No?"

"Just what I said, no." She rubbed a finger through the condensation on the glass she held. "Guns kill people."

He glowered at her, slanted his head to one side and then the other. "Guns ain't gettin' the fuck up and start shootin' on their fuckin' own. Motherfuckers *with* guns pull the trigger and kill other motherfuckers."

"Point taken," she agreed. "*But* the principle is the same. If you didn't have a gun in the first place, people wouldn't be killed."

He snorted in disbelief.

"You and the guys have an entire arsenal at your disposal. There's no reason for me to have to get near a gun."

"Except it's the luck of the fuckin' draw, baby. My ass might have a entire fuckin' army and if another motherfucker get a fuckin' drop on us—"

"Whether I know how to shoot a gun or not, someone could still get the drop on you." She didn't want to think about anyone besting her husband, so she shifted in her seat to dispel images of the past carnage she'd been subjected to. "I understand why you want me to learn how to shoot. To protect myself and CJ." She couldn't imagine ever picking up a gun and pulling the trigger to kill someone else. "Just teach me self-defense techniques."

Knowing he wouldn't win the argument, he grabbed the bottle and drank it dry. "Keep the doors fuckin' locked when you here 'til I get everyfuckinthing in place. I shoulda put you over my fuckin' knee when I walked in and found you naked and the door un-fuckin-locked."

"Christopher, there's not even a driveway here. I have to keep my car at the club. There's only one entry gate to the property."

"Ain't givin' a fuck if you needed airdroppin' in the middle of this motherfucker to get on the property or if a helicopter needed to land your lil' ass on the fuckin' roof so you could get the fuck in the house."

He scratched his shoulders, drawing Meggie's eyes to his newest tat that covered the healed wound in his shoulder. He'd had her name tatted on his left wrist and Little Man on the right one. She flirted with the idea of getting his name inked somewhere on her body and smiled when she imagined his surprise. She glanced at his shoulder again and the smile slipped away. The day Christopher had been shot was one of the most horrible days of her life and just another reason she wanted to stay far away from guns.

"When a motherfucker wanna get you, they findin' a fuckin' way," he continued, picking up on the conversation again. "With dickheads advisin' you to go on fuckin' trips and you fuckin' listenin' to *them*, my ass need to fuckin' know you able to protect your-fuckin-self."

"You're right, but I'll learn some type of martial art."

The remaining dampness in his hair rubbed onto his fingers when he thrust them through the gleaming strands. "We continuin' this conversation another fuckin' time, Megan. I ain't wantin' to ruin your Valentine dinner with this shit." He got to his feet and Meggie went to follow suit. "Stay there. I'll be right back."

He sauntered to the bathroom, allowing Meggie to admire the tautness of his buttocks. His long, strong body gave new meaning to the word hot. A moment later, he swaggered back in, his penis rising from the thick nest of black hair trailing from his belly button and down to his groin. He smirked at her when he noticed where her eyes focused.

"Raise your gaze from my cock long efuckinnuff to get your Valentine Day present, baby."

"Your body mesmerizes me," she admitted.

"I know." He didn't allow her to respond, instead, dropping to one knee and drawing in a deep sigh. "Megan, baby, when we tied the fuckin' knot, I just kinda told you we was goin' to City Hall. So, you already own fuckin' rings and you ain't takin' them off 'til the day we marryin' in church so I can put them back on you—"

He paused and scowled at the thought of their big wedding, then heaved another breath.

"Fuck me, anyfuckinway," he went on, scrubbing a hand over his face and opening the velvet box he held to reveal a diamond tennis bracelet. "Do my fuckin' ass the greatest fuckin' honor of bein' my wife for all fuckin' time?"

It took a moment for her shocked brain to process Christopher was down on one knee, proposing to her. Her heart stuttered with emotion, and she swallowed. "Oh my God! Christopher," she screeched, launching herself into his arms and bathing his face in kisses. "I love you so much! Yes. Of course."

She held out her wrist so he could attach the bracelet. After he fastened it, she stared in awe at it.

"Motherfucker set in platinum," he told her.

The band of round cubic zirconia sparkled and gleamed like real diamonds, illuminated by the lights in the room. A butterfly-shaped clasp consisted of more cubic zirconia. Meggie had never seen anything like it.

"I saw some shit 'bout butterflies a coupla months ago. What I was readin' defuckinscribed the motherfucker symbolism. Romance. Liveliness. Strength. How it help calm assfucks 'round you. They might mean promisin' a better fuckin' future. You all the fuckin' article describe, Megan. One fuckin' look atcha and I see my present, my future, my fuckin' everything. I ain't into no totem pole spirit animals and the meanin' of butterflies all wrapped in that." He shook his head, his green eyes earnest, tender. "Ain't matterin'. You bringin' light, *life*, to my dark fuckin' world and romance to whatever small bit of fuckin' soul I fuckin' got."

Sniffling, Meggie hugged him. "I love you so much."

He scooped her into his arms and carried her to bed. Once he had them both under the covers, he rolled onto her and pinned her hands above her head. "My ass did this Valentine's bullshit right, Megan?" he murmured and sank into her.

Meggie lifted her hips. "You did it just perfect, Christopher."

He grinned, the look in his eyes vulnerable, his face boyish. "I love you, baby."

"I love you—"

He captured her mouth with his own, drowning out her response with the heat of his tongue, and holding her gaze the entire time he made love to her with slow, gentle strokes and tender kisses.

Meggie wouldn't soon forget this night.

Chapter 10

Meggie

EARLY THE NEXT AFTERNOON, MEGGIE RUSHED ALONG THE pathway and away from her house. She, Dinah, and CJ had attended church and she didn't have time to go to their room at the MC to change out of the leather-hemmed tuxedo dress she'd purchased in Seattle before she had to get to the meeting in the board room. As usual, Christopher skipped services and his lack of cooperation worried her because if he didn't adhere to the requirements, their wedding wouldn't take place. Not only wasn't he a parishioner, but he was also Agnostic, a fact she'd kept from the priest.

Somehow, he'd gotten Father Wilkins to agree to her having the Wedding March—secular music—and the lone stipulation of attending pre-marital counseling. Father Wilkins was rumored to be a stickler for his rules—the demand that couples live apart for at least six months before their marriage; the requirement that they were parishioners; the preference that the couple not have children out of wedlock.

Though she'd met the priest, she hadn't dealt with him one-on-one yet. She'd worn her bracelet to Mass. At communion, Father Wilkins's eyes lit up at the sparkles, the cubic zirconia reflecting in his black eyes like an omen.

Meggie suspected just how Christopher had gotten the priest's agreement for the music, but she didn't want to dwell on it too much. Assuming her husband had threatened a holy man wasn't something she wanted to sit around and think about. Not only from a moral standpoint but, because doing his business in his world was bad enough. Having it spill over into mainstream life was horrifying and the quickest way to get Christopher behind bars.

Waving to May, Gurly and Bin, she hurried through the main room and down the hallway, knocking on the door to the board room, where Christopher said he'd be waiting for her with the brothers she wanted to talk to. She heard all sorts of juvenile snickering and rowdiness on the other side and knew their church had ended as well. Or *their* version of church.

"Come in," Christopher called.

Opening the door, Meggie smiled as she stepped in, laughing at the greetings thrown her way. A headcount revealed all the guys she'd requested were present. She headed to where Christopher sat, bent and kissed him, wishing she could smooth away the frown marring his brow. For a few hours last night, he'd let go of some of his anger toward Cee Cee—his father—not even mentioning him or the newfound connection to the man. But Meggie saw the rage seething in him and the wall he was dropping between them in the light of day. His father had always been a sore spot with Christopher because of the violent way his mother had conceived him.

Meggie couldn't make it better for him, but she could let him know she was there for him. If he'd listen to her.

"Megan, baby, hurry the fuck up. I gotta do shit."

Johnnie glared at Christopher, who, thankfully didn't notice. Christopher was spoiling for a fight—bloodshed, actually. With anyone.

"All right. I'm not going to keep you guys long," she said on a sigh, her gaze falling on Val. Shoot. She hadn't had a chance to show him his son's photos. Grabbing her phone from the pocket in her purse, she held up a finger. "One second, gentlemen."

Everyone but Christopher, Johnnie and Mortician crowded on Val's side of the room. Christopher sat at the head, his chair positioned in such a way that he blocked her from passing. Scooting between Johnnie and Mortician while pulling up the photos, she leaned across the table and slid her phone to Val.

"These are for you," she whispered.

"What—" His words choked off when his gaze slid down. For a long moment, he stared in silence, then swallowed and peeped at Meggie.

She grinned, happy to see his smile. "Scroll through," she encouraged. "There's more."

"Where'd you get these, babe?" he asked.

His gruff tone and scary demeanor could frighten a bear. Meggie took it all in stride.

"I took them," she answered.

"That's some fucking ice on your wrist, Meggie," Shady observed, staring at her bracelet.

She grinned, bursting with joy, even if he mistakenly thought real gems sat atop the platinum band. "Christopher gave it to me for Valentine's Day."

"Oh," Shady responded, tugging his beard. "Outlaw gave it to you."

"Even if I ain't give her the motherfucker, what she got befuckinlong to *her*," Christopher said coldly.

"Shady, bruh, why you noticing anything on Meggie?" Digger demanded as if Christopher didn't have enough ammunition. "Sound to me like you want to take that motherfucker for yourself."

Christopher growled.

"Um, *no*," Meggie inserted quickly, throwing Digger a look of admonishment. "He was just admiring it. Right, Shady?"

Instead of allowing Shady to respond, Cowboy focused on her bracelet. "Must be worth a pretty fucking penny."

Folding his arms, Christopher glanced between the two men. "Worth 'bout you motherfuckers chopped and boxed to 'bout a thousand fuckin' pieces each."

Meggie gasped. "Omigod, first Father Wilkins looked at it in a way that made him seem anything other than priestly. Now, you all are about to throw punches. It's a beautiful, thoughtful gift from my husband. Just a bracelet that has sentimental value to me."

They ignored her.

"Outlaw, I like living." Shady laughed nervously. "I was just saying."

"Ain't remember a motherfucker askin'. If you ain't tired of seein' and like them motherfuckers in your goddamn head, keep your fuckin' eyes offa my woman." Christopher scowled at her.

"Ain't bought that motherfucker to have you flashin' it all the fuck 'round."

"Prez—" Mortician stated as Meggie blurted, "but we're on club grounds and this is my engagement bracelet."

"We fuckin' married alfuckinready," Christopher snarled.

"It's a real pretty bracelet, Meggie girl," Mortician said kindly, his gentle smile soothing her hurt feelings and helping her to suck back her tears.

"Can I see it, sweetheart?" Johnnie asked in a tone that sounded suspiciously suggestive.

She stood between him and Mortician, wedged in on each side by their thighs, but Johnnie shifted, leaning toward her. One more move and his arm would press against the underside of her breast. That…that would be a catastrophe, so she folded her arms.

"Meggie, you know that's real fucking ice on your wrist, don't you?" Digger asked, cocking his head to the side.

She frowned at him, shook her head slowly, then unfolded her arms and held her hand up, gasping. Staring at the bracelet, she counted the stones, starting on one side of the butterfly clasp and ending at the other. Thirty-six round gems, plus four more to make the butterfly.

"Oh, my," she whispered, heat sweeping through her. She wasn't sure if she'd gone into shock or suffered a severe case of embarrassment for not knowing she wore real diamonds.

"Christopher," she breathed, awed by his generosity, humbled that he thought her worthy of such a gift. He must've spent five or six thousand dollars. The thought made her gasp again. She'd never ask outright. For one, Dinah had taught her it was rude to ask the price of a present, even from your husband. Also, the number in her head seemed exorbitantly high.

"Meggie?" Digger called again.

Still unable to form words, she lifted her gaze to him.

He scratched his jaw. "How much you think that motherfucker cost?"

She'd be a blatant liar if she pretended no curiosity about the price. How was she supposed to answer that with all the guys, except Val, gawking at her. She glanced at Christopher, but his expression gave nothing away.

"You wanna fuckin' know, yeah?" he finally relented.

Yes, badly.

"Girls curious," Mortician told her. "Nothing wrong with that."

"You fuckin' say how fuckin' much you fuckin' think I dropped on the motherfucker," Christopher told her.

Figures swirled in her brain. The house he was building for her was massive. Whatever she wanted, she got. She knew he'd founded the medical lab, but it also laundered club money. Then there were his hydrogrows, and the club-sponsored CBD storefronts. Beyond that, they moved a lot of other merchandise through Dweller chapters across the country, with help from a vast network of support clubs. He supposed he could spend…

"Ten thousand dollars," she announced, her heart sinking at the way they stared at her. "Five?" she squeaked.

"That price a fuckin' lot to you, huh, baby?" Christopher asked.

She nodded. "I don't need diamonds when I have you and CJ, Christopher."

Tenderness flickered in his eyes, before he lowered his lips. He raised his gaze again and the gentleness had extinguished.

"I love this bracelet," she confessed. "It didn't dawn on me the stones were real because I never thought someone would see me as deserving something like this."

Fury burned in his eyes at her words. She decided she didn't want to know the price.

Licking her lips, she unclasped the bracelet she hadn't intended to ever take off and walked to Christopher, holding it out to him. "Keep it safe for me." Her voice cracked because she didn't want to stop wearing it, but she kept her smile in place. He was angry with the world right now. "I'll wear it as part of my trousseau."

He opened his palm and she dropped the bracelet into it. His fist closed around it and her lips trembled, but she cleared her throat and glanced away. Her gaze fell on Val, still enraptured by the photos she'd snapped.

"He's gorgeous, isn't he, Val?" she said softly, walking back to her position between Mortician and Johnnie.

"You want your phone back, Meggie?" Val asked gruffly.

"Whatcha fuckin' got?" Christopher snapped, leaning forward and resting his elbows on the table. He looked ready to launch himself at Val and snatch her phone away.

Val held the device up. "My kid." His brows drew together, and he glanced at Meggie, shrugging. "Um, what's his—"

She wouldn't tell him that his son had been born prematurely. Not knowing all the details, she didn't want to worry him. Besides, it wasn't *her* place to share that news, so she'd keep her answer simple. "Ryan Matthew Taylor," she supplied.

"No fuckin' shit?" Christopher said, standing up and pulling her out the way to grab her phone. He scrolled through the photos himself, then handed the phone back to Meggie.

Val looked as if he wanted to snatch it back from her, but he knew better.

Meggie glared at Christopher and huffed. *I have you covered,* she texted to Val and fired off the photos. Immediately, his phone started vibrating with incoming text messages.

Christopher threw her a dirty look. "You ever fuckin' listenin' to me?" he demanded, pocketing her bracelet in his cut.

She shrugged. "Of course, Christopher," she responded without hesitation. "If I agree with you."

"How did you come about those, Megs?" Johnnie asked.

"I visited Zoann yesterday."

Christopher and Johnnie exchanged glances, then Christopher shrugged, too. Johnnie shook his head and Meggie knew he had his own opinion about his bitter cousin. Swallowing, Christopher directed his gaze to the wall on the other side of the room, where a huge photo of his mother and two smaller ones of Ellen and Kiera—all victims of Meggie's brother—hung.

While she'd shared a very strained relationship with the two women—considering their relationship with Christopher—they'd been killed in cold blood, and they'd been regulars at the club for years. Meggie had thought it only fair for their memory to be honored in some way. Deep down, she knew Christopher had had a soft spot for both women, but most especially Kiera. He'd always vehemently insisted Kiera had never been his girlfriend, even to this day. Meggie maintained otherwise just as fervently. He'd tracked down their families and paid for their funeral services. He'd even sent Traveler and Bin with a lump sum of money and a message that the relatives contact him if they ever needed anything.

Christopher had had a life before he'd met her, so she didn't begrudge him his grief over their deaths. They'd been her competitors and, yet they'd shared an odd kinship. Frenemies, she supposed. Whatever they might've been to her, she'd grieved for them as well. Hanging photos in their memory felt right.

Christopher had made the decision to place them in the board room. "Don't want every piece of fuckin' Club Ass thinkin' they gettin' some fuckin' monument if they die."

Right.

Meggie hadn't argued. At least, she'd gotten him to put it to the vote before the brothers on whether to hang the photos in the first place.

Now, as he continued to stare at his mother, she knew the mention of Zoann had brought the circumstances of Patricia's death front and center.

Traveler cleared his throat. "Me and Bin got a run to make, Meggie. Can you hurry up?"

Christopher narrowed his eyes at Traveler and the man flushed. "I didn't mean any harm," he said defensively.

Meggie placed her hands on her husband's shoulders. Tension bunched his muscles and she searched for ideas to draw his feelings out, keep him calm, and, somehow, prevent the bloodbath in the making. Whether Christopher or Cee Cee struck first didn't matter. Neither outcome would be good. If—and when—she had another run-in with Cee Cee, she'd either keep her mouth shut or go to Val, Johnnie, Mortician, and Digger.

"Talk, baby."

"I'm not going to take too long," she started, squeezing Christopher's shoulders. He looked back at her, reached a hand behind her, and pulled her closer to slant his mouth over hers. After she'd had her brains fucked out last night, his touch rocketed through her system, and she opened her mouth for his onslaught. When he let her go, her breath came out in short, little pants and her skin felt flaming hot. She groaned when she felt the letdown of her milk and stepped behind Christopher's chair, using his body to cover the rapidly spreading wet spots.

She licked her lips, tasted the mint from Christopher's mouth, and tried to arrange her scattered thoughts.

Christopher sidled a sexy half-smile to her. "The weddin', Megan."

"Yes. Right," she mumbled, flushing to her toes. It didn't help that her gaze fell on Johnnie, and she recognized the heat and jealousy in his eyes from the kiss Christopher had given her. She rubbed her forehead. Not that that helped either. Even the tips of her fingers burned like a fever invaded her body. That fever was Outlaw. Christopher. *Her man.*

"Get on with it, Megs," Johnnie said in bored tones. He leaned back, not bothering to hide his semi-erect state, his heavy-lidded look enough to send a sane man into a jealous fit.

"Motherfuck you, John Boy."

Everything she needed to say crashed back at Christopher's growl. In this powder keg of on edge testosterone, someone needed an excuse to throw the first punch. She refused to allow it and glared at Johnnie for provoking the flames of Christopher's jealousy.

"So the wedding's about a month away," she announced with a sniff. "Just as promised, I've only asked for measurements, so far. I've also chosen everything. Now, you have to go for your fittings. First thing tomorrow."

Grumbles, as she'd expected. But Christopher's thought of fighting had been deflected. For now.

"Meggie, I don't want to walk around in no fucking monkey suit all fucking day," Shady called.

"Yo, fuckhead," Christopher growled. "Watch your motherfuckin' mouth and how the fuck you talk to my old lady. She ain't gonna be here for-fuckin-ever to calm my ass the fuck down. Curse at her again and Ima fuck you up."

"Shady, Bowlie, Traveler, Cowboy, as the ushers, why don't you wear your cuts, over a white tuxedo shirt and the black tuxedo pants."

"I'll take that, babe," Bowlie agreed with a smile. He flipped Val and Mortician the bird because he knew she still wanted them to wear tuxedos, collectively referred to by them as *monkey suits.*

Mortician pulled a rolled cigarette out of his cut and Meggie backed away.

"Ima break your fuckin' fingers if you light up that fuckin' blunt."

"I'm not lighting the motherfucker, Outlaw. Just getting inspiration from it."

"Yeah, strength," Digger agreed.

"A plea for mercy," Val inserted, glancing between Christopher and the phone where he flipped through the photos over and over again.

Meggie sniffed. "It isn't that bad, boys."

Johnnie shifted his long legs in front of him, pulled out a pack of cigarettes, took one out, then passed the pack to Mortician. "It's even worse, Megs. I wear suits on a regular basis and even I hate the thought of a fucking tuxedo." He puffed on his cigarette then released the smoke, shaping his mouth in an 'o' still in search of the perfect smoke ring. The action drew her focus to his lips, and she cleared her throat, glancing away.

"You try my ass, motherfucker," Christopher bit out, balling his fists on the table. "One fuckin' day, Ima rearrange your fuckin' face."

Johnnie blew another smoke ring. "You're just jealous of my god-like beauty, Outlaw."

Meggie rolled her eyes.

"Or, maybe, you're jealous you don't have anything to suck on right now."

"I got more than you, motherfucker," Christopher shot back, not even hesitating. "Courtesy of my son, I got something to suck on every fuckin' day."

Meggie squeaked, mortified. A muscle ticked in Johnnie's jaw, and he glowered at his cousin. But, judging from Christopher's taut muscles, he felt not a shred of remorse. In fact, Meggie suspected the moment she walked out the door, the brawl she'd managed to divert would commence. She knew, though, Christopher was lord and master here. To put their hands on him in anger courted death, even though Christopher could beat the brothers to a bloody pulp for infractions. Or even kill them.

She threw Johnnie a pleading gaze. His eyes burned silver but roamed between her and Christopher before he turned away.

"My mom said she's baking chocolate chip cookies later," Meggie announced through tension so thick it would bring a bullet to a screeching halt. "She loves our new kitchen. If anyone wants to come over—"

"For cookies?" Stretch asked. When Meggie first arrived, he'd been a Probate.

After Snake hit the club and took out half the club officers, an interim election had been held. By the time, regular elections took place, Johnnie had given up his Nomad status and Stretch was a full-patch member.

He was the quietest of all the officers. Really, of all the brothers, outside of Bin. But Bin gave Meggie the heebee jeebees that she tried to hide. It shamed her to think his appearance spooked her. White hair. Pasty white skin. Reddish-brown eyes. Stretch, though, fit in with all the rest of the officers. Gorgeous. Even K-P, missing an eye and fifty, was handsome.

Shady and Cowboy, on the other hand, had thick beards, beer bellies, and a generally scruffy appearance.

"It was just an idea…" to remove the building hostility. "Forget it."

"I'll be there, babe," K-P called. "For sure."

She smiled and nodded. "Okay. So, guys, my ushers," she amended, "I still expect you to wear the bow ties."

Traveler's face fell, the corners of his greenish-blue eyes crinkling. He shoved the red bandanna along his hairline and scratched through the pieces of hair sticking out. It was rare he went without something on his head, but she knew he had a crew cut. "For real, babe?"

"For real," she echoed, thinking Val's eyes were also green and blue, but there were golden undertones, turning an ordinary combination to an outstanding turquoise

"Suppose I get a bow tie tattoo?" Traveler suggested. "I can wear my cut and the bow tie will show."

"Can we at least wear our boots?" Cowboy inserted. His features drooped like a lost puppy.

"Yes, *you* guys can."

"Fuck me," Christopher said, glaring at her. "You sayin' us motherfuckers ain't able to?"

"You're the groom, Christopher, and they're groomsmen. Your tuxedos won't look right with motorcycle boots."

"Megan—"

"Please, Christopher?"

He sighed and yanked at his hair, throwing her a sour look, a wordless capitulation.

Happiness danced through her, and she bent and kissed him. "Thank you. I love you so much."

"I love you, too, you lil' pain in the ass motherfucker," he grumbled. "That's the only fuckin' reason my ass agreein' to what the fuck you presentin'."

"And here I thought it was so we could go on our honeymoon."

A half-smile curved his mouth, turning his expression into pure wickedness and he winked at her. "That shit, too, babe."

"Fittings are Saturday," she announced, shooting out the time and location. "Thanks for giving me this time."

"Ain't like them motherfuckers had a fuckin' choice, baby."

Her phone rang and she saw that it was her mother. Since there'd been no mishap last night, she thought it would be fine to leave CJ with her for the few minutes it took to impart the information. She should've known it wouldn't be so easy, having to make her announcements through the comments from the boys.

"Momma?" she asked in answer. In the background, CJ whined, and she forgot about everything else. "What's wrong?"

"CJ's hungry."

"I bought formula for him." She had to start weaning him because she'd be away for two weeks on her honeymoon. After explaining what she wanted her mother to do, she disconnected and saw that Shady, Bowlie, Cowboy, and Traveler had left.

She still didn't trust an argument not to break out once she left. For whatever reason, Johnnie had decided to taunt Christopher with *her*. Never a good idea and if Christopher wouldn't have flipped, she would've taken Johnnie aside herself and had a word with him.

"This 'bout it, baby?" Christopher asked, tapping his fingers on the table, his body language telling her he wanted her gone.

Shoving aside her twinge of hurt, she slipped her fingers through his hair. "Yes. I need a word with you in your office."

"I gotta talk to John Boy."

"What I have to say is really important, though."

"Then say—"

She leaned close to his ear, breathing in his scent and the leather from his cut, loving his smell and warmth. As a girl, she thought of breastfeeding as a baby's nourishment. Christopher saw things a little different, so she'd dangle one of his favorite pastimes in front of him. "My breas…*tits* are full. I need you to suck them for me, then I want to suck you."

He shot to his feet and grabbed her hand, throwing over his shoulder, "meetin' fuckin' adjourned. Ima catch up with your fuckin' ass later, John Boy."

Not if she had anything to say about it. By the time they left Christopher's office, she'd see to it he remembered he owned her body and soul.

Chapter 11

Christopher

CHRISTOPHER HALTED HIS HARLEY IN FRONT OF Dippin' Sam's, hangout for one of the bigger black MCs in the area. Bikes lined the front and side of the place and music and the babble of a big crowd floated in the cold night. He hoped he didn't run into any bullshit since he'd brought Megan along.

Unlike the previous two nights. He was on the hunt, and he didn't want her caught in the fucking crossfire, so he'd duck out right after dinner, not inviting her along as he had started to do since she'd recovered from her stabbing.

While he'd been out last night, he'd been invited to the birthday party for the Night Flyers' president, a friend of Christopher's who had informants outside of Christopher's network. He'd considered leaving Megan behind this time, too, then decided against it. On a fucking Tuesday evening when some motherfuckers had to get the fuck up early tomorrow for their jobs in the civilian world, shit should be much fucking tamer. He also wanted her to see what took him away from her every night. Besides, though the Dwellers and the Flyers didn't actively socialize, they were on friendly terms, and it never hurt for Megan to acquire new contacts.

"Are we going in, Christopher?"

He looked up at the velvet black night at the sound of her sweet little voice. Getting himself a smoke, he nodded. Her phone rang and she sighed. "It's Momma. Let me take this. Go on in. I'll catch up to you."

"I ain't leavin' you out here by yourfuckinself."

"Outlaw?" a voice from the shadows called.

"Mouse, that you assfuck?" Christopher called with a smile and a drag on his cigarette.

Mouse, the Flyers' enforcer, stepped beneath one of the floodlights. He was a small, muscled man, earning his road name Mouse after that old cartoon character Mighty Mouse. Mouse and Stretch were friends. Christopher had met Stretch here, before the motherfucker started hanging around with the Dwellers.

Christopher and Mouse slapped their hands together and clutched in the universal sign of brotherhood. "Where the fuck your ass been, motherfucker?"

Mouse smiled. "Around, bro. Your old lady gonna be fine out here. Go in. I'll watch over her and escort her to you myself."

He glanced back at Megan who stood next to his bike, deep in conversation. He wanted to get some intel, have a few drinks as a show of respect, then get the fuck gone and in bed with Megan. He nodded. "Thanks, brother."

When he walked in, he saw people scattered about. Most of the motherfuckers were heading out the back door and into the yard, where he knew the party was taking place. The room was half the size of the Dwellers' main room. Photos of their Free Bird members hung on the wall to the left of him, a greeting to everyone who walked into the place. He received nods here and there, but nothing overwhelmingly welcoming. As he approached the bar, two bitches he hadn't seen in ages rushed up to him.

"Outlaw," the taller one breathed, planting her mouth against his. Rail thin and model like, she had smooth, dark skin, close-cropped hair, and wide, luminous eyes. "Where've you been, baby?"

She grew eight fucking hands because she touched him everyfuckingwhere.

He pushed her away. "Get the fuck offa me, bitch."

"C'mon, baby, don't be like that," the other one said, licking his ear, having the same octofuckingpussy hands as the other bitch. She was shorter, her figure fuller, and had quite a luscious rack topped off by plum-colored nipples. Thick braids framed an oval face with a smooth brown complexion. "Let's find a spot where you can watch me eat some of her chocolate pussy pudding."

Fuck, if he could remember their names. He *did* remember fucking them several times, though. "I said get the fuck offa me."

Two guys he didn't remember being members the last time he'd visited narrowed their eyes at him as they crowded him in. "Yo? Rose, Chantal, this white boy giving you problems?"

Fuck him, he wasn't in the fucking mood for this bullshit. "No, motherfucker, this white boy ain't givin' these two fuckin' bitches problems. More like these two bitches givin' this fuckin' white boy problems, so get them the fuck outta my fuckin' face."

"Don't sweat it, baby," the tall one said, and Christopher didn't fucking know if she was Rose or Chantal and he really didn't give a fuck. "Boy and Outlaw tight. And Outlaw don't fuck around, so drop it if you don't want trouble."

Dumb Ass snickered. "You can't do fucking math, you dumb slut? There's two of us and one of him. What the fuck can he do?"

"This," Christopher snarled, punching the fuckhead in the throat and pulling his nine, pointing it at fuckhead's friend. "You motherfuckers got 'bout two fuckin' seconds to get the fuck outta my fuckin' face befuckinfore you missin' yours. My old lady 'round, so you gotta defuckincide now cuz I ain't wantin' your fuckin' blood dirtyin' her pretty outfit."

"Who the fuck in here disrespecting my club?" another voice boomed across the sudden silence.

Yeah, Christopher sure the fuck was disrespecting another man's club, something that could start a turf war, but fuck it, he'd been involved in them before.

"It's Outlaw, Boy," Christopher called through gritted teeth.

Silence. Yeah. Boy always called him cray-cray. Christopher hated that fucking term, but he'd fucking take it right about now. Of course, the man still had to look like he knew how to hold his own fucking balls in front of his boys, so anything could happen.

"What seems to be the problem?" Boy stopped next to Christopher, his own piece in the hand he held at his side and scratched his bald head.

"We was just wantin' to fuck Outlaw," one of the girls explained. She thrust her chin to Dumb Ass still on the floor and the fuckheadChristopher trained his gun on. "And them two got involved."

"In *my* motherfuckin' business," Christopher added, "which ain't ever a good fuckin' idea."

Boy glared at the two pretty girls. If Christopher remembered, he had once tag-teamed the taller one with Johnnie. Or both of them…? Fuck, hadn't he fucked them with Mort too? Fuck, who knew? That was many fucking condoms ago.

"The two bitches displeased you in some way, Outlaw?"

Christopher scowled. "Nope."

"He say he brought his old lady," the tall chick volunteered.

"She can always join in," the shorter one offered.

He switched the gun from his left hand to his right and showed his ring finger. "Nope, babe, she can't."

Tall chick's dark eyes widened. "You're married?"

"Legally?" Short chick squeaked.

He nodded.

"How long?" Boy asked.

"Seven months."

The girls snickered. "We won't tell her. We can sneak out back and fuck and the boys will keep her in here."

"She'll never find out," the tall chick promised, raising her hand. "Cross my heart and hope to die."

"Since this is my birthday, let's let bygones be bygones. Don't want us to become enemies on what should be a celebration." Boy indicated the two women using his gun. "You two bitches, get the fuck out of the man's face."

The women scurried off and Boy rocked back on his heels. "I'd appreciate it if you put your piece away, Outlaw."

For a moment, Christopher stared into the eyes of the other man, hoping he got the message not to fuck with him ever again. Then, he stuck his nine back into his jacket. The dumb ass Christopher knocked in the throat staggered to his feet.

"It's his fault, Boy," Fuckhead complained, flicking his thumb toward Christopher. "Come in here wearing fucking colors that's not ours." He looked him up and down and sneered. "And with him being who he is, we didn't appreciate the way he spoke to those two fucking bitches."

"I *fucked* them two fuckin' bitches," Christopher snapped. "We live in a diversified fuckin' world, motherfucker. Get the fuck in the 21st fuckin' century. You dealin' with me cuz my colors unrecognizable I underfuckinstand. You dealin' with me cuz of other fuckin' bullshit, piss my ass the fuck off."

"Outlaw not like that," Boy said, bristling, "and now, you're insulting one of our allies. If anything happened to this fuck or any of the Dwellers…"

Boy's voice trailed off.

"A reign of fuckin' terror happenin' to the motherfuckers responsible," Christopher finished.

"Get the fuck out of my face before I kneecap your asses," Boy ordered, gesturing toward the door with the gun.

The two men hustled away, and Boy pocketed his piece. Christopher and Boy greeted one another much the same as him and Mouse had, adding a brief bro hug.

"Here's your woman, Outlaw," Mouse said from behind him.

Christopher turned and saw Megan smiling at him. He bent and kissed her. "Hey, babe."

"Hey, you." She smiled at Mouse. "Thanks."

Mouse nodded. "My pleasure," he said and walked away.

"Where the fuck you been?"

"Talking to Momma, then Mouse and I got to talking. Before I knew it, twenty minutes had passed."

Christopher shrugged and cursed when he realized he'd lost his cigarette during the exchange with Dumb Ass and Fuckhead, so he lit another one and said, "Ain't nothin' to worry 'bout, baby. You ain't missed shit."

Letting his smoke hang from his lips, he turned Megan toward Boy and wrapped his arms around her waist. "This my wife."

Boy's gold grill gleamed when he smiled. "That's where you've been, huh?" he asked with a laugh.

"Yeah. Gettin' hitched and makin' my son."

"Yes, indeed, Outlaw." Boy gave Megan the once over. Three fucking times. "Always knew you were a smart fucking man." He held out a big hand to Megan. "I'm Boy."

Megan grinned and placed her hand in his. "A pleasure," she said. "I'm Megan."

"You two stayin' and partyin' a minute, right?" Boy asked with a shit-eating grin that Christopher felt like knocking the fuck away.

"Yes," Megan answered. "We came for your party."

Boy nodded and lifted an eyebrow. "You don't fucking say? Mighty strange. I recall having a birthday last year and the year before and don't remember seeing Outlaw around."

Christopher glared at Boy and kissed the top of Megan's head, breathing in the scent of her hair to calm himself. "Ain't got a invitation," he responded, sucking on his cigarette and squinting his watering eyes when the smoke hit him the wrong way. "Ain't ever invadin' another man turf uninvited."

Boy laughed. "Still got that fucking silver tongue, I see."

"Ain't nothin' but a thing," Christopher said with a smile. "I gotta fuckin' talk to you. Mind leavin' your fuckin' party and steppin' in your amore private fuckin' office?"

"For you? Always." Boy beckoned a girl over, who wore a strip of silver material that concealed her nipples but kept her aureoles revealed. The outfit twisted across her belly in an 'x' pattern, met at her pussy, and just managed to cover it. "Take Outlaw's old lady to Danicka."

Megan glanced up at him.

"Boy old lady, baby," Christopher explained.

Tits bouncing, the girl sauntered past Christopher, revealing a bubble of an ass, round cheeks exposed, that was hard not to admire. "Follow me," she told Megan.

Biting down on her lip, Megan hesitated, but when the girl lifted a pierced brow, she went behind her.

Five minutes later, Christopher had a glass of tequila, a cold beer for a chaser, and the situation about Cee Cee on the table. "So far, me and my boys ain't found no motherfucker matchin' that description in no area club. Most recent fuckin' turnover for president happened at my club."

"Agreed." Boy leaned back in his chair. "You believe his claim?"

Christopher shrugged, not revealing Cee Cee's declaration of being his father. Listening to Megan's description and having Johnnie verify it made Christopher believe their blood ties.

The other shit? He didn't know. He kept his finger on the pulse of the activities of both his allies and his rivals, but green motherfuckers liked to test established outfits.

"Ain't able to fuckin' say. Might be a new fuckin' outfit, takin' balls in hands, tryna get word 'bout their fuckin' rep 'round and establish cred."

Boy rubbed his eyes. "Fuck. That's all the fuck we need."

"Yeah, stupid motherfuckers challengin' the hierarchy." Christopher tasted his tequila, held it in his mouth and sipped from his bottle of beer to chase it. "Usually, young dickheads without the sense to fuckin' know better pull bullshit like this."

Unless it was personal like Cee Cee claimed.

"I'll put some feelers out," Boy promised, pulling out a baggie and cigarette paper.

Christopher downed the rest of his alcohol. Fuck, he needed a blunt right now. "Pass, brother," he said, watching with longing as Boy began to lay the grass on the paper.

"You clean?" he asked, not pausing in his task.

Christopher chuckled. "Fuck, no. Just ain't fuckin' with Herb when I got my girl with me."

Boy waved away Christopher's reservations. "Danicka won't leave her, and she'd never make the mistake of coming back here unless I give her permission." He finished the roll and placed it in front of Christopher before starting on a second one. "Let's go in the alley. I'll have a couple whores brought to us to suck our dicks."

Christopher got to his feet and pulled out his wallet, taking out some bills and placing them in front of Boy, not only for the blunt but for the anticipated assistance in the Cee Cee matter. "No, motherfucker," he said, pocketing Aunt Mary. "Ain't happenin'. I love the fuck outta my girl and respect her too fuckin' much for a sneak fuck."

Boy gave Christopher an under-eyed look. "You saying I don't respect my bitch?"

Christopher folded his arms. "Ain't givin' a fuck if you fuckin' respect your woman. If I fuckin' did, my ass sure the fuck tellin' you, but since I ain't thought 'bout it cuz I *ain't* givin' two fucks, I ain't carin' if you respect that bitch. Befuckinsides, it ain't my fuckin' business, so I ain't commentin'. If you gotta problem with what the fuck my ass sayin', deal with it, motherfucker, cuz I ain't givin' a good fuck 'bout that either."

Shaking his head and pocketing the ten bills, Boy shook his head. "Still off the fucking chain, Outlaw."

"Just keep your fuckin' ears to the ground and send me what the fuck ever you hearin'."

When Christopher returned to the main room, he searched out Megan and saw her talking to a group of women, including Rose, Chantal, and Danicka.

He considered intercepting the conversation but whatever damage those bitches had wreaked was already done and pulling Megan away would only make the situation worse. Sighing, he went to the bar and ordered a setup. By then, Boy had joined Christopher and they decided to play a game of pool. At the end of the game, he'd had enough of those gossiping bitches keeping Megan away from him, so he removed her from the circle of bitches.

After buying a bottle of tequila and six beers, he guided her toward the back, where the *real* party was taking place. The moment they stepped outside, they heard moaning. Two bikers leaned against the back wall, getting their dicks sucked.

He slanted a glance at her, dying to know her thoughts. And just what the fuck those bitches had been telling her. Taking her hand into his own and keeping a firm grip on her, he weaved through the crowd of dancing people. Sprinkled throughout the group were one or two bitches getting fucked by two, three, or four bikers. Other motherfuckers passed blunts around and Christopher didn't doubt some of the shit had more than just fucking grass in it.

This was hardcore, a side of the life Megan hadn't been exposed to because he hadn't allowed it. He'd kept her away when things got too out-of-hand with the boys. Her head was swiveling in all directions, her wide eyes taking in everything.

He found a spot for them on the perimeter of the craziness. *His fucking world.* She loved him? But did she love this side of him? The side related to Cee Cee? No. Not Cee Cee. Sebastian fucking Caldwell.

"*Dirty, filthy little idiot.*"

"*Devil's spawn.*"

"*Evil little bastard.*"

His grandfather's voice floated in his head and Christopher's skin crawled at the names Logan threw at him from his earliest recollections. His mother had always sobbed her heart out from her daddy's meanness.

Because of Christopher.

His sisters had sobbed, too.

Because of him. Because his carelessness had gotten their mother killed.

Megan sobbed. Because of him. Because that's what he was good for.

He dropped onto the ground and opened the bottle of tequila before pulling out his blunt. He took a swig of liquor, narrowed his eyes at Megan. She was pale as a motherfucker and his heart hurt.

"My world ain't diamond fuckin' bracelets and church fuckin' weddin's. *This* my world, baby."

Her gaze fastened to his and she swallowed. "This had been my daddy's, too."

He glared at her, not wanting to think about her old man since that shit was as bad as thinking about *his* old man.

She reached over and took the bottle from him, bringing it to her lips and taking a small sip. Nothing happened, so she took in a mouthful and swallowed. Her eyes watered and she choked. Christopher pulled the bottle from her and patted her back until she caught her breath.

He drank from the bottle again.

"Any news?"

"What the fuck 'bout?"

"Cee Cee?" she supplied. "Isn't that why you've been leaving us every night? Looking for him."

Yeah. He'd also brought her here to ease her fucking mind and show she had nothing to worry about during his times away at night. He wanted to include her like she expected, but fuck him, whatever he told her, all the shit he already told her over the months, could be used against her if any of his rivals got to her.

"Ain't mattererin' why the fuck I been goin' out, Megan. We ain't able to stay joined at the fuckin' hip for fuckin' ever."

Her eyes watered and her chin wobbled.

"Why are you doing this?" she whispered.

Because his demons were chasing him and overwhelming him. Instead of answering—since he didn't have one—he lit up Aunt

Mary and sucked in, holding the smoke to allow it to seep into his head before exhaling.

Megan watched him, her head cocked to the side, not bothering to put a little distance between them. None of them smoked often around her, but, when they did, she stepped away from their group.

"I want to try it," she said, shocking the shit out of him.

A muscle ticked in his jaw. "No."

"I beg your pardon?"

"This shit ain't for you, Megan."

"I might like it," she argued.

"Fuck off the fuck off with the reverse fuckin' psychology." He shoved the roll at her. "Take a fuckin' hit. I ain't givin' a fuck. You a grown lil' motherfucker. You wanna get fuckin' high, fuckin' do it."

Instead of turning her nose up, she grabbed it from him, put it to her lips and inhaled, mimicking what he'd done a few minutes before. She held it in a moment before she started coughing like a motherfucker.

He snatched the joint from her and glowered at her. Fuck him, if she wasn't the most reckless fucking brat he'd ever met. "If my ass jumpin' the fuck from a fuckin' buildin' you fuckin' copyin' me?" he growled once her coughing fit passed.

She drew in a deep breath and swayed. "You're spoiling for an argument and I'm not going to give you your way."

Too fucking late. He was furious and he knew the bullshit he was feeling was directed at motherfucking Cee Cee. He knew taking it out on Megan was a fuckhead move, but he wasn't no paragon of goodness and she wanted to be with him, so she had to take him the fuck as he came.

Megan crawled closer to him, her pupils dilated, her eyes red-rimmed, the scent of alcohol and herb rising from her like steam. His sweet, innocent Megan was high and drunk.

She licked her lips before rising on her knees to kiss him. He despised the taste of her mouth right now, despised himself a little more for doing this to her.

She straddled his hips and rocked against his rising dick, thumbing his lips, even her fingers smelling like weed. "We're passed this, Christopher," she managed to slur. "Don't push me away. Don't beat yourself up for Cee Cee's actions. CJ and I need you. We love you no matter what."

Megan's words hit him straight the fuck in the gut and arrowed to his heart.

She clutched his cut, leaned back, and frowned up at him. "I just hope I learn how to please you in bed."

What the fuck?

"Rose and Chantal…they told me you had sex with them and how you like to watch two girls make love before or after you…and…them…" Her face crumpled. "I don't like girls that way and I couldn't stand watching you with other girls, either."

Jesus. He needed to be fucked up for what he was doing to her. He wrapped her in his arms. "Megan, baby, I ain't wantin' no other girl. Fuck, baby, when I'm thinkin' sideways, lookin' backwards, bowin' my head down, it's cuz of you I look up. Into the light. At all the goodness in you. You my sun and my moon, a bright shinin' star in my fucked up world." And he'd hurt her. By exposing her to this. By allowing her to get fucked up.

She blinked, licked her lips, on the verge of tears. "I love you so much," she whispered. "I'll stand by you all the days of our lives. No matter what," she added fiercely, and tears did escape then.

Growling in frustration, she swiped angrily at her cheeks. "I'll withstand anything for you. Endure it all." Her blue gaze caught his, held him captive. "Except cheating." She lifted her chin. Sniffled. Ignored her fresh tears. "That would break me, Christopher."

"I ain't ever stickin' my cock in no other bitch, baby," he promised, regretting his decision to have her with him tonight. Chantal and Rose wouldn't have fed the doubt that his behavior fucking planted. "I fuckin' swear."

She studied him for long moment, touching every plane and angle of his face, searching his soul as only she could. "I believe you. If you say it's so, then it is."

Because she trusted him. Believed *in* him. She had a faith in him that no one ever had. Not Boss. Or Mort. Or Johnnie. Not Val, K-P, or Digger. Not even Kiera or his ma. Megan saw in him what no one else ever had—goodness.

"You're a fine, honorable man, Christopher," she said as if she read his mind. "You have integrity and decency."

Fuck. He wanted to be the man she saw him as so fucking bad, if only for her.

She groaned and leaned her head against his chest. "I'm not feeling too good, Christopher."

He felt even worse. The kernel of hope that had rose in him disintegrated. Whether he liked it or not—whether she admitted it or not—he had every rotten cell of his father inside him.

All he needed to do was look at her current condition as proof.

T WO DAYS LATER, CHRISTOPHER GLANCED AT HIS WATCH AND cursed. He had one hour before he had to get to the church for the pre-marital counseling shit that dickhead insisted him, and Megan do before he married them. Motherfucker. They were already fucking married, so this bullshit was fucking pointless. But Megan wanted that church wedding. They'd already postponed it once, so Christopher had to suffer through that priest's advising them on shit they were better off figuring out on their fucking own.

What the fuck did he know anyfuckingway? Not like the motherfucker had ever been married. Probably never had pussy, either, with the vow of celibacy required of priests.

Christopher held up the ice pick and dangled it in front of the motherfucker strapped to the wall in the shed. He glanced at Mortician, hoping like fuck he didn't have to pass this job to him, Digger, Val or Johnny. To him, Cee was personal. He wanted to exact the vengeance on everyone connected to him. Like now, with this stupid fuck, who, so far had four holes in him, all courtesy of Christopher.

Christopher paced in front of the moaning fuckhead. "I ain't repeatin' this shit but one more time, motherfucker. It's been brought to my attention you the fuckhead that brought Cee Cee to my fuckin' club."

He refrained from taking a bigger instrument and making fuckhead feel real pain. Both Megan and his mother needed avenging for Cee Cee's actions and if he had to fuck up a hundred motherfuckers to get to *that* motherfucker, he would.

He shoved the pick into the man's thigh, scowling at the dickhead's bitchified scream.

"As far as I fuckin' know, ain't no new fuckin' presidents got elected in none of the Dwellers' local support clubs. Me and my boys spent the past four fuckin' days checkin' to make sure."

"Outlaw, pl-please. I sw-swear I didn't br-bring him here to cause trouble," the man cried.

Christopher poked his shoulder with the ice pick tip, red oozing from the white skin. "Then how the fuck he your guest?"

The man gasped. "I…he was at the Haven a couple weeks ago," he said around sniffles.

Fucking pussy. Sniveling like a fucking bitch-ass punk. Christopher jabbed his other shoulder—deeper—in pure fucking disgust.

What the fuck was this pussy's name anyfuckingway?

"He…he said he was an old friend of the family—"

Christopher let out a roar of pure rage. How many times had he heard about the family fucking friend that violated his mother then fucking came to sign his birth certificate? He stabbed the man's jaw and would've done it again if Johnnie hadn't stopped him.

"That's what Cee Cee said," his cousin reminded him. "Not this stupid fuck."

"Yeah, Outlaw, he just the fucking messenger," Digger said, nodding in agreement.

"At one time, messengers got fucked up for deliverin' bad fuckin' news," Christopher snapped, his vision blurring with the red haze of his anger.

"You have blood all over you." Val pointed to his jeans. "You and Meggie need to leave for the church in ten fucking minutes."

He stared at the bleeding, crying motherfucker, wanting to take out his rage and frustration on someone. The humiliation he'd suffered at the hands of his grandfather for years because of what that motherfucker had done to his mother. The shame and degradation his mother had suffered, for that matter. Now, Cee Cee, the man who'd provided the seed that had become *him*, had made the fatal mistake of fucking with Megan.

He blinked, needing to clear his head, needing to think.

His boys were shuffling, staring at him, and waiting for his final decision. Kill this stupid fuck for bringing hell to Christopher's doorstep? Or not?

Megan's face rose in his head, and he growled in frustration, administering one last stab in the man's knee before pitching the ice pick against the wall. He unfastened the man's restraints and watched as he sagged to the ground, sobbing at Christopher's feet. He kicked him away, satisfied at the crack of bone he heard.

"Listen up, motherfucker. Unless you a fuckin' moron, you fuckin' knew you ain't never fuckin' seen that fuckhead 'round here befuckinfore in your fuckin' *life*. He coulda been any-fuckin-body you invited here." He crouched down and pulled the man's head up by his hair, the weight of his nine heavy in his cut. The fuckhead deserved to have his piece shoved in his mouth so Christopher could pull the trigger. "And it fuckin' was. You brought a fuckin' demon to my door. But Ima let you fuckin' live. Know fuckin' why?"

"No! No!" he sobbed, holding out his hands as if they'd stop a bullet. Or prevent Christopher from shooting again.

Because I got a wife that think I'm better than a cold blooded killer. "Because your ass findin' that motherfucker. You got 'til the night befuckinfore my fuckin' weddin' to deliver that fuckhead to me. If you fuckin' ain't comin' through…if me or my boys gotta fuckin' find him, then they gonna have motherfuckers out lookin' for you and I swear to you, they ain't gonna be able to find a piece of your fuckin' ass usin' the best microscope in the world. You hear me?"

He nodded and Christopher jerked his head away, then got up, glared at Val, Digger, Johnnie, and Mortician, and ordered, "get him the fuck off premises. Have him fuckin' gone befuckinfore me and Megan come out."

He stalked into the fresh air, the cold not doing anything to lessen his anger when he thought about his *father.* Cee Cee, huh? His fucking ass. *Sebastian Caldwell.* The fuckhead was a rapist and no doubt every other vile thing there was. That's why Christopher *detested* the name Caldwell. He'd never wanted Megan stuck with that name.

Fuck him. He'd never wanted her stuck with *him.* He might not have been a rapist, but he was every other vile thing in the world. She'd hurled her guts out before they'd left Dippin' Sam's, then spent most of yesterday unable to do fuck but puke and stay in bed, greener than the fucking Jolly Green Giant. And now she wanted him to say vows in a *church*? *Him*?

No fucking way could he do that. He was rushing from the fucking meat shack—as it was known among him and the boys—to wash away another man's blood to go sit in front of a judgmental fuck and pretend he wasn't what he was.

He wanted to kill, and he felt sick to his fucking stomach thinking about Megan. Instead of going to the clubhouse, he headed to his Harley. He couldn't deal with shit right now. He needed a minute to himself.

Fifteen minutes later, he was rolling to a stop in front of the graveyard, and he scrubbed a hand over his face. He wasn't sure which way to go—to his mother or to his mentor. They both had graves here—even though Boss's was empty. No matter. They'd both loved him. His mother would tell him to let it go. And Boss? Big Joe would tell him to shove a canon up Cee Cee's ass and blow him the fuck away.

He stood, unable to decide, but admitting to himself he'd run away from Megan. He hadn't wanted her to see him with all this fucking blood on him. She never interfered in club business, but when worse came to worse and he had to put a motherfucker to ground on premises, he did his usual diverting attention bullshit.

This time, she'd been waiting for him. She would've been in their room, smelling like heaven and looking like salvation. Waiting for him. Tending to his son. Planning their wedding. Talking about the decorations for the other rooms in their house.

She was feeling better today and didn't blame him for the other night. "I'm a big girl, Christopher. I made the decision to smoke that joint and drink the tequila."

It shamed him to think he hadn't protected his girl.

He pulled out his smokes and lit one up before entering the gates of the cemetery. He started toward his mother's grave then stopped. Whenever he came, he always brought her flowers. And today he didn't have any. He hoped the gesture let her know how much he loved her. He wasn't even sure she could see him. Megan said she could, that she'd already met their boy.

Sometimes, Christopher wondered if his mother and Megan's father had met up somewhere in the afterlife, then decided, no. They probably hadn't, certain they'd gone in opposite directions—Patricia went northward while Big Joe took the Southbound Express.

He trudged toward Boss's grave, unable to go to his mother without her flowers. Reaching the black marble obelisk, he grabbed the cigarette from his mouth and released smoke. "Yo, Prez," he said quietly. He took another drag, wishing he had a different kind of cigarette. "My ass doin' the right thing? Listenin' to Megan? Goin' along with her church weddin'?" No answer. Not that he expected one. His phone started blasting out Megan's ringtone. It stopped, then started again. Fuck, what the fuck was he supposed to say to her?

Anything was better than hiding like a pussy.

He let it go to voicemail, then turned off the phone completely. He'd deal with her when he got back to the club.

Stop being a fuckhead, motherfucker. The thought pounded through his head, and he cursed, glaring at her father's obelisk.

The monument sat upon a small rise, the highest point in the cemetery. Since it held neither body nor casket, it was just a tribute to Joseph Foy for his daughter's sake and she had no fucking clue she knelt at an empty grave whenever she visited.

Christopher flicked the cigarette away. "Everyfuckinthing ever good in my life always go to shit. Usually in a real bad way." *Like death.* Because, really, before Megan and CJ, the only good in his life had been his mother. And he'd gotten her killed.

The man who'd fathered him showing up wasn't good news. It didn't take a fucking genius to know that. If he didn't get the motherfucker contained before the wedding, who the fuck knew what havoc the fuckhead would wreak during the ceremony.

A religious ceremony Christopher had absolutely no business being a part of. Until now, he'd pushed the shit to the back of his mind. Now, with Sebastian Caldwell circling, he couldn't stand in a church and pledge his soul to an angel when he was nothing but the devil.

Chapter 12

Meggie

HATS OFF TO WOMEN AROUND THE WORLD WHO BALANCE children, parents, outside jobs, and households. Meggie wouldn't have been able to do it. Without having a career, she had a hard enough time taking care of her son, her husband, and her mother while being the female all the other women associated with the Dwellers deferred to, keeping up and helping with the celebrations at the club, planning her rehearsal dinner and wedding, and decorating the remaining rooms in their house. Cooking, cleaning, and laundry didn't bear mentioning since that was a given.

So, it felt like heaven after she loaded groceries in the car to go in to the little coffee shop and wait for Bunny, one of the old ladies of a Dweller named Trader. She didn't know him very well, but she liked Bunny.

The MC dominated the southeastern section of Hortensia, along with a good swath of forested areas. At the intersection that led to the club's dead-end street, a right turn led to a forked road. One way led to a back entrance to the club, surrounded by trees and dense foliage; the other direction connected to a few backroads and farms, along with the continuation of the thoroughfare intersecting with the club's dead-end street. The cemetery was there, too, her father's final resting place, solitary and majestic, where several small houses and trailers could be found, belonging to women protected by the Dwellers. Residential neighborhoods pocketed the way, including Zoann's house and the home where Meggie and Christopher had been taken after his mother was killed. Hortensia General Hospital served as the cornerstone of this part of town. Shops and restaurants had grown around the medical facility.

She supposed because City Hall, the police, and fire stations, along with the post office were located nearby, the biggest supermarket in the area would be in that area, too. The distance between the motel she'd stayed at, and the hospital always surprised her. They weren't as close as she'd imagined, yet not that far away either.

Unfortunately, the coffeeshop Bunny suggested required Meggie to drive to the other end of Hortensia, past the turnoff to the MC. Once she veered right, instead of continuing straight to go to Portland, she met more forest, cut in half by winding roads. Here and there were other roads that led to more houses and businesses. Soon, she skirted the road that led to the creek she'd lived at for a month and fronted by a gas station and the minimart where she'd gotten her food.

She zoomed past a smaller grocery store, a recently built cinema and pizzeria, with a turnoff that led to a very nice apartment complex before coming to the elementary, junior high, and high school campuses, sitting side-by-side along the highway, the roar of Harley pipes ever present in her head.

Meggie's guard detail was firmly back in place, tailing her everywhere. She understood the necessity, so she didn't complain, especially because Christopher had returned her bracelet to her and told her to wear it whenever she chose.

Finally, after passing more businesses, her destination came into view, and she turned off the road, parking in a space near the coffee shop. It, along with an ice cream place, a drugstore, a bakery, sandwich shop, and massage parlor made it a crowded area. Just as her guards were rolling to a halt, she got out of her car and walked to the two bikers. The hairs at her nape stood on edge. It suddenly felt as if a thousand eyes watched her. Uneasy, she gazed around but saw nothing.

"Why are we here?" Bin demanded.

Seeing his frown, Meggie sighed. "I'm not going to be long." Anticipating the honeymoon Christopher had promised her, she began to slack off nursing her baby boy, but she missed him when she stayed away too long. "I do have groceries." No perishables, though they didn't need to know. They might order her back to the club.

Bin and Shady stared at each other. Somehow, she'd gotten stuck with Bin. At the last minute, Cowboy had bowed out and Bin stepped up to the plate, volunteering to shadow her. Christopher trusted him, so she hadn't put up a fuss.

Bin took the toothpick from the corner of his mouth and gestured with it. "There's a bar right down the street. We're going to hang there until you have your coffee."

Shady frowned. "Outlaw wants us here." He pointed to Meggie's wrist. "Especially with her wearing that."

"C'mon, Shady. Prez won't mind. I bet he would do the same thing."

"No," Meggie said. After her conversation with Christopher, she wanted Cee Cee caught. Until then, she wouldn't feel completely safe, even though she tried to go about as she normally would. "I'd prefer you to stay here with me where Prez ordered you to."

Bin's forehead moved, indicating he would've lifted a brow—if he'd had any. A chill slithered down Meggie's spine, and she gritted her teeth against her irrational unease.

She hadn't been feeling herself for the past few days. Tiredness wore at her and, last night, a bout of nausea so awful it shocked her she hadn't vomited. This morning, her head hurt, and she felt…*off*. She also felt studied, like the very air had eyes, which added to her irritation. She didn't need paranoia and illness to set in now when…when what? Christopher had determined there would be no big church wedding and she couldn't understand why. She'd gotten him to agree that the ceremony could go on, but as a much scaled-down version. Every time she thought about it, she wanted to burst into tears. She'd been so excited to have Lacey and Farrah down for their fittings, so she could introduce them to Christopher and the guys. They still could've come, but declined, citing discretion. Meggie couldn't decide if Lacey or Farrah's anger burned hotter. Since they wouldn't hold their opinions from Christopher, they chose to stay in Seattle.

"What can happen, Meggie?" Bin pressed, indicating the bright day. "The bogeyman won't jump out at you."

"Hey, babe," Bunny said brightly, walking into the midst of their trio. She bent and hugged Meggie. She was a tall, busty, brown-haired girl whom Trader had started bringing around the club about three months ago. She'd looked so out of place, Meggie had made it a point to introduce her to some of the other ladies. In turn, she and Bunny had become friends. "A little Powwow going on here?"

Meggie shrugged. "Um, yeah."

"We don't need them," another female voice said, and Meggie groaned. Gypsy. Derby's old lady.

Meggie avoided her as much as possible, even though she *really* liked her, too. Precisely why she avoided the woman. Derby cheated on Gypsy on a regular basis, and it just made Meggie sick. It also caught her between a rock and a hard place. Tattle on one cheater, the other old ladies would expect her to report their men, too. Gypsy and Derby's relationship wasn't Meggie's business. And, most of all, opening her mouth to the woman would cause problems for Christopher with Derby and trickle down to other men.

Lost in her thoughts, she hadn't realized Bin and Shady departed until she heard the roar of their bikes.

"They so should not have done that," she grouched. "They were supposed to wait for my dismissal."

Annoyed at her surliness, she spun on her heel and stalked into the coffee shop, her gaze zeroing in on a cheese Danish. She swore her tongue swelled with the need to taste the pastry and, suddenly, she felt ravenous. After ordering two Danishes and coffee, she waited while Bunny and Gypsy ordered. Once they collected their food and drink, they found a table right in the center of the laid back little place.

"Ready for your bridal shower?" Gypsy asked. Her eyes twinkled and she winked. "And the stripper we've hired to grind on you?"

Meggie paused in her chewing. "You're joking right?" she asked around a mouthful of food, the taste of the sugar and cream cheese exploding on her tongue in a burst of heaven. Once it hit her stomach, nausea careened through her. Crap. Gypsy ruined her Danish with the mention of a male dancer and Meggie's imagining her husband's reaction to another man swinging his penis in her face. She forced the last little bite down and frowned. "Christopher would kill the guy."

Bunny chuckled. "Shit, yeah, we're joking. He wouldn't only kill the guy, he'd never let us around you again."

Meggie didn't comment because Bunny was right. She chased another bit of pastry with a small sip of coffee, her mind easing. "In that case, yes, I'm ready for the shower."

"Geez, babe, excitement is just oozing from you," Gypsy said with a short laugh.

"I'm just not feeling good," she admitted with a shrug before biting another piece of Danish.

"Just nerves," Bunny reassured her and patted her hand. "I'm fucking nervous, too, and it's not my wedding. I don't want your big day messed up, you know? And…well…you know, it sounds like you're planning a big fancy wedding. And—"

"The boys aren't big, fancy men," Meggie finished, studying Bunny's cotton candy pink polish. For the wedding, she intended to get a blue nail color close to the blueberry bow ties and handkerchiefs the guys would wear.

Gypsy puffed out a laugh. "Except for John Boy. He's big and fancy."

And…cue her blush. She lowered her lashes and licked her lips, unable to prevent the image of her cousin-in-law or the memory of how big he'd felt.

"Omigod," Bunny squealed, wiggling a finger at her. "Meggie, you're totally crushing on Johnnie."

"Am not," she denied, her cheeks heating even more at being called out.

Gypsy giggled, sounding younger than Meggie ever remembered. A sadness always hung about her, though she masked it with throaty laughter and loud talking. "You are! Don't feel bad. We all crush on him and—"

"Christopher," Meggie finished with a giggle of her own. As if how women viewed her husband was new to her. Christopher Caldwell equaled wicked temptation. "My husband is a hot piece of man candy who I enjoy sucking on every chance I get."

The three of them roared with laughter and the release of tension felt good. Even her naughtiness freed the edginess within her. She'd had one of the toughest weeks in a while since her arrival at the club. Her responsibilities to everyone and her son kept her sane. Christopher only paid attention to her at night when he came to bed and made love to her. No. Not make love. She felt no connection to him; as he drove into her he refused to look at her and wouldn't hold her afterward. He turned his back on her. It seemed unreal that their Valentine's dinner had only been two weeks ago. Between then and now, a lifetime had gone by.

But this was part of being his wife and she'd weather this storm like she had all the others in her life.

Gypsy's bang on the table popped through her thoughts. "He's rubbing off on you, Meggie," she hollered.

They chuckled again, Meggie's laugh forced this time. Once more, she felt watched, a specimen under a microscope. She glanced around, seeing nothing out of the ordinary.

"Where's Little Man?" Bunny asked when their noise died down, buying Meggie's pretense of amusement.

Debating on buying a third Danish and determined to overcome her stupid unease, she said, "With my mom."

"Must be nice," Bunny said, a little wistful. "I admire your relationship with Dinah." She lowered her lashes. "Even envy it at times."

If she only knew.

Instead of speaking, Meggie combed her fingers through her hair, at loose ends. Nothing felt right anymore, and she didn't know how to repair whatever had happened. No, she knew what had taken place. Cee Cee.

Sadness hit her. She wished she could go to her momma, just to talk, find solace. But they didn't have that type of relationship. For as long as Meggie remembered, *she* gave the comfort, while her mother received it.

Sighing, she scraped her fingers through her hair again.

"Oh my God! Look at the bracelet," Gypsy said, her voice filled with awe.

Mixed emotions hit Meggie. Every time she looked at the bracelet, she remembered the magical Valentine's her husband had given to her. It had been so perfect. Until suddenly it wasn't. The very next night, he'd left her and CJ, and hadn't returned until the early morning hours, before disappearing again later that day. He had allowed her to accompany him to Dippin' Sams, though it led to his further withdrawal. The bracelet symbolized everything she thought her marriage, her man, to be. Hope. Love. Romance. Happiness. Friendship.

The gems sparkled and glimmered, like the brightest light in a world of turmoil. Diamonds were tough to break, among the hardest stones in the world, despite their illusion of fragility. Except her marriage felt so very delicate, the bond she thought she and Christopher had as frayed as worn hemp.

In her heart, she believed when he'd gotten down on one knee and given her the bracelet, he'd meant every word he told her. Until his demons found him again and took their terrible toll.

"Look at the clarity of the stones."

At Bunny's words, Meggie realized she'd held her arm up for the two women to inspect her bracelet.

"Your guards shouldn't have left you on your own with a hundred grand hanging from your wrist," Bunny said with disapproval. "You need to tell Outlaw."

"A hundred *what?*" Meggie squeaked. "No way!"

"She's right, babe," Gypsy offered.

Suddenly, Father Wilkins, Shady, and Cowboy's interest made sense. She was inclined to agree with Bunny, though. Christopher never would've returned the bracelet to her if he didn't think she'd be protected at all times.

"Thinking you might owe him a little more pussy and cock sucks, huh, babe?" Gypsy laughed. "Whenever Derby gives me nice gifts, I put extra grip in my cooch. Fuck, if he ever gave me something like that, I'd throw in more ass action than what I currently offer."

Meggie swallowed, trying to join in with their chuckles. But Gypsy sounded so happy and carefree, seemingly clueless about Derby.

"Remember, when you saw my tat, you said you wanted one," Bunny said in a change of topic. She shifted in her seat and leaned forward.

"Yeah," Meggie said with a nod. "But I wanted to get a temporary tattoo." Bunny had a really cool tattoo of a manga girl with sad, teary eyes, filled in with color and highlights. In comparison, Meggie's would be much simpler. "To see if I liked it."

"No shit?" Gypsy said, her perfectly arched eyebrows rising. She was a very pretty woman with long platinum hair and a killer figure. She loved leather, stilettos, fake lashes, and long nails. "You with a tat? That'll be something to see, girl."

Meggie's smile and enthusiasm faltered at Gypsy's friendliness. She glanced away. Her mind surfed through the protocol of the situation. Probably no different than how it would be in the regular world, she decided. Some women would want the 411 on their man's infidelities. Others wouldn't.

"Hey, babe." Gypsy reached over and clasped Meggie's hand. "Are you angry with me about something?"

"No. Of course not." She squirmed in her seat.

Gypsy's lips thinned. "This is about Derby, isn't it?"

"No." She mumbled the lie.

"You lie for shit," Gypsy snapped, a fact Meggie already knew because her father had always pointed that out to her. "This *is* about my old man. Don't lie."

Meggie glared at Gypsy, applauding her decision to distance herself from the woman. With everything else going to crap, it didn't surprise Meggie she'd find herself in Gypsy's presence now. "I don't know how you think Derby is involved in how I'm dealing with you—"

"You think I don't know about the bitches he fucks?" she interrupted.

Meggie swallowed. Conflicting feelings bombarded her. She had no real friends anymore. Lacey really didn't like Christopher now. Farrah straddled the fence about Meggie's new life. The burgeoning friendship she'd had with Ophelia, her sister-in-law, had gone to smoke because of the girl's treatment of Christopher. And Gypsy…honesty laid the foundation for any true friendship and Meggie didn't have the option to tell Gypsy God's honest truth.

Gypsy grabbed Meggie's hand and squeezed. "I love Derby and he loves me in his own way." She shrugged, tossed her long hair over her shoulder. "I know what he does, Meggie. And I understand the position it places you in because I'm sure you know, too."

Bunny and Gypsy looked at Meggie with expectation, but she kept her face blank, refusing to confirm or deny the assumption.

"I hate it, you know, babe?" Gypsy whispered, pulling her hand away from Meggie's and rubbing her brow. "But I love him. We got two kids together. Eight and three."

Meggie took a small nibble on the last bit of her pastry, everything she'd consumed churning in her belly. The masochist side of herself tortured her with speculations about her future life with Christopher. Would this be her in seven or eight years? He'd already jeopardized their now scaled-down wedding ceremony by missing the counseling session with Father Wilkins. Her saving grace had been how awful she'd looked, courtesy of her hangover, so she'd fibbed and said she'd caught a bug from Christopher, and he was still sick. Not only did it give them a free pass, but the priest had also hastened her away. In two days, they had another session scheduled and she wasn't sure what she'd do if Christopher missed this one. There wouldn't be *any* service if he didn't cooperate.

She glanced at Bunny, who wore a sympathetic frown. Not because of Meggie's thoughts but because of the distress on Gypsy's face.

"You don't have to confirm it," Gypsy said without malice. "I already know, but, please, don't let that affect us. Our friendship. You're not responsible for Derby's roaming dick."

Almost Christopher's exact words.

"Is this what's facing me?" Bunny asked on a swallow.

"Not necessarily," Gypsy responded with a watery smile. "I-I mean look at Outlaw. He wouldn't fuck over Meggie if you paid him—"

"How long have you known Christopher?" Meggie hadn't been curious before but something about Gypsy's tone.

"About eight years—"

Bile rose to her throat, and she looked away. She'd have to get used to running into Christopher's past lovers. But it wasn't easy. First, those two really pretty girls, Rose and Chantal at Dippin' Sam's, had described to her all the things they'd done with him. Then, Meggie had listened as Boy's old lady, Danicka, advised her on how to sneak around and have her own lovers. Now, suspicions about Christopher and Gypsy settled into her. This coffee break was supposed to have been relaxing. "So…so you've slept with him?"

Bunny looked horrified at the idea.

Gypsy sniffled through laughter. "No, babe. I haven't. I-I wanted to. I've slept with Mortician and Johnnie, though."

Relief flooded Meggie and she sagged against the table, dropping her head in her hands. Her emotions were all over the place lately. She just wanted her marriage blessed. Was that too much to ask? Call her superstitious, but she wanted as much good karma in her life as possible. If it came down to it, she'd forget about a wedding ceremony in the traditional sense and just have her and Christopher renew their vows in front of the priest. No reception. No guests. Just herself, Christopher, two witnesses, and the priest. She'd tell that to her husband and then run the idea by Father Wilkins.

"Meggie, you have to be strong, babe," Gypsy went on. "You're in an awkward spot, but you make it clear your loyalty is to Outlaw and none of the girls are gonna expect you to rat out their men. Keep a neutral front. So far, you're doing fine. That's all any of us can ask for. Your man and the girls alike."

Meggie smiled, but her heart hurt for the woman across from her and she placed her hand on top of Gypsy's. "Thank you."

"Hey, Meggie," Bunny cut in, her mouth downturned. The gaiety they'd shared earlier had blown away. Discomfort and unease settled between them like dust in the wake of a sandstorm. "My kid brother is at his tattoo shop. You wanna swing by there and see if he's free to discuss your temporary? Maybe even draw it up and place it on you."

Meggie thought it over for a minute, then glanced at her bracelet, uneasiness still twisting her belly. Wearing it hadn't concerned her when she believed it cost a few thousand dollars. Knowing Christopher had paid six figures for it instead of five made a world of difference.

"Don't worry," Gypsy promised. "You're safe. Outlaw wouldn't have given it to you if he thought you'd be at risk."

"I wore it the day after he gave it to me and it caused somewhat of a commotion," she admitted.

"Honey, you're Outlaw's woman," Gypsy reminded her kindly, "a fact he's let the world know. He wants to spoil you. Give the man his fucking props and show off his gifts."

"We're going to another location anyway," Bunny said, "so you have to summon those two bozos that deserted you."

"You're right," Meggie said. A temporary tattoo wouldn't hurt, and it might ease Christopher's guilt over what had taken place the other night. Visiting a tattoo parlor, *without his influence*—she'd never mentioned getting a tattoo to him—would show him she'd made a conscious decision to smoke pot and swallow tequila. The man had to understand he wasn't responsible for everything that went on in her life. An idea of the tattoo she'd try formed in her head and she smiled.

"Do you want to go to my brother's shop?" Bunny asked.

Another night of loneliness faced her, so postponing her return to the club wouldn't hurt. "Yes, I think I do."

Before going to the ladies' room, she sent Bin and Shady a text, telling them to meet her at the coffee shop because they were ready to leave. After calling her mother and checking on CJ, then trying to contact Christopher without success, Meggie followed Bunny to the shop. Gypsy cried off, saying she had to get home to her kids.

Once Meggie parked, she waited for Bunny to do the same, while Bin stormed her way.

"I'm not here to be a babysitter, Meggie," he complained. "I have shit to do."

"You do," Meggie agreed. "And that is accompanying me wherever I want to go."

"You better back off, Bin, dude," Shady advised. "Prez'll rip you a new asshole if you don't get out of Meggie's face."

As much as she wanted to demand Bin stay, she'd had enough of his complaints, on what should've been her drama-free day. She waved him off. "Go then."

Bin flicked away a cigarette butt and stalked off.

"Prez is gonna hear about this," Shady swore. He thrust his chin toward Bin's retreating form. "About him, especially."

"Don't worry about it. Why don't you go, as well? I'll be fine."

Shady hesitated.

"Go," she insisted. "I'll be fine."

"Okay. I won't be too far away. If you need me, just give me a call. Okay? I'll be two minutes away, so—"

Meggie placed a hand on his arm and laughed. "Thank you. I'm fine. And I appreciate that you'll be nearby."

He smiled and nodded as he walked toward his bike.

Meggie was happy to find Bunny's brother, Gabe, was in fact free and able to draw a temporary replica of the Celtic cross entwined with the black roses that Christopher had on his left forearm arm. Right near the well-defined bicep that tempted the female population into craving a touch. She wanted a smaller one on her side to cover her ugly stretch marks leftover from her pregnancy. At the last minute, she told Gabe to add in two or three butterflies.

If she liked this tattoo and got permanent ink, she might choose another one for the other side later. And, maybe, one day she'd do something about the marks she'd made on herself.

"That sounds so cool, Meggie," Bunny said with anticipation once Meggie completed her description and Gabe had drawn her design on transfer paper. "I'll bet Outlaw is going to love it."

Meggie agreed and couldn't wait to see his face. She'd bet it would light up just as it had when she'd shown him his man cave. "I think so."

"I have an idea," Bunny said. "Why don't you let him draw the design. If you don't like it, just wash the markers away."

"Good idea," Meggie agreed, not knowing a lot about tattoos other than what she'd seen when she went with Christopher.

While Gabe prepared his pens, Meggie and Bunny chitchatted. Meggie discovered Bunny had met her boyfriend when he'd come in for a tattoo at Gabe's shop. Since Gabe's assistant had called in sick, Bunny promised to answer Gabe's phone while he worked on Meggie, who reclined in the tattoo chair, studying the drawings hanging on the wall in the room. The place consisted of this room and the reception area. Small but clean.

Finally, Gabe was ready. He wore a denim vest and matching jeans with chains hanging from the belt loops. Tattoos covered both arms in intricate designs that extended down to his knuckles. "You must have sat hours for your sleeves," she said, admiring them. "Did they hurt?"

Gabe grinned at her, mischief in his nut-brown eyes. "After the first two or three, you know when to expect the pain. Shading hurts like a mug."

She'd been with Christopher when he'd gotten his most recent tattoos on various parts of his body, including his shoulder and thigh to cover the scars from his gunshots. He'd kept a steady conversation, not even flinching.

"Shading hurts?" she questioned, giggling. "I'd think that would be nothing considering all your piercings."

Gauges measuring at least an inch stretched his earlobes. Tips of jewelry poked out from each edge of his nostril. "Do those bars go through your septum?" she asked faintly, her stomach queasy.

"It wasn't too bad," he said with a shrug. "My septum piercing was worse than these." He twirled his finger around his head.

Silver studs lined his brows, and six earrings, three on each side, decorated his bottom lip.

"You have a lot of piercings."

He stuck his tongue out, revealing a gold stud through this tip. "I have nipple piercings. Cock piercings, too."

Meggie's mouth formed an 'O' in surprise, and she burned in embarrassment. Bunny scowled at her brother, but he ignored her.

"You're blushing!" he said with laughter.

He was so engaging; it was hard not to chuckle with him. "You've offered too much information," she admitted. "I don't want to hear about piercings I can't see."

Gabe waved away her admonishment. "Wanna take off your shirt, Meggie? You can leave your bra on."

"How about I just lift my shirt out of the way?"

"You'll be more comfortable with it off. It'll also make my job more proficient. Easier access to your side."

"Trust the woman," Bunny offered, sitting in the extra chair. "Her old man won't like her taking her shirt off."

Meggie and Bunny shared a glance.

"To be honest, he probably won't like that you're touching her, but he likes tats, and you do excellent work, so that'll be your saving grace."

"All right," Gabe agreed, picking up his first pen as Meggie lifted her shirt.

Smiling, Meggie imagined Christopher's voice full of gruff approval when she showed him—

"MEGAN!" Christopher's voice blared through the small building, shaking the walls, and seeming to lift the roof.

Gabe's eyes widened just as the door burst open.

"Motherfucker."

Meggie scrambled from the table and barreled into Christopher before he punched Gabe.

"What are you doing here?" they both screamed at one another at the same time.

"What does it look like I'm doing here?" Meggie snarled. "Getting a tattoo."

"No, the fuck you ain't." He glared the promise of murder toward Gabe, then focused on Bunny. "You the bitch who brought my wife here?"

Bunny paled and inched closer to Gabe.

"No!" Meggie snapped, stepping in front of her charging husband. "I asked her to bring me here. I wanted to surprise you—"

"By lettin' some fuck touch you?"

"He was—"

"And marrin' your beautiful fuckin' skin?"

"I wanted to—"

"You ain't ask my ass if Ima afuckinllow a tattoo on you."

"You fucked, Prez," Mortician said from behind Christopher and Meggie realized they were probably all out there. "You can't order chicks around."

Christopher spun to Mortician. "Shut the fuck up," he spat. "Megan mine." He pointed to Gabe. "And you fuckin' dead for puttin' your fuckin' fingers on her." He glanced at Bunny. "I ain't ever lettin' your ass fuckin' set foot in my club afuckingain." And focused on Megan. "And you. Get the fuck in your car. I ain't ever lettin' you go nowhere on your own afuckingain. And the entire bullshit with that lil' fat motherfucker off. I ain't fuckin' goin' to no church for a fuckin' ceremony. Big or fuckin' small."

Meggie stared at him, swearing her surroundings had been painted red. Or, maybe, that was the color she was seeing because she wanted to kill Christopher. "Move," she said in a voice so deadly calm even Christopher blinked.

But, of course, he recovered too fast. "Go the fuck home," he ground out.

Meggie glanced around the little room for an escape, but Christopher stood right in front of her, blocking her way. Without taking her eyes off the furious face of her husband, she said, "Bunny, you're my friend, so you're welcome to visit me anytime. Or I'll visit you at your house."

"Megan—" Christopher barked.

"As for you," she spat in an icy voice, "if you don't get out of my way and let me pass, I'm going to hurt you really, really bad."

He snorted and lit a cigarette with infuriating smugness. "As fuckin' if."

Meggie stomped Christopher's foot, satisfied at his yelp. "You…you're…you…" She couldn't think of anything nasty enough to express her range of emotions. Hurt, humiliation, and anger. So, she snarled the first thing that shot into her mind, "*fuck off, you fucking asshole,*" shoved him out of her way and ran out of the shop, bursting into tears. She went through a wall of bikers—Stretch, Val, Mortician, Digger, Johnnie, K-P, Shady, and *Bin*. She glared at him, wanting to spit in his ugly face. She was sure he was the one who'd ratted her out.

"Megs," Johnnie called, reaching for her.

She shook her head and ran past him. She didn't need Johnnie's death on her conscience. If he touched her, Christopher *would* kill him.

Once she reached her car and got in, she sped away, needing space, and driving blindly. In the distance, she heard the roar of a motorcycle and felt herself edging closer to the limit of her control. She wasn't Christopher's possession, which was what he was turning her into, ordering her about as if she had no brain. Having her followed. Deciding once and for all he wouldn't go through with their church wedding.

She'd never used a curse word a day in her life, but he'd made her so mad.

Sniffling, she pulled into a gas station. Despite all the food she'd eaten not two hours ago, she wanted a Milky Way and some chocolate milk. After filling her gas tank and making her purchases inside the minimart, she started off again, frustrated when two bikes sped past her.

A moment. That's all she needed. Away from the MC and Christopher. When she neared the dead-end street that led to the clubhouse, she dialed her mother's number to check on CJ. If he needed her, she'd go to him. Thankfully, he didn't, so she decided to head to the creek, where she'd lived for a month before meeting Christopher. She hadn't visited there since she'd moved to the club, but she needed the fresh air. She could eat her candy, drink her milk, and think. Or not think. Just smell the freshness of the trees and feel the briskness of the air against her overheated skin.

She sat on a grassy slope and folded her legs, opening her milk and candy bar. She took a bite, then a sip.

Meggie needed to break through Christopher's rage. Everything set him off and it all went back to Cee Cee. Not that that excused his behavior from a little while ago.

She didn't know who to turn to for advice. She'd had no examples of supportive relationships. She only knew of her idea of what standing behind Christopher meant. And it certainly didn't mean he had license to treat her so crappy.

Meggie rubbed her temples and glanced at the peaceful flow of the water.

"I'd say you set my son in his place."

Meggie drew in a deep breath. Call her insane but hearing Cee Cee's voice didn't surprise her. She'd had a sense of being watched for most of the day. That's why she'd wanted Bin and Shady to stay. Otherwise, she would've been as unhappy about her guards as they were to babysit her. Even Mortician, Val, Stretch, and Digger, as much as she liked them and they liked her, didn't relish the task. Of course, Christopher never sent Johnnie with her.

Just as well, she supposed, since her husband was an insane, jealous maniac. Speaking of which… "Go away," she ordered over her shoulder.

"That's what I'm here for, girlie," he said, without elaborating. "I'm adept at disappearances."

A tremble shook Meggie.

"Outlaw's not my oldest," he told her conversationally. "It might be Bash." He shrugged, hooted with laughter. Insanity. "Maybe not."

If she stayed silent, he might go away.

"I hear tell Outlaw's gunning for me. I've had to lay fucking low so I don't get my ass shot off all because he doesn't see the humor in my run-ins with you."

Meggie drew in a breath. She wished Cee Cee would leave. Maybe, if she kept him talking, she might discover information useful to Christopher.

"My goal isn't to be his enemy, but my contact has warned me he's not asking questions. Never had to fucking sneak anywhere before. Motherfuckers converging on the Burning Hounds MC for a barbeque. It wasn't fucking easy getting here. I had to circumvent the whole fucking area and come the back way." She vaguely recalled Christopher mentioning Derby's club hosting something.

"Imagine my fucking surprise when Outlaw showed up at the goddamn tattoo shop cuz his cunt went there. Fuck, if I hadn't recognized some of their bikes…if he hadn't been so focused on you, I would be dead right now and that would be such a travesty."

Meggie thought otherwise. She wished he would've rolled off a bridge and carried downstream. Even better if he would've been stopped by a police officer and taken to jail.

"Then another surprise: you storming away. All by your lonesome. Like a gift from above."

Or below.

Out of her peripheral vision, she caught sight of his boots as he stopped next to her and stepped on her candy bar. She jumped to her feet and brushed over her backside, flinching when he kicked her milk hard enough for it to land in the water.

Cee Cee leered at her. "You love my boy, right?"

She hated hearing Cee Cee referring to Christopher as "his boy". But, as much as she wanted to deny the claim, he resembled her husband. And her son. Where they had all that black hair, Cee Cee's tattooed bald head made him look like a scary criminal.

She turned to run to her car.

He grabbed her arm and pulled her back. Her bracelet glinted in the sunlight. Stark anger lit his eyes before he covered it with a smile.

Silence surrounded the lonely creek. During the weeks she'd found shelter here, she'd not seen one visitor. Months later, Christopher had revealed the locals stayed away because it had once been a club hangout in the early days of the Dwellers.

Even though they'd long ago given up their claim here, it didn't matter. Shrouded in Dweller lore, it remained deserted, with no one to hear screams or cries for help.

Fingers shaking, she pulled her cell phone out of her pocket. Shoving her away, he laughed again. She swallowed. She couldn't blame him. Her actions were stupidly amusing. Before she dialed a digit, he'd have her subdued. Or dead.

He folded his arms. "I really want to fuck you."

"I'd really rather die."

He shrugged again. "I can oblige you in that, too."

She bet he could and when he finished, he wouldn't lose sleep over it.

He moved closer to her. She had so many questions going through her head—none of which mattered because he wouldn't be interested in answering why he'd decided to drop into his son's life and challenge his authority.

"We could run away together," he offered, glancing at her bracelet again. "Me and you."

She frowned at the unexpected words but saw an opportunity. "You didn't just show up to run away with me. So why are you here? What do you want with my husband?"

He roared with laughter. "Don't want nothing from my boy. A man couldn't ask for a better son." His nostrils flared and he spat a stream of…*something*…right near her feet. "Thought he'd finally be free when his fucking mother chewed on that bullet. Stupid cunt. Led Rack right to her. Years ago, I told all those motherfuckers back away from my kid. Pig-eyed motherfucker's lucky Outlaw got to him before I did." He glared at her. "You're the problem now. Otherwise, Outlaw would be willing to listen to my proposition about forming an alliance with him. My MC and his."

"What's the name of your MC?"

Right then, her life came full circle. She'd run away from her mother's house to get protection from her abusive stepfather. And found love. She'd run away from her love to clear her head. And found abuse.

Cee Cee slapped her across the face and she saw stars.

He shook her and narrowed his eyes. "You don't get to ask fucking questions, you little slut. You stay with him, you'll make him weak. His enemies want something from the club, all they have to do is threaten you—or get to you—and they'll get it. I don't want some cunt coming in and fucking up all my son's built."

Her phone started ringing. Cee Cee jerked it out of her hands and pitched it. A moment later, it plopped into the water, along with dozens of stored photos of CJ since the moment she'd brought him home.

Cee Cee shoved her back and she stumbled. Grabbing her arm, he hooked his thumb underneath her bracelet and yanked. The clasp didn't give, it's resilience kindling fire within her. She jerked her hand away, scooting sideways, bursting around him. It seemed only a second before he looped her waist and dragged her against him. His erection pressed into her back, and she trembled. Unlike her stepfather who'd never been able to get hard enough to penetrate her, Cee Cee suffered no such affliction.

She trembled. Her insides turned to glass, threatening to crack her apart and she gasped, the pain and humiliation of her past slamming through her.

Nosing her hair aside, he licked the shell of her ear, before biting her lobe, one of his hands covering her breast.

"Please," she whispered, her voice as shaky as her limbs.

"You're his biggest liability. The whole club's. *You*, Megan Foy."

Cee Cee had a point, she thought with a shiver, careening over the edge she'd been teetering on since this man had landed in their lives with the force of a tsunami. She was Christopher's liability. He'd agreed to a church wedding when he didn't want it. Agreed to dress in a manner he'd never dressed in—without his cut during the ceremony. For her. He'd stopped hanging out in the main room as often or too long. *Everyone* knew how he felt about her.

He squeezed her breast, still covered by her shirt and bra, but she knew if she didn't do something, he'd rip her clothes away. Grabbing a handful of hair, he twisted her to face him, his grip so brutal she feared he'd tear her scalp away. His head tilted, his mouth aiming for hers. The moment his lips touched her own and he loosened his hold on her hair, he bit into the tender flesh. Pain sliced through her, and she cried out. A trail of blood warmed her chin…

She needed help.

He forced his tongue between her lips, filling her mouth with the taste of alcohol, weed, and blood. Her stomach turned and she couldn't hold back a heave.

It seemed as if he hadn't noticed her gagging, then he stilled in a delayed reaction that proved as detrimental if not more. Lifting his head, he stared at her, his green eyes filled with hate and lust and fury.

He seized her hair again, backhanding her but holding her tight, thereby not allowing her to fall. The side of her head and face stung. Terror burrowed into her. She needed to go. She needed to make her fear go. Go. *GO!*

But she had nothing at her disposal. Not a knife or a blade. She didn't have Christopher or any of her guards.

Cee Cee pushed her to the ground. A knife glinted a moment before he covered her with his body and pinned her in place. She screamed, despite herself.

"Shut your fucking mouth," he snarled, laying the blade against her throat and grinding his hard penis into her belly. "If you want to live a few moments longer, don't make another fucking sound. I want to slit your fucking throat while I come in your mouth, but if you don't behave, I'll find another cunt to have fun with."

He moved away from her and grabbed her hand, then inspected her bracelet. Since the diamonds were set on a platinum band, the knife didn't cut it away. The blade was too big for Cee Cee to put between his teeth. If he coveted the bracelet that much, Meggie knew he'd have to set his weapon aside. She knew she had one shot at survival, a single chance to get back to her son, husband, and mother.

Setting the wickedly long knife aside, Cee Cee rotated the bracelet to the clasp. The moment he released unfastened it, then pushed the button to fully open it, Meggie rammed into him with all her might. Caught off-guard, her movements propelled him back and he landed on his side.

Ignoring her pain, she scrambled to her feet. But he was so quick, his height and muscles no hindrance to his agility. Growling, he caught her leg and she stumbled and fell. If she didn't fight, if he pinned her down, she was dead. Wanting only to live, she kicked and screamed and punched, until he had no choice but to release her. Even if he did so momentarily, to get a better hold on her.

Her breath sawed out and her body ached. He stood in the way of her freedom, staring at her with frenzied eyes, as winded as she. "You do Big Joe proud, girl," he told her. "You wild little cunt."

She lowered her lashes, afraid she might give away her escape route in some way.

"Look what I have, Meggie?" he taunted.

A quick glance revealed her bracelet dangling between his fingers.

"Look at me," he snarled, and she jumped, but complied.

Grinning, he fisted Christopher's gift and flung it over her head. She flinched as it plopped into the creek.

He took a step toward her, his gaze flickering to her right side for the briefest of seconds. He reached for her, but she'd learned how to survive years ago. Anticipating his move, she went the opposite way, almost losing hope when he readjusted his advance and backhanded her. Her ears rang, more stars dancing in front of her eyes.

That fuckin' bitch had to get up close and fuckin' personal so I could shove her the fuck away. That's what Christopher had said about the woman who'd been at his bachelor party.

When he came for her again, Meggie shoved her fingers into his eye and brought her foot up, kicking him as hard as possible in the groin. She shot forward to her car, barely able to get in and lock the door because Cee Cee trailed her, though the last hit she gave finally him slowed him. Maybe, he was almost as exhausted as she was. Otherwise, he would've caught up to her. He banged on the window and Meggie clutched the steering wheel, tears almost blinding her. Her hands trembled so violently she barely shoved the key into the ignition and started it. When she did, Cee Cee stopped kicking her door and pounding on her window to lunge toward the hood.

God, please! Don't make me have to run over him. But, she knew, if she had to, she would; to get away, back to Christopher, back to her son, but Cee Cee jumped out of the way at the last minute.

Meggie gunned the car forward and sped away, hating that she had to bring evidence of Cee Cee's violence to Christopher and wishing she could somehow hide this incident from him.

But knowing that wasn't an option.

Chapter 13

Christopher Outlaw

WHEN CHRISTOPHER REACHED THE CLUBHOUSE AND THEN checked his own house, it pissed him off not to find Megan. His boys all gave him the silent treatment for the way he'd gone off on her. Maybe, his words had been fucked up and they'd come out wrong like a motherfucker and made him look like an assfuck. He'd just been so fucking furious when Bin called and reported Megan had gone to a tattoo parlor with Bunny.

Christopher couldn't imagine anything—even ink—marring Megan's beautiful skin. Yeah, it was her body, and she could do what she wanted with it, but, to him, she was just so perfect. Then, to discover a *man* was touching her body.

Fuck him if Megan wasn't his handicap. She made him wild with jealousy and one insecure motherfucker. He couldn't keep her in a fucking cage, but he was afraid like a motherfucker that she'd open her eyes one day and realize he was nothing but a piece of shit. And leave him.

But he wanted her happy and, if it took leaving him to make her happy, he'd step the fuck aside and let her walk away. After the scene in the parlor shop, it wouldn't surprise him if she'd pack her shit once she returned. Before her, if a chick had gone all psycho fuckhead on him, he would've told her she'd lost her fucking mind and then left her the fuck alone.

Sitting at the bar, Mortician placed a beer in front of him. Dinah waited at the house with CJ and Christopher knew Megan wouldn't leave without their boy. That meant, sooner or later, she'd return to the club.

It was quiet tonight. The Burning Hounds was throwing a barbeque, where Christopher had intended to go before Bin's call. Derby had also invited Boy and his Night Flyers on Christopher's instructions. Cee Cee had gone underground, but Christopher wanted that motherfucker so bad, he could see the rivers of blood running from his eviscerated body.

Yet, he'd be a motherfucker in a barrel before he ignored news that his woman needed him. Fuck. Well. Need was a fucking stretch in this instance. But the sentiment was the same. Bin had called because he didn't have the authority to stop Megan from doing whatever the fuck she wanted to do.

If she told a motherfucker on her detail to fly her to fucking Mars, then that's what the fuck they'd better do.

"Hey, Outlaw," Val called from his place at the bar.

Christopher glanced over his shoulder, glowering a warning to him.

Mort slid Val a bottle of tequila, before drinking from a pint of vodka. Stalking to the far end of the bar, away from those motherfuckers, Christopher sat on a stool.

"We all know how you been leaving Meggie. Changed your mind about the wedding she's been wanting just to have her marriage to you blessed. Today was a fucking travesty, though. Your girl don't do nothing but love you and look after you. She not responsible for motherfucking Cee Cee showing the fuck up. Neither are you, Outlaw. Fuck."

"Fuck you," he ordered, unable to figure out why the fuck else could Cee Cee show up, if not because of Christopher.

That demon motherfucker had violated Patricia and, until the day Logan Donovan fucking died, he never let Christopher forget he'd been responsible for his mother's constant humiliation. Every time she looked at him, she had to see Cee Cee and relive his assault. Patricia never quite disabused Christopher of that notion. She'd loved him, but even she, in her own way, resented him. Christopher tortured himself, imagining that Satan in the fucking flesh ambushing Megan, instead of fucking with her like he'd done on the plane and at the store.

He realized he'd hoped staying away from her as much as possible, allowing his plans to be known in advance, he hoped to draw Cee Cee out of his sewer and force a confrontation.

"You're an asshole, talking to Meggie the way you did."

"Go back to Derby fucking MC, Val." He swept them with a glare. "All you motherfuckers. Leave my ass in fuckin' peace."

Digger guzzled a beer, then sat the empty bottle on the bar. "We *your* boys, Prez. Why we want to stay with other motherfuckers if you not there? We been through shit together, bruh. When you going to realize, you not alone? We got your back. Your woman got your back."

"Right in her scope, to plunge the same knife in yours that you thrust into hers," Johnnie said savagely.

"I ain't repeatin' myfuckinself," Christopher snarled, to no one in particular, just angry with the fucking world. "Back the fuck outta my shit."

Johnnie glared at him, stalking behind the bar to get a bottle of whisky, wanting to jump in his shit. Christopher wished he would. He needed to do something to get this fucking sick anger out of him. It had been lingering ever since Cee Cee had fucked with Megan, ever since Christopher discovered the man who'd given him life—given him the name he fucking detested—still breathed. Just knowing they both drew in air on Planet Earth sent equal parts of shame, humiliation, and fury through him.

He dialed Megan's number again. When it went straight to voicemail, he drew in a deep breath.

"This is Meggie. Leave a message."

Even her voice was bright, the light to his darkness. She'd brought sunshine to his life, pulled him from the pits, and made him think. Made him feel.

"Where the fuck you at?" he demanded, then disconnected the call.

"As far as I know, Meggie haven't turned into a chick into BDSM, Outlaw," Digger said woefully. "You calling and barking like a rabid dog not the best way to kill her anger."

Christopher growled.

"Prez," Mort said quickly, close enough to thump the side of Digger's head. "What Val, Johnnie, and this fool—" he nodded to his brother— "trying to say is…" His voice trailed off and he glanced away. "Your mama didn't have a choice in what Cee Cee did, Outlaw. But you had even less than that. You didn't fucking ask to be the product of that motherfucker. It wasn't fucking up to you. I fucking hate Lowman."

"Hate misfuckinplaced on a dead assfuck," Christopher snapped.

Mortician cleared his throat. "Hate die fucking hard," he said quietly, glancing at Johnnie.

At another time, the unease and guilt might've sunk into Christopher, but it was a passing blow to his turmoil, barely felt and easily ignored.

"You one of the smartest motherfuckers alive, Prez," Mortician continued into the silence. "You letting motherfucking Logan win. You turning into what the fuck he said you was. Cee Cee son."

Christopher stiffened. "I ain't that motherfucker and fuck you for sayin' that shit."

"You not like him, Outlaw," Mortician said with annoyance. "We're trying to get you to see that. You got a fucking heart, first of all. Sooner or later, the motherfucker crawling out of his hole. We turning this state and the next and the next upside down looking for him."

"My ass ain't lookin' in the right fuckin' places. We missin' something. I ain't able to fuckin' figure out what the fuck though."

"So fucking what?" Val asked. "Unless he a fucking snake, slithering from hole to hole, he not nowhere around. Not a motherfucker seen him in days."

"Meanwhile, you doing exactly what Lowman said you would and fucking up the best fucking thing ever happened to you," Mort told him.

"Assfuck ain't say that shit, Mortician. Fuckhead said my ass was the fuckin' fuck up. A fuckin' blight and stain on the fuckin' world."

Johnnie looked at him. "Christopher, fuck…Logan tortured the fuck out of you. With years of physical and emotional abuse, I understand how his belittling corrupted your psyche. If I hadn't witnessed it in the years before you met Mort, I might not understand either. You're not the stupid, filthy, dog Grandda—"

At Christopher's glare, Johnnie drew in another breath.

"Prez, John Boy right," Mort put in. "You already was a grown motherfucker when we met. I stayed clear of Lowman. Motherfucker didn't see me as human. For a different reason than you. First day I fucking met him, I wanted to fucking kill him. He made me feel…fuck, I can't even put it into words. I didn't know if Big Joe would've fucked me up, or even you, but I never felt hate toward no motherfucker the way I did for Logan Donovan."

Johnnie's mouth tightened.

"That's your one fucking flaw, motherfucker," Mortician grumbled to Johnnie. "Loving a crazy old fuckhead like Lowman."

"I always hated what he did to Christopher," Johnnie said coldly. "No matter what I told him, he never stopped his abuse."

"Yeah, motherfucker, and you never stopped visiting him," Val scoffed.

"Never stopped loving him," Digger said.

"Fuck you. I defended Christopher and told Grandda to fucking stop. He didn't listen to me. What was I supposed to do? Turn my back on a lonely old man?"

"Yes," Mort, Digger, and Val chorused.

"Motherfucker was insane, Johnnie," Mort said, slamming his palm on the bar. "Fucking evil."

Johnnie's nostrils flared. "Christopher, I have always admired you and looked up to you. That's why I'm here, in the club. At your disposal." He blew out a noisy breath. "I don't know how it feels to have endured what you did at his hands." He swallowed and scrubbed a hand over his face. "*Their* hands. Neither Aunt Patricia or Grandmother ever stepped in. To his beatings and his putdowns and his rage."

Christopher shrugged. "They was afraid of him."

"And you were a child," he retorted.

"So was you, John Boy."

"Even after I became a man, Logan devoted himself to me. When you had the chance for revenge, when I fucked up and we both knew he would've turned on me, you saved me. You never let him know what I did."

"Motherfucker already hated my ass, Johnnie," Christopher said tiredly. He got up and moved to the stool between Johnnie and Val, facing Digger and Mortician who stood on the opposite side of the bar. "Afuckinnother fuck up from me ain't makin' a fuckin' difference. As much as my ass fuckin' hated Logan, motherfucker was yours. Knowin' you was happy and thrivin' was one fuckin' thing I wanted most of fuckin' all." Outside of protecting and seeing the same for Patricia, Zoann, and Ophelia. "Befuckinsides, I ain't begrudgin' you Logan. Mort had K-P. My ass had Big Joe."

"Now, you have Megan," Johnnie told him.

"And the son she gave you," Val added.

"Until Cee Cee turn up, stop worrying about that motherfucker," Digger said. "Maybe, he dissolved back into the hell cloud he came from."

He nodded and grabbed his phone from his cut. An hour had passed since his last call, and he hadn't heard from her yet. Fuck, he'd fucked up so fucking bad.

His call went to voicemail.

"Baby, come home. We gotta talk. Ima try to rein in my fuckin' hate for that assfuck and stop actin' like a assfuck like him. It ain't gonna be easy cuz I wanna fuck him up so fuckin' bad, Megan."

"Didn't Bin say she hung out with Gypsy and that chick, Bunny?" Digger asked. "Maybe, she decided to hang with them again."

Heaving in a breath, he disconnected the call. Waited. Five minutes passed and nothing.

"Fuck, why I ain't put trackin' on Megan fuckin' phone and in her car?" he asked to no one in particular.

Christopher dialed her number again. "Megan—" he began gruffly after the beep.

"Outlaw," Mortician interrupted.

Christopher looked up and the man pointed his thumb in the direction of the monitor that showed the gate. Stretch was opening it to let Megan in. Hanging up, he got to his feet, watching as she gunned her car forward, momentarily out of camera range.

Anticipating the moment she walked in, he walked to one of the tables close to the door. He'd embarrassed her in front of everyone, he'd apologize—

"Holy motherfuck," Mortician growled. "What the fuck happened to her?"

Before Christopher could turn to the monitor, the door blasted open and Megan ran in, screeching to a halt when she saw them.

Christopher stared at her, the tears streaking her face. The terror in her eyes. The motherfucking *bruises* on her face and neck. Her bloody lip and broken nails. Mud and grass stained her clothes, and her bracelet was gone.

"Jesus Christ, Megan, what happened to you?" Johnnie demanded harshly.

"A motherfucker jumped you for your bracelet, Meggie?" Digger questioned.

"Where you went, Meggie girl?" Mort asked. "Tell us. Describe the motherfucker that did this to you. We'll get Outlaw present back."

Her face crumpled and she let out a small sob.

"Your bracelet not gone," Val swore.

She didn't answer any of the questions thrown at her. She drew in a deep breath, barreled into Christopher's arms and clung to him, trembling in his arms.

He held her tightly, allowing her to cry, refusing to think about her state or what else might've happened to her.

Closing his eyes, he nosed her hair, not caring that it smelled of sweat and dirt. "Megan, baby, what the fuck happen to you?"

"N-nothing."

"Nothin'?" he echoed, caressing her back. When he took her face between his hands, she flinched. He would've released her, but she placed her fingers over his and held him in place. "A motherfucker jump you for your bracelet? That's what the fuck happen?"

"N-nothing happened."

He saw her broken nails again, her dirty fingers, and knew she'd put up a vicious fight. He searched her face. "How the fuck you so fuckin' bruised then?"

Silence. Tears rushed to her eyes, but she could no longer meet his gaze. As if she hid something. Had news she didn't know how to share.

His mind immediately went to Patricia and what had happened to her. "Megan…?" He stopped and cleared his throat, trying to find the right words. "Megan…was you…you got…"

"No," she said hoarsely, glancing at him briefly to shake her head, then looking away again. "I didn't. Nothing h-happened."

His fucking ass. It was motherfucking obvious shit *had* happened, so why the fuck wasn't she revealing the facts, so he could find…

He stepped away from her, all the better to stare and study her. To read what the fuck she couldn't put into fucking words. He narrowed his eyes, felt his blood pressure rise. A thought emerged in his fucking head, only too motherfucking insane to entertain because he was like a fucking bogeyman, lurking in the fucking shadows, unable to be fucking found. Trying to control his temper and feeling to his bones he knew what the fuck had happened, he wrapped her in his arms again, stared at Johnnie and nodded.

Johnnie scratched his jaw. "Er, Megs, sweetheart, does this nothing have a name?"

Silence.

Yeah, infuckingdeed, that motherfucker had a name. If that motherfucker had followed Megan from here to Seattle, then back to here and hid in plain sight until he could strike, he didn't only have a death wish, he had a wish to die slow, violent, and gruesome.

"Uh, Meggie," Val said, "not many motherfuckers we know…fuck…*no* motherfuckers we know would fuck you up and jack your shit."

Nothing.

Megan didn't volunteer information, but she'd answer with a motherfucking yes or no.

"It was fuckin' Cee Cee, huh?" Christopher snarled, tightening his hold on her and resting his chin on the crown of her head.

She nodded.

Motherfuck him. He'd fucking known that motherfucker was lurking. He'd felt it in his fucking gut, but he hadn't been able to find him. "Where?" he roared, pulling away from her to tip her chin up. He winced at her battered face.

"At the creek. H-he took my phone and my bracelet and threw them in the water."

He tossed her things in the water, huh? Christopher supposed pieces of Cee Cee would soon join them.

"Here, Prez," Mort said, setting a bowl with water, clean towels, and antibacterial soap on the table.

Christopher guided her to a chair and tenderly cleaned her lip, clenching his jaw at the cut on her earlobe. He washed her fingers, then patted them dry with the second towel. She had more bruising and swelling then actual open wounds, not that that shit mattered.

"What the fuck he say to you, baby?"

Her lips trembled, her blue eyes filling with more tears. "That he wanted to f-f-fuck me," she whispered. "I'd told him I'd rather die." She let out a little hysterical sob. "He said he could oblige me with that, too. He wanted me to go away with him. He said I made you weak. I was your—the club's—liability."

Christopher had to draw in a breath to keep all the images from his head. Images of Cee Cee raping Megan, strangling her, and then dumping her body in the creek.

"What the fuck else?" Christopher demanded. "I wanna hear everyfuckinthing from start to fuckin' finish."

Clenching her jaw, she stared at her hands. "Why?" she finally asked.Oh, yeah. Fuck, she was probably fucking thinking about his soul. "For inforfuckinmational purposes, Megan."

Her look called bullshit, but he didn't give a good fuck. "Spill, baby."

"O-okay," she said in a small, tired voice as Mortician handed her an ice pack. She sniffled out details. The hits. The knife to take her bracelet. The theft. How she compared Cee Cee to her step fuckhead.

"A penis?" Digger blurted when she got to that part. "What the fuck is that?"

Christopher glared at him. "Megan name for a cock," he growled.

Val blinked. "Well, fuck, Outlaw, I haven't had one of those since I was nine or ten."

"You fuckheads do know that's the proper terminology for the male anatomy, don't you?" Johnnie asked.

"Ain't givin' a good fuck right now. Call the motherfucker a lil' smokie. Shut the fuck up so she can fuckin' continue," Christopher ordered.

Go on she did. On and on, torturing him and infuriating him.

"You did Big Joe proud?" Johnnie repeated upon hearing her.

"Motherfucker right," Christopher said in a tone he barely recognized. "You Big Joe girl and you got the fuck away. Ima fuckin' leave Cee Cee cock, nuts, and asshole infuckintact, so Boss got shit to rip the fuck apart when that motherfucker join him."

"How the fuck you finally got away?" Digger asked.

"I jabbed my fingers in his eye and then kicked him in the groin and ran for my car. He almost got me though. If I would've stumbled—" She shivered. "I barely had time to lock the door—"

How could he be a sane motherfucker when fuckheads would always go for Megan? Because that walking fucking dead man was fucking right. She was the first one motherfuckers would go for.

Crouching down, he flicked a thumb over the side of her face, and she flinched, her tears falling onto his hand and pissing him off like nothing else—besides Thomas Fucking Nicholls—ever had. If he had to have a body count stacks high, he fucking would. For every motherfucker who fucked with Megan, Christopher would fuck them up and wipe them off the face of the earth.

He'd already had more than enough hate filling him up toward Cee Cee. This shit just sealed it all up nice and tight. He bent and kissed her, relieved she didn't pull away. In fact, she stood on her tiptoes and kissed him back, wincing at the contact of their lips.

Christopher threaded his fingers through her hair. "I'm sorry, baby. For earlier. All that shit I said. And you was fuckin' right callin' me down. If you was a easy motherfucker to boss the fuck 'round, I ain't sparin' a fuckin' minute for you. But you gotcha own mind and you ain't afraid to tell us motherfuckers. That impress the fuck outta me, Megan. And, baby, you had to efuckinscape that motherfucker." He let her go and paced in front of her. "But, fuck me, Megan. He coulda hurt you bad fightin' back, baby."

"He would've hurt me if I hadn't fought back, Christopher." She sounded exhausted. "The creek was right there. He probably would've…once he finished with me—" She shrugged, and he knew her thoughts mirrored his.

Horror dawned in all their faces at the thought of Megan at the bottom of a fucking creek.

"I had to try," she went on. "I had to get back to you and CJ. Momma and…and…Johnnie and Val and Digger and…and—" She swiped at her tears. "And Mortician—"

"I know, baby. I know." Christopher smiled at her. "And you here, yeah? See? Our ugly fuckin' faces here—" He drew in a deep breath. "Ima call Stretch to bring Dinah and our boy here. I ain't got efuckinnuff security measures in place at the house to live the fuck there yet. Okay?"

She nodded, her lack of argument or disappointment pissing him off even more. He knew how bad she wanted to get the fuck out of the MC and live at their own house.

"Can you…I need a few minutes to pull myself together before I see CJ," she admitted as if it shamed her. "Can you give me thirty minutes to take a shower and make the tears go away?"

She got to her feet and backed away, the look in her eyes…distant, far off, like she'd floated away into her own world. He'd deal with whatever way she coped with this another time. If she needed to cut herself to take away her trauma, he'd let her.

Because he sure the fuck intended to murder to take away his anger.

Mortician

LUCAS "MORTICIAN" BANKS LOOKED AT THE MESS HE'D made and frowned at how gruesome things had gotten. But, hey, a bunch of stupid fucks roamed hereabouts, and they had to get said fucks in line, especially when said fucks had information about the motherfucker named Cee Cee.

And if they didn't fall into line and give up the info?

Mortician wrinkled his nose at the clean up facing him, the result of a fuck not giving up the info. Needing air for a moment, he removed his gloves and apron and left the gore behind.

It had been two weeks since things had gone down the shitter. Two weeks since Outlaw had lost his mind in the tattoo parlor. Two weeks since they'd almost lost Meggie. Two fucking weeks. Outlaw's refusal to have their church wedding was even more adamant now, which made Meggie even more miserable. And because Meggie was miserable, Outlaw had turned into a fucking beast. To everyone.

As a result, stupid fucks ended up like the corpse in the meat shack. Outlaw was leaving a path of bodies and destruction that made motherfuckers tremble. Any hint of an association with Cee Cee was cause for annihilation. Meanwhile, the motherfucker in question had gone underground again. Mort knew with the justice the club was meting out, if a fuckhead knew where Cee Cee was, they would've given him up.

Outlaw was fucking wild in his rage. John Boy wasn't much better, but Mort kept his opinion about that shit to himself. Besides, they all wanted to avenge her. She was Outlaw's woman, but their friend.

Once Meggie's bruises faded enough that makeup would completely cover all evidence, Mort thought Outlaw would've gotten a little better. That hadn't happened. Two days after she came back to the club so worked over, Outlaw had turned into a fucking ogre to *her*, of all fucking people.

If they could just find fucking Cee Cee. But the motherfucker had MCs for miles scratching their fucking heads. Some of the best enforcers and trackers around were looking for him. Nothing. Dude had once again dropped the fuck off the face of the earth. That left Meggie vulnerable. In turn, it made Prez defenseless.

Mortician adjusted his cut and dug out his cigarettes.

Bitches like Meggie was the primary reason he never intended to tie himself down. He struck the match, lit his cigarette, then flicked his wrist to get rid of the flame. He liked Meggie, too. He also tried his best not to eyeball Prez's old lady and he'd just bleached the fuck out of his brain to remove the memory of a naked Meggie. Remembering shit like that or admitting that he'd gotten a couple boners over her was the quickest way to get his dick fed to him for breakfast. He understood Outlaw's dilemma. Meggie was the sweetest little thing they'd ever met and *that* was the problem. Sweetness like that reached out and touched hard motherfuckers and drove them crazy. They couldn't see the light of day for sweet bitches.

Mortician doubted Meggie acted the way she did on purpose. She just demanded the things all good girls demanded. Like their weddings blessed and sanctioned by churches. That was cool, unless a good girl hooked herself to the ultimate bad boy.

And Outlaw won the prize for bad boys.

Usually, Prez and Meggie found a way to compromise. Not this time. Not with all this peripheral bullshit going on. Fuck it. It was what it was. Prez had to accept her just as she had to accept Prez. One of them had to give in and Mortician doubted it would be Meggie this time around. He loved the fuck out of Outlaw but, sometimes…all Mortician was saying was the dude had tied himself to Meggie, so he needed to get his head out his ass and realize the girl loved him even with all his faults. She believed him worthy enough to vow herself to him in front of God and man. Didn't much matter Outlaw wasn't spiritual and didn't believe anymore in that stuff. *Meggie* did and that's what counted.

She was the type of chick who grabbed hold of a problem and decided on a plan to fix it, never losing faith it would be rectified.

Instead of standing around in the cold, he walked along the pathway to take a peep at Meggie's house. Yeah, the shit was Outlaw's, too, but he'd built it for his girl. Now, they'd move in soon and Mortician wondered what other changes would happen after Outlaw moved out of the club. The house was a five-minute walk, but Prez still wouldn't live at the club anymore. What the fuck did that mean for the rest of them?

The dogs were trained. They'd started with them as puppies and Outlaw even had clothes with Meggie's and Little Man's scents, so they'd know they were supposed to protect them and not chew them the fuck up.

John Boy had suggested they let Meggie interact with the dogs as they grew up, but Outlaw had immediately vetoed the idea, pointing out his wife would coddle the animals. Not that the dogs were mistreated, but they needed a firmer hand to follow commands and protect rather than roll over to have their fucking bellies rubbed.

Taking one last drag on his smoke, he threw it onto the ground, then crushed it beneath his boot. Noticing the bloody footprint he'd made, he glowered and lifted his leg to inspect his boot sole closer. Motherfucker. He'd just paid a mint for these cold ass boots, and they were already spattered with other people's DNA.

Ain't this a bitch?

Frustrated, he headed toward the clubhouse instead of back to the meat shack to change his boots. He had some dirty ass work to get through and he didn't want to ruin his boots any more than they already were. He noticed a bunch of cars in the parking lot and saw Stretch and Bin on gate duty. He waved at Stretch, the recently-elected club secretary, and gave Bin a two-finger salute when he wanted to give him a fuck you. But one of the club's lifers, Traveler, had brought Bin in. Traveler was in good standing, so they trusted him not to bring any riff-raff into the club.

Maybe, it was just Bin's appearance. *Albino motherfucker.* Mortician still remembered that Albino from *The Da Vinci Code.* Maybe, that's why he got such bad vibes from Bin.

Stepping into the warmth of the club, it surprised him to find so many chicks so early. It was about three in the afternoon. Upon closer inspection, he saw these weren't the normal hangers-on, but some old ladies the brothers were slowly acquiring again and one of Outlaw's sisters, Ophelia. He continued to take inventory of the faces, smiling and nodding to those who acknowledged him.

He squinted, not that he needed to with all the lights on. It just shocked him to see a gorgeous woman with a head of rich brown hair. *Zoann.* Another one of Prez's sisters. Mortician couldn't stand that bitch, though. Didn't even matter that she'd popped out Val's son. Zoann was the most self-righteous, judgmental cunt he'd ever met.

Meggie's bridal shower for a wedding that should be a week away from taking place. The realization dawned on him when he saw all the decorations—ridiculous crape bells, balloons, streamers. Despite the pile of gifts on the table in the corner, the shit resembled a funeral rather than a celebration for an upcoming ceremony that probably wasn't happening.

Outlaw walked out of the kitchen, chewing on a rib. It didn't surprise him when Val, Johnnie, and Digger followed, close on Prez's heels. They'd agreed to keep a close watch on him until things settled down.

Meggie stiffened in her chair and slanted an evil glare toward Prez.

Mortician caught Johnnie's eye, then blinked as he watched the blush creeping over Prez's skin. *Well, I'll be a motherfucker in a chicken coop.* So, his ass knew he was being a total dick to Meggie. Interesting. And just another example of the power of sweet girls and young pussy.

The door opened and before Mortician could move, someone barreled into him. He turned and met K-P's glare. "What the fuck you doing in the doorway, you little fucking runt?"

Mortician snickered. At six feet, he could hardly be considered a runt. K-P liked to jerk everyone's chains, though.

"'Scuse me, Kitchen Bitch," Mortician responded, heading to the bar and leaning on it. "Wassup?" he asked the other guys.

Val didn't respond, too busy staring at Zoann. The way she sat so straight, Mortician guessed she knew her baby daddy eye fucked her. Bitch went out of her way to pretend he didn't exist. One day, the brother would realize he was better off without that sadity bitch.

"This here's my daughter," K-P announced from behind Mortician in a voice filled with hard to miss pride. Most dads thought their daughters beautiful, even the bitches whose nicknames should've been Bowwow and Needa…as in need a mask to fuck your ass. "Bailey. Meggie said it was okay to invite her to her wedding shower."

Outlaw nodded and grabbed a bottle of tequila. Val didn't say a word. Digger and John Boy exchanged glances. But it was the look in John Boy's eyes—the one that had girls falling all over themselves—that really made Mortician turn around.

Jesus H. Christ. A pair of greenish-brown eyes met him. Dark brows turned down in a frown and, somehow, drew his gaze to her rosy lips. Glossy black hair fell around her in waves and Mortician sat in the stool, punch-drunk. If a seat hadn't been there, he would've fallen right on his ass.

Purple sequined leggings clung to her hips and her white leather jacket hung open to reveal a cropped pink sweater and a flat belly that tapered to a small waist.

Her skin looked like vanilla with a hint of caramel, beautiful and smooth. Wanting to feel every inch of her, he swallowed and cocked his head to the side. "You got a little coffee in your cream, girl?"

She stiffened at his words.

K-P lifted a brow. "Say again…?"

Mortician stalled, needing a minute. Just one. To get his pounding heart and the awareness flowing between them under control. He shrugged with false nonchalance, swept his gaze over her and estimated her age to be between nineteen and twenty-two. Definitely a young bitch. Definitely a sweet chick.

Definitely a no-no. Not only because of the 100Gs on the line, a bet made in the heat of the moment when he'd been noticing how miserable Outlaw was without Meggie around. He'd been so fucking caught up, he hadn't even bothered with an expiration date. Which meant, he could be fucking ninety and run across some young pussy and he'd have to pay up.

"You plan on answering me about the comment you made to my daughter?"

Ignoring K-P, he continued his staring contest with Bailey and folded his arms, lightheaded when her lips parted. He scratched his temple and cleared his throat. "You a black chick?"

His question earned him a hard hit on the back on his head.

"She a human chick, fuckhead," Outlaw growled, using a bar towel to wipe away the barbeque sauce from his lips and fingers.

"My mother's black," Bailey clarified and licked lips he wanted to taste nice and slow.

Mortician's dick went rock hard and he balled his fists to keep from reaching out to touch her.

"Does it matter?" she asked. "Aren't you black?"

"Am I?" he goaded. He wanted her in his bed and, when he got her there, he intended to lick every part of her. "Guess I need to go look in the mirror and see if I changed colors since this morning."

She narrowed her gorgeous eyes. "Whatever else you are, asshole is front and center."

"Don't mind my brother, babe," Digger called, winking at her.

Mortician wanted to drive his fist into the man's mouth. Maybe, snatch off an eyelid so he wouldn't flirt with her again. Wait, *what? Scccrrreeeecccchhhh!* He backed his thoughts the fuck up.

"You got him pegged anyway, so now you know to stay far away from him," Digger said with a wider smile.

"Him on the other hand—" Mortician began. He needed a bud to slow his fucking mouth down. Obviously, his brain was losing the fucking race to the finish line because his fucking tongue kept wagging.

Johnnie's eyes twinkled. "Him, what, Mort?"

K-P rounded to the other side of the bar and glared from Johnnie to Digger before his warning gaze landed on Mortician. "Any of you fucks touch her, you die."

"Dad!" Bailey whined, her skin adapting a red tint and Mortician shifted, his dick hurting.

"Not playing, babe," K-P went on. "You're a virgin and—"

Bailey gasped. "You so didn't just out me like that," she complained.

He *so* did out her like that.

Remorseless, K-P went on. "Stick close to Meggie. Or, better yet, sit next to Zoann. If you're not careful, you'll be in one of their beds before I can get you off premises and then your old man would get in bad standing with his brothers for killing one. And you don't want that do you, babe?"

"You're all idiots," a voice chirped from behind them.

Meggie scooted around him to glare at K-P. Mortician squeezed the bridge of his nose, so *not* noticing how Meggie's brown suede pants and cream-colored silk blouse showed off her tits, ass, and hips. He *so* didn't notice the hint of a pink lacy bra beneath her shirt. Her black hi-tops gave her a casual look.

Maybe, he noticed—didn't notice, he meant—that bullshit because he'd been thinking about how well she was handling Outlaw's fuckuppedness. And, because, Bailey had him hyperaware. And both Meggie and Bailey were gorgeous chicks.

"I'm Megan Caldwell," Meggie said to Bailey, who seemed to have been mortified into speechlessness by her father's casual announcement. "You must be Bailey."

"Y-yes." She stared at Mortician, her greenish-brown gaze ringed with thick lashes and filled with heat and curiosity.

He winked at her, and Meggie thumped his shoulder.

"Don't mind them," she bit out, giving him the stink eye. "They're all party-poopers."

"Hey, Meggie babe," K-P said. "I'm her old man."

"She's…" Meggie's voice trailed off and she lifted a blonde brow at Bailey. "How old are you?"

"Twenty-one," Bailey supplied, her gaze flickering to his and roaming from head to foot and back again. She heaved in a deep sigh, the movement drawing his attention to her breasts.

"She's twenty-one," Meggie announced. "Old enough to party."

Twenty-one? *No, Mort, don't go there, man.* But she was legal and only nine years younger than he was.

"Twenty," K-P corrected, glaring at his daughter. "You won't be twenty-one for another three months."

Okay, so ten years older.

With a huff, Meggie led Bailey away.

"C'mon," Outlaw grumbled. "Let's leave these bitches the fuck alone. I need a fuckin' drink."

Mortician remembered he'd left unfinished business in the meat shack. "Uh, I'll come to your room in about half hour," he called.

He headed for the door, feeling the weight of a gaze on him. Just before he stepped outside, he turned and found Bailey had tracked his every move. For some reason, the thought made his body tighten and his head race with images of her in his bed, all that black hair spread out over his pillow. Have Bailey look at him the way Meggie drank in Outlaw…

Wasn't happening, so he didn't need to waste his fucking brain cells thinking about it. Her virginity had sealed his decision. He'd *never, ever* get inside of her.

Later, he'd find a bitch to fuck and forget Bailey existed.

CHRISTOPHER NEEDED TO DO SOMETHING WITH HIS tangled emotions besides sit in the bedroom with his boys while Megan enjoyed her bridal shower and hated on him.

He sucked on the blunt they were passing around, knowing he was the motherfucker to blame for the wedge between him and his girl. Fuck him, but he'd tried to take a cue from her and live his life in the present, not the past.

His fucking past kept a motherfucking chokehold on him, though, and insisted on fucking him up the ass.

He knew him and Megan could get through anything else together. Like they were meant to be. Now, he couldn't get past this bullshit. He'd offered to buy her another bracelet. She'd turned him down though, without explanation, and he hadn't pressed the issue.

On the other fucking hand, he wished he'd kept his fucking mouth shut and never asked her if she'd held anything back from the story she'd told upon her return to the club. It just hadn't made sense why she'd thought about Thomas Nicholls if Cee hadn't tried to force himself on her.

He'd discovered the entire truth and, yeah. Fuck. She had left a bunch of shit off. Cee Cee forcing his mouth on hers. Squeezing her tit. Holding a fucking knife to her throat, and too much other shit. He couldn't fucking help her cope because he was too fucking angry.

Angry with the fucking *world*. The entire fucking *universe*. If he could've only been lucky enough to get one fucking break in his life. He knew he was headed to hell for the shit he'd done, but the least hoof-foot could fucking do was wait until Christopher *arrived* down there before he sank him in a mire of fucking shit.

But no. Hoof-foot motherfucker wasn't happy he'd gotten his grip on Christopher's soul and ripped it away years ago. That bullshit wasn't enough. He couldn't allow him one fucking ounce of happiness. Not one. Not even when Christopher had sent down so many motherfuckers to cohabitate with him.

Three nights after her run in with Daddy fuckhead Dearest, she'd asked Christopher if he was serious about canceling their counseling sessions, holding onto CJ as if she'd never let him go.

"What the fuck you think?" he'd snapped.

"Okay," she'd said, surprising him. "We can ask Father Wilkins to marry us in his office. We don't need a formal service."

He didn't, but she did.

"Megan, fuck—"

"I just want our marriage blessed and I never should've pushed you for something so huge."

"Unless my ass fuckin' stupid, askin' one fuckin' time ain't pushin'. I was the motherfucker that said yes without thinkin'. So now after I fuckin' thought shit through, we ain't havin' no type of church ceremony."

"Talk to me, Christopher. Please," she'd whispered. She hadn't been angry.

Yet.

"I ain't gotta tell you my every fuckin' thought, bitch."

And, yeah, that had pissed her the fuck off so much, she'd padlocked her fucking pussy and kept the combination to her fucking self.

"Christopher?"

Ophelia's voice calling his name snapped him back to the present. He frowned and blinked at the closed door. His sisters hadn't spoken to him in months.

Johnnie lifted a brow in question and Christopher shrugged. "You got something to say to your young cousin, John Boy?"

"No."

Another knock. "May I come in? Please?"

"Come the fuck in," he growled, scowling at how uncertain she sounded.

The door pushed open, and his little sister stepped in. Her short hair was slicked back, and a frown creased her brow. She waved at Digger and Val.

"Hey, Johnnie," she greeted.

Johnnie nodded and gave her a half-smile. "Fee."

"What do you want, Ophelia?" She and his other sisters had turned their backs on him, so he didn't need more bullshit from them. Especially now when he was dealing with so much other bullshit. He wanted her gone because, despite how angry he was, he couldn't help how her eyes were beginning to water from the strong scent of the blunt. He folded his arms. "Lemme guess. You want more money from me."

She shook her head. "I babysit Ryan and…" She rocked back on her wedges and glanced at Val.

"You ain't doin' that band thing and still in a school for filmmakin'?"

She refocused her attention to Christopher at his statement. "I haven't been doing too well this last year," she mumbled and bowed her head. "I-I'm glad things worked out for you and Meggie."

He glowered at her, refusing to give an inch.

"I wanted her to tell you that I was sorry," she continued.

That was news. "Yeah?"

Swiping at tears, Ophelia sniffled and nodded. "She invited us to her bridal shower, so I could tell you myself."

Megan. His soft-hearted, determined Megan. He needed her so fucking bad but he needed Cee Cee dead more. Until then, Christopher would have no peace.

"I'm sorry, Christopher," Ophelia whispered in a trembling voice. "The way they—" She swallowed— "I treated you," she amended. "Can you please forgive me?"

He considered refusing her heartfelt plea. She'd been the bitch who'd delivered the messages for the other fucking bitches. She could've taken a stand against them. But, no, they'd all turned their backs on him when he'd needed them.

Fuck. Him. He couldn't send her away when she looked so vulnerable and sounded so sincere. "Fuck me," he mumbled, under his breath. He threw her a dirty look. "Apology fuckin' accepted. Now, if you ain't got no more to fuckin' say, get the fuck outta my room, and leave me and my boys the fuck alone."

Even with his harsh words, relief brightened Ophelia's features. She looked as if she wanted to say or do something else. Instead, she sighed and said, "thank you." She glanced at Val again. "Er, um, V-val. Zoann…Meggie…we talked, and Meggie suggested Zoann let you visit Ryan while she's on duty at the hospital."

Val straightened, anticipation spreading over his face as he waited for Ophelia to continue.

"Whenever she goes on duty, I'll give you a heads-up and, if you have time, you—"

Val didn't need to hear anymore. "When's the next time she goes on duty?"

"Tomorrow afternoon."

"I'll be there." He smiled at her. "Thanks."

Ophelia cleared her throat and turned to leave. At the door, she looked back. "Don't thank me, Val," she said softly. "Thank Meggie."

The words hung in the air after she left, and Johnnie, Val, and Digger stared at him.

"You motherfuckers shut the fuck up and don't open your fuckin' mouths."

Not that they had to. Their accusatory looks said it all.

He was being an assfuck to Megan.

Chapter 15

Meggie

MEGGIE KEPT A SMILE PLASTERED ON HER FACE, throughout the day, though inside she felt wrecked. She'd asked Christopher not to announce that their church services had been canceled, so she pretended to be happy in front of all the women when she and Christopher were at such a crossroads. When the shame of the fresh cuts on her thighs stung her physically and mentally.

If Christopher gave her attention only during the good times, then their relationship wasn't at all what she thought it to be. That hurt more than anything.

During her bridal shower, she managed to get some music going and got some of the ladies to join her in dancing. They discussed her wedding gown and their bridesmaids' dresses. Only Lacey and Farrah knew the full truth and thought Meggie insane when she didn't cancel the shower. She asked them to come down, but they refused. Instead, they tried their best to convince Meggie it was time to walk away from Christopher.

Meggie refused to entertain that idea. She forced herself to enjoy the day. She, Bunny, Gypsy, Danicka, and Bailey danced, then they played a few more games that Zoann and Ophelia led in between May and Gurly's raunchy jokes. At some point, the loss of her bracelet came up. News of her run-in with Cee Cee had made the rounds, but she didn't want to talk about him or her lost Valentine's Day gift, when things still seemed so perfect between her and Christopher. He'd offered to purchase her another bracelet. She'd declined. His treatment of her would make such an expensive present meaningless.

Then, finally, her bridal shower was over. Before her guests departed, she handed them each a sealed envelope and asked they read her note as soon as they could once they left.

Inside, she explained the church wedding had been canceled. If they wanted the gifts returned, she'd understand. She reminded them that she and Christopher were already married and it was her with a silly superstition about having their union blessed to ensure years of happiness. She'd waited to tell them because she had hoped Christopher would change his mind, but since they were receiving the note, that wasn't the case.

She handwrote each note for a personal touch. Tears spattered the ink on one or two, but that couldn't be helped as hurt as she was over not only the wedding but his treatment of her, too.

After the women left, she rushed to the bathroom. Her bladder felt on the verge of bursting, then she splashed water on her face to wash away fresh tears before returning to the main room and gazing at the decorations she, Bunny, and Gypsy had placed. Blue and peach silk rose petals, floral garland, crape pompoms and lanterns, candles and balloons turned the normally masculine area into her own fairytale.

She wasn't living in a magical kingdom with princesses and knights. This was her life and she'd chosen Christopher to share it with. That meant she had to take his feelings into consideration too. At the moment, he was suffering. He didn't need her pressuring him for an unneeded ceremony. As she'd written to her guests, she was already his wife.

Maybe, one day, their marriage would be blessed. In the great scheme of things, Christopher always found a way to give her whatever he thought she might want or need. It was rare that she asked for anything. That she'd *asked* for a church wedding and he had decided against it told her what she needed to know.

If not for extenuating circumstances, he would never have backed out.

Silence surrounded her and Meggie grit her teeth, fighting her sadness and loneliness. Drawing in a deep breath, she shoved some of her hair behind her ear.

Though only eight women had attended, she had a mountain of gifts on the table that Christopher and his officers always sat at. Even when Christopher was gone, Johnnie, Mortician, Digger, Val, K-P, and Stretch would be if they were at the club. If none of them showed up, the table remained empty.

The place needed to be cleaned. Maybe, Dinah would help out. Her mother hadn't wanted to attend the shower. She'd said it was because of CJ. But Meggie didn't really believe her. Momma was less than pleased that Meggie was married at all.

Sighing, she decided to bring her gifts to Christopher's room. Despite the stillness, the overwhelming quiet, Meggie still knocked at the door. It didn't matter that she shared the room with him. She didn't want to barge in.

She waited. Knocked again. This time, she opened the door and found it empty. The guys had left. *Christopher* was gone again. Was their marriage over? Not only didn't he want a church wedding, it seemed as if he no longer wanted her. Her heart fragmented, pieces of it falling away, but all of it hurting.

Turning, she left the room and headed down the hallway, rounding the corner to reach Dinah's room. She discovered her on the floor, playing with CJ. Since their return from Seattle, Dinah acted better, different, and more self-assured and in the present. Dinah had even shocked Meggie and prepared the mac and cheese that she had loved at one time.

Backing out of the room and not wanting CJ to detect her, Meggie decided to go for a drive, so she returned to the room for her keys and wrinkled her nose. Thanks to the boys, the room smelled like smoke and alcohol.

Ugh! She couldn't bring CJ in there until she freshened it up, so she changed plans—cleaning instead of leaving to clear her head.

First order of business…allowing the door to remain open. Next, she removed the empty beer and tequila bottles. No wonder Christopher could be so difficult. He'd pickled his brain with all the drinking.

It surprised her but restoring the room didn't take as long as expected. It helped that she cleaned it daily. Grabbing her keys and her ID, she headed out. Her car was kept around the side of the club, toward the back. Christopher always sent a Probate to get it for her, but she didn't feel like talking. Smacking her husband, yes. Conversing with anyone else, no.

The cloudy afternoon was morphing into early evening, and she wondered again where Christopher might be, not wanting to consider his possible activities. She tried to keep his dark side from haunting him and, most of the time, refrained from asking questions because she didn't want to know. But she *did* know. She'd seen the do-or-die situations firsthand, months ago. She hated to think about murder and retaliation. She always wished there could be a way for the police to intercede. Yet, she knew what side of the law Christopher fell on. That meant club vengeance. It was awful of her, but she preferred Christopher to get his enemies before his enemies got him.

When she drove to the gate, Stretch stopped her, pinning her with his blue eyes. He scratched his mop of brown hair. "Where you going, Meggie?"

At her response, his eyebrows almost touched his hairline. "Out."

"Er, Prez will want to know—"

"Where's Christopher?" she snapped.

He blinked in confusion, and she suspected Christopher's whereabouts were as big a mystery to him as they were to her. Not having an argument under the circumstances, Stretch looked at the ground.

"Open the gate."

"Cee Cee hasn't been caught."

She swallowed.

"You're probably still healing. I know it's important to pretend everything is fine."

"I'm not pretending," she said quietly. "Please. I just need a moment to think."

"Meggie—"

"This is what I know, Stretch," she whispered. "When I lived with Momma, I had to get up every day and smile, no matter what else had happened the night before. I had to leave, knowing my mother needed me so I had no choice but to go home to take care of her. I'm okay. I just need away from the clubhouse."

"Outlaw's going to be so fucking mad."

"You're doing nothing wrong."

"He doesn't want you leaving."

"Has he told you to force me to stay here?"

He groaned but shook his head, then opened the gate.

Once she left, Meggie didn't have an exact destination in mind. She just needed a break. For months, someone was always around her. At first, she appreciated the protection and loved the fact Christopher kept her so close and held her in such regard that he wanted her guarded even when he couldn't do it. Now, though, she realized he could take a break whenever it pleased him. He had a battalion of men at his disposal to foist the duties of protecting her in his stead. He ordered her safeguarded as his woman, the president's old lady. Dweller property. Not only was he always out, vulnerable to injury or death, he rarely called her anymore to say 'hi'; 'I love you'; 'I miss you'; 'are you okay'.

She was okay in the sense that she'd lived under the threat of Thomas's violence for years. She'd been Dinah's nurse and bodyguard. Men like her stepfather and Cee Cee thrived on a woman's fear. One had been a law-abiding citizen and the other was a ruthless criminal, each as dangerous as the other. Perhaps, Thomas had been more treacherous. Cee Cee didn't bother to hide his menace.

Craving a chocolate fudge milkshake, she pulled into one of her favorite restaurants, surprised at the early crowd. Finding a spot near the exit of the parking lot, close to the road, she hurried inside, stood in line to order, then slid into a booth once she'd gotten her shake.

The chocolate tasted so delicious, and she closed her eyes in bliss. For a few minutes, she just enjoyed her shake and the hum of the crowd, the laughter of the little kids.

Thoughts of Christopher crept into her head again, and she set her shake aside, covering her face with her hands. She bit her lip to keep from giving into the urge to sink her teeth into her wrist, so her uncertainty and fear trickled away as she bled.

She breathed in half sigh and half-sob and refocused on her chocolate shake. Supposedly, she was so much stronger now. She *was* stronger. But she was still human. And, sometimes, people took three paces backward before they leaped ten steps forward. For the first time since she started cutting, she wanted to talk to someone about it and admit what she did to herself.

She already knew her triggers—violence against her person—where she had no control over her body or if she lived or died.

She'd tried talking to Dinah last night, but when she blurted that she injured herself to take away pain and humiliation, her mother had looked at her and said, "It's a simple decision. All you have to do is stop. It isn't like cutting yourself will prevent men from doing what they want to you." She'd hugged Meggie and kissed her cheek. "I hope this has helped."

Then, she'd started talking about something else.

Meggie winced, her shame deepening at the bluntness of Dinah's words and wishing with everything in her that it was so simple.

BY THE TIME SHE LEFT, NIGHT HAD FALLEN, AND Christopher hadn't once called or texted her. Though CJ was being weaned, she nursed him at night, so she needed to get home.

"Meggie?"

At the sound of her name, she paused in the opening of her car door. Bin stepped into the brightness of the parking lot light and smiled at her. He held a box in his hand.

She raised her chin and brushed some of her hair behind her ear. "Hey, Bin."

He nodded and held the box out to her. "Prez asked me to find you and give this to you. An apology, he said."

Meggie debated on whether to take the big shiny box with a golden bow from Bin. Christopher usually gave her his gifts himself, especially for an apology. Then, again, he hadn't been acting normal toward her, so this was probably legitimate.

She grabbed it from him, surprised at the weight. "Thanks."

"No problem, Meggie." With a last smile, he backed away. "See you around."

More like see you tomorrow.

Grumpy, Meggie opened the back door of her Beetle. She sat the gift next to CJ's car seat since it was too big to fit inside it, got in the driver's side, and sped back to the compound, relieved to see her husband's Harley. Not that they'd talk much, but, at least, he was home.

Most of the bikes she recognized, so it looked like nothing big was going on tonight. Fine. Maybe, she could take Christopher to the room and open the present with him since he'd sent Bin to give it to her. Unlikely. This was just Christopher's way of checking up on her.

Holding the gift, she rushed inside. Christopher stood at the bar and glanced over his shoulder, narrowing his eyes at her.

"Megs!" Johnnie called from their usual table where he and Digger sat playing dominoes.

Christopher stalked to her. "What the fuck you got, Megan?"

She stomped around him, to the nearest table and set the box down. "What do you think?" she snapped, yanking the bow off and lifting the lid, barely paying attention to the dark plastic bag. "The gift you sent Bin to deliver to me."

She jerked the bag open and staggered back.

"I ain't send no motherfucker—"

Meggie's ear-splitting scream cut him off.

Inside the box, a severed head stared at her.

Chapter 16

Outlaw

G RABBING MEGAN, CHRISTOPHER WRAPPED HIS ARMS around her. His boys were already swarming around the gift while he tried to calm his wife down. She was shaking like a fucking leaf.

He threaded his fingers through her hair, grabbed each side of her head and forced her to look at him.

"Megan, baby, calm down. It's okay." It sure the fuck *wasn't* okay. Motherfucking Bin was a fucking dead ass. He sent a fucking *head* to Megan? That motherfucker would soon fucking miss his. "It's okay," he repeated, the pieces finally fucking falling into place. No fucking wonder Cee Cee always seemed one fucking step ahead. Bin was clueing him the fuck in.

She pounded on his chest. "A head? I was given somebody's head! A head." He forced her head against his chest and kissed her crown while she sobbed against him. "H-he g-gave me a head. That's not okay."

"No, baby. You right. It ain't."

"Hey, Megs." Johnnie held out a glass of alcohol. Whisky, probably, since that's what he preferred. "Drink this to calm yourself."

She didn't move, just clung to Christopher.

"Oh my God," she shrieked. "I had that in my car. Next to CJ's baby seat. I can't ever get back in that car again."

"C'mon, Meggie, sit down, babe," K-P offered, reaching out for her.

Christopher knocked the man's hand away and threaded his fingers through Megan's hair, murmuring soft words to her.

She buried her face against Christopher's chest like she could make the fucking image of a motherfucker's dead head vanish, but her heart pounded hard enough to break her fucking ribcage. Wetness spread over his stomach, and he knew immediately her milk was letting down.

He guided her to a chair and sat her down, then waved Johnnie over. He took the drink, crouched down, and held the glass to her lips. "Drink," he ordered.

She took a sip, swallowed, and coughed.

"Drink it all," he said again.

She held her breath and finished it in two gulps, gagging after the last drop. "Why would Bin do that?" Her blue eyes looked at him with all the trust in the world, like he had all the answers to life's biggest mysteries. "Is he working with Cee Cee?"

Probably. No use lying to Megan. She always figured shit out. "That's what the fuck my ass thinkin', Megan."

She threw her arms around him and started to sob all over again. "Oh God! Oh God! Oh God! What…Oh God, suppose that had been you?" she cried. "Suppose he'd sent me your head?"

The moment she said the words, she leaned over and hurled.

Not that he blamed her. He'd hurled once or twice himself after kills. He scooped her into his arms, needing to comfort her in private. He indicated the vomit with a nod. "Clean this shit the fuck up. Ima be back soon."

Inside their room, she stood in silence and allowed him to undress her, just Zombie fucking staring straight the fuck ahead. He unbuttoned her shirt, the swells of her breasts rising from her pretty lace bra. Her chin wobbled, tears slipping from her eyes. He thumbed them away. Urging her down on the bed, he crouched and untied her sneakers, pulling them off her feet and repeating the action with her thick brown socks.

"Up."

She sniffled, her lips trembling. "I can do this myself."

He cursed at the distance in her tone. Fuck him, if he didn't get his shit together, he'd lose her. He saw it in her frown and the complete withdrawal in her features. His phone beeped a text message alert and Megan pulled back further, her gaze accusing. He hadn't been spending time with her and she hadn't been fucking him. It wasn't a big fucking stretch to imagine the conclusions she was reaching.

He remained in front of her, so she wouldn't use the distraction of his reading the message to slip the fuck away.

Hello, boy. Smiley fucking face and then, son. *Your cunt got her present?* A winking fucking face. *She's your weakest link. SMH.*

What the fuck? SMH? Smah? What the fuck ever that bullshit meant.

I wanted her to see how I'm going to send her head to you.

"MOTHERFUCKER!" Christopher snarled.

She served her purpose. Gave you a son. Me, a grandson. Now, it's time to get rid of her. I'll give you the chance to do it. Or I'll have to do it myself, son.

Another motherfucking smiley face.

Christopher trembled with rage." Go take a fuckin' shower, Megan," he ordered.

She didn't utter a word, just got up and stumbled to the fucking bathroom.

Christopher didn't have time to do bullshit fucking texts, so he dialed the fucking number. Motherfucker didn't answer. It went to fucking voicemail and Christopher's stomach curdled, listening to the man's fucking voice.

It beeped.

"Listen up, you motherfuckin', dirty dog, fuckin' fuckhead." Christopher drew in a harsh breath, fury pounding through his body. "I fuckin' owe your ass for a lotta fuckin' shit. Ima see you pay for every infuckinfraction. You havin' a walkin' dead fuckhead from my fuckin' club terrorizin' my fuckin' wife? A lil advice, assfuck. Start diggin' your motherfuckin' grave. If efuckinuff of your fuckin' ass left, I'm handpickin' a fuckin' hole and droppin' pieces of you in that motherfucker."

Christopher disconnected the call, breathing deep and kicking his desk chair into the entertainment center. What fucking good was his network doing if none of them had smoked out one fucking shithead?

Thrusting his hands through his hair, he listened for sounds of the shower. Heard no fucking water running. Started forward. And stopped when another fucking message came through.

Your tone was disrespectful to your old man, son.

Christopher growled. *Fuck off, motherfucker.*

Your brothers would never talk to me like that.

He had brothers? *You a punk ass bitch, fuckin over women cuz you ain't got the fuckin balls to stand up to men.*

You're pissing me off, boy.

And? Did he really think Christopher gave a fuck? *Tough fuckin shit, old man.*

I came in peace. The Dwellers are big. I wanted our clubs to form an alliance. Your attitude is heading us to war instead. All because of pussy.

My ass your worst fuckin nightmare, motherfucker. You ain't knowin what the fuck you done threatenin my girl. When I get my fuckin hands on your fuckin ass, Ima start off poundin you with a meat fuckin tenderizer. You feel me, motherfucker?

Loud and clear, Christopher Caldwell.

I fuckin hate you, Sebastian Caldwell. The fuckin universe ain't fuckin big enough for us to share fuckin space.

Sad face.

Stop with those stupid fuckin faces, fuckhead. That's some pussified, fucked up, pissin-me-the-fuck-off-more type of shit.

Well, my boy, you just bought your bitch some time. For now. So bring me whatever you have.

Tell me what fuckin rat hole you hidin in and Ima fuckin' bring everythin I got.

Nothing. After twenty minutes of fucking texting, the motherfucker just—

Megan is safe. For now. Until the best man wins, so, if you want me so bad, fucking find me.

T HE SOUND OF THE SHOWER BROKE THROUGH Christopher's rage. He realized he'd been standing up and wrestling with the urge to *kill* for five minutes after the final text came through.

He needed to see to Megan. Stalking to the bathroom, he threw open the door.

And screeched to a fucking halt, the air whooshing from his lungs fast enough to cave in his chest.

Megan stood in the bathtub, out of reach of the showerhead, her thighs and arms dripping blood. She held the small knife in her hand, fingers trembling. Just staring.

Christopher wondered if she even saw anything.

His anger died and his entire focus zeroed in on his wife. He swallowed and tugged at his hair, unable to think of the right words to help her. He'd read up on self-injury four or five months ago. Should he demand she stop? How could he demand something that eased her hurt and pain? Her trauma. Besides, it would only add to her shame.

The knife clanked to the bottom of the tub and Christopher jumped, his heart hurting for his Megan.

"Christopher?" she gasped and shielded her body with her hands and arms, bending over to hide her thighs. The water rained on her head, but blood still dripped from her arms and legs. She turned her back to him. "Go away."

He backed two steps away then halted. Instead of leaving, he undressed and joined her in the shower. After turning off the water, he picked up the knife and tossed it to the bathroom floor. Placing a hand on her shoulder, he turned her to him.

"Get out."

"Ain't fuckin' happenin', Megan."

She blinked away the tears rushing to her eyes. "You can't see—"

He took her into his arms and kissed the top of her head. "I already fuckin' saw, baby," he said quietly, his dick rising between them. Fuck him, but she'd chained the gate to her Promised Land for two fucking weeks. He couldn't help his fucking cock stand now that he held her so close.

"I-I don't know what to say. Please. I-I'm sorry. I can't answer—"

Christopher leaned away from her and tipped her chin up, but she kept her lashes lowered. "Look at me."

Her nostrils flaring, she raised a miserable blue gaze to him. He bent and kissed her lips.

"Explain shit when you fuckin' ready. And, if you ain't ever ready, I gotta accept that shit, too." He sighed. "I drink like a motherfucker, baby. Yeah, the shit taste good, but it get me through what the fuck I gotta do. Hear me?"

She nodded. "Yes."

"Aunt Mary my favorite fuckin' relative in the whole fuckin' world. I just pull her out her lil' baggie, roll her the fuck up, suck on her, and all my fuckin' issues go. I cope my way. You cope your fuckin' way. Ain't meanin' I ain't wanna fuckin' help you. And it ain't fuckin' mean I ain't feelin' each of them cuts I see on your beautiful skin, straight the fuck in my gut. Now you see why I ain't wantin' to stand in a church next to you? *My* ass the fuckin' blight causin' you to do this shit—"

The words seemed to snap her out of the safe place inside of herself she'd gone to. She stood on her tiptoes. "No. Never. I love you with all my heart and soul. But…but…God, Christopher…a…a h-head. Only the whites of his eyes—"

He shut her up with a kiss. "Shh. You fine. I saw that dead fuckin' head too, refuckinmember?"

She pounded her hand against his chest. "Suppose it had been you?"

It could've just as easily been her. That was Cee Cee's ultimate goal.

Fuck! Christopher wouldn't fucking think about that shit because he couldn't afford anything to distract him. Leaning forward, he turned on the shower and urged Megan under it. He soaped her and washed her hair, then raced through his own shower.

By the time he finished, Megan had stepped out. His knife remained on the floor. Grabbing a towel, he scrubbed it over his wet head and settled it on his neck before wrapping another one around his hips.

He wouldn't comment on the state of his dick.

When he walked into the bedroom, she turned from where she stood in the middle of the room. She came to him and reached up to touch his jaw. He kissed her fingertips and smiled at her. Tears filled her eyes again. "I love you, Christopher," she whispered.

He bent and kissed her, not wanting to admit how fucking shaken he was. This was a message for him, and he was fucking grateful it hadn't been her head in that fucking box. He crushed her to him. "I love you, too, baby."

She stood on her tiptoes and kissed him, her hand grasping his dick and jerking it. He lifted her up and she wrapped her legs around his waist, her mouth devouring his. He buried himself inside her hot body and thrust hard in and out of her, the sting of her nails in his biceps and the bite of her teeth on his lips pushing him to deeper drives.

He shoved his hand between them and rubbed her pussy to make her come. When she did, he plunged into her one, final time, exploding inside her as she sucked his neck. Once he reached the bed with her, he got her comb and pulled it through her damp hair, kissing down the side of her neck, around her shoulders, along her hairline. Setting the comb aside, he guided her onto her back and entered her again, blocking out everything but the blueness of her eyes telling him all he needed to know about how she felt about him.

His conscience pricked him that he'd used this opportunity to fuck her, but he flipped it off. They both needed the connection and the comfort of each other's bodies. Now, though, he held her, her head in the crook of his arm, massaging her scalp.

"It makes everything go away," she said in a small, soft voice. "The cutting."

He rearranged their bodies, so they faced one another. He settled his hand on her hip. "Yeah?"

She nodded. "Just for a little bit. Whatever I'm going through, what I do takes is all away." She drew in a deep breath. "The sting washes it all away and I can refocus on that. I have control in those moments. It's the only way I knew how to cope. It's…I shouldn't be doing this now. I should learn to shoot the gun. Instead of something so…so…I'm so sorry, Christopher."

He knuckled her cheek. "I gotcha, baby. Don't ever think otherfuckinwise. If you gotta apologize to me cuz you goin' through shit, my ass some fuckin' fucked up pussy."

She giggled.

"There's my girl," he whispered. "And her beautiful fuckin' laugh." He kissed her again. "I'm your man, Megan. You like the air I need to breathe, so Ima be the strength you need to carry you."

HALF AN HOUR LATER, CHRISTOPHER PAUSED AT THE bedroom door. "Be right back, baby."

He'd hoped she would've fallen asleep, so he could get to work and tear this motherfucking town apart to find two motherfuckers at the top of his hit list.

But she wasn't going to sleep, leaving him little choice with what he needed to do. Once she nodded, he headed to the main room. His boys were waiting for him at the bar.

"How's Megs?"

"How the fuck you think, John Boy? Shook the fuck up."

Johnnie scowled at him. "I'm as worried about her as you are."

Fucking doubtful. Instead of answering, Christopher signaled Mortician to the end of the bar.

"Prez?"

"Fix me up your fizzy special," he ordered, low. "But make the shit light cuz Megan just needin' to sleep a few fuckin' hours. Hear me?"

Mortician's eyes widened.

"Do it, motherfucker." He spoke through gritted teeth, not wanting to be overheard. Christopher felt shitty enough that he was about to drug his wife.

"You sure, Outlaw?"

Christopher rubbed his eyes. "Yeah, Mort. I gotta get them assfucks and Megan ain't 'bout to fall the fuck to sleep." He pounded on the counter. "Fuck off and follow my order."

While Mortician prepared Megan's sleeping potion, Christopher stalked to Johnnie. "Time for different fuckin' shit,

John Boy. Get a investigator. Relyin' on just member recommendations ain't cuttin' it no more. I want full fuckin' background checks on every motherfucker involved in our operations. Put a fuckin' attorney on the payroll. A fuckin' girl lawyer to dick whip and do legal work if we fuckin' need it. Hear me?"

"Here you go, Prez," Mortician announced before Johnnie answered.

His cousin lifted a brow when Mortician slid the Styrofoam cup to Christopher.

"You hear what the fuck I say, John Boy?"

Gaze focused on the cup, Johnnie gave him a curt nod.

"Be fuckin' ready to ride in thirty."

Megan didn't do shit like what he held in the cup. Once she drank it, she'd be out in minutes. Christopher sighed. Just another fucking sin to add to his list of many.

Chapter 17

Outlaw

CHRISTOPHER HADN'T BEEN ABLE TO JUST GIVE MEGAN the drink. Instead, he'd let her nurse CJ first and get his boy to sleep. Once she finished, he'd given her the potion, now watered down, which made him feel a little better.

"What's this?" she'd asked, sniffing it in suspicion.

"Somethin' to relax you." When it looked like she was going to argue, he added, "make you forget them images in your head."

"Okay."

Watered down or not, she'd been out within fifteen minutes. He'd ordered Dinah into the room and told her not to disturb Megan under any circumstances, although he doubted she could. Megan was out fucking cold.

With his wife seen to and after determining the head belonged to the dumb ass he'd used the ice pick on, Christopher called

Traveler and ordered him to the clubhouse, demanding he bring Bin along. Not surprising when Traveler arrived, he'd been unable to find Bin.

"Mortician, take this motherfucker to the meat shack," Christopher ordered now, close to midnight.

"The meat shack?" Traveler said, losing every drop of his color. Or, maybe, the fucking blood evaporated from his head. He looked like he'd fucking faint at any moment. "Why?"

Christopher grabbed him by the neck and banged his head against a table. "Cuz I fuckin' say so, motherfucker."

"Please." Blood slid down the side of Traveler's face from the cut that opened. "I swear. Please. Whatever I did, give me a chance."

Mortician nodded toward the door. "You can walk. Or I can get you there my way."

Traveler swallowed. "W-walk."

"Smart man," Mortician said.

Christopher took out a cigarette. "Strap him up the fuck up when he get there, Mort."

"No!" Traveler screamed, falling to his knees. "No! Please."

Lighting his cigarette and taking a drag, Christopher pushed forward. He paused in front of Traveler, took another drag, then kicked him in the nuts. "You brought that motherfucker in, yeah?"

"I don't know!" he sobbed between his gasps of pain. "I…who?"

"Bin!" Christopher snarled. "Who the fuck you think?"

"Yeah, but—"

Christopher kicked him again. "But fuckin' nothing. You protectin' him. You know where the fuck he at."

"I don't! I swear! God, I swear. I didn't have time to stop at all the places he might be. You told me to come here as soon as I could."

Christopher flicked ashes and let them rain onto Traveler, then waved Val over. The Road Captain handed the bag containing the head to Christopher.

Hanging his cigarette between his lips, Christopher pulled it out, crouched down and sat it in front of Traveler. He screamed at the top of his lungs.

"Shut the fuck up, pussy," Christopher snarled. "You wake up Megan and Ima cut your fuckin' tongue out." He shoved Traveler back down and held him there by placing his booted foot on the man's neck, leaving him no choice but to lay next to Megan's gift. "John Boy?"

"Yeah?"

"This motherfucker eyes open?" *He* sure the fuck wouldn't have *his* open with a dead fucking head staring at him.

"No."

He applied slight pressure to Traveler's neck. "Open them motherfuckers, Traveler."

"Please, Outlaw. My girl having a baby and—"

"Bin brought my girl this fuckin' prop for a horror movie. Only it ain't a prop. The shit fuckin' real. How the fuck you think Megan reacted seein' this?" He shook his foot. "Huh?"

"I swear…I swear…I didn't know nothing—"

"You fuckin' know now. You gonna spill the places where Bin fuckin' hang, then hope like a motherfucker he at one. You takin' his place if he ain't. While we out bein' private fuckin' investigators, you and the head sharin' space in the meat shack."

Outlaw

I T TOOK ALMOST ALL NIGHT, BUT THEY FINALLY FOUND Bin across state lines in Portland, fucking some bitch.

He pulled out of her and raised his hands, while the chick scrambled to close her legs and cover herself.

Christopher trained his nine on Bin, frowning at the scent hanging in the air. Sex musk and body odor. Johnnie wrinkled his nose and leaned on the plain wooden dresser. Val shook his head while Digger searched through Bin's wallet and pocketed the man's piece. Afterwards, Digger snatched the bitch's purse from the top of a chest and poured the contents on the bed.

Bin swallowed and held up his hands. "I can explain," he said, his voice trembling.

"Ain't rememberin' askin' you to." Handing his gun to Johnnie, Christopher snatched the man's pants and threw them at him. He got his boots and removed his blade before picking up

Bin's cut and folding it over his arm. Wouldn't fucking need it where he was going. "Get fuckin' dressed."

Bin's hands shook and his erection deflated like a pin had been stuck in it. The idea had merit. "Prez, please. I needed the money."

Christopher glared at him. "We got efuckinnuff business to keep everyfuckinbody flush with bills and I pay you a fuckin' mint as one of Megan guards."

"Outlaw—"

"Shut the fuck up. Enjoy these last moments while your body infuckintact and stop fuckin' blubberin'."

He grabbed Christopher's hands and dropped to his knees. "Prez, please."

Apparently, he thought Christopher was a fucking moron and he needed the words switched around for understanding.

"Please, Prez." He sobbed, grabbed Christopher's legs and began kissing his boots. "Please."

Christopher kicked him away, embarrassed on behalf of the dickhead. "What the fuck wrong with you? Have some fuckin' dignity, assfuck."

"Pride goes out the door when you're begging for your life," Bin sobbed. His dignity dropped ten degrees further when snot dripped down his nose. He rubbed his arm across his face.

Christopher shook his head, disgusted.

"Cee Cee's from the East Coast," Bin volunteered. "Somewhere in Virginia. His MC is the American Scorpions." He rubbed his snotty ass arm on his shirt. "He just wanted me to show you how fuckin' weak your bitch is. That's it. I swear! God, I swear!"

Christopher backhanded him. "What the fuck he here for?"

It took a moment for Bin to answer. Christopher's blow left him stunned and blinking his eyes to stay focused. "For an alliance with you," the motherfucker sniffled.

"Ain't ever happenin', but you ain't fuckin' thought my ass needed that fuckin' information. A motherfucker skulkin' the fuck 'round, with fuckin' designs on the fuckin' club?"

"Outlaw—"

Christopher hit him again. "Where the fuck he stayin'?"

Bin rattled off the address of the motel, two fucking states away in Northern Cali.

"Time for your fuckin' dissection," Christopher announced, knowing he had calls to make in Cali.

Bin sobbed again. "Please, Outlaw, I gave you the information to find Cee Cee."

"Ain't givin' a fuck. Befuckinsides, you holdin' back, so we takin' our time in the meat shack 'til you give up the fuckin' all the info you got."

Bin shook his head, his reddish-brown eyes filling with tears, his chalky white skin turning pink. Fucking Vampire motherfucker. Christopher might need a fucking stake to fuck him up.

Bin pointed to the bitch. "Her. The bitch there. She working with Cee Cee, too. She was supposed to get Meggie and bring her to him."

Christopher drew in a deep breath and narrowed his eyes at the whore.

"You fucking asshole!" she screamed. "Telling on me." She glared at Christopher, hatred brimming in her black eyes. "Not like you're going to do anything, but give me a warning," she spat. "We know the Dwellers don't hurt women."

Yeah, when a motherfucker got on the bad side of other clubs, they jeopardized everybody close to them, females included. Wives. Girlfriends. Sisters. Mothers. Dogs. Cats. And just like that was known, the Dwellers' stance was known, too. *How fucking ever…* "Bitch, you was comin' to hurt my wife. Ain't no fuckin' forgivin' that."

Snatching his nine from Johnnie, he pointed it at her head and fired, glad he'd attached his silencer before riding out.

Bin stared at the bitch, sprawled back, the side of her head gaping open from the hollow point bullet.

The scent of urine hit Christopher's nostrils and he glanced down. Fucking Bin. He'd pissed himself.

Christopher rolled his eyes. "Val," he called, watching as the man began to wrap the girl in the comforter. "Stay befuckinhind 'til one of us bring a vehicle for transport and disposal."

"No problem, Outlaw."

Once they were outside, Johnnie grabbed Bin's shoulder and guided him to his bike. "You a lucky fuck. You ridin' bitch with me." He pulled on his gloves and helmet. "Try not to piss me the fuck off, so I ain't accidentally pushin' you off and in the pathway of the boys' bikes."

"Damn, man," Digger said, securing his helmet on his head. "I might fucking prefer getting run over, then ending up with parts of my ass as some present for Cee Cee in a fucking box."

Chapter 18

Meggie

THE NEXT EVENING, MEGGIE PICKED AT THE MASHED potatoes and fried oysters she'd cooked for herself and Christopher. The two of them sat alone in the main room. Most of the day, the place had been empty. Unless invited, only the officers were allowed on the premises. Christopher had been on his phone when she'd awakened in the early afternoon.

She still dragged with fatigue from whatever had been in the fizzy Kool-Aid-looking drink Christopher had asked her to drink.

Rigid with tension, Christopher sat next to her, one of his guns right in front of them. He'd just gotten through cleaning and reloading it. The door opened and Meggie snapped her head in that direction. She smiled in relief when Stretch escorted Traveler in. The man's face was bruised and bloodied. Her smile faded and her belly clenched.

"Thanks, Stretch," Christopher grumbled.

"Meggie," Traveler said after Stretch left.

She swallowed. "Hey, Traveler."

Christopher pointed to Traveler. "Sit the fuck down," he ordered, then focused on her. "Go."

Traveler glanced between them, then gazed around like he was looking for something. "Where are the others, Prez?"

"Aintcha fuckin' business."

Anger rushed across Traveler's face. Anger—and hatred. Alarm raced through Meggie, but the looks dropped from the biker's face so fast, she wondered if she'd hallucinated.

"Brought me in to finish me off?" A muscle ticked in Traveler's jaw. "Having to watch Bin get—"

"Shut the fuck up," Christopher snarled, distracted by her presence and another text message. "I say fuckin' go, Megan."

Having to watch Bin get…Don't go there, Meggie. She didn't have to be told what Traveler must've had to watch. The sight of the head in the box flashed in her mind and her stomach churned.

Traveler scrubbed a hand over his eyes. He looked exhausted, plain wrung out. "Can I have a drink, Prez?"

"Fuck no."

Traveler stuffed his hands into his pockets. "Just one before you put me to—"

"Stop bein' a fuckin' idiot, Traveler," Christopher snapped, throwing his phone aside. "If I wanted you fuckin' dead, I woulda done it earlier." He climbed to his feet and glared at her since she hadn't moved, but he turned away and unease slid through Meggie.

He trusted Traveler or else he wouldn't have turned his back. But the mean way the man was looking at her husband scared her.

Christopher made for an easy target right now. He wasn't even armed. Meggie licked her lips, her heart beginning to pound.

"Get the fuck out, Megan. I gotta talk to Traveler 'bout a run."

In slow motion, Christopher's words reached her. In a fast blur, Traveler opened his cut and pulled out a gun.

She squeaked, but no sound came out.

But, then, Traveler raised the weapon and she reacted. Doing the only thing she could. She grabbed Christopher's gun, copied what she remembered seeing him do.

And pulled the trigger just as Traveler fired.

Outlaw

CHRISTOPHER SPUN AT THE SOUND OF THE GUNSHOTS, one bullet flying right the fuck past his head, his sudden movement putting him out of the bullet's deadly path. And the other?

The other?

Fuck him, Megan stood, sheet-white, his nine in her shaking hand. Hand? Her entire fucking body shook.

Traveler wheezed on the floor, blood blooming on the front of his shirt, gun still clutched in his hand.

"He was going to shoot you," she said in a high, I'm-about-to-lose-my-shit voice. "I killed him."

Christopher reclaimed his gun, fired two shots in Traveler's head, and said, "Nope. I offed the motherfucker. Your conscience clear, baby."

She stared at him a moment, her mouth moving but not one fucking sound coming out. Her eyes rolled back in her head, and he just managed to reach her before she fucked herself up with a fall to the floor.

He brought her to their bedroom and laid her on the bed, staring at her. Right now, he was too jacked up with adrenaline from the past twenty-four hours to feel any regret on her behalf. She'd shot a motherfucker to save Christopher's life and that impressed the fuck out of him.

Tucking her in and kissing her lips as her eyes fluttered open, he called Mortician. He and Digger had their hands full already, but Traveler had to disappear, just like the other two.

After he explained the situation to Mort, Christopher disconnected the call and sat next to Megan.

"You okay?" he asked gruffly. She was still pale as well as droopy from the fizzy hangover, but she nodded.

"I-I'll be fine," she whispered and blinked. "I guess I failed the test for Bad Asses."

Christopher frowned. "What the fuck you talkin' 'bout, Megan?"

"Sh-shooting somebody to s-save your life and then f-fainting."

He stretched out next to her and gathered her in his arms. "In my book, you the baddest lil' motherfucker alive, baby."

She smiled sleepily at him and curled against him.

Stroking her hair, he kissed the top of her head, then sighed. "Megan, if I gotta get a fuckin' shrink on the payroll, lemme know. 'Cuz shit like this fuck with people. A lil' life-long therapy might be on the menu for you. Fuck what happened to you befuckinfore we met. The past day been one tough fuckin' problem after a-fuckin-nother, startin' with that fuckin' dead head." He tightened his grip on her, Cee Cee's intentions for her…Nope, wasn't going there. "Lemme make this shit clear 'bout that shot you gave Traveler. You disabled the motherfucker. That's all. He coulda survived. Okay?"

Until he saw exactly where the wound Megan had given Traveler was found, he couldn't be sure.

She remained silent for a couple minutes and then, "I would do it again to save you, Christopher," she said softly. "I aimed for the biggest area on his body to increase my odds of hitting him."

Christopher processed her words for a few minutes, nuzzling her neck when he felt her tremble. "You tellin' me you woulda capped him in the head if you had better aim?"

Instead of answering, she pulled away, dark circles around her red-rimmed eyes. More effects from what he'd given her. "I stabbed Thomas. Remember? To vindicate my mother."

"Yeah, I fuckin' remember." Christopher didn't mean to sound so annoyed but the thought of her step fuckhead put him in a bad mood on a good day. He urged her head back to the crook of his arm. "You the lil' pain in the ass motherfucker tellin' me letcha step fuckhead live. I fuckin' stuck to your fuckin' wishes and look what the fuck happen." He'd almost lost her. "Now, you sayin' you stabbin' him cuz of Dinah."

"I would prefer if everybody that does us something could be handled through law enforcement and the courts. Bad guys should be dealt with legally."

"My ass a fuckin' bad motherfucker—"

"No, you're not!" she said fiercely. "You're not understanding what I'm saying."

"I sure the fuck ain't," he said as gently as possible, but her explanation just reminded him of how different they were. She was young and idealistic, with her whole life ahead of her. He was a cynical motherfucker with a big fucking target on his back. He wasn't sure why he was holding onto her so tightly. She deserved a life of peace and happiness. Safety.

"I'm glad I didn't kill Traveler. I didn't really want to kill Thomas, even though I always said if I had the courage I *would* kill him. But it was just in the heat of the moment. You know how that is? When someone does violence against you, you overreact and make threats you don't intend to follow through on."

Nope, he sure the fuck didn't know. He had not a fucking problem offing a motherfucker.

She shuddered. "If-if…Traveler was a threat to you. I didn't think when I saw him with his gun. I reacted. To protect you. Save your life. I don't know if I was sure of my aim, if I would've fired at his head."

A part of Christopher hoped not. Call him a crazy, contradictory motherfucker, but he wanted her to keep her innocent sweetness. He *needed* her to keep it. That's why he protected her as much as possible, especially from other bitches.

He'd asked her to learn to shoot a gun and, yet he didn't want to look at her and know she was carrying.

"You couldna shot that motherfucker in the head," he said with certainty, still shocked that she'd even think such a possibility. "You ain't even wantin' a fuckin' piece."

A little snore reached his ears and he couldn't stop his chuckle, despite his annoyance at her conflicting ideas. She'd fallen asleep, well-deserved after playing Annie fucking Oakley. Easing his arm from under her head, Christopher got up and made his way back to the main room, where Mortician and Digger had arrived.

Mortician snapped his plastic gloves into place and looked at Christopher, reclaiming the cigarette hanging from his lips. "You always got to do head fucking shots, Prez?"

"Yeah, Outlaw," Digger grunted, maneuvering Traveler's body onto the tarp they'd brought in. "This chest wound would've done the job and only left us to deal with blood right now."

"No the fuck that chest wound *ain't* woulda done the fuckin' job," Christopher snapped, advancing on Digger, "and Megan ever hear you say that bullshit, Ima cut your fuckin' tongue out. She feelin' bad efuckinnuff 'bout shootin' this motherfucker."

Digger's eyes widened, before his brow creased into a frown. "Meggie shot Traveler?"

Christopher glared at Mortician.

"Sorry, brother," he said with a shrug. "Didn't get a chance to clue him in to all the details." Mortician finished his cigarette while he filled Digger in on what Christopher had told him. "So, Prez right," he concluded. "We can't have Meggie girl thinking she killed this dumb fuck."

The door opened and Val stomped in, sparing a brief glance at dead Traveler, then stomping toward the hallway.

"Hey!" Christopher called, concerned at Val's attitude. He never ignored workplace situations. "What the fuck your problem?"

Val spun around. "A bitch named Zoann my fucking problem," he roared.

"Say somethin' I ain't fuckin' knowin'," Christopher said with a snort.

"I explained to her I couldn't visit Ryan today like I promised Ophelia because of club business. That shit set her the fuck off more than anything else."

Christopher didn't respond. Val needed to get his anger off his chest. When his Road Captain fell silent, he nodded to Mortician and Digger, then pointed to Traveler. "Get him the fuck outside. We got another two or three hours before he start stiffenin'. I need a fuckin' drink." Which was what dead ass had interrupted Christopher from doing in the first place.

Val remained in the entryway, clenching and unclenching his fists, pissed like a motherfucker.

"Sit the fuck down, assfuck. If talkin' 'bout the bitch help, I'm all fuckin' ears." Christopher grabbed a couple bottles of tequila and headed for his favorite table, in the corner, where he could observe every-fucking-thing.

Digger opened the door while Mortician hefted Traveler's tarp covered body into his arms and carried him outside, allowing frigid air to blast in for the moments it took the two brothers to complete the task.

Val slammed four glasses on the table, grabbed the bottle—swigged from it—then filled the glasses to the brim. "Don't mind me. I'm ready to head to Cali whenever you ready to roll, Outlaw."

"Just waitin' for the confirmation call, Val." Christopher drank from his glass before getting a smoke. "I ain't trustin' fuckin' Bin and what dead motherfucker sayin' before he got fuckin' fucked up. I think the motherfucker helpin' Cee Cee set some type of fuckin' trap for my ass."

"Once Cee Cee taken care of, you going to be…" Mortician's voice trailed off and he drew in a deep breath, so Christopher guessed what the question might be.

"Stay outta me and Megan business."

Digger stretched, then stood and shook his leg. "I've been sitting five fucking minutes and the bitch fell asleep on me." He shot Christopher an irritated look. "You need better workplace conditions, Prez. The meat shack not big enough to handle the volume we saw today."

Mortician slapped the side of Digger's head. "Stop being a pussy."

"We not trying to get in your business with your woman," Val began, squirming in his seat. "But Meggie don't deserve the shit you been handing her. She don't do anything but love you and your boy and care about us motherfuckers."

"And that whiny bitch K-P sniffing after," Digger added. "I can't see how he even think about fucking her. Instead of screaming when her pussy feeling good, she probably burst into fucking tears."

Christopher frowned and released smoke through his nose. "Yo, fuck face, you *is* talkin' 'bout Megan Ma pussy. Somethin' I ain't even wantin' to think 'bout in any way, so shut the fuck up." He glanced at Val. As much as he should step back, so her and his boy could leave and have happy, safe lives, he couldn't. He loved her, his sweet angel. "As soon as Cee Cee fuckin' grounded, Ima make everythin' up to her. Big Joe grounded. After Cee Cee fucked up, we gonna be all outta fathers needin' groundin' for one reason or afuckinnother, so we gonna be straight."

Chapter 19

Meggie

EGGIE HAD HAD ENOUGH OF CHRISTOPHER'S DISTANCE AND attitude. After being so sweet to her after *The Incident*, he'd withdrawn completely. And, now, two days later, he wasn't spending any time with her. Or even at the club. He hadn't been responsible for any of what had happened and neither had she, so she couldn't understand why he'd retreat from her again.

Fed up, she decided to follow him in one of the spare cars on this particular cold, drizzly morning. She wasn't sure what she expected. Deep down, she didn't believe he was being unfaithful, but, then again, Christopher always did the unexpected. Her heart beat in a painful rhythm at the thought of *her* Outlaw putting his body inside someone other than herself. Even discovering he was confiding in another woman would break Meggie's heart. He was a man who held a lot close to the chest, but she also knew he'd confided in Kiera and Ellen before he'd met her, so, whether he realized it or not, he liked having the softness of a woman to lean on.

She swallowed and nausea bubbled to the surface, tears lurking at the corners of her eyes. Perfect. Just freaking perfect. The best way to get Christopher's attention would be to burst into tears after suffering a bout of morning sickness. Morning sickness he knew nothing about since he hadn't been around when it began.

Somehow, while ruminating and driving—*yes, really smart Meggie*—she'd managed to lose sight of his Harley. She sniffled and glanced around. The only reason—other than a woman—Christopher would be on this side of town was to visit the cemetery. Doubting he'd be there, but deciding to pass by anyway, she swiped at her tears. Within minutes, she was pulling in front of the place where both her father and his mother were buried. She squinted her eyes and started when she saw the chrome in Christopher's bike brightening the dreary day.

Placing a hand on her belly to will the nausea away, she sat for a few moments. Reasonably certain she wouldn't throw up everything and her guts, she stepped out of the car and slammed the door. The cool droplets hit her warm skin and the wind lifted her hair. She wished she'd remembered to bring a jacket, but she'd been so determined to find Christopher. After getting CJ to her mom and throwing up, she'd run out of the club in time to see which way Christopher had turned, glad he'd already chosen a temporary car for her. She didn't have to wait on someone to find her a vehicle, since her tainted Beetle had already disappeared. She'd probably broken a few speeding laws to catch up to Christopher, but now, she'd found him.

Wrapping her arms around her waist, she made her way to Patricia's grave, surprised when she didn't find her husband there. She turned and glanced at the small rise in the distance where her father rested. She couldn't see the expression on Christopher's face, but she saw him staring in her direction, the wind whipping his black hair back and forth.

She scowled when she saw him take a long drink from a bottle. It was so early in the morning for him to be drinking. For the past few months, he'd waited until late afternoon before imbibing. As she glanced between the pathway and her husband, she walked toward him, reaching him moments later. A frown creased his brow, drawing his dark eyebrows together, the obscene length of his lashes ringing guarded green eyes.

"What are you doing here?" she asked, a graveyard the absolute last place she'd expected to find him. "Is this where you've been disappearing to every day?"

He shrugged and tasted his tequila again, his big body tense. "Yeah."

Meggie heaved in a breath. It was obvious he didn't want to talk. They'd been through too much for him to just shut down like this. Blocking her out was unfair. At least give her the benefit of the doubt and share his problems.

She frowned. "Why?"

"Best place for me to be, Megan."

"A graveyard?"

He rolled his eyes. "Ain't this where the fuck my ass at?" he growled.

"*Jerk!*" she snapped. "I don't need your sarcasm, Christopher Caldwell."

"*Christopher Caldwell?*" He stepped closer to her, finally allowing only inches to separate them instead of three feet. "You my fuckin' ma or some shit?"

"No, but I am your *wife.*"

He flinched and Meggie's heart sank, the fight draining out of her. The new baby was already taking a lot of her energy, so she didn't have the heart to battle its father. "You don't want to be married to me anymore?"

He thrust a hand through his hair and pulled the ends. "Fuck, Megan. What the fuck kinda question is that?"

"A legitimate one," she returned. Try as she might, she couldn't hold her tears back.

"Don't fuckin' cry, baby." He pulled her into his arms and hugged her. "'Specially over a motherfucker like me."

She stood on tiptoes, breathing in the leather he wore and him, her husband. Her Christopher. "I love you," she whispered, nausea roiling through her.

He pressed his lips on the top of her head. "Why? That's what my ass wanna fuckin' know. Why the fuck you love me, Megan? I ain't even guaranteein' you protection against Cee Cee cuz I ain't able to find the motherfucker. My ass supposed to fuckin' protect you. Motherfucker slipped back to Virginia. Which pisses me the fuck off cuz instead of groundin' him myself I had to put a fuckin' hit on that motherfucker." He cursed, his shoulders heaving with disappointment. "So, afuckingain, why you love me? I ain't even takin' care of a motherfucker threatenin' you myself."

She wiggled out of his arms and stepped back to breath in fresh air and stare him in the eyes. He looked uncertain and disgusted. Meggie was sure he was both. He was a strong, willful man and he hated feeling vulnerable. "I love you because of the man you are.

You're strong and no-nonsense, but for those you care about and love, you're always right there. It's your heart and your soul—"

"My soul?" he scoffed and drank again, glaring at her. "My soul, if I got one, blacker than the pits of hell. My soul? What fuckin' soul?"

And, suddenly, Meggie got it. She understood why he'd pulled away and why he'd hurt her and insisted they not have a church wedding. She stepped closer to him and rubbed his cheek, freshly shaved but still so masculine. "If you didn't have a soul, Christopher, you wouldn't have a conscience."

He opened his mouth to speak but she placed her fingers over his lips to forestall his words.

"Shhh," she soothed. "You have both. Whether you know it— or like it. If you didn't have a conscience, the things you do wouldn't eat at you."

"You got me pegged wrong, baby." He finished off the tequila and swiped his hand over his mouth, glowering at her. "Ain't started givin' a fuck 'til I met you." He stomped around her. "Take off your fuckin' blinders, Megan. See my ass for the motherfucker I really be."

"I *do*," she yelled and marched up to him, shoving him backward. "How long have I been living with you, you moron?"

He glared at her, stepped closer. She planted her hands on her hips and raised her chin, narrowing her eyes.

"If you comin' here to—" He raised his hands in the air and spun on his heels.

"I came here for *you*, Outlaw," Meggie called, desperate. To her, he was Christopher. He was human with a heart and a soul, but she had to let him know that she loved *Outlaw* just as much.

He paused and glanced over his shoulder. "What the fuck you call me?"

So now they were playing *that* game? "You're right there. You heard me."

He turned back to her, the rise she stood on giving her a slight advantage in height. Emotions raced across his face, and he swallowed. "Megan, you ain't knowin'—"

"Don't I?" she said quietly. "I know who and what you do, Outlaw." She rocked back on her heels. "Life isn't all sunshine and roses. Do I like to *think* about that side of you? No. I try not to. Even living at the MC, I try to ignore the other side of your activities." She chanced a closer step to him. "If I have to choose you or them, I choose you every time. This is the reality of my life with you. You're not holding me hostage here, Outlaw."

His nostrils flared. "I love you, Megan. I do but—" He stopped, looked into the distance and raised his empty bottle. It was clear he wished he had more.

"But?" she prompted.

"Baby, the day we was supposed to go for that counselin' session…" He closed his eyes and shook his head. "It don't matter, Megan. It don't fuckin' matter. I am who the fuck I am."

"You know what? You're right. You are who you are. Outlaw. Cold blooded killer. MC President. Tough ass. Christopher. Bad boy. Sex god. Husband. Man I love. And father of my children," she said softly, placing a hand on her belly and staring at him.

"You havin' another baby for me?" he whispered, his eyes wide, his expression as incredulous as his voice.

She nodded. "Yes."

He looked up at the cloudy sky. "And you out here in all this fuckin' drizzly weather?"

"Aren't you?" She wouldn't point out she'd also consumed alcohol, smoked a joint, and drank whatever else besides liquor that was in the fizzy drink he'd given to her the other night.

"I ain't like hearin' you call me Outlaw," he admitted, rocking back on his heels.

She cocked her head to the side. "Why not?"

He shrugged. "Cuz I ain't fuckin' Outlaw to you. You ain't never called me fuckin' Outlaw, so you ain't startin' now."

"Then stop acting like Outlaw with me and I'll stop calling you him."

Christopher glowered at her. "I ain't nowhere fuckin' near—"

"You are," she insisted. "Word around town is Outlaw is cold blooded and mean. Doesn't care about anything but his club and his brothers. His word is law and final. He's feared and respected."

Christopher drew in a deep breath. "Fuck me, Megan." He closed his eyes. "How the fuck you do this shit to me?"

"Don't know," she said with a little sniff. "Since I don't know what you're referring to."

"Yeah, you fuckin' do, baby." He walked up to her and set the bottle next to her, then bent and kissed her. She tasted the alcohol on his lips and groaned. He pulled back and sighed. "You gonna fuckin' hurl, aintcha?"

She nodded and turned, falling onto her knees, and throwing up for the third time that morning. Only this time, Christopher crouched beside her and held her hair out of the way, stroking her back until she finished. He pulled her into his arms and drew her onto his lap, kissing her forehead.

"I'm sorry, Megan," he whispered.

Her head lulled against his chest, and she felt drained. "For?"

"For hurtin' you. I'd rather cut off my dick than hurt you."

"No, please," she said. "If you can't cut off any other part of your anatomy, I'd rather you hurt me than you cut off your dick."

He hooted with laughter and leaned back against the grass. Megan felt too sick to be embarrassed.

"Christopher, you realize we're in a graveyard?"

"Ain't nothin' but a thing, Megan," he said, lifting up on his elbows. "A graveyard peaceful. Don't have no motherfuckers comin' up to talk to you."

"Let's hope not," she mumbled.

He stroked her cheek. "You really wanna stand with me in a church?"

"More than anything."

He blew out a breath. "Thought I found a way to get us outta wearin' them fuckin' monkey suits."

"Christopher, you're sooo bad."

His arms tightening around her, he got to his feet, his strength amazing her. Not that she was heavy, but he stood as he held her without even appearing to strain.

"You're probably safe anyway," she said glumly, another thought occurring to her.

"Yeah?" he asked, zigzagging to sidestep graves. "Why the fuck that be?"

"Father Wilkins. He won't marry us until we've finished the required pre-counseling. Our wedding is supposed to happen in three days. I don't think any of the guys finished the tuxedo fittings and there's so much—"

He kissed the tip of her nose. "Stop worryin', baby. Ain't nothin' can't be fuckin' done. Priest ain't no problem. Brothers ain't a problem neither."

Not them, maybe, but…Suspicion welled inside her. "You can't threaten a priest, Christopher."

"Who the fuck said anything 'bout threatenin' the fat lil' motherfucker? He agreed to your weddin' song, ain't he?"

"True."

"Just trust me, baby."

"I always do," she whispered.

Outlaw

Christopher

"**N**o."

"I ain't likin' that fuckin' word," Christopher growled, later that afternoon. After escorting Megan back to the club, he'd called Johnnie to meet him at the church, before texting all the motherfuckers the wedding was on again, so be fucking prepared. He also called Derby for security assistance from the Hounds.

"Father Wilkins, is there anything we can do?" Johnnie asked with the kind of patience Christopher didn't have. "Out…Chris…Mr. Caldwell had some urgent business—"

"There's nothing more urgent than pre-marital counseling."

"We married alfuckinready. What the fuck we need counselin' for?"

Father Wilcunt sniffed and puffed up his chest. "Because that's my requirement for anyone to marry in my parish."

Christopher glared at him. "We got three fuckin' days to the weddin' and—"

"That isn't my problem, sir. You should've thought about that when you canceled." He shoved his glasses up on his nose. "Furthermore, I'd already made concessions for you by allowing the Wedding March—"

"Fuck you. You ain't doin' that cuz of me. You fuckin' doin' it cuz I told you I was cuttin' out your entrails and feedin' them to my fuckin' dogs, Father Wilcunt."

The priest jumped to his feet. "Out."

Johnnie scowled at Christopher. "Father Wilkins—"

Christopher stood and pulled out his piece.

"Jesus! Put that the fuck away," his cousin snarled.

"Shit goin' this fuckin' way. You marryin' me and Megan in three fuckin' days *in this church* with whatever fucked up bullshit music Megan want." He raised his gun. "Or I'm blowin' you the fuck away right fuckin' now and takin' my case to your replacement."

The priest swallowed. Fuckhead was finally realizing how serious Christopher was. He'd fucked up enough with Megan and, although he still didn't believe he belonged anywhere in a church, he owed this to her.

"Do you realize how inappropriate this is, Mr. Caldwell?" the priest sputtered.

He had to give it to the old geezer. He was determined to show he had balls. Motherfuckers might be useless, but they were big.

"Ain't givin' a fuck if the shit misappropriate or not." He narrowed his eyes at Wilcunt. "My ass the most misappropriate motherfucker you ever meetin', so this ain't nothin' but a thing."

Johnnie cleared his throat and beckoned Christopher closer. Probably to complain about his bad language to Father Wilcunt.

"What, fuckhead?"

"Er, Outlaw," he whispered. "Misappropriate isn't the right word. That means misuse of shit. Inappropriate means not suitable—"

"The word mean whatever the fuck I want it to mean, motherfucker," he snarled, jerking away from his cousin. "Ain't needin' you to give me no fuckin' definitions."

Johnnie only wanted him to make as much of a good impression on Father Wilcunt as possible, but that fucking ship had sailed. The man didn't like him, and he didn't like the man. Besides, it reminded Christopher that he only had a ninth-grade education. It reminded him he didn't speak proper English because he'd always been more interested in running the streets than sitting in a classroom.

That boat had floated, too, and he was what the fuck he was.

He scowled at Father Wilcunt, who continued to glower. The priest slanted a quick glance to the phone—thinking Christopher was fucking blind—before he nodded. "Fine. The wedding can go on."

Christopher lowered his nine. "If I was you, I'd shove them thoughts you got of callin' the cops right the fuck out of your head."

Not having any more to say, Christopher stalked out, leaving Johnnie behind to give the man some monetary incentive to keep his fucking fat trap shut.

Chapter 20

Mortician

SERVING AS MEGGIE'S BODYGUARD SHOULD'VE BEEN THE easiest fucking assignment Mortician ever had. Considering his current role in the club—his former chores on behalf of Big Joe, watching over Outlaw's woman *could've, should've* been a piece of cake. It would've been. The day started fine until shit fell apart.

Later, he'd blame it on the fact that they'd gotten a late start. Instead of leaving first thing in the morning, Meggie didn't come out to the main room until early afternoon. For the first time ever, he'd been so fucking annoyed with her. He had shit to do, *enforcer* shit. His text hadn't been answered and his call went straight to voicemail. When he'd seen Dinah with CJ, he'd been hopeful that Meggie would soon come out. Nope. Hadn't happened. And Dinah's shit-eating grin had doubly irritated him.

He'd waited another ninety fucking minutes before she'd brought her little Smurfette-sized ass out.

Once they left the club, Meggie dragged Mortician to the butcher, the baker, and the fucking candlestick maker, attempting to *uncancel* her fucking wedding. She believed Outlaw when he said their ceremony would take place on March 14th, a date that had already been rescheduled from Valentine's Day. Mortician thought otherwise. Although out of all the motherfuckers in the nursery rhyme, she only visited a baker, she *did* go to a florist and her dressmaker. Out of the three, only her seamstress reassured her that her gown would be ready because she had only a final fitting. With a huge tip, the woman canceled her other appointments and saw to Meggie then and there.

"You got your gown," Mortician told her, escorting her to Prez's cold ass pickup.

"I know," she said on a sigh, sliding onto the passenger seat once Mort opened the door. She snapped her seatbelt into place. "But we need a cake and flowers. Food."

"Alcohol," Mortician added with meaning.

She smiled, humor sparkling her eyes. "That goes without saying," she retorted.

Mortician grinned. "You a teetotaler so I had to make sure."

"I'm not a drinker, but Christopher is." She worried her bottom lip. "Do you think he's had success at the tuxedo shop?"

"He Prez, Meggie. What you think?"

Her brows snapped together. "He's not threatening anyone, is he?"

Like a motherfucker.

"Nope," Mortician lied with a straight face.

"I'm going to call him then and ask if he can talk to the florist and baker. Hopefully, the caterer, photographer, and DJ will be more flexible."

Sighing, Mort debated on clueing Meggie the fuck in. The long guest list Dinah came up with had turned what was supposed to be a blessing of Meggie and Prez's marriage with a celebration afterward into a huge motherfucker. While he knew Prez was working overtime to unfuck his fuckup, Mortician doubted the wedding would take place in two fucking days.

Prez couldn't threaten, but if he fucked up the service people if they couldn't meet his deadline, then that would defeat the fucking purpose. But Meggie believed in Outlaw. He told her their wedding would happen on the original rescheduled day and she trusted that it would.

"What?"

Her question broke into his thoughts.

He gave her an under-eyed look. "What you mean *what?*" he asked.

"I can see it in your face, Mortician," she said, sounding close to tears. She sniffled. "You don't think the wedding's going to happen in two days."

Horror washed through Mortician. If Prez found out he'd made Meggie cry, Mortician was fucked. "Awww, Meggie girl," he said quickly, "don't go by what you read in my ugly mug. I was just thinking about other shit."

"You're not ugly," she said, swiping at her wet cheeks. "You're really quite beautiful, just like Johnnie and Christopher."

Mort nodded, pretty fucking sure commenting on Meggie's observation might be as badly taken by Outlaw as her tears.

She placed a hand on her belly. Something about the way her fingers splayed over the area raised Mort's suspicions. He cleared his throat. "You having another baby?"

She nodded. "Morning sickness delayed me this morning. Momma didn't tell you? When she got CJ, I asked her to. I told her to have you call or text me if you had other things to do and wanted to reschedule."

"It's okay. What happened to your phone?" he asked, internally wincing because his thoughts had been quite rough on her, when he *should've* targeted her ratchet ass mama.

"It was charging. The battery had died." She looked on the verge of tears again. "Mama did let you know, didn't she?"

Mort nodded. He didn't want her upset. Today was stressful enough for her. He wouldn't add to it by telling her about Dinah's games. "Where to next?"

"The mall," she said. "One of the department stores. I have several things I need. It'll save time going to one place instead of specialty shops."

He glanced at his watch. Fuck, he liked to snatch motherfuckers during the day, so he'd be free in the evenings. Sometimes, he needed to scope out other fuckheads. Or he had disposal duty. Or a girl to fuck.

"We don't have to go today. Besides, it isn't as important as the caterer, DJ, and photographer."

Mort scowled at her sad tone. *Young bitches.* No wonder she wrapped Prez around her finger. "How about I text Outlaw when we get to the store, so he can take care of the DJ and photographer. We go to the department store and the caterer. Sound good to you?"

She nodded.

Relieved, Mortician shut her door, walking around to his side, and admiring the pickup. Gleaming black paint rivaled the shiny chrome rims on the low rider with a bumping sound system. Years ago, he'd stopped liking the closed-up feeling of automobiles. He'd begun to feel caged up. Referring to cars and trucks as cages took on new meaning for him. But, fuck, the pickup was the shit. He'd offered Outlaw triple the purchase amount, but he'd declined.

Twenty minutes later, Mortician was guiding Meggie into the department store, thankful for the separate entrance. Otherwise, he would've had to take her through the mall, and anything associated with spending money or shopping wasn't his thing.

Meggie's brother, Snake, had been a fucking shopaholic. For some reason, that always amused the fuck out of Mortician. A fucking psychopath like Joey Foy loved to hang out at malls and shop.

Yeah, he was throwing stones like a motherfucker. He handed out vengeance and justice to club enemies and wrongdoers, and he loved music. Loved it so fucking much it had been one of his majors in college.

Inside the store, Meggie paused and sent a text before heading to a perfume counter, then the vast section that included makeup, hair care, and skincare products. Shoes and handbags came next. Toddlers. Casualwear. Dresses. Jeans. Swimsuits.

The number of items she chose in a short amount of time blew the fuck out of Mortician's mind. She was definitely related to Snake, but that dead ass had nothing on his little sister. She hit the different areas like a general with a war plan. Either she'd looked online and already knew what she intended to buy, or she was choosing random shit in consideration of his time.

"One more section," she said an hour, and thousands of dollars, later. She swept her gaze over him. "I can carry some of that. You're carrying about five shopping bags in each hand."

"I'm fine," Mort told her, unable to stop his smile at her bright, happy eyes. "Let's just go to the last place on your list."

"Follow me."

The moment they stepped off the escalator, displays of bras and panties greeted him. Mannequins wearing lacy thongs. Sheer bodysuits. Sexy bra and panty sets with strappy shit that would crisscross ass cheeks. Maybe, even disappear between the crack. He saw Meggie as Prez's woman. Even though Mort had thought to kill her when she first arrived, he really liked her now. He'd even pushed out of his head the day he'd seen her buck naked. But he wasn't a fucking saint; he'd never been a candidate for a monastery; and he sure the fuck wasn't a eunuch.

"I'm going bring these bags to the pickup and grab a smoke," he told her.

And that was when the fuck shit fell apart.

"Meggie!"

Mortician froze at the sound of that voice. He'd only met her once, but he swore he knew who it was, but he couldn't bring himself to turn his ass around. His heat thumped in a frantic beat and anticipation rose in him. He couldn't wait to see her face again.

Meggie giggled, and Mortician blinked. They must've already exchanged greetings, yet she still hadn't walked into his line of vision.

"Do you remember Bailey, Mortician?" Meggie asked.

Mortician decided he'd be a fucking asshole and pretend to have forgotten her. Fuck, even if he hadn't made the fucking bet—

which he was in *no* goddamn danger of losing—Bailey was K-P's daughter. K-P had been better to Mort than his own father. He couldn't disrespect him by fucking his little girl.

Clearing his throat, Mort glanced next to him. Bailey's hair cradled her face, falling around her like black silk. Some of it rested against the swell of a tit. Mort swore he wouldn't have noticed it if the little green dress she wore didn't draw his attention to her chest. The short hemline revealed almost all her pretty thighs. Her shoes gave her height but also made it hard not to look at her legs.

He could imagine her thighs cradling him and her legs wrapped around his back.

His balls tightened.

She smiled at him, licked her lips. "Hi, Mortician. I'm K-P's daughter. I met you at Meggie's shower."

K-P's *twenty-year-old* daughter. A young bitch. The type that would cost him 100Gs.

Only if he fell for her, he reminded himself. The bet said nothing about *fucking* one.

She laid her fingers on his arm and her touch burned him. "Hey, um, I was wondering if you wanted to hang out one evening? We can go to the movies. *Or* you can come to my place, and I'll make us New Orleans-style daiquiris." She grinned, her face sweet and gorgeous. "I can't legally drink in bars for another couple months."

Her house. Yes definitely. They could drink and talk and he could steal kiss after kiss from her pretty mouth. He could eat her pussy, watch as her lips wrapped around his cock. Afterward, they could fuck the rest of the night.

The color of her dress turned her eyes more green than brown.

A tug on his sleeve drew his attention away from Bailey. Turning, he met Meggie's amused face.

"We're not going to be long. Can you wait for us?"

It came to him that he hadn't said a fucking word to Bailey. But fuck, he felt lightheaded, as flushed as a new motherfucker on the hunt for his first piece of pussy. He didn't know what to say. To him, Bailey was the most beautiful girl he'd ever fucking laid eyes on.

His phone beeped, the sound of an incoming message. Realizing he still held Meggie's shopping bags, he set them on each side of him and got his phone from where he kept it in one of the inside pockets of his cut.

Seeing Prez's text reminded him he needed to tell him about talking to the DJ and photographer. On second thought, he'd see to the DJ. Outlaw could handle the photographer.

Bailey's hair brushed his arm as she peeped at his screen.

He glared at her. "Stop being fucking nosy." He looked at the place where Meggie should've been standing. Instead, she wasn't there. She stood at a rack, sliding hangers from one pair of panties to the next. He set his phone on the shelf next to him, so he'd remember to send the message to Prez. "Why you here, Bailey?" he demanded, his entire body prickling with awareness of her.

Clenching his jaw, he met her gaze, then really wished he hadn't. What he saw made him want to take her in his arms and promise he'd never let anything hurt her. On the surface, she looked calm and friendly, but her pulse beat wildly at the base of her delicate neck. She was fucking nervous.

"I sent Meggie a text to tell her I was able to get fitted for a bridesmaid's gown, although the seamstress said she couldn't get it done in two days," she said. "She texted me back to say she'd call me later."

"And? How the fuck that message turn into you being here?"

"She told me she had to stop here, but she couldn't be long because she'd kept you out long enough."

It hit him suddenly, all making perfect sense. Forgetting the packages, his phone, *Bailey*, he stalked to Meggie. She held a handful of selections, busily choosing from another rack and humming under her breath.

"I know Prez don't like to lose, Meggie, but I don't appreciate you playing fucking games on his behalf."

She blinked, her hand on a pair of lacy black panties stilling. "Wh-what are you talking about?"

"Bailey," he snarled, his teeth clenched.

Glancing over her shoulder in Bailey's direction, Meggie looked at him in confusion. "What about her?"

Shaking his head, Mort wagged a finger at her. "Don't play fucking dumb. You told her to come over here on Outlaw behalf. You think my cock going to overlook the bet."

"What bet?"

"Enough with the fucking dumb bitch act, Meggie. Fuck the 100Gs on the line. My cock want Bailey and I want *him*. K-P'll hack the motherfucker off when I touch Bailey." His brain homed in on the word *when*. "*If* I fuck Bailey." That implied there was a chance he would. Fuck, he couldn't think straight right now. "I thought you were my friend, but your fucking scheming showing me you not."

At the end of his rant, her eyes were wide and watery, her nose reddening and her lips trembling. She set the items she'd intended to purchase on the rack in front of her, then sniffled.

He suddenly felt so fucking low. Fear surged into him, sweeping away his regret. When Meggie told Outlaw about this, Mortician would have his tongue cut the fuck out.

"I'm sorry," he said, meaning it. "Seeing Bailey threw me off, Meggie." He scrubbed a hand over his face. "Fuck. I thought Prez…I got a hundred grand on the line." He'd never dream of spending so much money at once. *Losing* that amount sent cold chills through him. When he'd made the fucking bet, he hadn't had a doubt in the world he'd win, *whenever* one of them called it. Five months? Not a fucking problem. Five years? Still good. *Fifty* goddamn years. He intended to throw it in all their fucking faces how immune to young pussy he was. If K-P had been in on the bet, he would've sworn he'd brought Bailey in as a set up. But he knew his old friend wouldn't use his daughter in such a way.

When Prez's ringtone blasted from Meggie's phone, she turned and walked away, in the opposite direction from where Bailey stood.

Fuck, he deserved whatever punishment Outlaw handed down. Maybe, it would be so fucking severe, he'd be in a coma for ten or fifteen years and win the bet by default.

Sighing, he returned to where Bailey stood. She now held some of Meggie's bags, while others sat on each side of her. Unaware of the scene that had just taken place, she smiled brightly at him. "Your phone is behind me," she reminded him. "Meggie's purchases were left unattended, so I thought to safeguard them until y'all got back."

"Thank you," he said, sounding like the preacher's son who'd been taught manners by his mother. He glanced to where Meggie was pacing on the other end of the department. "We can't be friends, Bailey," he stated in no uncertain terms. "We can't be *nothing*."

Her face fell. All her happiness faded. If he felt bad about his treatment of Meggie at her reaction, watching his words affect Bailey ruined his entire fucking day.

What the fuck was wrong with him? This was the second time he'd seen her in his entire fucking life. She was just a fucking girl, like so many he'd come across over the years.

"Daddy won't mind if that's what you're worried about," she told him quietly.

Mortician begged to differ. K-P definitely would fucking mind. He knew Mortician, sometimes better than Mortician did.

"I don't know why I've thought about you so much since we met." A flush swept over her skin. "It isn't as if I haven't had a boyfriend before."

Mortician frowned at her. He didn't think Meggie had ever had another motherfucker other than Prez, but he almost understood why Outlaw refused to let most of the motherfuckers guard her. Especially Johnnie.

Bailey's pulse started thumping again. Mortician wished they were alone so he could lean down and lick that particular spot, before sucking the tender skin.

"I was going to make strawberry daiquiris from my mother's recipe. She uses real strawberries. She also makes these Pina Coladas that are to die for."

"I don't like sweet drinks."

"You wouldn't have to drink a lot. I've made them only once and the guy I was dating…" Her voice trailed off and she swallowed. Something about the look in her eyes put Mort on alert. "He didn't like them, and we got into an argument." She forced a laugh. "I was hoping you'd have a little taste and tell me if you think they're completely disgusting."

His nostrils flared, but he made himself focus. "Why you here?"

"I, uh, I told you why," she started with uncertainty.

"No, fuck. I mean why you moved to Portland?"

"I don't live in Portland. I live in Hortensia."

Fuck.

"In the apartments around the high school."

"I don't want to fucking know where the fuck your place is," he snapped, catching himself before he clapped his hands over his ears like a ten-year-old fuckhead.

"You asked me where I lived."

"No," he snapped, as much irritation in his tone as he'd heard in hers. "I fucking asked you *why* you moved here."

"It was time to move out of my mother's house." She glanced away, her vulnerability returning before she shrugged. "It was time."

"Why? You don't get along with her? Is she mean to you?" Or whiny and manipulative like Dinah.

Bailey shook her head. "Mama is the best. She didn't want me to move. She even had my sisters and brother talk to me. MeMe."

"Who the fuck is that?"

"Her mother. My grandmother." She shifted her weight. "I had to go, so I transferred my credits to the University of Portland."

"You should live on campus. Get the full college experience."

She laughed. "Is that what you did?"

"Who told you I went to college? I don't sound like I went to high school sometimes," he said with a snigger. "At least according to Johnnie."

"The blond biker I met?"

Mortician nodded.

"That isn't very nice of him. It's what's inside of a man that's important, not whether he sounds educated. Or *is* educated, for that matter." She lowered her lashes. "Besides, you just seem really smart. Like you know a lot of stuff."

"Don't need college for that. Life teach you shit you wish you didn't have to fucking learn."

"Hey." The sound of Meggie's voice interrupted whatever Bailey had been about to say.

Mortician told himself he needed the intervention before he did something stupid. Like ask for Bailey's number. He could've talked to her for hours. There was so much he wanted to ask her. Body language spoke volumes and hidden inside her was a story that needed to be told.

He was fucking certain. That's what she had K-P for, though.

"It's okay, Meggie," Bailey said.

The two girls had been talking and Mort completely missed the conversation again.

"No, you didn't barge in on me," Meggie promised, apparently in response to something Bailey said.

"And you didn't ignore me," Bailey countered. "I should've gone with you, but I chose to stay here."

Meggie nodded, but all her bubbliness was gone. She looked at him. "I need to find a bathroom, then we can head home."

Meggie, with her soft heart and tender feelings, wore Mort the fuck out. But *Bailey* with her beautiful face, gorgeous eyes, and sweet voice, tore him the fuck up. He wanted her. More than he'd wanted any woman in years. Between the two of them, the last fucking thing he felt like doing was lugging bags around while keeping watch over Meggie. Fuck, if Cee Cee popped the fuck out of nowhere, the packages would handicap Mort.

"I think there's one straight ahead and turn left, then walk all the way to the back," Bailey volunteered.

Meggie's phone chimed and she glanced at it. "Digger wants to know if we can bring him a spinach and mushroom pizza with curry sauce, red onions, sardines, and feta?" She wrinkled her nose, turning a little green, but another incoming text distracted her. "Along with a twelve pack," she added.

"Tell him fuck no," Mortician barked. "Remind him he didn't give me no goddamn money to bring that shit to him and even if he had, I wouldn't get that fucked up combination. Shit would have his breath rancid as hell."

"I really have to pee," Meggie said, then held her phone out to Bailey. "Can you text whatever Mortician wants to tell Digger?"

Bailey nodded. "I'll watch the stuff too," she told him as Meggie scampered away. "Go with her."

Mortician smiled with gratitude and rushed after Meggie. By the time he rounded the corner, she was running down the aisle in the direction Bailey had sent her. He reached the area with the restroom moments after she did. As the door closed, he saw her leaning over the sink and vomiting. He ended up waiting for over five minutes for her to reappear.

When she did, she was flushed, and her shoulders sagged.

"I think I'm ready now. Just don't mention that pizza…"

Her shoulders heaved.

Mortician made a zipping motion over his lips. "I won't say a word."

She started off, without responding. When they reached Bailey, the two girls hugged. Mortician offered to drive Bailey to wherever she was parked, but she declined. In the truck, Meggie sat silently in her seat.

"What Outlaw said when you told him what a fuckhead I was to you?" he asked, when they were almost to the club.

"Nothing, because I didn't tell him."

"I got to apologize to you again."

"It's okay, Mortician. Really. We all have bad days. Today was one of yours."

But she still sounded off. "If you not mad at me and Prez not describing in grisly detail how he fucking me up, why you so sad?"

"I'm worried about the stupid nausea and if it'll ruin my wedding day." She twisted her hands, and her diamond ring caught a sparkle of light. "Christopher also told me that we might have to push the wedding back again. There's so much to be done that it probably isn't possible to have it when it was supposed to happen."

"I'm sure Prez going to do everything possible to see your wedding blessed as close to the date you want as is feasible. But look at the bright side. You get more time to remember little hanging details that you might have overlooked."

She nodded. "You're right. I didn't think of that."

At the club, Outlaw was standing outside talking to Johnnie, Val, and Digger when Mort and Meggie arrived. While Mort got her bags, she went straight to Prez. They simultaneously moved. She lifted herself up as he leaned down to kiss her before he wrapped an arm around her and pulled her close to his side. He bent and whispered in her ear. A pretty blush bloomed in her cheeks.

Johnnie's jaw clenched and he sent her such a look of longing that Mortician squinted.

Outlaw smirked. "My woman got another lil' motherfucker in her," he announced, his gaze hard and brutal.

Meggie smiled at Prez, her look as sweet as the one Bailey had given to Mort.

"Congratulations, Megs," Johnnie said, ignoring Outlaw's glare.

"You a cold motherfucker, Mort," Digger said after he too congratulated Meggie and Prez, with a bit more sincerity. "My mouth was watering especially for the curry and sar—"

"Shut the fuck up, fool," Mortician warned, nodding to Meggie as she began to turn green again.

"It's th-that combination," Meggie said weakly as Prez turned her and dragged her to a small patch of grass, holding her as she dry-heaved.

Her stomach was empty. Mortician hadn't seen her eat at all today.

"C'mon, baby," Outlaw said, guiding her to the door and disappearing inside with her, but not before shooting a glare at Digger.

Val stared at all the shopping bags. "What the fuck she bought?"

"Stuff," Mortician answered. Even if he'd paid attention earlier, which he hadn't, after his encounter with Bailey, he would've forgotten. "I have to hit the fucking road. I got shit to do."

"I was wondering when you was going to call me for my job," Digger said, then sighed. "That fucking pizza would've been delicious."

"Motherfucker we grounding happen to be in Portland," Mortician said, shaking his head at his younger brother. "We taking the van since it's evening. We can get your fucking pizza on the way back. You're gonna need a dozen breath mints after that nasty shit."

At the mention of the mints, Digger actually wrinkled his fucking nose. "I don't like breath mints, motherfuckers nauseate me."

"You need to extract information?" Johnnie asked, perking up and redirecting the conversation away from Digger's eating habits.

Mortician nodded.

"If you get him back to the meat shack, I can help."

"This got to do with Cee Cee?" Val asked.

"Not this time," Mortician answered. "It's a fucking Torp."

Johnnie lifted a brow. "Spoon's club?"

"He been a stupid motherfucker," Val growled.

"He claiming no fucking knowledge of the doings of the motherfucker I'm scooping up," Mortician admitted. "Spoon the one that named him."

"Spoon been a shady motherfucker," Digger said.

"Right now, he not an enemy," Mortician said. "That might fucking change. Only time will tell us the real deal." He held up the bags. "Let me bring these to Meggie, then we can hit the road."

Walking through the club, he nodded to Stretch. He sat at the bar, talking to a motherfucker with curly, black hair, the two of them whispering to each other in an oddly intimate way.

Mortician decided he was tired. Stretch wasn't fucking stupid. Motherfuckers loved whoever the fuck they chose, but *this* wasn't the place to have any other partner but a woman. He'd talk to the motherfucker later.

Leaving the main room, he went down the hall to Outlaw's room. Meggie's giggles coupled with Outlaw's snickers made Mort hesitate. But fuck she might want her shit later.

"Fuck it," he murmured to himself, manning up and knocking on the door.

"Come fuckin' in," Outlaw called.

Opening the door, Mortician walked into Prez's room. Meggie leaned against a pile of pillows on the bed, in the spot closest to the brick wall, dressed in the T-shirt Outlaw had been wearing, nibbling on saltine crackers. Meanwhile, Outlaw went bare-chested under his cut as he lounged next to her.

"Where you want this?" Mort asked, lifting the bags as if they couldn't see all the motherfuckers he held.

"On the fuckin' desk," Prez responded as Mort complied. "What the fuck you buyin', Megan?"

"Stuff to take on our honeymoon. Clothes for CJ."

Outlaw scowled. "All the shit my boy got, he ain't needin' no more. And the lil motherfucker ain't goin' on the fuckin' honeymoon."

"I know, Christopher. But babies grow really, really fast." Meggie nibbled more of her cracker. "I also bought a couple outfits for our new baby."

"Fuck me," Outlaw groaned. "You buy CJ new shit every goddamn week. Babies don't grow that fucking fast."

Meggie smiled innocently.

"Fuck. Fine, you lil' pain in the ass motherfucker."

"I'm really happy with everything I bought," she said huskily. She lowered her lashes. "I'll show you just how happy when we're alone."

Leaning over, he kissed her, then got off the bed. "I ain't too sure, baby. You been hurlin' like a motherfucker. What the fuck my cock down your throat gonna do?"

She gasped and turned beet red, while Outlaw lit a cigarette, her reaction amusing the fuck out of him.

"I'm going to hit the road, Prez," Mortician told him, not giving away how much Meggie's blush entertained him.

Silent, Outlaw took a few drags on his cigarette. "Bailey part of the weddin' now."

Mortician's humor fled.

"You seen her afuckingain since the day you met her?"

He couldn't read Outlaw. The question sounded mild, but Mort didn't know what Meggie had said.

"Bailey not even on my fucking radar, Prez." He told the blatant lie with a straight fucking face.

Outlaw stared at him, his expression unreadable, the type of look Mortician didn't like. He just smoked and glowered, smoked and glowered, sending a chill down Mortician's spine.

"Baby, when was the last time you seein' Bailey?"

"Why?" Meggie asked with suspicion.

"K-P gettin' a call earlier from her when we was out," Outlaw said, never taking his gaze from Mortician. He finished his cigarette before he spoke again. "She was tryna surprise you at the mall or some shit."

"Surprise me?" Meggie echoed.

Outlaw dragged his attention away from Mortician to look at Meggie. "Yeah, baby. Meanin' she ain't wanted you knowin' her plans to meet you there and hopin' you happy seein' her."

Meggie nodded. "Umkay," she said faintly. "Yeah, um, she…she missed us."

"Yeah?" he said.

"Yes," she mumbled, unable to meet his gaze, reddening once more.

Folding his arms, Outlaw leaned against his desk, his gaze cold enough to freeze fucking Yeti. "Guess what the fuck I'm bettin' Mort, Megan?"

She cleared her throat. "What?" she asked, leaning forward to reach her pack of crackers.

"He fallin' for young pussy like my fuckin' ass."

The announcement stopped her from pulling out the saltine. "Huh?"

"You fuckin' heard me right. He so fuckin' sure he ain't ever tumblin' head over fuckin' heels for a young bitch like my ass did." Outlaw snorted. "Like I was expectin' you walkin' in my fuckin' life and turnin' my fuckin' world over. It ain't nothin' you controllin', assfuck," he imparted to Mort, then turned back to Meggie. "Bet started with 5Gs. Motherfucker upped the fuckin' ante to 25Gs. Digger, Val, and Johnnie staked up, too. Mort riskin' a hundred large."

"Ummm," Meggie responded, noncommittal.

"So you ain't seein' Bailey tofuckinday, huh, baby?"

"Nope."

Outlaw glanced between Meggie and Mortician, none too pleased.

"You ain't just sayin' that shit to protect this motherfucker?"

Meggie drew in an irritated breath and flopped back onto the pillows. "The bet is ridiculous," she grouched. "The four of you cornered him into it."

"*You* wasn't there, so you ain't knowin' if we cornerin' the motherfucker or not."

"Uh, yeah, I do," she retorted. "All you've done is guaranteed he'll dig his heels in and deny any feelings for whoever it might be."

"Ain't so, Megan," Prez countered. "If he lovin' on a bitch efuckinnuff motherfucker'll pay a hundred bands."

Folding her arms, Meggie sniffed.

"You ain't protectin' no motherfucker bettin' against my fuckin' ass, Megan."

"If I don't agree with your stupid bet, I'll protect anyone I choose to," she snapped.

"I ain't cancelin' it."

"I didn't ask you to," she said evenly, glaring at Mortician.

Earlier, he'd given her shit about the fucking bet, too.

"*You*, Christopher, aren't telling me whose side to be on."

"You bettin' with Mort?" Outlaw asked, outraged.

"All five of you are juvenile, so no, I'm not, but I'm not helping you to prove a point just because he couldn't keep his mouth shut. You're saying you wouldn't allow a bet to stop you from being with me, but your pride alone would've made you dig your heels in."

"You lie for fuckin' shit, so Ima ask you afuckingain, you saw Bailey at the fuckin' mall?"

"Even if I did, doesn't mean Mortician did," Meggie said sweetly.

Outlaw grit his teeth.

"Christopher," Meggie said on a sigh. "I'm not begrudging you your bets, even if I don't agree with them. But Mortician's my friend. He's looked out for me since I got here. I think him and Bailey would be great together." She beamed a smile between them. "As a matter of fact, I'm pairing you and Bailey at the wedding."

"What?" Mortician barked. "No. Fuck no, Meggie girl. I'm not—"

Outlaw's attention returned to Mort, stopping him fucking cold.

"Fine, Meggie," Mortician grumbled.

Satisfied, Outlaw looked at his woman again. "You playin' both ends to the fuckin' middle, Megan. How the fuck you *protectin'* the motherfucker then turnin' 'round and *temptin'* him?"

"I'm Switzerland. Neutral," she added. "I make decisions about this situation as I see fit."

"You ain't agreein' with none of us motherfuckers, so you interfuckinferin' and sabotagin' all us assfucks?"

Meggie weighed Outlaw's words, then beamed a smile at him. She didn't give him a direct answer.

Shaking his head, he laughed. "You ain't able to tell no other motherfucker," he told her.

She threw him an evil look. "I know you mean Bailey. I haven't and I won't, although she should know. After all, she might be wasting her time on one idiot because of four other idiots." She glared between them.

"Club fuckin' business, Megan," Outlaw replied, unrepentant. "Meanin' you ain't able to open you fuckin' mouth 'bout it, without betrayin' the club."

She snatched one of the pillows from behind her and threw it at his head, hitting her mark. As it bounced off Outlaw and fell to the floor, she huffed out a breath, turned her back to them, and drew the covers up to her chin.

He winked at Mortician. "Be right back, Megan. Ima step out a minute. Dinah probably bringin' my boy back soon."

She glanced over her shoulder. "I'm going to text K-P and ask if it's okay if he watches over Momma and CJ a little longer."

"Ain't gonna be long."

Outlaw looked at Mortician and nodded to the hallway.

"See you, Meggie girl," Mort told her.

"Bye, Mortician," she responded.

Heaving in a breath, Mortician followed Prez out of the bedroom, watching as he closed the door, anticipating a blow to the ribs or a punch to the throat.

"Ain't fuckin' you up, Mort," Outlaw announced in low tones, standing in the doorway of the ajarred door. "Was gonna, but ain't got a lotta time befuckinfore my boy here and I been waitin' all fuckin' day to fuck my woman. Johnnie tappin' a photographer he know, by the way."

"I'm going to get the DJ," Mort said, relieved he wasn't going to have to do his job in pain. "My wedding gift to you."

Outlaw grunted. "I ain't hopeful no more the ceremony happenin' in two fuckin' days. We seein' the next date the church got, then we workin' like a motherfucker to make it work. Fuck, my ass shoulda infuckinvited a bunch of motherfuckers for all the fuckin' hotel and airline cancellation fees and shit."

"Sounds fucking awful," Mortician said, meaning it.

"It ain't," Outlaw said, suddenly serious. "Cuz she worth it, Mort. Hear me? She worth every fuckin' dollar, every fuckin' gray hair she gonna put on my head cuz she ain't ever fuckin' doin' shit my way if she ain't fuckin' wanna." He grinned. "But love like that. It make me go grab a motherfucker, cut his fuckin' head off, then hurry and clean the fuck up so she ain't seein' cuz I ain't Outlaw to her."

"What you saying, Prez?" Mort asked.

"Megan ain't a fuckin' liar," he responded, instead of answering the question. "K-P alfuckinready tellin' my ass Bailey seein' you and Megan. At fuckin' first, her coverin' for you pissed me the fuck off. Then I got to fuckin' thinkin'. Me and you been fuckin' tight. I trust you with my life. My fuckin' wife. You takin' care of her so fuckin' good she see you as her friend, too."

He held out his hand. Smiling, Mort clasped it and shook it.

"So infuckinstead of punchin' the fuck outta you, I wanna say thank you for bein' a good motherfucker, Mortician."

Mort nodded, unsure what to say.

Outlaw began backing into the room. "That's what the fuck my ass sayin'. Ain't nothin' like Megan lovin' me to help me see welcomesome of the good the world got."

Without saying anything more, Prez stepped into the room and closed the door. Mort stared at the spot where Outlaw had stood, and Bailey's image rose in his head.

She wasn't for him. No matter what gris-gris she fucking sprinkled whenever he fucking saw her. Turning on his heel, he headed into the main room. Stretch and his friend were gone. Cowboy, Shady, and Bowlie sat at one of the tables. They waved at Mort and he responded in kind.

After the wedding, he'd fucking forget Bailey, he determined as he walked into the cold night and headed to his bike. An incoming message alert sounded on his phone. He snatched it out of his pocket and frowned at the unfamiliar number with the word 'Image' next to a picture icon.

Tapping the message, he stared at Bailey's photo. As pictures went, this one was quite tame compared to the raunchy photos he normally received. Bailey wore a catsuit with platform boots and her hair in a high ponytail.

He didn't know how she'd gotten his number. Meggie might've given it to her or she could've gotten it from Meggie's phone. It didn't matter. Another line of communication had opened up. No one had to know about it. They were both fucking grown anyway. They could talk, text, drink, date. *Fuck.*

Then, common fucking sense returned, and Mortician scowled at her photo, hitting his finger against the cursor to open the message screen and keyboard. He intended to tell her to lose his fucking number. Before he followed through on his plan, she sent another message with five, simple words, even more meaningful because he knew they were sincere.

Hi. How are you tonight?

INSTEAD OF THE WEDDING HAPPENING ON THE DATE PLANNED, IT TOOK place ten days later. It was just too fucking much left to do to suddenly resurrect fucking plans. Motherfuckers needed final tuxedo fittings; bitches needed bridesmaid's dresses. Megan had to make sure her gown could be finished. Food had to be ordered. Her fucking besties, Lacey and Farrah, had to be convinced to attend. Dinah had to suck about twenty fucking lemons to get that pinched fucking look on her fucking face when Megan told her the wedding was back on. He tapped Gypsy and Bunny to help Megan plan the reception and rehearsal dinner since her fucking Ma refused, just as that bitch told his girl she wouldn't walk her down the aisle. Christopher had to arrange their honeymoon.

The rehearsal and dinner both happened last night at the club, since Wilcunt was a fat, little assfuck and wouldn't open the church for the bridal party to practice what the fuck they needed to do today.

Thinking back, Christopher was so fucking glad their wedding hadn't happened on March 14th, the day CJ had turned eight months. They used it as family time and Megan had been happy spending time with Christopher, their lil' motherfucker, and the new baby in her.

"It would've been nice if K-P escorted Megan down the aisle," Johnnie whispered as K-P appeared in the double entryway, his arm linked with Dinah's.

Scowling, Christopher nodded. "Megan always givin' that whiny bitch her fuckin' way. She shoulda told that cunt to fuck herself when she pitchin' a bitch cuz K-P was gonna bring my woman down the fuckin' aisle to my ass."

"K-P should've put his foot down and ignored Dinah's complaining."

"You right, John Boy," Christopher said, watching as K-P whispered to Dinah as they walked down the aisle. He had to admit she dressed up quite nicely, with her hair colored to hide the gray and makeup to hide her wrinkles. Nothing masked that fucking sucky lemon expression and her fucking gown pissed Christopher the fuck off. Megan had wanted her ma in peach. That cunt chose fucking black.

Once they reached the halfway point, Mort appeared in the doorway, Bailey at his side.

Bowlie prevented them from starting down the aisle by squeezing around them and seating himself on the last row. Shady and Cowboy, the other two motherfuckers Megan picked as ushers stood at the door, like sentinels on duty. Traveler should've been one of the ushers. The betraying assfuck wouldn't be nothing ever again.

Shady drank from a fifth of rum and Cowboy held a can of beer. Christopher wasn't sure if Megan had been that lenient with her ushers or if the motherfuckers disrespected her day.

"Mort looks like he's ready to spit bullets," Johnnie snickered.

Yeah, the motherfucker looked madder than a motherfucker, escorting K-P's girl toward the altar. Although he held onto her, he stood as far apart as he fucking could.

K-P reached the pew where Dinah would sit. Instead of following suit as his fucking ass should have, assfuck stood, arms folded, glowering at Mortician.

Glaring, Mort flipped K-P off as Christopher left his place, stomping to K-P and tapping him on the shoulder.

"What, runt?" K-P growled.

"Sit the fuck down," Christopher ordered. "Megan ain't sayin' a motherfucker standin' there."

"I'm not moving until my baby girl reaches her place and Mortician lets her go."

Hand on K-P's shoulder, Christopher forced him to move to where him and Johnnie were supposed to stand.

"Assfuck ain't able to put his cock in her in this motherfucker," Christopher snapped.

"Mister Caldwell!" Father Wilcunt hissed, preventing K-P from responding.

Christopher ignored him.

"My girl's so gorgeous," K-P said with pride, rocking on his heels.

Bailey was a gorgeous fucking chick. Her black hair was shining and the peach gown she wore made her skin glow. With each step, the flowy skirt swirled and the long split exposed her legs.

When they got to the altar, Mortician released a visible breath, snatching his hand from Bailey's. She looked up at him, her eyes more green than brown. They had the look of a girl completely fucking spellbound. Mort knew her gaze stayed on him. As much as the motherfucker tried not to, he couldn't help but glance at her, the entire scene amusing the fuck out of Christopher.

K-P led Bailey to where he thought she should be as Mort reached them.

"25Gs extra gonna be so fuckin' sweet in my pocket," Christopher chortled. "Gimme mine in straps of 20s, 50s, and 100s, hear me, motherfucker?"

"I want all 100s," Johnnie added.

Mort gave John Boy a dirty look.

"Hey, Prez," Stretch greeted, reaching them.

He'd been so fucking focused on Mort, he'd missed Stretch marching with Lacey. She stood next to Bailey, her Big Bird yellow hair clashing with the blue fucking gown she wore. Her black fucking lipstick fucked up her look even more.

"You married Meggie once, Outlaw," Derby said as he walked up, while Gypsy went to the bridesmaid side. "I can't believe you're doing it again. You won't see me walk my bitch down the aisle at all."

"Shut the fuck up," Christopher commanded. "Megan want Gypsy in the fuckin' bridal party. Your woman ain't walkin' without your fuckin' ass."

Derby grinned. "Just her way of keeping tabs on me, Outlaw. If I'm here, another bitch isn't with me, sucking and fucking me. Women have all kinds of fucking tricks, brother." He shook his head. "Let me plug her asshole to get me to agree. Licked another broad's cunt while I fucked her so I'd wear this fucking tux."

"I hear you, brother," Boy said, walking up and catching the tail end of Derby's conversation.

"Look at Zoann," Johnnie said.

She was already halfway down the aisle, on Digger's arm in her gown, her order in the processional calling for peach. Her chestnut hair was swept up, like all the other women, and the makeup she wore only enhanced her beauty. It reminded Christopher of how proud he'd once been of her. Even now, when their mutual dislike went fucking deep, he couldn't deny how fucking impressed he was by her self-sufficiency and good looks.

At the altar, Digger kissed her hand with a loud smack and winked at her. Zoann narrowed her eyes, so Digger raised his hands and backed away, while she stomped to the women.

"Zoann going to stomp your fucking cock, son," Mortician said mildly, sneaking glances at Bailey, thinking motherfuckers didn't see. "If she don't, Val will."

"Val don't want her, bruh," Digger said with certainty. "He the motherfucker that switched when Meggie asked me to walk Little Man down the fucking aisle. If he wanted the woman, he never would've left her to swoon at my pretty fucking face."

"Fuck, when you started needin' glasses?" Christopher sniggered, while the other men joined in.

"Prez, that shit cold blooded," Digger said mournfully.

"I'm warning you for the last time, Mr. Caldwell," the priest interrupted. "Cease and desist with your offensive language."

"You been pacing up and fucking down, priest man," Digger said. "I saw you doing it when I was standing in the door. Get to hoofing across the altar again and leave us the fuck alone."

Wilcunt's jowls shook.

"Ain't fuckin' sayin' this shit but one fuckin' more time," Christopher warned, "you fuck up my woman day and my ass fuckin' up your fuckin' life."

"Prez!" a voice inserted, drawing Christopher's attention away.

It was Trader, a Dweller who'd joined about three years ago.

"I'm honored to be part of your wedding. My old lady's beside herself. I told her if it wasn't for me, she wouldn't be in the bridal party." He laughed when Christopher didn't hear anything fucking funny.

"Megan want your woman as a bridesmaid, Trader," Christopher said, tension starting to knot his gut. The fucking procession seemed never fucking ending. He just fucking wanted to see his girl coming down the aisle. "If it ain't for Bunny, *you* wouldna been in this motherfucker."

Trader glanced at Bunny, then nodded to Christopher.

"Fee is Megan's maid-of-honor?" Johnnie asked in confusion.

Christopher looked away from Trader to see his youngest sister, Ophelia, walking toward them without an escort. "No, Ghost backin' the fuck out at the last fuckin' minute."

"McCall?" Johnnie said in surprise.

Christopher nodded.

Once Ophelia got to them, she blew Christopher a kiss, made the sign of the cross, then joined the other women.

"Prez, the women standing diagonal," Mortician said. "Us motherfuckers all crowded together. We supposed to be like this?"

"Step the fuck in position," Christopher ordered as Farrah, the actual maid-of-honor got to them."

Throwing Christopher a look, she raised her chin and turned away.

"Bitch don't like you, Outlaw," Digger pointed out.

"Ain't givin' a fuck. Megan do. Case fuckin' closed."

"Meggie love you," Digger corrected.

"She like my ass too, so shut the fuck up."

"She do," Mort agreed with a nod. "That shit important too. Love don't mean shit if you don't have like too."

"So you like Bailey or love her?" Digger questioned casually.

"How can I love her when I don't even know her that well?" Mortician demanded.

"But you do know her, huh, bruh?" Digger said, grinning as it dawned on Mortician just what the fuck he'd let slip. "I could use those 25Gs."

"What 25Gs?" Boy asked.

"Which one's Bailey?" Derby questioned.

"Bailey's the one with the black hair," Johnnie said.

"Goddamn," Boy blurted.

"She K-P girl, motherfucker," Christopher said with a laugh.

"No, she *Mort* girl," Digger said, guffawing like the rest of them. All except Mort.

Wilcunt marched his fucking ass back over to glare at them like the motherfucker he was.

"Mort accepted a bet that he wouldn't fall for young pussy like Outlaw did," Digger explained when they stopped their laughing, ignoring the priest's displeasure and the guests' curiosity.

"He don't have to fall for her to fuck her," Derby said with a shrug.

Christopher thumped his shoulder. "Ain't tellin' you afuckingain. She K-P girl."

"If we can't talk about that young bitch, can we discuss yours, Outlaw?" Trader asked.

"If you fuckin' tired of your fuckin' head on your fuckin' shoulders, go right the fuck on," Christopher snarled.

A small body caught him off-guard and flew into him. "Hey, Uncle Chris."

Glancing down, he saw his niece, Sasha. She would be six soon and had taken a shine to Megan. She was the flower girl, so pretty in a cream-colored dress, a floral wreath on her brown hair.

Christopher hugged her. "Hey, Sasha," he greeted, glancing at the guests, and finding his other three sisters, Nia, Avery, and Bev, on a pew along with his remaining three nieces. Two girls belonged to one sister and two belonged to another. Fuck him if he knew who. For that fucking matter, he only knew Sasha's name.

"Sasha, baby get back over here," Zoann called, though Fee scampered over, grabbed Sasha's hand and guided her to the spot she belonged.

"Who the fuck all these motherfuckers, Prez?" Mortician asked. "They wasn't at the rehearsal."

"Dinah and Meggie friends got these fuckheads here," Digger volunteered. "K-P told me how Dinah demanded Meggie let her see the list, then when Meggie left, Dinah dialed up her bitchy girlfriends."

"Fuck, civilians," Johnnie spat with disgust. "We better be on our best fucking behavior."

"Fuck them and fuck that whiny bitch," Christopher said, stiffening when Wilcunt walked over again.

"Does your bride ever intend to show her face?" the priest asked.

Christopher frowned and stole a look at his watch.

"The entire bridal party is here." Wilcunt indicated Sasha with a flourish. "The flower girl usually heralds the bride entry." He nodded to the empty doorway. "Do my little eyes spy her? I think not, so where is she?"

"She comin'!" he snapped, glaring until the motherfucker roamed away again, to continue pacing.

Suddenly painfully aware of the time, Christopher glanced at his watch again. Two minutes had passed.

Three minutes ticked by.

Four.

Seven.

"What the fuck holdin' Megan up?" Christopher finally asked, glancing toward the windows. Most of them were stained glass, except for two that centered each side of the church.

She should be on premises. Low clouds blanketed the air, but the rain held at bay. When he'd arrived it had been as cold as it had been the day Megan found him in the cemetery. The weather wasn't holding her up, he thought, rocking back on his heels. So, where the fuck was she?

The organist continued to play and he considered shooting the fuck out of her at the noise she fucking pounded out. When Megan appeared, the woman would rest her fucking fingers and a CD of the Wedding March would begin. "I'm gettin' tired of lookin' and feelin' like a trussed up fuckin' penguin, John Boy."

Johnnie scowled, while Christopher tried to remain level-headed. "Give Megs a break—"

"Shut the fuck up with callin' my woman Megs on my fuckin' weddin' day, assfuck, cuz I'm 'bout to fuck you up," he said, on edge suddenly, all his humor and goodwill evaporating.

A stern clearing of the throat interrupted Johnnie's retort. "I've had it, Mr. Caldwell," the priest began with tight disapproval, "we're in the house of the Lord and I'll expect you to refrain from foul language within my church."

Christopher glared at the older man. "Ain't givin' a fuck who fuckin' house we in. If my fuckin' wife ain't walkin' the fuck down that aisle in two fuckin' minutes, Ima fuck something up."

"Yo, Outlaw, if the priest call off the ceremony and put us out, Meggie girl going to be pissed. I'll even risk my life and say she might decide to lock her pussy up and keep it to herself a while," Mortician explained. "Women funny like that."

Johnnie cleared his throat and sent a pleading gaze to the priest. *What the fuck ever.* Christopher would let John Boy convey how fucking much it would mean if the wedding went on. He'd see to it the parish received a hefty donation.

"She said she had a surprise for you, Christopher," his cousin said.

Christopher stilled and frowned. "Maybe she changin' her mind cuz...cuz…" *I'm still me.* Pussy-whipped or not. Loving the fuck out of Megan or not. He couldn't fucking change and the last month some intense fucking bullshit had happened. Worse, it looked like the Dwellers and the Scorpions were headed for war. Cee Cee remained under the radar, but to smoke him out, Christopher had ordered a hit on another one of Cee Cee's sons. The fucker—who happened to be his half-brother—had gotten plugged two days ago. Had Megan discovered the extra bullshit he tried to keep away from her? What if…?

"She already your wife, Prez," Mortician reminded him. "All this bullshit just because Meggie want a big wedding. The girl not going nowhere so stop fucking tripping."

Like a pussified motherfucker. The sentiment went unspoken but hung in the air like a motherfucker. Even the priest scoffed at him.

Christopher growled low in his throat, glaring at the man. What the fuck did he know anyfuckingway?

Johnnie rolled his shoulders, making Christopher all the antsier.

Just over one year had gone by since any of them had last set foot in a holy sanctuary. That time had been for his Ma's funeral, and she was all up in his mind today. He wondered what she would've thought of how the church looked today. Megan had made it so fucking pretty, helping Christopher to blot out the memories of Patricia's funeral.

Unlike then, peach, cream, and blueberry-colored gauze, silk, and lace decorated the church today. Bouquets of peach, white, and blue flowers hung on each side of every pew. Rose petals littered a long blue carpet emblazoned with their names that was laid on the white marble floor. Small candles in holders made of motorcycle gear chain lit the altar, reflecting on the bridesmaids who stood on the left in gowns alternating between blue and peach. The groomsmen wore tuxedos with blue bow ties and matching cummerbunds, adamantly refusing Megan's request that some of them wear peach instead.

It had surprised and pleased him to find bullet lapel pins containing flowers in their wedding colors for him and all his motherfuckers.

Johnnie glanced at his watch and Christopher mimicked the action. Megan was almost fifteen minutes late for the church wedding she'd been so excited about.

Johnnie tugged at his collar and Christopher wanted to knock the fuck out of the motherfucker. John Boy's fucking jitteriness was making Christopher's skin fucking crawl.

"Fuck me," Christopher whispered. "She realized what type of man my ass is and ducked out, John Boy. Took my boy with her."

The men all shifted, uncomfortable, looking from one to the other, beginning to agree that she was going to be a no-show.

Shady handed Cowboy the almost empty bottle, then nodded toward the same pew Bowlie sat on. Motherfuckers joined him.

Balling his hands into fists, Christopher went rigid.

"Keep it together, Outlaw," Johnnie said under his breath.

If she'd used this opportunity to leave Christopher, it would destroy him. He thrust his fingers through his hair. Megan wouldn't fucking do this to him. She loved him as much as he loved her, so if she wasn't marching the fuck down the aisle…it was because she didn't have a choice in the matter. A boulder of anxiety pressed in on Christopher's chest, something unsettling him. Everyone had already marched to the altar, even the flower girl. Not the ring bearer, though. The ring bearer…CJ…aided by Val…because an eight-month-old couldn't hold a motherfucking thing. He couldn't even fucking walk. The lil' motherfucker might've started to try, but it hadn't happened yet.

So, where the fuck was Megan? CJ? Val? Val valued his fucking life. He wouldn't runoff with Megan and CJ, even if that was what the fuck Megan wanted. Christopher knew fucking well she didn't.

Val would've walked the fuck down the fucking aisle by now, if—

"Prez, where Val?" Mort asked as if he read his mind.

The guests were beginning to get restless, too. Murmurs and movements were rippling through the pews, harping on his nerves like chirping birds. And that fucking organ music. Fuck him. Megan was going to get her Wedding Song, so he should've requested Insane Clown Posse in the meantime. He'd prefer to hear *Another Love Song* play on repeat, rather than having this boring shit pounding through his fucking brain.

Johnnie narrowed his eyes. "Where the fuck *is* Val, Christopher? *She* might've ducked out on you, which is as unlikely as the sun falling from the sky by the way, but *Val* wouldn't."

John Boy and Mort had the same fucking idea as Christopher. And it wasn't as if Val would run away with Megan and CJ, so what…Holy motherfuck him. How could his head be shoved so fucking far up his ass? This situation stank of…Cee Cee. Sebastian fucking Caldwell.

"Cee Cee," he snarled, and the men standing with him focused on him with dawning realizations.

"Motherfucker wouldn't dare," Derby said.

"Derby, Boy, Trader, still in this motherfucker. Civilians fuckin' here, so don't pull your pieces unless you gotta. Ain't no assfuck leavin'," Christopher warned. "Mort, Digger, Johnnie, Stretch, fuckin' follow me," he ordered. He kept his back to the wedding guests and pulled his nine from the holster beneath his jacket. Removing the silencer from his pocket, he attached it to his piece as Father Wilcunt spluttered in outrage.

"Mr. Caldwell!" the priest began.

Christopher shoved the gun in his pocket. "You! Shut the fuck up. And if you goin' one fuckin' place befuckinfore my ass gettin' the fuck back, Ima fuckin' gut you."

"If something's happened, we don't want a bloodbath in the church," Johnnie warned, turning to Father Wilkins. "Please. Bear with us. I hear the church daycare needs a few renovations."

The priest glared at him but nodded. Assured that that had been taken care of, Christopher rushed down the red-carpeted stairs that led to the altar and headed down the aisle, the fury wafting from him discouraging anybody from stopping him.

Meggie

AFTER ALL HER COMPLAINING ABOUT THE GUYS NOT wearing their cuts, it came down to this—Megan pacing in a small room, her beautiful wedding gown hanging on a wall hook, her second wedding outfit hidden behind it.

She couldn't wait until Christopher saw her in that dress at the reception. He hated when she sexed herself up with skimpy clothing. It brought out a particularly possessive side that had their normally hot lovemaking sizzling.

Grinning, she gazed around. Small room? Actually, the place looked like a storage closet with a hastily thrown-in floor-to-ceiling mirror and a cheap vanity with a stool to sit on.

She sighed. Something else courtesy of Christopher's persuasions.

CJ giggled at the mooing of a terrycloth cow when he slapped the toy attached to his bouncer in an arc of farm animals. Christopher had wanted her to find one with motorcycles. Even if they'd had such a toy, Meggie had refused. CJ's motorcycle and gun lessons would arrive soon enough. He was already well on his way to cursing sixty-nine ways to the moon. She was sure his first word would be one of Christopher's favorites, '*fuck*' or '*motherfuck*'.

She peeked out the blind for the thousandth time, wondering where Val could be, strands of organ music reaching her even from where she was in the church. It must've been quite loud in the sanctuary and driving Christopher insane.

Hopefully, the guests found the noisy music entertaining while they sat through the delay.

Retrieving her and CJ's cuts was a simple matter of going to her house and into her bedroom closet to get the box with the cuts, then making it back to the church. She, her son, and bridal party had gotten a hotel suite in Portland. She'd texted Val on the way to the church about the cuts. He hadn't been pleased, answering the message with *I'm nearly at the church.*

Meggie had apologized but told him he had to go back for her box.

If Val didn't get back soon, their entire schedule would be thrown off. Christopher had said they were going straight to the airport from their reception and wouldn't have time to return to the club for her suitcase, so it too crowded the space.

She looked with longing at her beautiful wedding gown. She loved every detail of the glittery tulle ball gown, from the plunging V-neck and open back to the beaded lace appliqués, cathedral train and wide skirt. She'd paired it with a two-tier lace and tulle veil embellished with seed pearls. Her pumps had dainty lace details with pearls and a cross strap. Her entire outfit had been cream-colored.

Christopher was going to be livid, but she was a woman and women had every right to change their minds. Especially pregnant ones who were worried about puking all over their silk and lace.

Instead of wearing the cut over her gown as she'd intended, she wore a black vinyl catsuit with and tall moto boots. Tasteless, yes, but vomit could be wiped away from vinyl. This was supposed to have been the outfit she wore to go to the airport, but after throwing up three times before heading to the church this morning, Dinah insisted she find something else to wear, so Meggie had finally given up on her dress.

Not completely since it's staring at you and tempting you to wear it. True, but her mother was already seated, and Bunny, Gypsy, Farrah, Lacey, Bailey, Danika, Zoann, and Ophelia had already marched. Yes, she'd made some last minute changes to her bridal party, but her wedding would really be the big one of her dreams.

So why not wear her gown?

This should've been settled. As a matter of fact, she should've been almost to the altar. She'd given the go-ahead for the bridal party to begin the ceremony because she thought Val would've gotten back with her cut.

A knock sounded on the door.

"Finally," she grouched and snatched it open. She sagged in relief when she saw Val, her new leather cut with the Death Dwellers' rocker and the words *Property of Outlaw* in one hand and the tiny cut for CJ, designed much the same way as hers but for the words: *Little Man, Son of Outlaw,* in the other.

"What the fuck, babe?" he managed, examining her up and down and sideways. "You in that shit and we in this bullshit?"

He sounded pissed and she couldn't blame him. She shrugged before stooping down to lift CJ out of his bouncer. She giggled because even he wore a tuxedo. Placing him in Val's arms, she put his miniature cut on him and stepped back, beaming with pride. She couldn't wait until Christopher saw this. "I've been throwing up all morning and I didn't want to ruin my gown."

"Tough shit," he growled and glared at her. "Hear me, Meggie? We not doing this shit again, so I'm thinking you should put your gown on. After all this bullshit, you'll be disappointed to see yourself in pictures with us dressed up and you not."

The same thought had crept into her head. "Too late now. I'd need someone to help me into the gown and button me up."

He grunted. "You know, babe, sometimes you're too fucking blonde for your own good."

"Matthew Ryan Taylor!" Meggie chirped, planting her fists on her hips. "Did you just give me a read using a blonde joke?"

The edges of his mouth kicked up and his eyes twinkled. "Did you just call me by my Christian name?"

She poked her tongue out at him and he barked a laugh. He scratched behind his ear. "I gotta admit, babe, you look hot as a motherfucker."

"And I gotta admit, Matthew, you still know how to go all pervy on me."

He laughed again and held CJ in a one-armed snuggle while holding his free arm out to her. "Ready, babe?"

"Yes, Val. Both me and the boys are ready."

"*Boys*?" Val snorted. "Give him another son and he's gonna be impossible to deal with."

"Just be prepared," Meggie warned, though she was uncertain since it was too early to tell. According to her mother, she would have a girl because of all the morning sickness. "Now, go. Take my son and march him down the aisle to his daddy."

"I'm surprised that motherfucker not storming in here when he didn't see me with Little Man when that little flower girl marched up the aisle."

"We're in church, Valentine," Megan sniffed. "Have some respect."

"Don't give a fuck. I have this fucking monkey suit on for you. That's about as much as you get from me, babe."

"God, you guys are impossible. Just go. Because you're right. Christopher is going to cause chaos any minute now."

"Fuck! I forgot the little pillow thing in my saddlebag."

"Really, Val? We're already twenty minutes late."

"I know, babe, and I promise you I'll make it up to you for being late with those cuts, but I'll look fucking ridiculous just carrying Little Man down the aisle without his pillow."

"Okay," Megan huffed in frustration. "Just hurry up. The pillow isn't so important since Johnnie has the rings."

CJ gave her a gummy grin and she kissed his cheek, the black hair on his head curly, his bright green eyes hard to miss.

"Uncle Val is silly, huh, my little potato?"

He smiled at her and grabbed her nose.

"Daddy's is going to cause a riot if we don't hurry. Maybe, I should walk down the aisle with you myself? We don't need a silly old pillow. What do you say?"

"I say stop calling me silly, Meggie."

She laughed at Val's mock irritation, and he shoved CJ into her arms, then turned. Blood sprayed on Meggie and Val dropped to the floor. A gun with a silencer attached cut off her scream when Cee Cee shoved it into her mouth.

"Well, well, well, if it isn't the dick bruiser and my grandson." He smiled at her and held out his free hand. "Give him to me or you're going to be missing the back of your head."

And he'd take him anyway. Meggie's heart banged against her chest. Val's blood dripped down her cheeks and mingled with the tears in her eyes. She hadn't heard a sound since he'd dropped to the floor. She didn't even know where he'd been shot. Was it his head? His heart?

"I'm counting to three, Meggie." He slid the release back and Meggie shook.

She'd prefer to die than just hand over her son.

"Two."

Reaching out, she flattened her palm against Cee Cee's chest and his gaze fastened to hers.

"One."

She didn't know if he wanted to look her in the eye as he blew her head off or if her touch affected him.

After uttering 'one', he didn't pull the trigger, so she took that as a good sign. Another tense heartbeat went by before he pulled the barrel out of her mouth.

"You want to say something?"

She wanted to say so many things, none of which she had time for, and most of them to Christopher. She settled for the next best thing. "If you let me put CJ in his bouncer and we leave him here, unharmed, I'll go with you."

Interest flickered in his eyes, and he glanced at the swells of her breasts, the indentation of her waist, the vee between her legs.

"Take that cut off. You're nothing to my son but a fucking liability, cunt. Bitches are only good for cleaning, fucking, and popping out kids." He pointed the gun at her head. "Put my grand boy in that contraption and let's get moving."

Meggie couldn't think of how she'd get out of this latest situation. Probates guarded the cars and motorcycles in the parking lot, but, if Cee Cee so readily agreed to take her, he must have a contingency plan.

Crouching down, she slipped CJ into his bouncer and his little face screwed up in preparation to cry. She kissed his forehead and Cee Cee slapped the side of her head, grabbing her shoulder and yanking her to her feet. He shoved her forward and she stumbled over Val, his big body cushioning her fall. She saw then he'd been shot in the bridge between his shoulder and neck. Blood was pooling beneath him. If someone didn't find him soon, he'd bleed out and die.

"Back away from him, now."

Rising to her feet, Meggie slipped her cut off. She was pregnant, just like when Snake got to her. One of these days, she or her baby wouldn't survive. She only hoped today wasn't that day.

Cee Cee pushed her again. "Walk real close to me," he ordered. "Don't want nobody seeing this gun planted against your back."

As big as it was, she wasn't sure how it would escape notice. The moment Meggie stepped out of the utility closet, CJ released an ear-splitting wail. Not that anyone would hear him with that woman banging on that God-awful church organ.

"Loud little motherfucker, huh?" Cee Cee asked with a snicker, slamming the door shut. "Walk. Your pretty head is going to be a nice reminder to another bitch who's trying to weaken one of my sons."

At his words, Meggie stumbled. If she didn't think he would've pulled the trigger, she might've taken her chances and made a run for it. Shady, Traveler and Cowboy were serving as ushers. They'd intervene.

If Cee Cee was taking her in that direction, but he wasn't. Instead, he dragged her toward a corridor with a glowing *EXIT* sign. She dug her heels in.

"Cooperate," he snarled, low, slowing down instead of stopping as Meggie wanted. "I have plans for you and me before I turn you into an example."

She shivered at the idea of Cee Cee violating her.

"I'm losing patience, cumrag," he continued. "If you don't fucking walk normally, I'm leaving your bullet-riddled body right here."

Like Val's body was in the utility closet. Meggie shuddered. She prayed the organist took a break to turn her music book. Anything, so CJ's cries would be heard. Her absence would be investigated. She knew that, but if help took too long to arrive, it would be too late to save Val.

At the door, Cee Cee cocked the hammer of his gun. "One fucking peep and you're dead. If a Probate sees us, you're telling him you're leaving willingly."

"I'm going to b-behave. Pl-please. One wrong move and the gun will discharge."

"Good of you to note."

Using a hip to open the door, Cee Cee wrapped his free hand around her arm. The sudden brightness blinded Meggie for a moment but didn't stop Cee Cee. Cold air whooshed around her face, the breeze whipping the curls allowed to escape her swept up hair. Her vision adjusted. Bursts of sunshine broke free from the low clouds. Still, her heart sank. He'd found a back exit. Probates were nowhere to be seen.

He tugged her toward the right. A short distance away at the edge of the walkway, a utility van waited. Somehow, she had to get away before he took her off premises. Otherwise, she was dead.

Chapter 22

Outlaw

BEFORE HE REACHED THE PLACE WHERE MEGAN should've been getting ready, he heard his boy's wails.

"What the fuck?" Johnnie inquired.

Weapon out and ready to fucking fire, Digger rushed ahead of Christopher, taking his duties as sergeant-at-arms seriously. But Christopher wouldn't have any of it. Not allowing Johnnie, Mortician, or Stretch to rush ahead of him, Christopher stormed in and screeched to a motherfucking halt.

Val lay in a pool of blood, pale as a fucking ghost, while CJ screamed in his bouncer thing, red-faced, arms and legs flailing. If he hadn't been strapped in he would've tumbled out.

"Megan!" Christopher called, scanning the small area and processing the scene in seconds. "Get K-P," he ordered to no one in particular, hurrying to his son and freeing him, holding his boy close. He was so fucking relieved to find the lil' motherfucker here. Except his woman was gone.

Although CJ was still in tears, Christopher had to find Megan. He turned to hand his boy over, but Mortician was rifling through Megan's suitcase, while Johnnie knelt next to Val. Digger and Stretch must've gone for help.

"What about Zoann?" Johnnie asked as Mort rushed to Val's other side, holding terrycloth wraps that Megan sometimes wore after her shower. "She's a nurse."

"She find a fucking gun and finish him off," Mortician said with a snort, jerking off his belt, then looping it over the terrycloth and angling it around Val's body.

CJ continued to cry. If Megan was here, she wouldn't have left their boy.

"Take CJ. I gotta find Megan." And he didn't want to put his son back in the fucking bouncer thing. He was already crying the way babies do when their feelings are crushed. Sniffling. Gasping. Wailing. Small shoulders shaking. "Megan gone," Christopher said again because Mort and Johnnie were speaking among themselves, ignoring him.

"What the fuck's happened in here?" K-P demanded, rushing in.

"Cee Cee," Christopher said, fear for Megan's safety uppermost in his mind. At this moment, he didn't even feel anger or hate. He was scared Cee Cee would kill her before Christopher could save her.

"How do you want to handle this, Outlaw?" K-P asked.

"John Boy, you in charge," Christopher said, unable to wait another moment to start searching for his woman.

"Christopher, I can't—"

"Prez, wait—"

"Outlaw, the guests—"

Johnnie, Mortician, and Digger's voices bounced in his head. Didn't they understand—

"You have to run the club," K-P said kindly, but there was something in his eyes. Pity. Sorrow. "Your president first and foremost, then father, then husband—"

"I'm Megan husband first." Christopher walked to Stretch and thrust his still-screaming boy in the man's arms, turned and started for the door. Val's body sprawled in the middle of the small fucking room, no bigger than a closet. Christopher clenched his jaw. "Get Val to the hospital. Ain't able to call it in cuz the badges'll interfuckinfere when I'm findin' Cee Cee. Delay motherfuckers, 'til I get my girl." His voice cracked. He'd been such a motherfucker to her. Now, she might not be alive for him to make it up to her.

"Prez, Meggie might not be in shape for a ceremony," Mortician told him.

It dawned on Christopher that CJ had stopped crying.

Megan was a fucking fighter and he loved her with everything in him. He'd know if she'd been taken away from him. She had become a part of his very essence, his heart and soul. "She fine," he said sharply. "She wantin' her weddin'. She gettin' it."

"Outlaw—"

He'd done his duty, given orders as the club president. He wouldn't listen to another goddamn thing. Too much time had already been wasted.

Meggie

THREE OR FOUR MORE STEPS AND THEY'D REACH THE VAN. Cee Cee would crowd her against it, gun jammed against her, open the doors at the back and shove her in. She would be trapped, a guaranteed casualty of Cee Cee, when she'd fought so hard to survive Thomas *and* this maniac the last time he'd gotten her.

She had a son and husband who needed her. She could *not* allow Cee Cee to take her away from them.

Her pulse thumped so erratically she felt lightheaded before energy surged through her.

"Omigod, it's him," she said, infusing as much awe and hope in her voice as she could, not knowing where those words came from but rolling with it.

"Who?" Cee Cee said, his hold slackening a tiny bit, his steps slowing.

Shoring up courage, Meggie elbowed his gut with all her might. He was a hard, honed beast, so she didn't damage him at all. The element of surprise served her purpose and freed her.

The gun fired, the bullet so close to her, it whooshed past her in a burst of heat. Screaming, she vaulted around the van. If she went in the direction they'd come, she'd have no cover.

"*Bitch!*" he snarled.

As she reached the front fender, another bullet whizzed past her. A row of trees, interspersed with shrubbery marched down the church's east side.

"I'm going to kill you while I fuck you," he shouted.

She weaved around the trees, screaming, praying none of the bullets Cee Cee continued to fire hit her. He was such a liar. If he wasn't trying to kill her now, he would stop shooting at her.

"I despise a hard-headed slut. I want to watch you suffer. Hear you moan in pain from my gunshot. Do you fucking hear me?" he yelled, shooting at her again.

Too breathless to scream any longer, Meggie finally rounded the corner and reached the edge of the parking lot. Her shoulders heaving, Meggie lowered her body, praying he ran out of bullets and barreled down a corridor of vehicles. She couldn't imagine the type of gun Cee Cee had. He fired round after round.

Windshields exploded. Windows shattered. The air was acrid and thick.

Cars and motorcycles took up almost every available space. Who had come to her wedding? It was a random thought, but it reminded her that people, *regular* people were in the church, not only bikers and their families. Even more distressing—they were *in* the church, waiting for her. It seemed as if no one had left or went to check on her delay and found her missing. The Probates were nowhere to be seen. Except for her labored breathing, it was silent.

Silent.

It was silent. No bursts of gunfire.

Cee Cee had finally run out of bullets.

Buoyed by the realization, Meggie straightened again, a grassy knoll between her and the open area that led to the church's entrance. A late model car halted at the end of the pathway. A moment later Father Wilkins exited.

"Help me!" she screamed, glimpsing Johnnie and Mortician carrying Val from the church as the priest froze. She estimated only about ten minutes had passed since this nightmare began. Val might have a chance to survive.

Mortician saw her before Johnnie did. "Meggie!" he cried, drawing Johnnie's gaze her way.

Her foot touched grass. Cee Cee rammed into her simultaneously wrapping his arm around her waist and lifting her off her feet. She had to buy herself time while the guys got Val into the car, so she dug her nails into Cee Cee's arms, earning her freedom for the briefest of moments. He caught her too quickly, grabbing her hand and jerking her to him, his fist poised to strike her. He was crouched, almost eye level with her.

Her foot shot out, but he scooted back, laughing like a wild man.

"Fuck, Meggie move!" Mortician yelled.

"Megan, get out the fucking way," Johnnie ordered.

"Big, mean rhinoceros," she snarled to Cee Cee, realizing he was using her as a shield. Balling her own fist, she crashed it against his jaw.

"Little cunt!" he said, the hit she gave him angering him. She stumbled back. Bullets whizzed past her, but they were going wide in an effort not to wound her.

Cee Cee dug into his cut and pulled out another gun, pointing it at her and cocking the hammer.

"No, no, no," she said, trying to dodge his grasping hand, but he grabbed her and shoved the gun against her head.

She stilled. If he'd shot her in the back, she might've been paralyzed but she *could've* survived. If he pulled the trigger now, purposely, or accidentally, she'd have no chance.

"*MEGAN!*" Christopher yelled, appearing at the opposite end from where she and Cee Cee had emerged, his own gun in hand. K-P stepped out of the church.

"Kaleb Paul," Cee Cee called, his breath hot on her neck from where he crouched.

"Megan, baby, stay fuckin' still," Christopher told her, then looked past her. "Ima go fuckin' easy on your fuckin' ass as long as you releasin' my wife."

Cee Cee turned the gun from Meggie's head and fired, shattering the car's windshield. "Don't seem like you're in control, boy. If one of you move, she's dead. I'm not in a charitable mood, so I don't think I want that motherfucker in the car to survive."

K-P walked to the driver's side. "Val done nothing to you, Sebastian," he said coldly. "Outlaw. John Boy. *None of them.*"

"Every motherfucker alive has done something to me," Cee Cee said, unconcerned there were three men pointing guns at him. Nor did it matter that he was holding a conversation without looking at K-P. He wouldn't move from behind Meggie. Despite his height, he'd somehow positioned himself perfectly.

"He got a new kid," K-P said. "A son. A boy need his father. If any fuckhead knows that it's you."

Cee Cee growled. "I still don't like you."

"And I still don't give a fuck," K-P replied. "I'm not pulling my piece, motherfucker. I just want to get this man to the hospital to try and save his life."

"A cunt for a motherfucker," Cee Cee spat. "I'll let you take this motherfucker, if those fuckheads lower their weapons and let me and Meggie leave with no fucking interference."

"You outcha motherfuckin' mind," Christopher snarled.

To Meggie, he'd inched the barest bit closer.

"Shut up!" Cee Cee exploded. "I don't fuck corpses. She's alive because there's nothing in this world like coming in a bitch while I fucking kill her."

"That's Joe's girl, you sick fuck," K-P snapped, losing his patience.

"I don't give a fuck!" Cee Cee screamed, sounding like a rabid dog.

Christopher had come closer still. As much as she wanted rescue, Val needed medical attention. She had faith in her husband.

"Let me talk to them," she whispered to Cee Cee. "I swear I won't resist any more if they agree and you let K-P take Val."

He shoved the gun against her head again. "Talk, cumrag."

He'd agreed easy enough, but she'd lived with Christopher long enough to know that she had to consider all possibilities.

"And you have to let us stay here until K-P's driven away with Val."

He hooted with laughter. "You think I was born yesterday. I know what you're doing."

"It isn't a trap," she said quickly. Just as he ran out of bullets in that first gun, maybe he'd start to feel the effects of crouching. "I don't trust that you won't use your stupid van to renege on your word and block K-P from leaving or catch up to him and prevent him from going."

He touched the back of her head and made a sound as if he were spitting. A warm glob slid down her neck. "I fucking swear to you if you're pulling a fucking stunt or trying to get Val out of the way so I'm a lame duck, you'll be sorry. You'll get your husband, Johnnie, and Mortician killed. And your death will be so much more gruesome. Do you understand me?"

"Yes," she whispered, almost losing her nerve. If her plan didn't work or if Christopher didn't realize her intentions—

Valuable time was wasting. Val might already be dead. Twenty minutes must've passed since he'd been shot.

She was exhausted and tired and scared, but Christopher wouldn't even think about allowing her to go with Cee Cee. He'd let Val die first. She stared at her husband, hoping he read the message in her eyes, the belief that he'd get to her before Cee Cee killed her.

"M-Mortician, J-Johnnie." Her voice trembled so she paused and cleared her throat. "Please, go and see to my guests before they decide to leave and find this. Not everyone will understand."

"Meggie—"

"Megan—"

They spoke at the same time.

"Please?" she said, looking between them and Christopher. "Val *has* to be seen to or he'll die." For the first time since this started, she choked up. "I love you, Christopher, so much. Lower your gun—"

"No, drop the motherfucker completely," Cee Cee ordered. "All of you."

"They don't have to surrender their weapons," Megan said in frustration, not caring that her voice had risen. She'd hoped talking quietly and privately to Cee Cee would lull him into believing she wasn't in fact trying to send a message. "I already told you I'd leave with you."

"Ain't no fuckin' way—"

"If you just let K-P and Val drive away," she went on, over Christopher's angry words, "while we stood here and watched so you want try to block him."

Cee Cee grabbed handfuls of her hair and shoved the gun in her mouth, jerking her against him. She was vaguely aware that he wasn't hiding behind her anymore.

"You fuckheads get the fuck inside as she said. Go, Kaleb. Take that motherfucker." Cee Cee jiggled the gun. "I fucking swear if you think you're fucking smarter than me…you're a fucking live one."

Taking his gaze off Meggie long enough to nod to Mortician and Johnnie, Christopher stared at her, while K-P rushed into the car and swerved away. It had been idling, waiting to be driven.

Cee Cee began dragging her away.

Outlaw

*T*his. Was. NOT. Fucking. Happening. A. Fucking. Gain.

And on his motherfucking wedding day.

And with Megan pregnant. A-fucking-gain.

And with a motherfucking relative who also happened to be a motherfucking lunatic. What kind of shit was this? All in the Fucking Family? Keeping Up with the Fucking Killers? Last time, Snake, Megan's fucking brother, had taken her. *This time*, it was Christopher's fucking father. And he hated that motherfucker with a passion so purple it looked like that stupid fucking Barney that deserved fucking up just for being a pain in the fucking ass.

And if Christopher hated any-fucking-body more than he despised motherfucking Snake, that shit said a lot.

When he'd gotten outside after leaving his boy, he'd found a sea of cars and motorcycles. No Probates. No Megan. No fuckhead. He'd thought to use a shortcut and veered left from the open court. The breezeway led to a line of doors on one side and the rectory on the other side.

Annoyed as a motherfucker at losing precious time, he'd started back the way he'd come until he noticed a fucking booted foot sticking out from a partially opened door.

Fuck him, but he'd found the missing Probates. Cee Cee had capped five motherfuckers. *Five.* Against one assfuck. If the fuckheads couldn't beat those fucking odds, then they fucking deserved fucking death. He hoped a fucking civilian didn't wander this way like his dumb fucking ass had done. He'd shoved dead motherfucker's foot inside wherever the fuck the door led to and started off again.

Instead of going fucking left, he'd taken a right, passing the church's entrance and reaching the west side, where a fucking utility van waited at the end of the breezeway. Images of Cee Cee in the cargo hold with Megan propelled Christopher forward. It had been empty, so he'd gone forward.

It was then that he'd heard Megan's screams and Cee Cee's gunshots. When he'd reached the edge of the parking lot and saw Cee Cee firing and Megan ducking and all the fucking vehicles in his pathway, Christopher thought it would be easier to go around and meet the motherfucker head on from the opposite direction.

Now, she'd risked herself on Val's behalf, trusting Christopher to save her.

If Val died after she did this shit, Christopher would fucking kill that motherfucker.

Once Mortician and Digger disappeared inside and K-P sped out of the parking lot with Val inside the car, Christopher stood still, gripping his 9mm at his side as Cee Cee began dragging Megan away. That fucking gun was still in her mouth and all Christopher imagined was Cee Cee pulling the trigger.

The sun glinted off the piece in his old man's hand. They were farther away now.

Christopher was going to have to take his fucking chances.

Cars filled this parking lot to fucking capacity, and not just with vehicles belonging to brothers and the old ladies, but fucking civilians, locals and motherfuckers from out of town that could rat them the fuck out or even get injured themselves. The Probates had died protecting the integrity of the club. Still, the odds had been in their fucking favor but what the fuck ever.

Cursing the fucking tuxedo and realizing Megan didn't have on her wedding gown, Christopher hauled ass in the opposite direction from where Cee Cee was bringing his girl. He was going to cut that motherfucker off head on. At the end of the walkway, a van was parked. He'd seen it earlier and gave it a quick inspection to make sure she hadn't been put in it.

Halfway down the walkway—midway to the van—a door burst open. Mort, Stretch, Digger, and Johnnie spilled out.

"Church doors are locked, Christopher," Johnnie said. "No one can come out."

"Probates fuckin' filled with fuckin' holes in a fuckin' room near the rectory," Christopher returned, because what the fuck could he say to holding wedding guests fucking hostage?

Not a motherfucking thing.

They descended on the van and swarmed it. While they opened the driver, passenger, and back doors, Christopher ran to the front of the vehicle.

Then, he saw them, the man propelling Megan down a path lined with trees and shrubs, using her body as a shield, the gun nowhere in sight, although that didn't mean anything.

Cee Cee's gaze fell on Christopher.

Raising his nine, he fired, hitting Cee Cee in the shoulder and the right side of his chest. He dropped like a sack of shit. If the motherfucker died befuckingfore Christopher got him to the meat shack, oh-fucking-well. He'd fucking targeted areas so he'd stay alive awhile, but it was what the fuck it was.

Megan ran toward him at the same time he started for her. Reaching her, he pulled her into his arms and clutched her to him, his heart beating as fiercely as hers. They clung to each other, before he pocketed his nine and lifted her up, cradling her in his arms. She leaned her head against his chest.

"Stretch, put assfuck in this fuckin' van and take him to the club," Christopher ordered when he reached his boys. They were all staring at him, at her.

Mort's shoulders visibly sagged in relief, his breath escaping him. Johnnie leaned against the van and bent, hands on his knees. Digger squeezed the bridge of his nose.

Frowning, Stretch hadn't moved, rocking on his heels, his gaze falling on the back of Megan's head.

Christopher nodded.

"Meggie, are you okay?" Stretch asked.

"I'm fine," she said, although she sounded so fucking far from fine she could've been a little fucking space bitch just landed from Mars. "Where's CJ?"

"With your mama," Mort answered.

She lifted her head. "Okay. She might decide to leave with K-P gone, so we have to tell her the ceremony will start soon because I still want us to have our marriage blessed."

"You want to what?" Digger asked, his eyes widening in shock.

"I want the wedding to take place. I have to clean up. Cee Cee spat on my neck." She turned green at the words. "Down," she moaned around a gag.

As Christopher was setting her on her feet and placing his hands at her waist, she was bending over and fucking hurling.

"Baby, your lil' fuckin' ass need to fuckin' rest." Besides, if he had to get through a wedding, motherfucking Cee Cee *would* die. And he needed extra fucking torture added in for spitting on Megan. Nasty motherfucker.

"Please, Christopher. We can cancel the reception and postpone our honeymoon for Val. Until he's out of danger."

"This your day, Megan," Christopher said softly. "We havin' our marriage blessed, going to the reception, *and* going on our honeymoon, baby."

"Val going to understand, Meggie girl," Mortician told her.

"He's alive then?" she asked, hope in her eyes.

"He was when we put him in the car, Megs," Johnnie told her.

Christopher glared at the assfuck for calling her Megs.

"I'll give Dinah your message," Digger volunteered, starting down the breezeway.

Megan's lips trembled, but she nodded and glanced at Christopher. "I love you."

"I love you too, Megan."

She plastered a smile on her face, grabbed his hand, then started behind Digger, tugging Christopher forward.

"Fall in fuckin' line, assfucks," Christopher ordered, sweeping her back into his arms.

She sounded as if she'd burst into tears at any moment, but if she needed their ceremony to go on, then go the fuck on it would.

Chapter 23

ONCE HE REACHED THE CHURCH ENTRANCE, HE SAW THE DOORS TO the sanctuary were opened and Derby was standing at the front, holding CJ and addressing the crowd.

Mortician and Digger met Christopher halfway to the utility closet that had been turned into a dressing room for Megan. Although she hadn't let him see her beautiful gown before today, he hadn't wanted it ruined since he couldn't be sure about the weather, so he'd suggested Father Wilcunt find a place for Megan to dress on the premises.

The fat little fucker had given Megan a fucking utility closet.

Johnnie was at the sanctuary entrance, but instead of going in, he backtracked and joined them. The look in his eyes when he stared at Megan let Christopher know his cousin still carried feelings for her. He didn't care. She was alive. That was the most important thing.

"People are getting really restless, Christopher," Johnnie said with meaning.

Soon, motherfuckers were going to walk the fuck out and with bullet casings in the parking lot and Val's blood in the church lobby along with the delayed ceremony…yeah, shit wouldn't look good.

"Get the fuck in front the motherfuckers, Johnnie," Christopher ordered. "Send Derby with my son. See what the fuck takin' Digger so long to bring Dinah."

Johnnie nodded, gazed at Megan again, then walked away because she hadn't lifted her head from Christopher's chest.

"Megan, baby, putcha fuckin' dress on."

She drew in a teary breath. "I need help with the buttons."

"Dinah comin'," he promised, setting her on her feet and gently holding her arms until he was sure she was steady.

"Momma might not want to help."

"She ain't havin' a fuckin' choice," Christopher said as Derby strolled out of the church with CJ.

CJ reached for Megan. Her eyes lit up and she took their son in her arms, hugging him tightly to her.

"Your woman good?" Derby answered. "Shit seen to?"

Christopher nodded but sent him a meaningful look.

"I'm going take a smoke before the ceremony begins," Derby said. "Want to join me?"

"Yeah," Christopher answered. They needed to move the dead Probates. Clear away all the evidence. "Gimme a fuckin' minute."

Once Derby strolled away, Christopher turned to Megan. She was cooing to CJ. "Can I hold the lil' motherfucker, baby?"

She responded by walking to Christopher.

He took his boy and nosed his little neck, just then realizing he wore a cut. He turned him around and saw the inscription.

"Th-that's what h-held us up." She hiccuped. "I wanted to surprise you with our cuts, and I forgot them and Stretch took forever to get here and then Cee Cee—"

Christopher hugged her again. "Shhh. Shit okay, Megan. You fine. *We* fine. Keep it tofuckingether for me, baby. Putcha pretty dress on to buy a lil' fuckin' time 'til other shit seen to so no motherfucker seein' shit ain't for their fuckin' eyes." He guided her to the utility closet and realized how bloody she was. "Fuck." He placed CJ in the baby thing. "You doin' so fucking good, Just continue holdin' it tofuckingether, a lil' longer. Hear me, Megan?"

She nodded. "Okay," she mumbled.

Hating to leave her, he backed out and closed the door, hurrying outside to where Derby stood talking to Mort and Boy. It didn't take long to tell them what needed doing. Christopher and Mort left Derby and Boy calling their respective members to follow Christopher's instructions.

Digger was just leading Dinah into the lobby. Christopher wouldn't ask what took her so long, so he walked to her and jumped straight the fuck to the point. "Listen up, Dinah. I ain't wantin' one fuckin' question from you. Underfuckinstand? Not a fuckin' tear or squeal…*fuck all*," he gritted in warning. "Help Megan with her fuckin' dress and shut the fuck up 'bout anything else. Hear me?"

Eyes wide, she nodded, her face paling and her lips tightening into a thin line.

"See to my woman and you better not fuck up."

She bustled away and Digger settled a hand on Christopher's shoulder.

"Your girl fine, man."

Christopher swallowed and nodded. "Yeah."

Digger dropped his hand. "Now what you need from me?"

Christopher heaved in a breath, his heart just settling back into his chest. Megan was fine. His boy was fine. The new baby inside her was fine. "Do what the fuck ever she was makin' Val do with my boy in the weddin'. Then, after them fuckin' pictures took, Ima duck out, so you assfucks distract Megan while I'm keepin' my appointment with Cee Cee, the meat shack, and our special tools."

MEGAN HAD HAD A POINT, INSISTING ON THE CHURCH ceremony, one Christopher couldn't deny after they got through all the readings and Alleluias, and he was taking her little hand into his to guide her back to the altar.

She looked like a princess in her pretty wedding dress with the long train behind her. She didn't have the cut on and that was fine. This was her day and she'd have many opportunities to wear it. Right now, it made him proud as a motherfucker to stand next to her to pledge his life, heart and body to her in front of everybody.

He'd written her a letter that he'd give her while they were on their honeymoon and hoped she understood what he was trying to say to her.

Because, for once in his life, he'd gotten something right.

Meggie

"CHRISTOPHER AND MEGAN, HAVE YOU COME FREELY AND without reservation to give yourselves to each other in marriage?"

"Yeah," Christopher said without hesitation.

"Yes," Meggie echoed softly, trying her best to conquer her overwhelming emotion. After everything else that had happened today, she was getting her marriage to Christopher blessed, in her fairytale gown. Want of her cut had delayed the ceremony, then led to the nightmare that followed.

She couldn't bring herself to wear it right now with her almost kidnapping—and probable murder—still so fresh in her mind. She'd reached the altar almost two hours late. Despite begging her mother to walk beside her down the aisle, Dinah refused. By the time Meggie marched to Christopher, their son had fallen asleep in her mother's lap.

Meggie wondered if Cee Cee hadn't found her where he had, would he have walked into the sanctuary and shot up—

"Answer the fuckin' man, Megan," Christopher whispered, nudging her elbow. "He fuckin' askin' if we gonna honor each other as man and wife for fuckin' ever and ever, amen."

Father Wilkins glared at Christopher. "I did not say that, Mr. Caldwell." He transferred his look to Megan. "I asked if you would honor each other as man and wife for the rest of your lives."

"Same motherfuckin' thing," Christopher snapped.

Meggie groaned, glad she'd opted *not* to have microphones attached to them, so everyone could hear the exchange of vows. "Yes, of course," she said, sending Christopher an imploring gaze to behave. She'd decided to go on with the ceremony, so she had to focus.

"Ain't whatcha supposed to fuckin' say, baby. Your lil' ass shoulda said I do. Ain't that right, Father Wilcu…"

Megan gasped, knowing what he'd been about to say. Christopher tugged at his bow tie.

"Yeah, Rev?" he said instead.

Father Wilkins narrowed his eyes, his mouth thinning in disgust.

"Twenty large," Johnnie said with a cough.

Clearing his throat, Father Wilkins turned to Meggie, his piggish nose and hanging cheeks red. "Mr. Caldwell is right, Megan."

"Er, I do. I'll honor him as my husband for the rest of my life."

Christopher bent and kissed her. "Fuckin' right."

"NO kissing," Father Wilkins snapped, knowing it was a losing battle to make Christopher stop using bad language.

"Ain't no fuckin' reason for jealousy, Rev. Just cuz you gotta jerk—"

"Christopher!" Meggie and Johnnie chorused.

"Yo, Prez, remember what I said?" Mortician offered. "Pussy lockout."

Meggie cringed, deciding not to ask.

Johnnie shifted next to Christopher and cleared his throat. "Father Wilkins, er, can you get on with it? We can only behave for so long."

"You mean act like civilized humans?" Zoann called, and Meggie realized the woman didn't know about Val. "We're already missing two of you, K-P and Val. At least these Cro-Magnons are still here."

Meggie scowled at Zoann. "Shut it," she snapped. She couldn't blurt the reason for the men's absences in front of…of *civilians*. They wouldn't understand. And whether Zoann liked it or not, she wasn't a civilian. She was as much a part of the biker lifestyle as Meggie. "Father Wilkins, please get on with it."

The round, little man sniffed. "Will you accept children lovingly from God—" His mouth pursed, and he frowned at Meggie, not taking his gaze from her as he continued. "Will you bring them up accordingly to the law of Christ and *His* Church?"

Omigod, the priest did not just take a dig at Christopher. Yes. Yes, he had. But hopefully—

"Listen up, assfuck. I ain't fuckin' you up for that cuz I ain't wantin' Megan day ruined. But keep your fuckin' opinions to your fuckin' self."

So much for hoping Christopher hadn't realized the potshot.

"Christopher, please," Meggie implored, grabbing his hand, and squeezing. "He didn't say a word other than—"

"Ain't fuckin' had to. His fuckin' look and where he put the fuckin' emphasis on the fuckin' marriage rite. The motherfucker think I'm hidin' a holy sanctuary somewhere? Where the fuck else our kids worshippin' but a place like this?"

"Oh, for God's sake!" Father Wilkins growled. "Mr. Caldwell—"

"Shut the fuck up," Christopher warned. "Do the Rite of Marriage and keep your fuckin' opinions to yourfuckinself. Don't say nothin' else cuz your ass takin' His name in vain and that shit a sin, too."

Father Wilkins gave him an under-eyed look. "I'm actually impressed enough that you know that much to continue." He gave Meggie another tight-lipped scowl and began. "Since it is your intention to enter into marriage, join your right hands, and declare your consent before God and His Church."

Christopher took her hand into his and smiled at her, his green eyes burning with passion. His black hair curled at his nape, pieces falling onto his forehead. Meggie knew she'd never see him in a tuxedo again but would never forget this day when he'd worn one for her and looked like every woman's dream.

"I, Christopher, take you, Megan, to be my wife." The surety of his voice as he echoed the priest's words resonated through

Meggie, his gaze capturing hers and holding her captive as he spoke. "I promise to be true to you in good times and in bad, in sickness and in health. Ima love you and honor you all the days of my life."

"Wonder of wonders, you actually didn't use the 'f' bomb," Zoann muttered.

"That is cause for celebration," Father Wilkins said dryly.

Christopher raised his hand and Meggie knew he'd flip off both his sister and the priest. She caught his hand and held tight. "My turn."

Johnnie shifted next to Christopher, the light falling on his blond hair, sad resignation in his eyes. He nodded and gave her the barest of smiles. Meggie hoped he found a woman to love and who loved him just as fiercely in return. No one deserved it more than Johnnie.

Or Christopher, who was finally accepting she'd stand by him no matter what and protect him with everything in her.

She gazed up at her husband. "I, Megan, take you, Christopher, to be my husband. I promise to be true to you in good times and in bad, in sickness and in health. I will love you, obey you, and honor you all the days of my life."

"Obey?" Lacey hissed.

"Notice he didn't put that in his vows?" Zoann taunted.

"You bitches ain't—" Christopher began.

"Christopher, do you take Megan to be your wife?" Father Wilkins interrupted, the ice in his voice telling Meggie he wouldn't suffer them a moment longer. "Do you promise to be true to her in good times and in bad…"

"Pssst," Meggie whispered, noticing the hostile glares Christopher and Zoann were exchanging.

Father Wilkins lifted a brow and sighed. "What?" he asked through gritted teeth.

"One moment," she begged. She'd use her bargaining chip, something she'd kept in her arsenal to keep them in line. "Boys, if we can get through this smoothly, you can change out of the tuxedos as soon as the photos are done. No waiting until after the reception."

"I can live with that," Digger called. "I don't even care we got to go back to the club to get my cut."

"You assfucks hearin' her." Christopher grinned wider than he ever had, his eyes gleaming with real happiness. He winked at her. "I love you, Megan.

"I love you, too, Christopher."

"Okay, Rev, we behavin'," Christopher promised. "Finish up the ceremony so I can get the fuck outta this monkey suit."

Unable to stop herself, Meggie burst out laughing and Christopher joined her, everything they'd endured to get to this moment more than worth it.

Chapter 24

Johnnie

"**W**HERE THE FUCK DIGGER?**" FRUSTRATION FILLED Mortician's rhetorical question as he stood with Johnnie in the vestibule of the hall where Megan and Christopher's reception was taking place. "She wanted to change to her second wedding outfit. We been here thirty minutes already."

Johnnie shrugged, on edge as much as the enforcer. There'd been no word on Val's condition. Christopher hadn't arrived yet from burying Cee Cee once and for all. Now, Megan was fucking taking forever to get here herself, when she'd assured them, her husband included, it shouldn't take long to change into the other dress.

Fuck. He'd almost lost her today.

Seeing Megan in the clutches of Sebastian Caldwell had affected Johnnie more than it should have, considering she belonged to Christopher. But only once or twice in his life had he ever felt so fucking helpless. Ironic both those times involved Christopher as well.

It wasn't only that. It was fucking Cee Cee, too. When Christopher had first given the orders to find information on him and then find the motherfucker, he hadn't known who he'd been searching for.

Then, it all fell into place in fucking Seattle. Sebastian fucking Caldwell.

All Johnnie wanted was for that motherfucker to disappear. It seemed as if he had. Of course, life wasn't that fucking easy.

Anything to do with Big Joe, Cee Cee, and Grandda had always been a fucking nightmare.

Big Joe's drug-induced psychosis had forced Johnnie to go Nomad. He'd worried about Christopher's safety but hadn't been able to talk him into leaving. Johnnie had claimed his new status had been for his girlfriend, Iona. While she *had* asked him to leave the club, the Death Dwellers had become embedded in his soul. He couldn't imagine life without the club. His new role as the manager of Christopher's medical lab fit him as well as his cut. Maybe, even better, because he had a business degree.

Johnnie hadn't realized how much he'd missed business suits until he'd put one on for his new position. Iona had been beyond pleased; Johnnie had still been miserable, without the anchor of belonging to a chapter. The mother chapter at that. His rocker no longer had a designated territory. He was simply 'Nomad'.

He'd deeply cared about Iona, believing he'd one day propose to her. Over time, that idea faded. They'd never lived together and because he threw himself into running the lab, he saw less and less of her. By the time she called with the news she'd met someone else and was leaving him, Johnnie had fully disengaged from the relationship. Over the duration of their relationship, he'd stayed faithful to her. Their parting had been cordial. He'd apologized for taking her for granted and she'd thanked him for all that he'd given up on her behalf.

"Meggie probably needed help in the new gown," Stretch decided, stuffing his hands into his trouser pockets, walking to the door and glancing out before returning to the place where he stood, away from Mort and Johnnie. As usual, uneasiness hung about him as if he hid a secret he didn't want exposed.

Mortician grunted. "This shit right here another fucking reason I'm never attaching myself to young pussy."

"A woman will be a woman no matter her age, fucker," Johnnie said, somber for so many fucking reasons.

"Older chicks more practical," Mortician said. "Two fucking wedding dresses? What Meggie girl need that shit for? She already married."

"She didn't need her wedding today either," Stretch said with a shrug. "She was already married."

Mort dug in his jacket pocket, pulling out a pack of cigarettes. After he lit his and offered Johnnie and Stretch one, he looked at Stretch. "Young pussy, son. That's the only fucking reason Prez married her not once but twice."

Johnnie dragged on his cigarette, grinning despite his thoughts running amok. "You want to up the ante on our bet? A hundred grand each."

"Fuck you. Fuck no," Mort snapped around plumes of smoke.

"Why not?" Johnnie challenged, stuffing his cigarette in the corner of his mouth to dig in his pocket for his phone. After checking for messages, he returned it to its place and took hold of his cigarette. "You're so sure you're not losing. You're immune to young pussy."

Mortician glowered at him.

"What say you, Stretch?" Johnnie goaded, glad to have something else to focus on. "Do you think he's wavering because of one Miss Bailey Andrews?"

"I believe you're right, John Boy." Stretch looked at Mort. "Are you sure betting is closed? I really want in, Mort."

"I'm fucking positive," Mort snapped. "Even if I was open to upping the ante, I couldn't do it, Johnnie. Val not here." He sighed, the banter of the past few minutes dying away. "I can't believe he down. The trip part about it is anyone of us could've been him." He glanced away. "Digger."

If it wasn't for Val not wanting to march with Zoann, it would've been Digger. And so went the vagaries of life.

The redhead he'd fucked the night of Christopher's bachelor party came to mind. He thought about her from time to time, wondered what had become of her. Wished he could've conceded to her request to kiss. He would've spent more time with her and gotten her number. He just hadn't been able to bring himself to do it.

It was too late for fucking regrets. She was lost to him forever. After he saw her to her car, he'd gone back inside and made inquiries about her with some of the men who'd been in attendance when she'd strutted into the club. Some motherfucker suggested he talk to Spoon, president of the Torpedoes. They weren't sure, but she reminded him of a girl who he'd seen at the club in Portland.

That made sense. Spoon put his girls on the pole, so maybe she'd been sent as a gift to Christopher, courtesy of the Torps. Still, something didn't sit right with Johnnie. Every motherfucker around knew Christopher didn't want another woman. As a club president, however, Spoon might've thought he was honoring another president whose clubs were on cordial terms. Yet, Johnnie's lingering doubts stopped him from continuing his search for the redhead. Besides, if she was one of Spoon's girls that meant she belonged to the Torps.

Days went by where she didn't cross Johnnie's mind. Then, suddenly, without warning, thoughts of her would intrude and he ached to have her in his bed again. Predictably, Megan's image came to him with a vengeance as if he betrayed her with thoughts of a woman whose name he didn't know and who he'd probably never see again.

"Any more word from K-P?" Stretch questioned.

Mort nodded. "He just sent me a message saying Val in surgery and is critical. They still don't know if he'll make it."

"Fuck," Johnnie grumbled, the image of Megan with Cee Cee invading his head again. What she did to get Val to safety could've so easily backfired.

"K-P also said he texted Meggie something different and we better not tell her the truth," Mort said quietly.

"Val's tough," Stretch declared. "He *will* pull through, so he can thank Meggie for risking her life."

"Fuck, son, I never been so scared in my fucking life, seeing Meggie in Cee Cee hands," Mortician admitted, pinching his cigarette to extinguish it and then walking to the trash can to throw it away. "Then listening to her volunteering to go with that mad motherfucker…fuck, she not even mine."

Johnnie didn't respond. Though he was happy he hadn't been the only one horrified by what had happened, he couldn't verbalize his feelings. None of them had spent as much time with her, had gotten to know her so in-depth, as Johnnie had. Aside from Christopher.

Johnnie had stepped out of the way, Fuck, he'd gone to the club to inform Christopher of her pregnancy and to warn him. If he didn't claim her, Johnnie would.

He often told himself that he would've done no different if she hadn't spurned him. Their time together seemed like yesterday, but still so fucking long ago. He'd never expected Christopher to marry her. Any woman, for that matter. Christopher just didn't seem the marrying kind.

When Johnnie heard about the courthouse ceremony, he'd been shocked. In the end, he was happy Christopher found a woman to love. He'd been happy it worked out for Megan. She'd been so brokenhearted when Christopher had walked away from her.

This ceremony was different for Johnnie. It seemed so final. If there'd ever been a glimmer of hope or doubt in his head, it had been rudely swept away. She'd pledged herself to Christopher before God and sundry.

Grimacing, Johnnie discarded his cigarette. He was still fucking *thinking*.

"One of you better get Meggie here," Derby said as he walked toward them from the hallway that led to the reception. "Outlaw not here. Neither's Meggie. Where the fuck she's at? If my bitch wasn't with her, I'd fucking leave now."

"Changing into her second wedding outfit," Mortician said.

"She's not going to have a fucking reception if she doesn't come," Boy put in as he appeared at Derby's side. "I don't know her well, but she didn't seem like such a fashion horse."

"Meggie's as girlie as they come," Stretch said, walking toward the trash can to get rid of his cigarette, where he paused and shook his head. "The brothers still whisper about some of her more infamous outfits."

"Fuck, don't remind me," Mort said. "Having her in a long gown with a wide skirt is fine with me. Prez not here to throw his Outlaw looks and I do want to fucking enjoy myself, instead of watching over her and pretending I don't have fucking eyes when I look at her."

"I just realized none of you fucks have your cuts on," Derby said. "A fucking sacrilege. Of course, motherfuckers won't take you fuckheads seriously. Come at me with fucking tuxes and I'd laugh in your fucking face."

"I didn't want to leave my cut in my saddlebags," Mortician explained. "I was going to run back to the club and get it after the ceremony then all the bullshit happened."

"And you two assholes?" Boy asked, glancing between Johnnie and Stretch.

"What Mort said," Stretch answered.

"I concur," Johnnie added.

Mort scowled at Johnnie. "Why the fuck your ass can't just say I fucking agree? Why so fucking fancy most of the time?"

"Why not?" Johnnie said. "It's who I am, Mort."

Johnnie decided to focus on the conversation and stop fucking thinking for a while, about any fucking thing. It was all combining and beginning to drive him insane.

The glass door opened, and Digger walked in.

"Where the fuck Meggie?" Mort demanded, watching as the door closed.

"She in the car with Bunny and Gypsy. They coming," Digger grouched. "Fuck." He scrubbed a hand over his face. "I hope you ready for this shit, bruh."

"What shit?" Stretch asked.

"Her fucking second wedding outfit," Digger said. "Outlaw a fucking wild man behind her. With him still not here, we going to have to stay close to her to keep other motherfuckers away."

"I don't know if I fucking like that sound of that," Mortician said.

Johnnie agreed. Her metallic blue skirt set she'd worn to a club party was fucking infamous.

The door opened again and Gypsy stepped in. She wore her 'Property of Derby' cut over a silver jumpsuit and chunky heels that sparkled.

"Hey, boys," she greeted, heading to Derby and planting a kiss on his lips. "Hey, baby."

"Ummm, sweet as candy," Derby responded.

The door opened, this time to Bunny, who leaned against it so it wouldn't close.

Mort had a view outside from where he stood, so he saw Megan first. He choked.

When she stepped into the lobby, the first thing Johnnie noticed was her loosely curled hair. He glanced at her makeup, dramatic eyes, contoured cheeks, and red lipstick that made his cock throb. His gaze flickered down. Rows of lace-ups lined her black sleeveless mini dress. Lace-ups ran to each hip, straight up the middle to her neck, and on each side of the front, going from her upper thigh to her panty line. Leather ties zig-zagged the holes, tied into bows, an insinuation of gifts waiting to be opened.

She wore no stockings. Johnnie would stake his life she wore no bra or panties. On her feet, she wore black stilettoes designed with chains and spikes.

A happy scream jerked Johnnie out of his shock.

"*Megster!*" the girl with the Canary yellow hair yelled.

"Who's the slut puppy now," her other friend said.

The two maneuvered through the men to reach Megan and grab her in a three-way hug.

"Guilty," Megan said with a laugh when they released each other. "I am the official slut puppy, Farrah."

"Turn, turn, turn," the first one demanded, spinning her finger as she chanted the words.

"Oh, um." Megan obligingly spun.

"God, Lacey, we haven't taught her yet," Farrah cried dramatically.

Megan frowned. "What do you mean?"

"Your hair," Lacey said. "It's hiding the back of the dress. "Turn around, miss."

"That's *Mrs.,* "Megan said with a sniff.

"Yeah, yeah, I know," Lacey said, busily lifting Megan's hair. "Mrs. Scary Biker Dude."

"Who you've sworn to obey," Farrah added sharply.

"And didn't have him say the same," Lacey said with clear disgust, deciding to braid Megan's wealth of hair.

Johnnie exchanged glances with all the men. They were Megan's friends, though, and Christopher had warned them not to interfere in their conversations because the three girls argued almost as they laughed and joked.

"First off, Christopher doesn't *obey* anyone," Megan said with annoyance. "Secondly, the traditional vows didn't have a man pledging that."

"The traditional vows also were for women whose lives revolved around marriage," Lacey said. "I wish I would've known you intended to say that. I would've had a thing or two to say to you."

"And I still would've told you to bite me," Megan snapped. "Whether I say obey, actually obey, or just wanted the word in my vows is neither your decision nor your business, so shut up."

"It's just—" Lacey started, but Farrah shook her head.

"Bunny and Gypsy already helped me with my hair," Megan said crossly. "What are you doing to it? I want to get to the reception to dance with Christopher."

"You can't dance with him," Lacey said, clearly still irritated. "He isn't here."

Megan went rigid. She thought for a moment, then nodded.

"This has been the weirdest wedding I've ever been too," Farrah said. "Delayed by almost ninety minutes. Now, the reception had been going on a couple of hours and neither the bride or groom is there."

"Meggie should wear her hair as she had it," Mort said, since she faced him. He nodded at her back.

Digger made a production of going next to Mortician to see why his brother made the suggestion. "Yeah, Mort right."

"Oh my God," Lacey gritted. "Is this the life you want? Being watched and controlled. Cheated on."

Megan fucking *growled* and spun toward her friend. The back of the dress had cutouts extending almost to her ass cheeks on each side of the long zipper. Johnnie was inclined to agree with

Mort and Digger. But he didn't say anything, staring at the anger on her face. Her eyes reminded him of Big Joe's when fury overtook him. Hers were narrowed and icy. "My husband is not with another woman. His whereabouts like my vows aren't your business."

"Fine. Not fucking a chick who isn't you," Lacey said with a snort. "He's doing biker stuff that I'm pretty sure had something to do with your delayed wedding."

Derby and Boy's faces hardened, but Johnnie kept his face as neutral as Mort, Stretch, and Digger. Any flicker of emotion might give the girl ammunition.

"Megster," Farrah said, raising her hands in supplication. "Meggie," she amended when Megan gave her a putrid look. "We've known each other since we were thirteen. What kind of friends would we be not to be worried about you? God, girl, you were so fucking sheltered. That's a shitty combination compared to a man like your husband."

Seeing Megan calmer as she listened to Farrah must've given Lacey an infusion of courage. She nodded with vigor. "Exactly. We thought he was taking advantage of you. Grooming you."

"Grooming me?" Megan echoed with a frown. "What does that mean?"

"See!" Lacey flared. "Grooming, Meggie. When an asshole targets a vulnerable woman, typically a *younger woman*, and pretends he's the greatest fucking thing on earth. Sir Lancelot reincarnated."

"Sir Galahad is better than Lancelot," Farrah inserted.

Lacey scoffed. "Does it matter? Either one of them. Father or son. Anyway, the point is we wouldn't be very good friends if we didn't worry about whether a man you've known less than a year and a half and is suddenly your everything, isn't with you for reasons that aren't any good."

"I told you when I visited in Seattle to back off. You should've gotten the message that I don't need rescuing. Christopher is a good man."

"He's a fucking criminal," Lacey yelled. "Thomas was a good man. A teacher who earned a decent living. He sang in the fucking church choir. Your husband is not, nor will he ever be anywhere close to the man your stepfather is. Dinah told me why he left, Meggie. Because of you. The stress of you running away took its toll on your mom and in turn destroyed her marriage. You should be fucking ashamed of yourself."

Face reddening, Megan stepped back and yanked the messy ponytail, furiously unbraiding her hair, although her fast movements were creating tangles.

"Here, babe," Bunny said kindly, stepping up and taking over.

"Lacey," Megan said, gladly surrendering the ponytail. "one thing I agree with you on. Christopher isn't like Thomas in any way. If he was, I wouldn't be with him."

"Why?" Lacey sneered. "Because he's a teacher? Sings in the choir? I never knew you had Daddy issues. Dinah told me you're with Scary Biker Dude because your biological father was a biker. He left you and her to go back to his whores and his biker life. You're a fucking fool if that's what you want."

Groaning, Farrah covered her face before dropping her hands. "Let's take a walk, Lacey. You're getting all work up. Meggie is already married, so—"

"You're also the worst fucking daughter in the world to do what you're doing to Dinah."

Megan trembled, flushed from head to toe. She looked at her two friends, then met Lacey's angry gaze with a furious one of her own. "You have a choice to make, Lacey," she said evenly. "I uninvite you to my reception and never talk to you again or you keep your stupid comments and ridiculous speculations to yourself. We've been friends for a long time, but you *will* respect my husband. Make your choice now. Stay—accept my marriage and my husband. Leave—forget I ever existed."

"There, all done," Bunny said.

Smiling at Bunny, Megan ran her fingers through her hair, then heaved in a breath, seeming on the verge of falling apart. Her anger was evaporating, and sadness was setting in. She glanced at Farrah. "I know you're trying to defuse the situation and I really appreciate it, Farrah. You're worried. I get it. I do. I…there are reasons I left home. I needed my father's help with something. That's all I can tell you out of respect for Momma."

"*Respect* for your mother?" Lacey shrieked before the other girl could respond. "That's rich. If you respected Dinah so much, you wouldn't be here."

"Lacey, shut up," Farrah snapped.

"No! Meggie knows Dinah didn't want her to get married today—"

"I was already married before today," Megan inserted.

Lacey snorted. "There are divorce lawyers for a reason."

"You have a beautiful son, Meggie," Farrah started, "and a husband you love very much—"

"And who loves me back just as much," Megan interrupted coldly.

Farrah nodded. "I can't understand why you chose to have a baby and a husband so young."

"That's it, Farrah, that one word you used," Megan said. "*Chose.* I *chose* to marry Christopher and to have his child, so—"

"I doubt that," Lacey said bitterly. "You were a fucking virgin."

Farrah winced, while Megan stared, mortification on her face, her skin flushing.

"No need to be all embarrassed," Digger said, shrugging. "You was just missing the banner that said never fucked pussy, Meggie."

As if that helped her. Johnnie glared at him, and Mortician rapped Digger on the side of the head.

"Shut the fuck up, fool."

"This is getting out-of-hand, ladies," Bunny said, stepping into the fray. "Meggie just wants to enjoy her big day." She smiled at the yellow-haired shrew. "Lacey, right? You've gotten your point across, babe. Back down a little. When Meggie returns from her honeymoon, you'll both see things a little clearer."

"No one asked for your fucking opinion, biker woman," Lacey spat.

"Her name is Bunny," Megan said sharply, "and you will respect her as one of my friends."

"Why?" Lacey demanded. "When I don't know if I respect you anymore. No, fuck that. I *don't* respect you anymore. You ran away, broke your mom's heart, looking for a man who deserted her and you to fuck whores—"

"*WHAT* did you say about my father?"

"Shut up, Meggie," Lacey ordered. "And you fucking heard me. Your mom told me and Farrah all about that deadbeat bastard. If it hadn't been for Thomas—"

"*Fuck* Thomas," Megan snarled, shocking her bitchy friend into silence. She took a step toward Lacey, her eyes burning with anger, but Farrah stepped in front of her. "Did Momma tell you she sold the house my father bought for her and me after she married Thomas? Did she tell you it was worth over a million dollars and she gave that money to her husband who spent it on God knows *what?* Did she tell you *she* was the one who barred my father from coming to see me? What about all the times Thomas beat her and me to a pulp, and I left to find Daddy so he could get Momma away because I didn't know what to do for her anymore? Every time I called the cops, she sent them away. Did she tell you Thomas was a big, mean rhinoceros who subjected her to all kinds of humiliation and the only reason he didn't sexually assault me was because I wasn't on birth control?"

Farrah had gone white as a ghost. Lacey looked unimpressed.

"You ended up pregnant because you had no way to prevent it from happening," Lacey said finally. "And, no, Dinah didn't tell us any of that. Do you know why? Because you're a liar. Thomas was one of the kindest men I knew. You forget I attended the same school as you. I never saw bruises on your mother. I never saw fear in her eyes whenever she was in Thomas's presence. Dinah still has thoughts of harming herself, ending her life, because Thomas left and because of *you.*"

"She what?" Megan said, setting aside all of Lacey's accusations.

"She took a leave of absence from school when you ran away because one of the teachers found her in a restroom sobbing uncontrollably and calling for you," Farrah explained, seeming as if she wanted to be anywhere else but there. "Lacey and me checked in on her that evening and—"

"And she'd gotten blitzed," Lacey said, "and had fallen. The side of her face was bruised and swollen. Her nails were broken. Her knees were skinned. Because of you, Meggie. *You.* You left her."

"She didn't fall because she drank too much," Megan said in a wobbly voice. "He'd beaten her."

"God, you're so fucking stupid."

"Enough with the name calling, Lacey," Farrah said tiredly. "We're just trying to look out for you—"

"Fuck, what the fuck you two bitches doing is you was trying to fuck her up?" Digger demanded.

"I don't remember talking to you, asshole," Lacey said angrily.

"I don't remember giving a fuck about you talking to me or not," he shot back.

"Yeah," Mort added. "We not concerned about you."

"Especially after all this," Stretch offered. "We have to keep Meggie safe when Outlaw isn't around."

"The reason we not picking neither one of you up and tossing you the fuck out is 'cause Prez said we can't interfere with the three of you," Digger said. "On Meggie orders."

"How kind of you," Lacey said sarcastically.

"Farrah, Lacey, Bunny was right," Megan started. "We can talk about this some other time. It's been a long day for me. Please, just back off for now. I don't know how much more I can endure. I appreciate your concern for my mom. You'll never know how grateful I am that you watched over her. And I know what you're saying to me is out of love and friendship for me. I didn't lie about anything I said. Momma didn't tell you the truth, but I know she's ill. Let's just go into the reception and enjoy the rest of the evening. When I get back from my honeymoon, Christopher and me will come up to Seattle and spend a week or so there so you can get to know him. You'll see what a good man he is. Right now, just let it go. I'm begging you. We can all be friends. You're *all* my friends." She raised her hands in supplication and looked at Lacey, a plea in her eyes. "Just give everyone a chance. Mort and Digger are actual brothers. They're funny and kind and caring. Stretch is quiet, but he's always interesting to talk to. When he says something, you want to listen. Val…" Her voice wobbled and she swallowed. "Val's a flirt," she said with a watery smile. "And a tease. He's reliable and advises me from time to time. K-P loves to cook and eat onions. He loves his daughter and he calls all the guys runts. He reminds me of my father." She fell silent and shifted uneasily, then glanced at Johnnie. "Johnnie," she said softly, nodding at him as she had with everyone except the absent Val and K-P. "He's charming and considerate, patient enough to listen to whatever I need to talk about, even if we'd just discussed it. He's loyal and the best friend anyone could ever hope for. Gypsy," she said, moving on as if she hadn't given him a tender smile to add an extra layer to her words. "Gypsy is a lot of fun. She'll keep you laughing. She's very *loyal*." Sniffing, Megan sidled a glare at Derby.

The asshole smirked at her.

"She has words of wisdom that you both would appreciate. And Bunny, the *biker woman*," Megan huffed, throwing Lacey a dirty look, "is a little reserved, but would be so quick to offer whatever help you need and would give you the shirt off her back. I haven't known Danicka long, but she loves a good raunchy joke. If I need anything at all, she has my back and she'd have yours, too, because you're my friends. I swear I'm okay. I'm around good, good people and I'm in no danger. As for my daddy…" Her smile was sad. "Daddy wasn't who Momma made him out to be toward me or her. He loved me and he loved her. From what I understand, he changed drastically at the end of his life, and I wouldn't have recognized him. But Big Joe, the man I knew, would've moved heaven and earth to help Momma, even if he didn't care about her. He would've done it for me. Because I asked him to. My father loved me, so whatever else you say or do, don't you *ever* disparage him again or I'll never talk to you for a long as I live."

Farrah dropped her gaze, but Lacey's look challenged Megan, until she began to clap.

"Wow! Wow, Meggie. You should've taken up acting. You're so fucking good, if a little melodramatic. Dinah told me not to mention that man to you. She said you'd defend him because of how much you hated Thomas."

The shock on Megan's face slowly morphed into anger.

"We're your oldest friends," Lacey went on. "We know you. You were spoiled and sheltered and frankly a little Mary Poppins that thought you were better than everyone, especially your mother. That cock and bull story you said. The accolades your spouted to all these people. Dinah told me and she told Farrah that you left when she and Thomas said you couldn't go with your father. He texted you and told you he was coming to pick you up to spend some time here, and they didn't want you to leave, so you ran."

"That's it. I'm done. You're a moron, Lacey," Megan growled and looked at the other girl. "Farrah, thank you. Whether you'll try to get to know my new friends or not is beside the point. You're at least backing off as I requested."

"Only because she's a chicken," Lacey said. "She thinks you're an idiot. Just on GP, but she's also called you a dick for brushing us off for fuckheads you haven't long known and an asshole for your treatment of Dinah."

"Oh my God, Lacey, shut the fuck up," Farrah hissed, unable to meet Megan's eyes.

"Kiss my ass, scary dipshit," Lacey flared. "As sick as Dinah is and as much as she struggles to make ends meet, you still expected her to pay for your stupid wedding and the reception."

"Right, because I'm such a bad daughter that I'd have no sympathy for Momma or what she'd going through," Megan said.

"You don't," Lacey said without mercy. "Then, you had the fucking audacity to vow to *obey* some old fucking dude when you've been so horrible to Dinah."

Instead of calling Dinah a fucking liar on all accounts, Megan narrowed her eyes. "Don't think I don't know what Momma and you two schemed up for the guest list. Half the people at my wedding, I wasn't even close to at school. After Thomas, my wonderfully upstanding stepfather, when she went to another school, Momma never developed friendships with the teachers." She rushed forward, starting toward the hallway. "Right there, you should've realized Momma wasn't paying for the wedding. Besides, I don't know what you three expected to do."

"We were just looking out for Dinah since you're so wrapped up in your *old* man," Lacey said innocently. "Sue us for helping your mom."

"I told you to tell Dinah to back off," Farrah whispered.

"Helping?" Megan screeched. "Momma wore *black* to my wedding, no matter how I begged her to change her color. You both knew that, so exactly what kind of help were you giving?"

Lacey and Farrah looked at each other.

"That's what I thought," Megan said darkly.

"Your mom just wants the best for you," Lacey cried. "We all do. Jesus, you've already had one baby and you're pregnant again, and you're not even twenty. What kind of life is ahead of you with that sexist jackass?"

Gasping, Megan's mouth fell open, then she took off one shoe and threw it at Lacey, hitting the girl's arm, before she sent the other one flying too, which Lacey dodged. Megan turned and stormed down the hallway in her bare feet.

"Uh, I think I'll bring her shoes to her and check on her," Bunny volunteered, a little nonplussed. "Trader's probably looking for me, too."

"I'll go with you," Gypsy said, with another quick kiss to Derby.

"Bitches, leave," Digger said, once the women had disappeared. "Meggie don't want you here."

"She never said anything to me," Farrah protested, then glared at Lacey. "I told you not to do what Dinah said, dumb ass. We both knew it would royally piss off Meggie."

"Meggie mama told you to say all this bullshit?" Mortician demanded.

Folding her arms, Lacey tipped up her chin. "She told me to express exactly how I was feeling." Fleeting guilt crossed her face. "Wh-when the priest got to the speak now or forever hold your peace part."

"Fuuuucccckkkk," Mort said, squeezing the bridge of his nose.

"I just feel so sorry for Dinah," Lacey admitted. "Meggie's her only child and she loves Meggie to pieces. I don't think Meggie should've married and become a mother so young, but I hate the way she ignores Dinah. She turns down Dinah's suggestions of spending time together. Anything her mom suggests, Meggie ignores. All for some old dude who shouldn't be with her in the first place."

At the same time, Johnnie, Mort, and Digger opened their mouths to speak.

"Dinah hasn't been telling you the truth," Stretch said, not enough venom in his tone to Johnnie's way of thinking. "Meggie has always been there for Dinah. I don't think she wants Meggie with anybody. Dinah was trying to sabotage her daughter's wedding. Think about that for a moment. A day that everybody knows is important to Meggie because she wanted her union blessed."

Drawing in a breath, Lacey started toward the hallways.

Digger planted himself in her path as Farrah put a hand on her shoulder.

"You not going back in that reception, girl," Digger said. "You upset Meggie once. I want pussy, and if Prez come and find his woman not enjoying herself 'cause we let a bitch already pissed her off back in, I'm not going to be in no condition to fuck."

"This is a free country," Lacey snarled. "I can go any fucking where I please."

"But this a private party," Mortician retorted.

"That I was invited to."

"Not no more," Digger said.

"We uninviting you," Mortician agreed.

"Come on, Lacey," Farrah said. "They're not letting us back in."

"You can stay, Farrah," Johnnie said, speaking for the first time since these two started in on Megan. It had lasted too fucking long, but he didn't know how intense their arguments got before they smoothed things over. "I believe you said everything Lacey accused you of, but at least you were classy enough not to open your fucking mouth in front of everyone."

"Farrah won't forsake me like Meggie has," Lacey said. "If I leave, Farrah leaves, too."

"Farrah has a fucking mouth," Johnnie barked, losing patience. "Let her decide. *You* shut the fuck up, Lacey. You've said enough to last a fucking lifetime."

"So much Meggie cussed," Stretch said, "and she's only done that one other time since I've known her."

Lacey threw Johnnie a violent look, but kept her mouth shut.

"I'm going to leave with Lacey. It might be a good idea anyway." Farrah glanced at the Wicked Witch of the Wedding. "You pushed every one of Meggie's buttons," she said with disapproval. "She was ready to tear you to pieces."

Lacey shrugged.

"Outlaw need to hear about his mother-in-law," Derby said after Farrah and Lacey left. "Bitch sound like she's going to be a big fucking problem."

Johnnie and Mort looked at each other. Though Johnnie agreed with Derby, he saw by Mort's look that he didn't and his words proved that.

"Don't say anything," he said, glancing from Derby to Boy. "Let's see how it plays out. Prez like Dinah as much as she like him. If he hears about this, he might put her out and Meggie love that bitch."

"If she love Outlaw, she'll understand," Boy said. "Her man warms her bed, so if she chooses loyalty to her momma over him, that's on her."

"Megan is loyal to Christopher," Johnnie said flatly. While he believed Christopher should know, he wouldn't show discord in front of brothers not members of his club. "Mortician is right. Megan has been through enough, especially with Dinah, to be placed in a position where she'll have to turn away from the woman because of Outlaw's orders." The fucking lying bitch leaving would make Megan damn unhappy, something Johnnie wouldn't stand for if he could help it. "What happened here goes no further. Agreed?"

Although Derby and Boy's agreements were grudging, they gave it.

Mort's phone beeped. He grabbed it from his pocket and looked at the screen. "Val made it through surgery. He in recovery," he said, relief clear in his voice.

"Fuck, you made my night almost as much as seeing Meggie in that lace-up dress," Digger said.

Mortician shook his head and wagged his finger, ignoring Derby and Boy's murmurs of agreement. "We don't see what Meggie got on. Fuck, for all we notice, she could be buck fucking naked. Understand?"

"Yeah, bruh, you right. Outlaw'll pluck my fucking eyes out."

"If Prez ever in a bad fucking mood and remember we saw her without clothes, he'll pluck our fucking eyes out," Mort complained.

"Shut the fuck up," Johnnie warned.

"You fucks act like she's the first bitch you ever saw," Derby said with disgust. "Nothing special about her. She has a cunt, a mouth, and an asshole."

It took effort for Johnnie not to strike or throw Derby the fuck out. The Burning Hounds was one of the Dwellers' biggest support clubs. Any move on his part would be an affront to the president. Since Johnnie was only VP and he wasn't sure if Christopher would start beef with another club for stupid words about Megan, he remained silent.

"She's everybody's golden princess now because none of them have bitches of their own," Boy surmised. "When other broads enter the picture, Meggie would become just another face."

"Outlaw's going to tire of her," Derby predicted. "You mark my words. First year or two after I met my bitch, I kept my cock exclusive to her, but feeling and tasting the same pussy is a bore."

Boy nodded. "Derby's right. Having one bitch for the rest of my life wasn't for me."

Mort shrugged. "I think it's for Outlaw. He crazy about Megan."

Derby waved Mort off. "She's young and immature. He'll tire of her."

"Take it up with Prez," Mort said casually.

"He's enamored of the little bitch," Derby replied. "All you fucks are. I'm tempted to send fresh pussy to the club to stop this fucking travesty. Call me the day you motherfuckers realize she's nothing special. Her pussy'll house your cock as good as the next bitch."

Mortician glared at Derby but heaved in a breath. Stretch and Digger didn't look too pleased either.

"Knock it off, motherfucker," Boy growled. "We're going a little overboard in our opinions on Outlaw's woman. The bitch's with him for now. Let's show her that much respect."

"The little cunt doesn't like me," Derby said in bored tones. "Fuck her."

Johnnie gnashed his teeth together.

"Guess what, bruh?" Digger inserted, looking at Derby. "Mort going down next."

"What the fuck you talking about?" Mortician snapped, already angry with Derby but having to hold back as much as Johnnie.

"Bailey," Digger said with a laugh.

"Another gorgeous bitch," Boy said.

"Another *young* bitch," Mortician snarled, scowling at Digger.

"She's both," Stretch said, always having so little to say. "Just like Meggie."

"You know what I would love to see?" Derby asked. "Meggie and Bailey fucking each other. "I could earn top dollar for a fucking show like that."

"I need another smoke," Mort grumbled. "I'm going outside. Air kind of polluted in here."

Derby smirked at him.

"We should go in the hall to watch Meggie," Stretch said.

"Gypsy and Bunny with her," Mortician said. "I waited for you to bring her. Now, I'm waiting for Outlaw."

Humor sparkling in his eyes, Digger cocked his head to the side. "You sure about that?"

"What the fuck you implying fuckhead?"

"I'm not implying shit. I'm straight up saying you not going in there 'cause Bailey in there."

"Mortician?" the girl in question called, as if Digger's words conjured her up.

She offered a little wave to all the men, then looked at Mort.

"Where the fuck your clothes at, Bailey?" he demanded.

She glanced down at the black fitted mini dress she wore, cut out at one side with a huge buckle slanting across her tits. High-heeled gladiator sandals, heavy makeup, and hair piled on her head completed her look.

"I changed before we left the church," she said, smiling at him.

Digger placed a fist underneath his chin, watching with avid interest.

Mortician swept Digger with a warning look and Bailey frowned, glancing over her shoulder at the sergeant-at-arms. "Um—"

Grinning, Digger stepped up to her. "What can I do for you, baby?"

"Meggie sent me out here to get Mortician. I suggested the Electric Boogie and she said we couldn't do it without him."

"Mort don't want to be bothered," Digger said. "Why don't you and me go and Join Meggie?"

"Fuckhead, you make it sound like I want to ignore Prez woman," Mortician snapped.

"I didn't say who you don't want to be bothered with," Digger replied, smirking.

Bailey's face fell, but she quickly recovered. "That's okay. I'll tell her you're indisposed, Mortician." She smiled at Digger. "C'mon. It's probably good that one of you come in anyway. The guys know she's married but they're swarming around her like flies. Bunny asked her boyfriend to help, but he said no. My date is too busy trying to sleep with Bunny."

"What fucking date?" Mortician demanded.

"My plus one," she said. "You know? The man escorting me."

"Mortician, out of all the shit she said you focusing on that?" Digger asked.

Mort stomped to her and grasped her elbow. "C'mon, Bailey."

"Meggie's been apologizing to everyone for the late start to her wedding," Bailey said, speaking between them, her gorgeous greenish-brown gaze looking from one to the other. "I told her not to worry. Maybe y'all should, too," she suggested, a hint of a drawl in her tone. "I went to a cousin's wedding a couple of years ago. It started three and a half hours late. She didn't estimate the right amount of time for her extensions. We thought it was canceled. Everyone was in church, waiting and waiting. Reverend Barnes threatened to cancel the ceremony because they had paid for only three hours. Momma threatened to stab him." She giggled in pleasure, drawing a smile from Mort. "He knew she would, so he shut up. Then, the wild child had a note in the program that all the guests needed to go to the store or stop at a fast-food place to order food."

They laughed along with her.

"I heard of BYOB but BYOF at a wedding?" Bailey shook her head. "No. Just no. I called Dad and he took care of the food. He called in a favor to friends he knows in New Orleans. By the time the service was done, and my cousin and her husband arrived at the hall, food was there. In comparison to that wedding, Meggie's was a piece of cake."

"Come on, pretty girl," Mort said softly, tugging her toward the hallway.

"Will you take my number now?" she demanded in her sweet voice.

"Nice fucking try, Bailey," Mort said with a laugh, "but nope."

"I'm going to get you to call me yet," she said, the rest of the conversation lost as they reached the door that would take them to the reception.

"Let's go find our bitches," Boy suggested, "and watch over Outlaw's 'til he gets his ass here."

"Prez should be returning soon," Stretch said.

Johnnie nodded.

"Want to go see my brother crash and burn and lose his fucking money?" Digger asked Stretch.

Stretch hesitated before reluctantly agreeing.

Alone in the vestibule, Johnnie walked to the glass door and glanced out. Night had fallen. Clouds remained, covering the moon and stars, somehow adding to his melancholy mood. It didn't help that Christopher was at the club, getting rid of a man who represented more problems than Johnnie cared to admit.

Years ago, when he'd first heard the name Sebastian Caldwell, he'd been curious about how the motherfucker looked. Grandda always said the mysterious man had been the spitting image of his fucking demon spawn, Christopher.

Yes, Christopher shared the color of Cee Cee's eyes, but in no way had the same maniacal light.

Johnnie continued to stare, waiting. Always waiting.

A cloud shifted, briefly revealing the moon before another one covered it once more. He'd been there, alone, for a while. Time was passing. Soon, Christopher would walk in to claim Megan. He'd take her to Europe, expose her to another world, and she'd fall deeper in love.

He wasn't there yet, however. Johnnie had one last chance to take her in his arms. Turning away from the door, he headed to the reception, determined to claim a dance with Megan before he shoved away his feelings for her and accept that she was Christopher's, now and forever more.

Chapter 25

Outlaw

B Y THE TIME HE DROVE ONTO CLUB PROPERTY AND PARKED in a patch of grass by the meat shack, went to his room to change out of his tux, then carried Cee Cee from the van, the motherfucker had went and fucking died on Christopher.

Lighting a smoke, he took a few drags, drank from his bottle of tequila, then jammed the cigarette in the corner of his mouth, thinking about which tools to use. Assfuck was already fucking gone so using the bone saw, skull chisel, rib cutters, toothed forceps, hammer with hook, bread knife, scalpel, toothed forceps, or his special scissors to open the intestines would just take up time, when Christopher didn't have any to waste. Using all his special tools might help get rid of the burning hatred he carried for Cee Cee. The motherfucker wouldn't suffer, though. He'd be just as fucking dead then as he was now.

"Assfuck," Christopher growled, glaring at the body, and puffing on the cigarette again. He'd died too fucking easy, for all that he'd done to Christopher's ma and then his Megan.

He would've started with his fucking teeth, yanking the motherfuckers out with one of the tooth forceps among the meat shack tools. Fingernails would've gone next. Eyeballs wouldn't have been dug the fuck out until after his cock was hacked the fuck off. A cracked rib here, a chopped off finger there. He would've had so many fucking choices to make this motherfucker suffer.

"Fuckhead," he snarled, throwing the cigarette on the concrete floor, and stomping it to make sure it was extinguished.

Walking around the table, Christopher took in every angle of Cee Cee, filled with loathing, furious he'd been denied the revenge owed to him. He reversed course, circling in the opposite direction, unable to look anywhere else but at Sebastian Caldwell. Dressed in jeans, T-shirt, and cut with the word *President* patched on. Worn motorcycle boots were on his feet. His eyes and mouth were closed. Yeah, motherfucker had copious fucking amounts of blood on him and two fucking gunshot wounds, but he'd maintained his dignity, when he'd taken it from every motherfucker he could.

Christopher stopped, his body shaking, cold sweat chilling him. He wanted to howl in rage and weep for the small boy he'd once been. The one his grandfather had despised because of the dead motherfucker laid the fuck out in front of him. He ached for his ma. She'd loved him, but she'd resented him, too. Even if she had been able to overcome how he'd been conceived, Logan never let it go.

"Motherfucker greet you in the fuckin' flames, Cee Cee?" Christopher demanded of the dead assfuck. "I fuckin' despise you, motherfucker." As much as he wanted to avenge his mother's pain, Sebastian Caldwell rode into fucking town and decided to target Megan. *Take* his wife from him. His sweet angel.

Megan.

"My Megan," he whispered. She was waiting for him, trusting he'd not take too long. She alone saw something in him that not one motherfucker ever had—good.

Christopher jerked the plastic apron from the wall hook, opened a drawer for a face shield, then walked to the counter and pulled latex gloves from the box there, before going to the cabinet to get the chain saw.

The meat shack wasn't that big. Mortician complained he needed better working conditions, but he'd rigged it out when he'd donated money for all types of upgrades in the club and on the grounds. It was a gable roofed shed with one window, one door, and a wall of cabinets in drawers, with the autopsy table in the middle. Of course, the motherfucker had been outfitted with restraints, a goddamn requirement since assfucks brought to the meat shack was on the way to being dead, instead of already in that state.

At the thought, he looked at Cee Cee and scowled.

"Fuck you, assfuck. Ain't lettin' you keep me from my Megan no longer than I gotta." Plugging in the power saw, he walked the short distance to the table.

He'd cut Cee Cee the fuck up, then go in and change back into his monkey suit.

He might've wanted to wear his cut, but she deserved to have him dressed in the way she wanted after all she'd been through today. He'd leave this fucking darkness in the fucking meat shack and follow her beautiful light.

Meggie

SOMEHOW, THE MARRIAGE OF A FAIRYTALE WEDDING incorporated with homages to the MC worked out well. Bouquets of blue, peach, and cream-colored flowers with two photo charms adorned each table inside silver motorcycle boot vases. Meggie hadn't been able to think of any other way to include her father and Christopher's mother.

She'd fumed all the way to the door after leaving Lacey and Farrah in the hallway, where she'd taken a moment to compose herself.

She could understand their concern for her and even appreciated the sentiment. Yes, she had been sheltered in some respects but exposed to too much in other ways. As her friends, she could forgive them for wanting to protect her. At the start of

Lacey's rant, her accusations against Christopher had infuriated Meggie. Then, she'd had to listen to one lie after the other spouted by her momma.

She'd intended to ask Dinah to leave and never contact Meggie again. Even if she didn't want the world to know about the real Thomas, she didn't have to assassinate Meggie and Big Joe's characters. Hearing her mother sometimes wanted to die reminded Meggie of Dinah's fragility. If Meggie confronted her about the way she'd manipulated Lacey and Farrah, and the stunt she'd pulled with all those strangers, it might tip Dinah over the edge.

Farrah and Lacey's thoughts about Meggie hurt her deeply. Even if they made up, their friendship was forever altered. They wouldn't even give her husband, and men she now saw as a part of her family, a chance. They wouldn't try to get to know Bunny or Gypsy or Danicka. Lacey had been so vocal, but in hindsight Meggie realized Farrah hadn't spoken up and taken her up on her offer to befriend anyone at the MC.

Yet, Meggie had pushed that aside, too after checking her phone and not having a message or voicemail about Val's condition. She wouldn't set foot into her reception until she knew something, so she texted K-P and waited until he responded with the news that Val was in recovery. The Road Captain was in critical condition, but K-P reassured her he would pull through. He'd ordered her to enjoy her celebration and that Val would've wanted her to.

But a day that should've been so happy, one that she'd wanted so badly, had exhausted her, emotionally, physically, and mentally. She wanted to go to the club and hide or cry or…or…do *something* to escape her pain and fear and grief. Before she'd been able to make her excuses and leave, the guys had come in and dragged her to the dance floor.

"You good, Meggie girl?" Mort had asked, taking Stretch's place as her dance partner.

She'd nodded. He must've seen something in her face, though, because he led her across the room to a spot quiet enough to talk.

"It's been a long fucking day," he'd said.

"Yeah."

"Your wedding been ratchet as fuck, Meggie. No fucking lie. A fucking mess. Full of fucking drama, maniac daddies, lying mamas, and mean chicks," he'd clarified. "A bride that didn't march when she was supposed to, a mama that wore black that invited motherfuckers amounting to strangers, a daddy that wanted to fuck the bride up and ended up fucked up, a priest taking potshots, a bride late to her reception, and a groom fucking missing from his reception. All that shit equal a ratchet ass wedding."

Meggie hadn't been able to say anything. She'd been too tired to think of a response, other than he'd forgotten to throw in Val's shooting.

"But you still fucking standing, Meggie. You tough. You got Big Joe genes and he looking up prouder than a motherfucker."

"Looking up?"

"I'm not going to talk about all the shit he did the last two years of his life, Meggie. That alone was enough to send him straight the fuck to hell. Well before that, he was fucking president of us motherfuckers. He was fucking feared. In your heart, you fucking know he didn't stay in his position by handing out fucking handshakes."

"I know."

"But he loved you, Meggie. He did. He carried a photo of you in his wallet. And you was right when you said he would've blazed up to fuck up Thomas, even if he never felt nothing more for Dinah, 'cause of you. You always going to be his baby girl. You can always live with the knowledge that he fucking loved you. You for Outlaw now. His woman, and he love you. Right now, he need you. He need you to go and hold shit down until he get here. I know you tired. Fuck, I'm tired, and I don't have a baby in my belly. I haven't gotten dumped on by a fucking chick you needed to slap until you beat out that bitch she had in her."

"That would've taken a lot of hits."

He'd grinned at her. "I know I'm a motherfucker for putting this responsibility on you, but if you give in to all the bullshit that went on today, tongues going to wag more than motherfuckers probably doing anyway."

"No, you're right. I wanted the ceremony to go on, so I have to do my part."

She knew she had to act normal, to greet her guests, smile, laugh, talk and enjoy herself. It was her duty as Christopher's old lady, so she'd stiffened her spine, straightened her shoulders, and done exactly that.

Once she and Mortician returned to the dance floor, she had one partner after another. Digger. Stretch. Boy. Mouse. A couple bikers she didn't know. Bowlie. She hadn't asked for a break until now when she was dancing with Mortician again.

She fanned herself. Besides, she had several romantic songs for her and Christopher to dance to, and she needed a rest for a bit so she'd be ready.

"I need a break from all the dancing, Mortician" she said, a little over an hour after her confrontation with her friends. "My feet are starting to hurt."

Mortician stepped back and dropped his gaze. "My fucking dogs would hurt too if I was wearing ten-inch heels."

Meggie giggled. "My heels aren't that high," she countered. "They're six inches."

"You still Smurfette size," he retorted.

Rolling her eyes, she laughed again.

"I need a fucking drink," he told her. "Sit down and rest a minute."

"Okay," she said, heading to the dais, where most of the wedding party had taken their places, except Johnnie, Ophelia, Zoann, and the groom.

Meggie didn't know Johnnie's whereabouts. Ophelia had returned to the club with Dinah, to watch over CJ. The moment Zoann learned about Val's shooting, she'd left.

And Christopher…Meggie decided not to dwell on his activities.

She hoped he liked how the reception turned out.

Each napkin holder was a ring of skulls. Wedding favors included keepsake albums that documented her life with Christopher and their son, flasks shaped like antifreeze jugs with her and Christopher's names and marriage date and motorcycle bottle openers. The club's insignia had been painted on the floors, just as it was on the dais skirt and the two specially made flags that stood next to the American and Washington state flags.

Her five-tier wedding cake looked traditional except for the 'road' running down one side from the bottom up to the topper consisting of a hand-blown motorcycle and heart and the bride in her biker groom's arms. Christopher's cake had been a massive undertaking that cost triple because of the short amount of time the bakery had to create it. A 3D Grim Reaper exactly like the club's stood next to a cake with 3D skulls ringing two layers a trio of 3D hearts rising from the bottom. White and black roses and strings of 'pearls' added the romantic touch Meggie wanted. Their names and a couple on a motorcycle imprinted the cake server while flames edged the knife. Open bars had been set up on each side of the room.

Meggie had also opted for a buffet rather than plated service, something Dinah vehemently protested. She'd predicted a lack of organization, long lines, and a veritable stampede. Meggie hadn't cared. Now, she applauded using her own judgment.

She couldn't imagine her guests waiting for food. Meggie couldn't have allowed anyone to eat until Christopher arrived. His absence would lead to more questions. Or accusations like Lacey's.

Despite her best efforts, her anger over the confrontation returned and churned in her. If her mother hadn't gone back to the club, Meggie might've asked her to leave. How dare her mother spout such lies about Meggie and then pull the stunt she had with the guest list. At least, the invitation list for the reception had been much smaller.

"Would you do me the great honor of dancing with me?"

Johnnie's voice drifted over Meggie's shoulder and she turned, glancing up at him.

"Hey," she said softly.

One side of his mouth kicked up, the half-smile sad. "Hi, sweetheart." He held out his hand. "Would you?"

"The DJ isn't playing. He might be taking a break."

"He's waiting for my cue. He'll play my requested song if we walk onto the dance floor, or he'll continue with his playlist at my very disappointed signal."

"You're so dramatic," Meggie said with a laugh, standing and placing her hand in Johnnie's.

Not releasing her, he guided her to the dance floor, drew her to him, and settled an arm around her waist just as *Claire de Lune* began to play. She'd danced with him in Long Beach, those many months ago when Christopher had left her there and Johnnie had not only kept her company but kept her spirits up. She smiled at him.

"I see you remember," he told her.

"How could I forget? You were the first man I'd danced with so…" She searched for the right word.

"Intimately?" he supplied, his tone low and rough.

"Johnnie, stop," she ordered, hating the heat rising to her cheeks.

He smirked at her. "You're blushing."

She didn't respond.

"It's not a crime to find me attractive," he said.

She scowled at him. "It's my wedding day, jerk," she snapped. "Have some respect for me and Christopher."

As usual, he was remorseless. "You didn't deny it," he pointed out. "And I said you found me *attractive*, sweetheart, not that you were *attracted* to me, so why the irritation?"

"I love Christopher. I don't know how many different ways I have to say that for you to understand it. I'm his."

After all she'd been through today, she was holding onto her sanity by a thread. She didn't want to remember her time with

Johnnie, and it had nothing to do with her husband. It was because of *Johnnie*.

"I'm being completely unfair to you," Johnnie said softly. "But I don't think I'll ever get the opportunity to hold you in my arms again. I wanted you to know what you mean to me. How much I cherish you and the time I had with you."

"I don't know what I would've done without you," she whispered, an admission that she'd sworn to keep to herself. "I would've been lost."

His hold on her tightened as the song came to an end. "One more," he said, staring at her.

She nodded, and Johnnie waved to the DJ. The next song didn't surprise her.

Everything I Do I Do It For You was a slow, romantic song that was older than her, and the second one they'd danced to that night in Hortensia. Meggie refused to look at Johnnie as she followed his lead. She hated to see the pain in his eyes, knowing she'd put it there. But she couldn't give him what he wanted, even then when she'd despaired the status of her relationship with Christopher.

"How are you? Truly, Megan."

"I—"

"The *truth*," he ordered, cold anger settling into his eyes. "I've never been so fucking scared in my entire life seeing you with that fucker. If I felt that way, how did you feel?"

"Terrified," she admitted, finally glancing up and meeting his stormy gaze. "But I had faith in Christopher."

He nodded, a muscle ticking in his jaw. "What about the argument with your friends?"

"I don't want to talk about them," she said coldly.

He smiled, and it was genuine. "The queen has spoken and I, as her most loyal subject, shall comply."

She poked his chest. "Stop it."

His humor fled, the intensity returning. "I am, Megan. I have never felt about any woman the way I feel toward you."

"Johnnie," Meggie whispered. "There's a woman out there for you. When you find her, you'll forget I ever existed."

"Unless I leave the club, I'll see you every day, sweetheart." He sighed. "I met a woman at the club a few weeks ago that I can't seem to get out of my head."

Relief surged through Meggie. "I told you—"

"I never got her name," Johnnie interrupted. "I let her walk away. It didn't matter at the time, but she still crosses my mind from time to time."

"There'll be someone else," she assured him. "Who knows? She might turn up again if you made the same impression on her as she did you."

"As you did me?" he countered, hunger in his eyes.

Meggie lowered her gaze again. "Don't do this, Johnnie, especially to yourself. I love Christopher. I'm happy. Can you ask for anything more? If-if you love me as you say you do, isn't that what you'd want for me? It's what I want most of all for you."

His arm around her waist tightened. "Are you saying you love me?"

"I'm in love with Christopher. I love *Christopher*," she reiterated.

"Megs—"

She wasn't quite sure what it was. Maybe, a shift in the air, or instinct, but she suddenly felt Christopher's presence. She turned her head and there he was, beautiful in his tuxedo, talking to Mortician, Digger, and Stretch.

"Christopher's here," she told Johnnie.

His hold slackened. "Megan—"

She couldn't wait for the song to end to go to her husband. She backed out of Johnnie's embrace. "Be happy, Johnnie," she said for the second time that day, turned and rushed toward her husband.

CHRISTOPHER

MEGAN WAS ALREADY FLUSHED FROM THEIR lovemaking and now, she turned beet red when the stewardess glared at her as Christopher led her back to their seats in the first-class cabin of their London-bound flight.

"You're soooo bad, Christopher," Megan chirped, plopping next to him in her seat by the window.

"What the fuck ever." He chuckled and stretched his legs out before him. "That ain't what you was sayin' when you was comin' on my tongue and my cock. As I recall, you was sayin' Christopher you're soooo good."

"Shut. Up."

He leaned over and kissed her. "Nope. When you cover yourself with that blanket, I'm gonna rub your pussy again," he whispered against her ear, nuzzling her hair.

Recognizing how much the idea turned her on from the deepening flush in her cheeks, he grinned. She didn't pretend, so, instead of protesting, she sniffed, snapped her mouth shut and faced forward.

He massaged the back of her head, remembering how gorgeous she'd looked in her wedding gown and all that she'd given him when she'd pledged herself to him in a church. The events of this afternoon—the disposal of Cee Cee—seemed like a dream. He kissed the shell of her ear. She fucking believed in him to the fucking depths of her soul. He'd ducked out after the photos. Some of them had included all of them, including Megan and CJ, in their cuts. Unfortunately, Val couldn't be in the photo and K-P had remained at the hospital until Val made it out of surgery. Once he'd left the reception, Christopher had gotten to the clubhouse and changed into some old clothes he didn't fucking need anymore. Once he'd finished in the meat shack, he rushed and cleaned himself and put his tuxedo back on.

He was glad Megan had insisted on having their reception away from the club. If it had been there, he would've tainted it with what went on in that fucking death shed. And he didn't want anything tainting his girl. She was sweet and good—despite everything—and he wanted to keep her that way.

When he'd walked back in, she'd been dancing with Johnnie. *Of course she had.* Motherfucker wouldn't waste a chance to take Megan in his arms with Christopher gone, but it satisfied him when she left Johnnie on the dance floor to come to him in a dress that almost made his heart stop.

"Thank you for not taking too long with whatever you had to do," she'd whispered.

He'd smiled and kissed her, then led her to the dance floor without a word.

Now, he took her hand in his and rubbed his thumb in her palm. "Megan," he said quietly, then snapped his mouth shut, not sure where to start. He was good as fuck at being dirty with her, but sweet words didn't come easy to him. Even when their sex was gentle, he still thought of it as *fucking*. Deep down, though, he knew he was making love to her. But he wondered if she knew. Did she understand how he felt about her even though he just said he loved her and none of the other romantic bullshit she deserved?

"Megan, I ain't a romantic motherfucker."

She looked up at him and gave him an uncertain smile.

He pulled an envelope out of the inside of his jacket and tapped her nose with it. "This letter here is from me to you." He shrugged. "Cuz I'm me and I ain't gonna walk 'round tellin' you no sonnets every-fuckin-day." He picked up her hand. "But I promise you, baby. On every anniversary, Ima give you a letter and Ima tell you." He swallowed. What he was about to say would put his feelings out there more than he ever had, even with Megan. "Maybe, some of your romance shit rubbed off on me. Ain't sure, baby."

She cocked her head to the side in that way she had when she listened intently to something.

He laid the letter in her lap, tempted to let her read it, and be done with it. "I love pussy—" He paused at her frown and pulled at his hair. "I love girls, Megan. I studied bitches as a pastime." He cleared his throat and winced at her wide eyes. Maybe, he should've stuck to the letter. The shit coming out his mouth wasn't the shit he'd written. He'd written the same words on the envelope that he'd addressed her as at the beginning of his letter: *My Megan.*

"This is—"

He held up a hand. "Wait, baby. Lemme finish."

Her look skeptical, she nodded.

"But ain't no girl I ever met make me as hot as you do just by thinkin' 'bout you. From the moment I met you, Megan, I ain't able to fuckin' focus on nothin' and nobody else. All I could think 'bout was you. Wantin' you and wantin' to protect you. I once told you you was gonna drive some poor motherfucker insane and I'm one lucky motherfucker that it get to be me. A girl that challenge her man, hardly never fuckin' listen to him, tell him to go fuck himself when he piss her the fuck off, worth every fuckin' minute of every fuckin' day. No matter what, baby, I'm always with you. *You,*" he emphasized and grabbed her neck to pull her close and kiss her. "Them pretty pink lips." He glided a hand down her arm. "Your beautiful lil' body." He bumped her nose against his. "Those gorgeous fuckin' eyes you got. All of you. We real with each other. Me and you. You don't gotta hide a motherfuckin' thing from me. You can be you. Scared. Happy. Wild. Angry. Kinky. I ain't givin' a fuck cuz I always got you. No matter how many times you need liftin' up—" He held out his hand and tapped his fingers against his palm— "Ima catch you and raise you back where you gotta be. I love the fuck outta you, Megan, and I ain't ever gonna stop."

Megan let out half-laugh, half-sob, tears streaking her cheeks. Christopher swiped them with his thumbs.

"I love you, too, Christopher. You make me hot and lustful for you, but it's more than that. It's about the two of us. You make me feel secure and loved and wanted. You're a wonderful father and husband." She placed a hand over his heart. "And you have a heart, Christopher. A heart that made me fall in love with you. I'll always be here for *you*. No matter how many times you fall—" She grabbed his hand and kissed the back of it— "I'll always be there to pull you up. You own me body and soul. You're my everything."

He wrapped her in his arms and kissed her with all the tenderness flowing between them. Fuck him, but the look in her eyes made him want her pussy. His nostrils flared. "I want some more pussy, baby."

"Why did you ruin our romantic moment?" she complained.

"Megan, everyfuckinthing I told you the God's honest truth, but I'm only standin' so much mushy shit and mushy time is fuckin' over."

She shook her head.

"C'mon, baby. Your lil' ass wanna gimme more pussy in that small fuckin' airplane bathroom. You a freaky little nympho."

She smirked at him. "Yeah, but I'm *your* freaky little nympho."

She sure the fuck was, and Christopher had never felt luckier.

YOU ROARED INTO MY LIFE AT FULL THROTTLE, AND I'll never forget the evenin I first gazed into your big, blue eyes. My world stopped in that moment. I didn't realize you would become by everything. The air I need to breathe and the angel who gives me a soul.

You accept me for who I am. Flaws and all. You believe in me even when I have a hard time believin in myself. You trust me. Your smile makes me believe I can conquer the world. You make me laugh. You make me think. You make me hot. You make me angry.

You make me *feel.*

You and me, we have each other's backs. No matter how many times we fall, we lift each other up. My heart, my soul, my life rests in the palms of your hands. No matter what you face, I have you, baby. I'll be your strength. Your rock. Your man.

Your Outlaw.

In your arms and in your body, you carry the best of me. The children you give to me are my pride and joy and I'm in awe that we've created somethin so perfect that's a piece of me. You've given me that. You're a wonderful mother, a sexy wife, and a great friend.

I'm not a hearts and roses type of man, Megan. I'm hard and rough, rude and crude. This letter took hours to do because I wanted to give my girl somethin she deserves, not what I know and what I'm used to.

But, for you, I'm willin to compromise and look up the correct spellins and grammar to send you a letter once a year, on our anniversary, the day I became the luckiest man in the world and put my ring on your finger.

I love you.

Christopher

p.s. I'm fuckin Outlaw, too. You said that shit yourself and he gotta send you a letter to, baby. Anyway, this was my original letter 'til the boys told me you might chain up the Promised Land again. Can't have that shit. Ever a-fuckin-gain.

Megan,

You have the best pussy in the world. I love that you now a freaky little nympho. I love fuckin you and lovin you and havin you in my life. I'm the luckiest motherfucker alive to call you mine.

I love the fuck outta you, baby.

Outlaw

Dear Reader,

ERRIAM-WEBSTER DEFINES MISAPPROPRIATE AS A *transitive verb: to appropriate wrongly (as by theft or embezzlement).* Synonyms on their website include *appropriate, boost [slang], filch, heist, hook, lift, nick [British slang], nip, pilfer, pinch, pocket, purloin, rip off, snitch, steal, swipe, thieve.* Cambridge Dictionary offers a little more leeway: *to steal something that you have been trusted to manage and use it for your own benefit.*

Originally, I named the book Misappropriate for two reasons. 1.) All the titles in the series forming in my head would begin with 'mis'. 2.) Most importantly, Cee Cee was there to rip Meggie away from Christopher. Bin was snitching, swiping information to feed to Cee Cee. Johnnie wanted Christopher to be happy, but he also would've stolen Meggie (again away from Outlaw) if she would've allowed it, after he had been trusted with her care. The word 'misappropriate' is a word normally used in finance and accounting.

In an abstract way, it fit what was happening in the story. I went back and forth with naming the book Inappropriate, but it just did not sit right with me, though the title would've been easier. It would not have required anyone to read between the lines to settle on a definition I twisted for my own purposes. In the end, I decided to add in Christopher using misappropriate in place of inappropriate and Johnnie correcting him.

Within weeks of the release of Misled and after encouragement from so many of you, I decided to write a novella to follow-up. I wasn't sure where it would lead me. I only knew I wanted it to feature Meggie and Outlaw's church ceremony. It was frustrating to me that I had wrapped everything up so neatly at the end of the first book. One other thing I was certain about—it's release date. Valentine's Day 2014.

I reached my decision on Christmas Day 2013. As a vague idea came to me, Christopher added his input. *My* story would be full of romance and wedding preparations. Fine for Meggie, but what the fuck about *him*?

Snake was gone. Big Joe seemingly had been put to rest, so I threw a question at him: What *about* you, motherfucker? After our (at times contentious) back and forth, I was reminded that he had an old man lurking out in the world somewhere. He fucking hated this assfuck. *Despised* him. The thought of laying eyes on him had always been Christopher's worst fucking nightmare.

To me, it was perfect. But who was Christopher's father? Other than a violent pig. Cee Cee was just that—a violent pig. He blazed into town with one goal and quickly settled on another: Meggie. Sebastian "Cee Cee" Caldwell was a ruthless man who thrived on brutality. He quickly identified Christopher's weakness and wanted her eliminated. He understood she would always be a handicap to his son and a liability to the club.

As I wrote the series, I begin to add in names at the beginning of each scene. When I made the decision to do this for all the novels during the update, I realized there were times throughout the series that Outlaw would always live in Christopher, and there were times when the biker and club president overtook the man he wanted to be for Meggie. As the story progresses, he won't have as many identity crises. Mostly, he will balance his roles as club president and Megan's husband, and he will usually see himself as Christopher because that is the way *she* sees him. He will conduct club business daily, kill as necessary, and put his woman everything always.

Speaking of Megan Foy Caldwell, Johnnie needed a resolution, his own HEA. Originally, the woman who barreled into Christopher's bachelor party wasn't Kendall Miller, attorney. She was Dr. Kendall Miller, Ellen's sister, out for revenge. Because she'd gone unidentified in the chapter in this book, she was a blank canvass at the beginning of Johnnie's story. *Dr.* Miller had come to kill Meggie. As a matter of fact, she hated Meggie because she had Outlaw, the man Ellen swore was going to marry her if Meggie hadn't stolen him away.

If that plot point sounds familiar, it's because it became motivation in a later book.

Johnnie was a complicated man, but he'd fallen in love with Meggie. It began as lust and the sure knowledge he'd eventually sleep with her because sharing was caring. He ended up truly loving her considering the constant time they'd spent together thanks to Christopher's decision to leave Meggie in Johnnie's hands.

In the beginning, Johnnie's concept of love had been shaped by his grandfather, Logan, but he learned tolerance and acceptance from Christopher. Outlaw, *Christopher,* chose to look at a man's character first, simply because of the way Logan, also his grandfather, treated him because he'd been born. Big Joe also had a great influence on how Christopher saw the world. Boss stepped in as father figure. Before drugs ravaged him, he'd been a solid man who demanded respect and loyalty but gave it too. One can only wonder what would've become of Christopher, and by extension Johnnie, if Big Joe hadn't rode into their lives when he did.

Christopher and Johnnie's backgrounds are explored more fully in the next installment in the series—Misunderstood. There, Johnnie's mystery woman will be revealed as my most controversial and divisive character is introduced.

Much love to everyone.

Ain't nothin' but a thing,

Kat

THANK YOU
… FOR READING MISAPPROPRIATE.

I hope you enjoyed Christopher's and Meggie's story.

Please recommend Misappropriate to the fellow readers in your life! Reviews at point of purchase and on Goodreads are much appreciated. Your thoughts and opinions mean a lot to me.

MUSIC FEEDS THE SOUL. I HAVE ALWAYS LOVED music. Pop. Rap. Jazz. Gospel. Country. Classical. Rock. Metal. Grunge. It doesn't matter as long as something in the words or the tune calls to me, I will listen to it. When I was younger, I had more time to devote to seeking out new music and new artists. I am so happy that I've passed my love of music to my daughters, as my mother did with me. Included in my playlist are songs mentioned within the story as well as those that I listened to and fired my imagination. Enjoy.

The Wedding March by Mendelssohn
Everything I Do I Do It For You by Bryan Adams
With Arms Wide Open by Creed
Another Love Song by ICP
Claire de Lune by Debussy
Come Undone by Duran Duran
Hit 'Em Up by Tupac
Hillbilly Bone by Blake Shelton (featuring Trace Adkins)
Badonkadonk by Trace Adkins
Firecracker by Josh Turner
Love Will Turn You Around by Kenny Rogers

Forever and Ever Amen by Randy Travis
Lovin' You by Minnie Riperton
Sway With Me by Saweetie & Galxara
Muwap by Latto
Laid Back Girl by Maze & Frankie Beverly
You're All I Need To Get By by Marvin Gaye and Tammi Terrell
You've Really Got A Hold On Me by Smokey Robinson and The Miracles
Tennessee Whiskey by Chris Stapleton
Timber by Pitbull feat. Kesha
Meant To Be by Bebe Rexha feat. Florida Georgia Line
Daughters by John Mayer
Love On The Brain by Rhianna
When I Think of You by Janet Jackson
Love Will Never Do by Janet Jackson
Juice by Lizzo
Venom by Little Simz
Pussy Talk by City Girls
Rodeo by Lil Nas X feat. Megan Thee Stallion
Little Bitty by Alan Jackson
Feeling Myself by Nicki Minaj feat. Beyonce
Rules by Doja Cat
Pussy Talk by City Girls feat. Doja Cat
Fancy Like by Walker Hayes
I Don't Want To Miss A Thing by Aerosmith
Dr. Feelgood by Motley Crue

Email: katkelwriter@outlook.com

24200 Southwest Freeway
Suite 402, #353
Rosenberg, TX 77471

Other Titles
by
Kathryn C. Kelly

Phoenix Rising Rock Band Series
Inferno
Incendiary
Scorched
Inflame
Ignite: My Perfect Pleasure Anthology

Death Dwellers MC Series
Misled
Misappropriate
Misunderstood
Misdeeds
Misbehavior
Misjudged
Misguided
Misalliance
Misconduct
A Very Christopher Christmas
Misfit

Mistrust

Misgivings

Outlaw's Dictionary

Death Dwellers: The Complete Series

An Outlaw Valentine

Misconstrued – Forever His Ride or Die Anthology

Dirty Boys Studio Series

Dirty Boy

Other Titles

All My Tomorrows

Dangerous

Riveted

Pink: Hot 'N Sexy for a cure: The

Books for Boobies 2015 Anthology

When Clubs Collide

Desire Me

The Marriage Monologues – Forever A Dark Obsession Anthology

Sexy Santa – All I Want For Christmas Anthology

Red Stiletto – Call My Bluff Anthology

Hazel & Grayson – Brothers Grimm Fairytales: An Erotic Anthology

Barebacked – Game Player Anthology

Breakfast & Bedlam – Happily Ever After Anthology

Drifter's Vow: Red Rum MC – Vow of Protection Anthology

How Innocent My Love – Secrets of Me Anthology

My One and Only – Goodbye Doesn't Mean Forever Anthology

Gods & Goddesses – Wicked Realms Anthology

KINDLE VELLA

Urchin of the Court

Ace of Spades – Red Rum MC

About
Kathryn C. Kelly

KATHRYN C. KELLY IS LIVING HER DREAM AND WRITING books. She's always been an avid reader and still devours books in her spare time. She also enjoys football, socializing, music, eating, and jokes. In her head, she's the ultimate biker babe. In reality, she's an ordinary girl-next-door and a native New Orleanian. Since the release of Misled in December 2013, she's been living her dream of writing books. In August 2015, her life took a dramatic turn with the diagnosis of Stage 2B HER2 Positive Breast Cancer. She underwent a double mastectomy, lymph node removal, and breast reconstruction in February 2016. The support of her family, friends, and fans helped her to stay strong and keep her head up. #F*ckCancer became her rallying cry. Now located in the Houston area, she's once again cancer free and is currently plotting her next novel.